Ela of Salisbury:
Do Justice, Love Mercy

Gary L. Patterson

Ela of Salisbury:
Do Justice, Love Mercy
by Gary L. Patterson

Prologue

I, Yolanda of Kent, have been commanded to give an account of how I came to be in my present circumstances. Before all else, it must be said that I have no regrets. Whatever fate the King may choose for me, I would not have acted differently, nor would I choose to have lived in blissful ignorance.

Every adult, if they take the time to look back upon their life, can point to a handful of days that truly decided the course of their time upon this Earth. If you are lucky, you can forever be changed for the better by even the briefest encounter with a single extraordinary soul. My tale begins with such an encounter, the day I met the woman who would rescue me from mediocrity.

It was the 24th day of August, in the year 1261 of our Lord and Savior Jesus Christ, and the year 15 of this humble witness. Mother Agnes pulled me aside as I entered chapel for morning prayers. I was to attend to the great lady that day. In all my eight years at Lacock Abbey, I barely set eyes upon the Countess; I certainly never spoke to her. Today, of all days, I was the one to be with her? It made no sense to me. No patience for questions was offered; I was to do as I was told without question and in a spirit of perfect obedience. That was the greatest of all characteristics a noble lady could possess, and my parents gave me over to the sisters because I could better learn such obedience from them.

During prayers, I dared scan the faces of the assembled sisters looking for Felicia. Though four years my junior, she was my dearest friend. She and I were an odd pair. First there was the age difference, but then too she was jovial while I was reserved, her skin always browned in summer while mine burned, her eyes appeared brown as acorns while mine were blue. Beyond the mere solace of a friend, Felicia spent much time with the Countess, experience I suddenly wanted to hear much more about. But Felicia had seemed troubled these last few weeks, a singularly strange state for such a perpetually happy child. When I could not find her amongst the gathered sisters, I guessed that Mother Agnes excused her from this day's obligations.

With the last Amen, I made my way out of the sanctified grounds to visit the bakery and then the brewery. Neither the baker nor the brewer said a word to me. Instead, both nodded with grim but knowing looks upon their faces. But what lay behind those knowing looks? Sadness, certainly, but what of my involvement? Was it simply the knowledge we all had, or did they possess some fact that would help me explain the odd circumstances I found myself in? Nothing was forthcoming, so I made my way along the western wall of the abbey from the brewery back to the main entrance.

Before reentering the sacred portion of the grounds, I took a moment to gaze upon the village of Lacock sitting at the base of a gentle slope. Lacock village was home to the peasants who worked the abbey's vast lands. There was an oddness about the scene, the nature of which finally occurred to me. It was so quiet! Not that Lacock is ever a particularly noisy place. After all, it complements the abbey. Lacock Abbey is a serious place full of serious women worshipping their serious God in a most serious manner.

But that day was different. No children played; they were kept inside the half-timber homes. Chores were begun as silently as possible. The tradesmen, even the smiths, went about work as quietly as their crafts allowed. No laughter came from the apprentices. Tremendous respect was reflected in the town's unnatural calm. Everyone from miles around must have known; this was the day we all expected the Countess to die.

And so I reentered the Abbey through the imposing gothic arch, made my way to the cloister, skirted along the southern aisle, and mounted the spiral stone staircase that led to the chamber belonging to Countess Ela of Salisbury. Once there, I waited some time for my eyes to adjust to the dim light, as the only window was firmly shut. When at last my vision was restored, I could see that I was in an ordinary stone room twelve feet by twelve feet square and eight feet high. There were only five things in the room: a table, a chair, a wardrobe, a bed, and a woman. All but the woman were made of the simplest rough-cut timber. All, including the woman, were unadorned in any way. The former Abbess lay on her bed perfectly still. At first I thought she already passed, but then I noticed her frail chest slowly rise and fall.

Having deposited the loaf of bread and mug of beer upon the table, I noticed a pool of light shimmering over the floor by the inner wall. Inquisitive by nature, and not knowing if or when the lady would awaken, I crossed to examine this small curiosity. Checking again, I was convinced that the thick wooden shutter was keeping sunlight out of the chamber. So what was the source of this glow? Getting down upon my knees, I could see that the light came up from below, rather than reflecting on the stone floor from above. When I placed my face into the light, I was amused to find myself looking down a shaft into the cloisters below. There was no roughness to the surfaces where the blocks were absent; this shaft was planned into the original construction.

Stories of the Abbess' extraordinary powers recurred to me. "She could smell sin," it was said. How many times did novices, thinking themselves in perfect privacy, exchange unnatural affections under the great lady's watchful eye? How many whispered conversations lofted up this narrow tunnel directly into her ear? As one who might well have been a victim of such spying, perhaps I could have been disturbed by such a discovery. Instead, I felt a sense of contentment one gets when you ascertain another's secret, especially a secret belonging to a superior. I chuckled.

"What is your name, child?"

After my childish yelp finished bouncing from the stone walls, I recovered enough to realize it was indeed Countess Ela who spoke. I remained surprised that a woman loitering at death's door could speak with such clarity and strength.

"Yolanda, Your Grace," I said.

"Yolanda… You are not here to take holy orders but to be raised as a service to your father are you not?"

"That is correct, Your Grace."

"And you have been at Lacock since you were a small child?"

I stood and walked to the bed, looking into her remarkable eyes as we spoke. From a face like wrinkled leather shone those emerald green eyes, speckled with copper. Before that moment, I did not realize that the former Abbess took any notice of me, much less interest. "Yes, Your Grace."

"Did they tell you yet that your father sent for you?"

They had not. I was never meant to become a nun. The

fact that my father now sent for me could only mean that a suitable marriage was arranged. I was about to reply when the woman continued. She read the answer in my face.

"I wish a good man for you my child. I was fortunate, my husband was a great warrior with a kind heart."

Still a bit shaken by the sudden news, I hesitated. I fought an internal battle between my curiosity and the sense of place that was beaten, sometimes literally, into me. But if I was to leave the Abbey, and the lady was going to die, would it hurt to ask?

"Your Grace, is it true what they say about you?"

The frail woman let out a giggle, that soon deteriorated into a pitiful cough. "That, my child, depends entirely on what they are saying about me."

"That you forsook vast wealth, that kings sought your council as well as your affections, that you were Sheriff of Wiltshire, that you killed a wicked man with your own hands."

She stared into my eyes with such intensity that it seemed she was reading my entry in the Book of Life, but I sensed nothing but benevolence and held her gaze. Finally, she spoke. "For twenty years I have been a mystery to those inside this abbey. In truth, I must now confess I rather enjoyed the game." The old woman gave me a mischievous wink, placed her chilly hand on mine, and asked in a conspiratorial whisper: "Would you like to hear about my life?"

"Oh yes, please!" The 'Your Grace' was dropped without a thought as we two became partners in some sort of rebellious alliance I did not yet even begin to understand.

"Then open the window and sit with me, child. I will tell you my story."

Part the First:

Daughter

Chapter One

March 4, 1196

Ela awoke in stages. Aromas of roasted ham and venison drifted up the spiral stone staircase to the top floor of the substantial courtyard house of Sarum. Her eyes were open, and she began to take in her surroundings in that purgatory between dreams and reality. Consciousness took hold enough for Ela to realize she was in her bedchamber at Sarum Castle. Something was odd, however, there was no daylight yet. Only the slightest silvery glow emanated from the arrow slit window of her bedchamber. Suddenly her memory engaged, and she knew why the morning meal was being prepared so early. This was going to be the most exciting day of her young life!

Voices of heralds drifted in from the streets. "Knights to the churches! Dress yourselves to seek God's grace and forgiveness of your sins, now is the time for worship!"

Vague memories of a dreadful dream momentarily troubled Ela. *True, today is a day of violence, but that can't happen. We're observing from afar.*

Within minutes, Ela threw off her plain woolen night

shift, squatted above the open hole of the garderobe, donned a flowing sea green gown, and crossed to the stairs that would deliver her directly onto the raised dais of the great hall. Ela descended, as she had so many times before, in a sort of game she called "graceful falling". The object of the game was to barely allow your foot to make contact with a step before shuffling off to the next. You descend thusly at the same rate as you would if you had simply jumped out a window, but as Ela would always assure any horrified adult who witnessed the game, always in complete control.

And so, with pride at her skill and obvious grace, Ela scurried out of the turret onto the dais. Hundreds of eyes fell upon Ela; a hush momentarily suppressed the low roar of dozens of conversations, which soon resumed with a little more volume and mirth.

This great hall was where her family sat for meals, and where her father would hold court. William FitzPatrick, Earl of Salisbury, was one of the wealthiest and most powerful noblemen in Britain; he was also Ela's doting father. Before she arrived in the great hall, her father sat engrossed in conversation with his cousin William Marshal, the Earl of Pembroke.

The Marshal was visiting in order to enjoy the tournament being held that day outside Sarum. Though his own tourneying days were now over, he was famous throughout the Christian world as the greatest knight who ever picked up a sword. With William Marshal having competed in over 100 tournaments without losing a single event, he was by far the greatest celebrity of his age. The mere presence of such a hero added to the excitement of the populace of Sarum, Wilton, and the surrounding villages.

"Aha! William, here is my birthday girl!"

"Prettiest flower in the realm. We should discuss betrothal

to my son before I leave your hospitality," the Marshal replied.

"Hang that. There will be plenty of time for you to steal her from me. For now, allow a father to enjoy exclusive right to his daughter's heart."

Earl Marshal turned his attention to the girl. "Take heed, Ela. You are eight years old today; if your father has his way, he'll see you an old maid!"

Ela curtsied with perfect deference to her noble and famous relative before throwing herself into the warm embrace of her father. Such extravagant displays of affection irritated the maternal half of Ela's parentage. No doubt this owed something to the fact that Eleanor de Vitre never gained such affection from the heart of the Earl.

"Good morning, Papa!"

"Good morning and happy birthday, my little cabbage. I have a present for you, but I will give it to you while we are waiting for the tournament to begin. Now you must fill your belly. It will be a long day out upon the field."

"Yes, Papa."

Ela curtsied to her mother and received in return a scowl of disapproval. "Ela, I never want to see you make such an entrance half dressed again."

"Yes, Mother."

A servant girl of twelve years set upon Ela, tying the threads of her sleeves about her wrists, then throwing over her a second sideless gown of contrasting yellow.

As the poor peasant girl fussed, Ela studied the large crowd in the hall. Sarum was a special place. Ever since they invaded the island little more than a century before, Norman nobles in England had lived within strong fortresses, called keeps, for safety. Sarum, on the other hand, occupied the top of a steep hill that towered above the Salisbury Plain.

Given that natural fortification, as well as ring ditches carved into the base of the hill uncountable centuries earlier, Ela's family was able to build a home with comfort in mind. The great hall, as well as her bedchamber, were in this stone courtyard house, thirty yards from the keep. Her home reminded her of her father, massive and fearsome on the outside, yet warm and inviting within.

With the open sides of the outer gown tied with golden thread, Ela was dressed to her mother's satisfaction and took her place at the main table. While those who faced the very real potential of death upon the field were in the chapel seeking favor from the Almighty, their retainers enjoyed the generosity of the Earl's kitchen. The families of the Earls shared a jovial morning feast on the dais, while their guests and servants discussed the merits of various knights between mouthfuls of pottage and fruit. Two rows of trestle tables stretched from the dais to the far end of the hall. The assembled crowd had easily and wordlessly arranged themselves in order of importance with the highest class closest to the Earls. These fortunate few ate from pewter plates rather than trenchers of stale bread.

Despite this obvious and unabated valuation by class, little variance existed in the nature of the debates raging at the top of the rows from those on the opposite end. While each man passionately extolled the strengths of his personal favorite, all in the hall were agreed on one thing. Their team held overwhelming advantage over those without.

A few miles away, in the town of Wilton, a similar, though less well catered, event was taking place. There the team that would be known as "those without" prepared to make their way to Sarum to meet the team of "those within" on the tourney field.

As the special mass ended, and the freshly sanctified knights made their way to the hall, the satiated made their way to the field, to be safely seated before the parade review. Squires went to prepare armor while spectators made their way to whatever observation point their station allowed.

In the case of Ela's family, and their esteemed guests, this observation platform was elaborate. Constructed for today's events alone, it would be dismantled the next day, the carpenter allowed to keep the rough timbers as his fee. A square tower, it stood three stories directly in the center of the tournament field. Its coarse construction was hidden behind colorful woolen tapestries, depicting old testament biblical scenes, borrowed from the castle's interior walls. On the second and third stories, windows provided the noblest born the greatest views of the day.

The scent of the freshly cut oak was a welcome contrast to the vile odor the family was forced to endure while making their way through the city streets. Climbing the plank stairs, Ela put the parcel of crushed flowers one of status used to mask city stench into the small purse tied at her hip. The smell of wood and leather could have no greater rival in her opinion.

Once assembled on the top floor, the families of the two Earls resumed conversation according to gender. With a sly look, Ela's father reached into the satchel at his feet. He handed a magnificently bound book into Ela's hands. "For you, little cabbage."

Ela stroked the soft brown leather. The hide covered thin wooden panels, studded with semi-precious jewels. The pages consisted of crisp velum. "Oh papa! Thank you! What does it contain?"

"It is a collection of lais from the pen of Marie de France. I ordered it crafted especially for you."

This was an extravagant gift indeed. Ela's mother held her tongue with considerable effort, in order not to cause an embarrassing display in front of the Marshal's family. This was, however, the fourth book Ela would own. As if a girl should be reading at all! This tally did not even include the Bible in the family chapel, which she knew full well the Earl encouraged Ela to read.

"It is beautiful! I love it Papa! Thank you so much!"

"I have the greater pleasure to see you so happy, Ela. Now please excuse me, the Marshal and I have boring matters of state to discuss."

"Of course, Papa."

Ela pulled up a chair by one of the windows where the light would fall just right upon the book. She wouldn't read now. A book of romantic poems must be savored, and she didn't want the tournament to interrupt when it began. She could, however, admire the craftsmanship of the bookbinder and the talent of the artist who painted the illustrations, as well as the flowery first letters. The calligrapher, she could tell, was especially gifted; the handwriting of this book was finer than the others in her collection.

A few minutes later, the sound of trumpet blasts rolled in through the windows. The distant voices of the heralds soon followed. All knights of consequence employed a poor boy of gifted tongue to shout his master's virtues to the crowds. In fact, those of exceptional talent could make a trade of it as adults. Ela set her newly acquired treasure aside carefully and watched as the knights of the team of those within assembled their line stretching between her perch and the hill on which the town of Sarum was built.

"We have one hundred and six knights on our side Papa."

"I wish I maintained as quick a counter in any battle I have fought!" The Marshal laughed.

"All the more reason I'll not hear of you stealing her away from me today you old fool."

"And who will be your champion, my fair maiden?" the Marshal asked Ela in lieu of a response.

A champion? Of course, why not? I am eight now. And papa whispered to me months ago that he chose this day for the tournament for it to be a celebration of my birthday. That was one of our many little secrets. So yes, I am a maiden of sorts. Why shouldn't I choose a champion?

Ela scanned the banners waving above each knight's head with increased interest. Each man was already fully encased in armor; she could not choose by looks even if she possessed the vision of a falcon. The banners resembled a tapestry of colorful pictures. Heraldry was a new addition to chivalry, but one that had grown rapidly in popularity. With all armor looking pretty much the same, heraldry was the easiest way for knights to tell friend from foe on the battlefield. Suddenly one banner straight ahead of her caught Ela's attention. It consisted of a blue background with six golden lions standing on their hind legs as if clawing at some unseen foe. This was not her first sighting of this symbol. Two years earlier, her father took her to the King's second coronation at Winchester.

"Papa! There's the banner of King Richard!"

"Well spotted, little cabbage; that is the symbol of the house of Plantagenet. But in this case it belongs to the King's brother— William Longespee."

"Half brother!" Her mother hissed. "His mother was not the Queen. He is a bastard."

"All's the pity, my dear woman. For of all Henry's brood, I'd venture that William would make the best king for England."

"Husband, I beg you to have a care! Even we are not

above a charge of treason, and there are ears about."

"Calm yourself woman. Richard would not be offended in the least. He doesn't care anything about England but the money and armies it can provide to fight France."

"Indeed, he once joked that he'd sell London if he could find a buyer!" added the Marshal, followed by a chuckle.

Ela listened to this exchange, and decided it presented an opportunity to side with her father at her mother's expense, albeit subtly. "Then William Longespee shall be my champion."

A moment of silence ensued, followed by belly laughs from the two Earls. A girl of more fragile feelings might have been crushed by the idea these men, including the dearest heart to her own, were laughing at her. Instead, Ela simply laughed right along with them. Her mother was not so amused, but then what else was new?

Down on the field, the freshly appointed champion of the eight-year-old Ela of Salisbury waited with thread-bare patience for the team of those without to arrive at the lists.

"Now you men remember. You are my bodyguard in the event, and ONLY the event, that a retinue targets me for capture on account of my flag. Under no circumstance shall you come to my aid in a fair fight!"

"Don't worry, William. If they fight with honor I will forget all about you and pursue my own glory!" replied the young knight on William's left hand.

"I would expect nothing else from William Talbot!" Longespee then turned to his right. "And you Peter, do you promise to forsake me?"

"As you wish," Peter of Warwick replied.

Longespee studied Peter a moment longer. It was impossible to decide whether the man simply missed the biblical pun, or if he possessed no sense of humor. In the end William conceded that his joke might not have been funny. Still, he felt less confidence in Peter's protection than that of his friend Talbot.

Moments later, those without appeared on the horizon and Sarum's team greeted them all the way in with their battle cries. When they formed up their own line, Sarum's contingent shouted one final cry: "Dex aie!" Which is to say: "God our help!" One portion of the line, however, followed this up quickly with "Dex aie li Mareschal!" Which is to say: "God for the Marshal!"

Within the tower, the Earl of Salisbury tilted his head toward the Marshal and looked at him from the corner of one eye. The Marshal brandished a surprised expression and shrugged his shoulders innocently. Eleanor made a noise with her teeth that resembled the sound of women knitting. The men and Ela smiled.

Senior heralds counted both sides and found that those without consisted of a few more knights than those within. Soon four knights were found with ties to either the Earl of Salisbury's holdings or those of the Earl of Pembroke. These men changed sides to even the lines at one hundred ten each. It was agreed to hold three jousts before the general charge; some young knights always needed experience. These individual encounters were quickly dispatched, with two going to those within, and one to those without.

At twenty years of age, William was becoming a seasoned warrior. Though he no longer participated in the individual jousts, this was only his third tournament. Experience from the first two did nothing to calm his fears. The noise and confusion of the melee was no less horrifying than an observer would believe. Now it was time to steel himself and act as nonchalantly as every other frightened man upon the field.

Anticipation permeated the field. It clung to, and chilled, participants and observers equally like thick morning fog. Knights, squires, spectators, even horses — who have memories too — awaited the inevitable trumpet blast that would hurl these lines of men and beasts at each other with fearsome fury. Skilled heralds knew that keeping silent at this stage increased the tension of the crowds. Sensing this calm preceded a terrific storm, Ela clenched the window's sill until her knuckles turned white.

The Marshal paid no attention; instead, he sucked on one of the imported exotic fruits on offer. He would obtain some lemons for himself at Pembroke. Dipped in the new spice brought back from the holy land, known as sugar, they made a pleasant treat. The fact that this fleeting delight cost enough money to feed an entire peasant family for several years only added to the enjoyment.

Just when the only sounds that could be heard were the occasional neighing and shuffle of a restless horse, a trumpet blast cracked the sky and rolled across the plain like thunder. Knights barked and cursed their steeds into motion, heralds bellowed warnings to the unfortunate souls who happened to line up against their masters, the crowd screeched unintelligible cries of pure excitement.

Above it all though, the resonance of horses' footfalls swelled. Soon it was beyond sound, the very earth began to shake. Eight hundred eighty hooves beat a rhythmic drumbeat into the Salisbury plain. Wine and beer in the Earls' sanctuary revealed ripples upon their surfaces. The wives began to doubt the integrity of the carpenter's labors.

Ela, however, could not be bothered with fear. She was enthralled. This first assault would be the worst of the tumult, and it would be over in a matter of seconds. What benefit did fear offer? Would being afraid keep the tower standing?

As the knights passed over an invisible line on the field, they lowered their lances from vertical to point directly at their chosen targets in perfect unison. Seconds later, the din of hooves was forgotten as a far greater turbulence buffeted the very air around the whole of Sarum. A great stew of noise left the most remote spectators taking inventory of their body parts, checking for injuries as if they themselves were just pummeled by giants. There was the sound of metal on metal, flesh on flesh, leather upon leather, wood on wood, and every possible combination of these materials. Above the cacophony rose the sound of great ash pole lances shattering into untold thousands of splinters. Ela, from her window, could see a cluster of at least a dozen such lances disintegrate into clouds of wood particles.

Unfortunately for Longespee, his nameless opponent was not one whose lance shattered. At that moment, William could see his horse's rump in front of him, tantalizingly out of reach and moving steadily forward. The crafty knight had used a ploy as old as it was underhanded. Rather than couching the handle of the lance under his arm, as all honorable contestants did, he left the butt of the lance in the feltrum, an anchor built into the saddle to rest the lance upon during parade. The effect of this deception was to put the entire weight of the horse, as well as the rider, behind the strike. Longespee's armor held, and the lance remained intact, resulting in the most inglorious sight of the prime of Plantagenet procreation dangling midair and traveling backward on the point of a spear.

Longespee wondered what was happening for a moment, but before his flight came to its inevitable end, he surmised the cause of his predicament. Landing with a protracted thump upon the ground, he sustained a further set of jolts as flesh rebounded within armor. His brain gave the order to stand and draw sword, but his body was interminably slow to obey.

Along the line of collisions stretching into the distance, Ela observed examples of many strategies for the grand charge. Some were more successful than others.

Twenty yards to the south of the central tower, two riders each relied on their horse's sense of self-preservation to make them veer away at the last second. The horses' training was regrettably successful, however, and both men had a leg crushed in the impact. A little further down, a rider swung around on the pass and grabbed his opponent by his mail hood, pulling the man off his horse. Next to them, an opponent from those without wrestled the reins away from his adversary, and could now trot him helplessly off the field.

Over half of the participants survived the initial charge unscathed. Most of those turned about for another pass, or to make for their own lines to replace shattered lances. Those who lost their mounts continued to fight on foot. Several groups formed, identifying safe ground for retreat. They would find a suitable area of concealment until opportunities to capture valuable prizes presented themselves. Charges would quickly grow smaller as the day's action diminished into minor group clashes ranging far and wide across the plain. Very little would then be visible to bystanders; reports of the heralds coming in from riders braving the mock battleground would be the only way the crowds could follow their favorites. Even that was enough to keep most in their seats.

"Coward!" Longespee shouted, as he staggered to his feet. He shook his head to stop the world from spinning. "You are not man enough to fight me honorably?"

The object of his rage dismounted and drew his sword, but he was not alone. Another knight had passed through the mass unscathed, and galloped over to join his compatriot.

"Trap!" Longespee shouted, looking around for his bodyguards. Talbot was engaged in a sword fight of his own. Peter was nowhere to be seen. The two stranger knights advanced slowly, swords drawn.

"Sir William, accept that you are captured, and we will make liberal terms for your ransom," the first knight said. "There is no need to risk further injury."

"Never, outlaw! I cannot accept your terms encumbered as I am with a sense of honor and of chivalry. I am the son and brother of kings!"

"Of course you are, bastard. Why do you think we have chosen you to ransom?" The second knight laughed. "If only you were worth what England paid to get your brother Richard back."

Longespee tactically retreated a few steps until he could see a corner of the Earls' observation tower when he darted his head to the left. He then shifted so that his back was to the tower, close enough to use it as a shield against an assault from behind, but not so close as to limit his mobility. The two knights allowed him this maneuver, stepping around so that they both stayed in front of him on either hand.

"Name yourselves and shame your families!" Longespee ordered.

Longespee was fully recovered from the shock of his dismounting. He was taller and stronger than most men. Hence he was gifted with the surname meaning long sword, as he carried a blade worthy of his stature. Above all, he possessed a full measure of the famous Plantagenet temper. Meeting a worthy opponent in battle, mock or otherwise, he would often follow the expected course like lines in a mystery play. These dogs would instead receive a share of hell itself for their trouble.

Feigning left, Longespee spun around and delivered a blow with the full strength of his blade against the helmet of right foe. Immediately, he raised the sword high above his head, then slammed the pommel down with a crushing blow that bent the noseguard of left foe.

The odds are even for a moment, William decided. This opponent was blinded until he removed his damaged helmet.

With renewed fury, Longespee landed three more unanswered blows before right foe fell backwards. In an instant, William disarmed his opponent. "Yield!"

"I yield," the unknown knight resigned.

Left foe recovered more quickly than Longespee anticipated. Using his partner's prostrate body for leverage, he threw all of his weight behind a leading shoulder, knocking Longespee to the ground. William's sword was under the foot of the enemy before he could react. Releasing his grip, he was allowed to stand.

"You yield!" the remaining rival demanded.

William Longespee was about to do just that. He comforted himself that he at least turned the skirmish into a somewhat fair fight. Just then, a yellow blur struck the fiend square in the face. For a moment, William stood transfixed as the man squealed like a frightened woman. Realizing his advantage, he crouched down, grabbed his sword, and came up with the tip pressed to the man's bare neck. The man, with eyes pressed shut, dropped his sword and cried out. "I yield! I yield!"

Having disarmed his own opponent, Talbot ran up to the scene. "You are unhurt, William?"

"Displaying your usual punctuality I see, Talbot!" Longespee jostled his friend's shoulder. "Gather our guests together and guard them closely. Assume they have no honor, for they have displayed none thus far. I will get the horses, then we must get our prizes to the lists before we garner further attention."

Peter rode up, holding the reigns of Longespee's horse. "I'm relieved to find you did not require my services, my liege."

"Fortune served me instead, Peter. Gather these rogues' horses and help Talbot get them all to safety."

"At once, me Lord."

Longespee stooped down and picked up a yellow mass that lay in the dirt at his feet. Bringing it to his nose, he was rewarded with a pungent scent he recognized. It was an exotic fruit of the Mediterranean he remembered experiencing at court. *A lemon?* He looked up to the window two stories above him. There his eyes met those of a young girl, he noticed their greenness from there. The girl pursed her lips and raised her eyebrows in a look of total innocence. She shrugged her shoulders and smiled. William Longespee bowed low, and when he stood again, he smiled back at her extravagantly.

Chapter Two

"Five pounds for the both of them," the Baron glared at his vassals. "Otherwise, you can keep them!"

"Plus the horses." Longespee gained eye contact and held it until the Baron looked away.

"Agreed."

Both men shook hands, thus bringing to a close Longespee's final ransom negotiations of the day. He was able to return to action within an hour of the incident of the grand charge. Riding across plains, over rivers, and through crops, his men and he managed victories in three more skirmishes.

"This day will be memorable for its profit as well as its glory." Talbot handed William a ceramic jug full of beer after the irritable baron was safely out of earshot.

"And then some," Longespee said, chuckled, then drained the jug.

"What does that mean?"

"Come, we must clean ourselves. We are invited to the Earl's banquet tonight." William held no desire to share with his friend suspicions of Sir Peter, or the unusual assistance he received that morning from a young girl.

A large man, in robes of scarlet velvet trimmed with ermine fur, approached William.

"A word, young man."

"Of course, my Lord."

"In private?" the man cocked his head toward Talbot.

"I'll join you shortly. See to it the squire has hot water prepared," Longespee instructed.

"Certainly, my Lord," Talbot replied, in a tone which the newcomer would think nothing of, but in which Longespee detected his friend's mockery of his sudden airs.

The raised eyebrow also indicated that the same question ran through each of their minds: *What secret does the greatest knight in Christendom want to share with William Longespee?*

"Knights! You are welcome here! Fill your bellies at my table." The Earl of Salisbury held his hands far apart as if in welcoming embrace before sitting at the head of his table. Careful observers noted that his smile vanished the moment he sat. He immediately entered into hushed conversation with William Marshal.

Servants were already setting various pots and trays brimming with delicacies, such as ground pork in spiced wine and stewed pheasant, on the tables.

"God reward you, my Lord!" one of the more senior guests yelled back. General shouts of agreement rumbled all around.

Raising his hands to silence them, the Earl traded one last silent communication with the Earl of Pembroke then stood again. "Friends and countrymen! I have received a message from our lord, King Richard, that I must convey to you. He is under renewed attack from Philip, in Brittany, and commands that all assembled here render liege service immediately. William Marshal shall take command of the army. You leave tomorrow morning."

The not unsurprising message sobered, but did not unduly depress, the crowd's spirits. General mumbling and anonymous complaints reverberated about the hall for only a few moments before being cut short by the voice of a woman.

"My lord and husband!" All eyes turned to the back of the hall to see Eleanor de Vitre standing side by side with Isabel de Clare. They were flanked by minstrels bearing instruments. "The ladies have reached a decision. If it pleases you, we would award the tournament prize. Please, dear knights, be seated so that your prize may be seen."

Pleased with the spectacle unfolding, as well as the squashing of any discordant banter, the Earl at once gave his blessing for the prize to be awarded.

Lady de Vitre nodded to the chief minstrel. To the music of the flute and psaltery, the ladies gracefully danced into the room. Parting, ladies and musicians alike performed an elegant turn, then bowed and curtsied toward the doorway from which they recently entered. A small figure darted through the doorway and onto the makeshift stage.

Ela's legs danced a spirited jig while her upper body remained perfectly still. Her left hand rested on her hip while her right arm extended horizontally to her side. Using her arm as a perch, a magnificent falcon settled its wings and scanned the crowd.

The entire assembly roared its approval at such a sight. It was wonder enough that such a delicate looking child could lift such a bird. This child, however, could not only lift it, she could dance while commanding the creature's respect as well.

Ela and the ladies then glided to a more restrained tune

as they moved from knight to knight amongst the tables. Some men smiled with avarice, believing they could truly be the 'flors des chevaliers.' Others averted their eyes in shame, believing the ladies to be mocking either cowardice or treachery displayed earlier in the day. Finally, the women came to a stop behind a tall young warrior with dark hair and brown eyes.

This time it was the Lady de Clare who spoke. "Sir William Longespee, of the house of Plantagenet, for deeds of exceptional skill and chivalry you have performed this day before our eyes, we the ladies of this land award you the tournament prize."

Ela walked forward and extended her arm toward her champion. In private counsel, the ladies unanimously agreed that Ela indeed chose well. None came close to matching the military exploits, nor the exemplarily conduct, of the late King's son that day.

After donning the leather glove offered by the Lady de Clare, William accepted the transfer of the falcon from Ela's arm to his own. He pinched hard on the bird's leash, or jess, and nodded to the girl thus assuring her that the prize was now "under his thumb."

William wanted nothing more than to have this ceremony be over and to slip back into the relative obscurity of the multitude. But he lifted the raptor above his head dutifully, and turned to acknowledge the congratulations of the assembly around him. When he had faced all points of the compass, and the applause was dying down, he began to wonder what he was going to do with such an unwieldy prize.

Ela read the confusion rising in the young man's face and smiled. His shyness was a pleasant contrast to the overt manliness of his previous persona. "I'll take it back to the cages for you if you'd like, Sir William."

"It seems I am obliged to you for a second time in one day, my lady." William passed the bird back over to the girl.

"It is a pleasure to aid a true warrior of Christ." Now it was Ela who was caught off-guard, and she gazed at the floor. With neither having anything else to say, Ela ended the awkward silence by curtseying and rushing off to dispose of the falcon.

Longespee climbed back into his place on the bench and, knowing Talbot's quizzical expression without looking at him, simply grunted. "Don't ask!"

Celebration festivities continued long after nightfall. When Earl William rose from bed late the next morning, his steward was outside the chamber to inform him that Bishop Poore had attempted to call on him three times already.

"Was the little vein in his forehead throbbing?" The Earl asked while striding toward the hall.

"I believe it may have been. Earl Marshal has also arrived to take his leave."

"Now him I will gladly see." Earl William replied.

Fires roared within all four hearths in the great hall, doing battle against an early spring chill. *God truly blessed our little tournament yesterday.* Earl William mused to himself as he walked out onto the dais. *That may be the last warm, sunny day we see for two months.*

He could see the red-faced bishop was back and striding purposefully toward him. Tall, but remarkably thin, the Bishop looked like a stick insect that could walk on pond water. Ignoring him altogether, William instead embraced his cousin the Marshal.

"God go with you, cousin. God's blood man, you look as if you've lived as a saint this past month; you always could

29

hold your drink."

"I wish I could say the same, William. I fear you look older than your days."

"Bah! I'll outlive you old man. Just see to it no filthy Frenchman proves my boast!"

"Unlikely," Marshal snuck a glance over the Earl's shoulder at the smoldering Bishop. "It would appear that Mother Church has business with you today, William."

"No doubt your men contributed greatly to the pleasure."

"My recollection is cloudy. Perhaps my men and I retired early out of reverence to the holy brothers."

"Ha! Less likely than your lucky Frenchman," Earl William said. "I wish he'd build his new church already. This hilltop feels like a bear baiting pit, and I am uncertain who is the bear and who is the dog."

"Have you seen the magnificent new cathedral at Wells? Poore won't move until he is certain he can do better... to the greater glory of God of course."

"Of course. Bring Richard this victory quickly and see us on your way back to Pembroke, William."

"I will endeavor to do both." The two embraced one last time before the Marshal marched into the courtyard to take command of the waiting army.

Each knight owed infantry as well. Those troops would take weeks to assemble. In the meantime, Richard meant to take full advantage of so many knights being assembled in one place. Troop ships were already waiting at Portsmouth, forty miles to the South.

Bishop Poore would not be ignored any longer. "Earl William, I protest the ungodly actions of this garrison!"

"What actions specifically?" The Earl sighed and took his seat at the table.

"At each prayer vigil throughout the night, the soldiers

were drunker than the last. My monks faced blasphemous ridicule from the castle ramparts."

"So what would you have me do? Most of the men are leaving the city as we speak on their way to France. They'll not bother you tonight."

"If you yourself had not been up all night drinking with them, perhaps you would have awakened in time to hear my complaint and to punish them."

"Fortunately, I was."

"At least punish your own men who remain."

"Why? Could you identify individual voices out of the darkness? I will not punish universally for the sins of a few."

Bishop Poore summoned up all of his ecclesiastical dignity for one last volley. "The Holy Father has stated that tournaments are sinful, and no good Christian would participate in them."

"This is true," Earl William conceded. "Which makes your performance of the special mass all the more gracious."

Bishop Poore bowed his head with his best semblance of humility. It was at that perfect moment that the Earl casually dealt the killing blow.

"I pray the silver deposited by so many wealthy knights in your collection box somehow soothes the injury to your monks' pride."

Poore shook physically under the attack, but as it was delivered couched in grace, there was no counter he could give. Instead, he made his leave and retreated from the castle conquered.

"I believe that vein looks worse," the steward said.

The roar of the Earl's laughter echoed over the hilltop. A stranger, dressed in a hooded tunic of the coarsest brown wool, listened to the laughter as he watched the Bishop stride through the gates with his purple face held high.

"Ah, William! I'd recognize your work anywhere," the stranger whispered to himself with a grin.

Ela sat with the ladies, struggling with a sewing frame in her lap, while her mother worked the loom. Lady de Clare asked to stay with them a few days before continuing to Pembroke to look after their estates in her husband's absence.

"Ouch!" Ela sucked her finger, only the latest to have been stabbed by her own needle.

"For crying in a bucket, child, you are worse than normal today. Be careful!"

"Yes, Mother."

Each time she would try to focus on the pattern her needle was meant to follow, her mind would drift to the excitement of the tournament. After yesterday's thrills, how was she to return to the soul-crushing boredom of women's pastimes? She was never any good at sewing, to the infinite disappointment of her mother. Thankfully, she was better at music, which promised to provide a tonic later in the afternoon. Ela was sure that if not for the Lady de Clare's presence, her mother would by now have happily been rid of her, and she would be reading the book of poems that she received from her father.

As if she could read Ela's mind, Lady Isabel broke the tense silence. "Perhaps Ela could be persuaded to read us one of Marie de France's delightful lais while we work?"

"What a wonderful idea," Eleanor replied. "Ela, fetch your new book and read the Lady de Clare a poem."

Ela knew that whatever Eleanor de Vitre thought of her daughter's literary endeavors, the Marshal's wife was a woman whose favor was worth currying. Her mother's motivations didn't dampen her response in the least. Ela complied, returning moments later with the precious volume in arm. With a silent look of thanks not lost on the dignified Lady de Clare, she settled in next to the window and found the starting point of a random lai.

> *'I'll tell you the lai of the ash tree now.*
> *Le Fresne as the story goes.*
> *In Brittany lived, in long past year,*
> *Two knights who were neighbors near...'*

Soon Ela forgot all about her audience; she was transported by the story unfolding from the verse. It told of a lady with an evil tongue. Out of jealousy of her neighbor's newborn twins, the lady swore that it was not possible to have twins 'unless two men had put them there.' Her own words would accuse her, as one year later she gave birth to her own set of twins!

A damsel of the household saved an infant daughter from the ultimate wicked act, which was the only path the mother could see to avoid being damned by her own words. Not far away there was an abbey of which the Abbess was known to be a virtuous woman.

> *'Outside the gates of the great abbey,*
> *the damsel laid the child in an ash tree...'*

The Abbess raised the child pretending that it was her niece. When she was old enough to understand, the Abbess gave the girl the two items that were left with her in the ash tree: an exquisite silk brocade in which she was wrapped, and a gold ring. The girl grew to be a beautiful young woman with full measure of every feminine virtue. Soon her qualities became famous throughout the region. Of course, this came to the attention of a wealthy bachelor knight.

'He saw her, so beautiful, wisely ruled,
By prudence, polite, well-bred and schooled.
If I cannot have her love, he mused,
He would curse Fate and feel abused...'

Here Ela's mother took issue with the lai as the bachelor knight took the girl's virtue without benefit of marriage. Ela pressed on.

'His vassal knights then came to say,
Take a noble wife, send this other girl away...'

By chance the noble wife who was found for the man turned out to be none other than his lover's twin. Without self-pity, the girl dutifully prepared the bridal bed for her rival. Finding the spread laid upon the bed unworthy for her lord, she replaced it with the silk brocade that was half of her inheritance.

The wicked mother seemed to have grown in character over the years. For recognizing the brocade, she questioned the girl and finding her to be their lost daughter, she immediately made a full confession to her husband.

'The lord replied, "I am glad of this!
Never before have I known such bliss.
Now we've found our girl that was lost,
God has given us joy beyond cost.
Before we could double your treachery,
Daughter," he said, "Come here to me!"...'

The unconsummated marriage was then annulled. Ecstatic with the news, the knight and his lover were married the next day. Even the newfound sister was well compensated with another husband closer to home. Ela completed the reading with the final lines:

'Le Fresne, the Ash Tree,
They named the lai after the lady.'

"Marvelous!" Lady de Clare smiled at Ela, having set her needlework aside several minutes before.

"Indeed," Lady de Vitre agreed. "Though I would prefer that wanton sin had not gone unpunished."

"Still there are many good lessons the story teaches. Perhaps another lai warns us against men's lustful advances," Isabel replied.

Ela recognized the way Lady de Clare's eyes rolled, and her lips quivered before the lovely face returned to perfect organization. The lady would likely realize her estates could not run themselves without her quite as long as initially thought. Guests of Ela's mother often experienced revelations of such a nature.

Ela was rescued from further discussion of the evils of sex by a servant bringing word that her father wanted her to visit him in his chamber. There was someone he wanted her to meet.

"You sent for me, Papa?"

"Come in, little cabbage. Please close the door behind you."

Earl FitzPatrick's private chamber was one of Ela's favorite places in the castle. Many pleasant hours passed in that room over the years, safe from prying eyes. The Earl could throw off all pretensions and duties, and be the adoring father, laughing and playing with her as if he were a child himself.

Today there were three chairs arranged in a circle in the middle of the room. Only one was free. Next to her father sat a stranger in coarse brown robes. Ela could tell that the stranger was tall and solidly built, he wore a warm smile and had kind eyes. Something seemed quite strange though, he appeared to be something Ela had never seen before: a poor priest. The cloth of his garment was frayed, and his sandals barely held together.

"Ela, I would like you to meet Friar Philip."

"A pleasure, my Lady." The stranger stood and bowed slightly.

"An honor to make your acquaintance, Father Philip."

"She's a fine girl William, a credit to the family."

"You're out to catch me in the sin of pride no doubt, Friar. Ela, this man seeks to cause us no end of grief with our godly neighbors." The Earl jerked his thumb behind him, in the direction of a window that overlooked Sarum Cathedral.

The hilltop of Sarum sat on three distinct levels. The castle occupied the very summit. The village spread out on the lowest area to the south and east. The cathedral clung to the hillside, below the summit, north and west of the castle. Thus, the ramparts of the castle were roughly even with the steeple of the cathedral, and looked down onto the clergy themselves, a situation considered intolerable to the monks, as well as the Bishop. 'Mother Church should never appear inferior to the warring class.'

"How so, Papa?" If the friar was a troublemaker, why did he enjoy the honor of the private chamber? Why would her father be saying such a thing so cordially?

"I've granted the serfs a fair since so many people from miles around were already assembled for the tournament. This rabble-rouser heard there would be crowds and asks permission to preach to them."

"Bishop Poore would not approve?" Ela asked.

"I dare say not. Friar Philip has some unusual views on

religion. Isn't that correct, Friar?" His tone was still warm and pleasant despite the words wrapped within it.

"Perhaps the Bishop would disagree with me on a point or two." The Friar frowned and nodded his head. "Or twenty."

Both men laughed, and the Earl slapped the Friar hard on the back. "Go ahead, Philip. Tell us, what will you be instructing my villagers?"

"I will tell them of the words of our Lord's brother James. He defined for us what religion is."

"Pure religion," Ela said, "is to care for the fatherless and the husbandless."

Earl FitzPatrick beamed with pride. The stranger smiled once again. "It seems I am not the only subversive amongst us." He looked at the Earl.

"Perhaps I mentioned to her some of those passages you gave me."

"Father Philip, why does the Church not want us to read a book which God has given us?" Ela asked.

"Because my child, there is power in being the gatekeeper of the words of God."

"Does that not make them enemies of God?"

"They can be a ..." the Friar scanned the chamber's ceiling for the right word, "a hindrance."

"Remember, little cabbage, that this is one of our little secrets," Earl William said. "If it were known, this conversation could risk all of our lives."

"Yes, Papa."

"Philip, a room is prepared for you. I will see you at evening meal. Now I am feeling tired, I will take a nap."

"Very good, William." The stranger stood and bowed toward the Earl before leaving Ela and her father alone in the room.

"Papa, who is he really?"

The Earl of Salisbury messed his daughter's hair and hugged her shoulders. "He is your uncle, my brother. That is another of our little secrets. I'll explain why another time. I have rescued you from your mother's tedium but now I wish to rest."

"Of course, Papa. Have a good nap."

The Earl stretched out on a chaise lounge that sat against one wall specifically for the great man's afternoon naps. Within minutes he drifted into heavy slumber, snoring noisily; half an hour later the snoring stopped. The Earl never woke up.

Chapter Three

Brother Walter was well familiar with the Prior's chamber by now. Obeying rules was never a strength tallied to his account, making Bradenstoke Priory a regrettable home. His options in life, however, were limited.

By bad luck or curse, Walter had a brother who inherited all of their father's land, as well as the title Earl of Salisbury. Landless younger brothers made their choice between becoming vassal knights in some other nobleman's household or entering the clergy. Though neither option afforded any measure of freedom, monasteries presented the far less dangerous choice. Safety suited Walter. Though ambitious, he didn't care for fighting. That is, he didn't care for fighting when it conformed to the inconvenient rules of chivalry and fair play.

Sitting in silence waiting to be acknowledged, Walter wondered why this interview was happening at all. It seemed a pointless endeavor. Prior Mark long ago made it clear that he had abandoned England's most reluctant monk as a project. Walter only remained in the abbey because the Earl donated large estates to secure a place for his younger brother. There was also the matter of the brothers' legacy at Bradenstoke.

And so Walter sat staring at the fire mesmerized by its lifelike motions. A draft chilled his bones, but he refused to scoot closer to the elusive warmth of the hearth. Was the furniture arranged strategically to produce this vulnerable condition in guests?

"You are aware, Brother Walter, of the priory's policy on work?" the Prior didn't look up from the charter he was studying.

"Which policy would that be, Father? There are so many."

"Those who do not work, do not eat."

"Ah yes. I do recall hearing such words before." Walter replied.

Prior Mark sighed. "Brother Andre informed you that your evening meal was forfeit yesterday."

"He did."

"Food was missing from the pantry this morning."

"Really? We must have a thief amongst us."

Prior Mark finally looked up, directly into Walter's eyes. "To the shame of this house of God, and to your grandfather's memory. I'm sure it must anger you that someone would steal from the priory he founded, where he spent his final years the most devout of God's servants. You will no doubt wish us to find and punish the culprit."

"Vengeance is mine, sayeth the Lord," Walter replied, meeting the stare. "We should let him sort it."

Both sat in silence several moments, neither willing to submit by being the first to look away from the other.

"I refuse to accept that there is no virtue in you, Walter. I may never see that virtue in this world; the search has grown far too tiresome. I would not have wasted my energy calling you in here, but for family news I must convey."

At the Prior's last words, something flashed in Walter's eyes, and their brows involuntarily raised. Father Mark did not continue, he let Walter sit in the silence wondering.

Walter blinked first. "What news?"

"I am grieved to be the one to inform you, Walter. Your brother William is dead." The Prior continued to stare him directly in the eyes, as if looking for something in them.

"I see. When?"

"The day before yesterday. He died in his sleep, without pain."

"Thank you, Prior. May I go?"

"You are excused."

Walter stopped at the door. "Oh Prior, would you excuse me from work today? I would like to be alone with my thoughts—and to pray for my brother's soul."

Prior Mark grunted. "I will inform Brother Andre that you are to be excused today."

Robert de Vitre arrived at Sarum Castle in the early afternoon, throwing the reigns of his nearly spent horse in the direction of the first boy to run into the courtyard.

Though Robert was at least two hours earlier than Eleanor had calculated possible, she was alert enough to hear the thunderous sound of hoofbeats pounding far too hard and fast across the moat's drawbridge. She entered the courtyard barely later than the servant boys.

After the briefest exchange possible to satisfy the formal greeting ceremony between close relations of their rank, Eleanor invited Robert to join her in the lady's reception chamber.

"Thank God the message reached you before you sailed for France." Eleanor said.

"The fleet sailed this morning. Unfortunately, news of

your husband's death sailed with it. Richard will know by next week." Robert absently rubbed a fresh wound on the bridge of his nose as he spoke.

"That is unfortunate?"

"It may complicate matters, yes."

"What will happen to us now?" Eleanor did not have a heart of stone; she did grieve somewhat. The death of an earl, however, brought substantial repercussions that directly impacted her. She needed to ensure she was prepared, for Ela's sake as well as her own.

"Ela is, of course, now a ward of the King," Robert replied. "As such, he will give her hand in marriage to some man at court he wishes to reward. The title, and all the wealth that goes with it, will belong to her husband."

"She's only eight, what will happen in the meantime?"

"It depends on if Richard has someone that he feels needs rewarding now. He could marry her off tomorrow. Most likely, though, he'll let the estates' profits flow directly into his own treasury for a few years."

"That is preferable to sending a child to the marriage bed before she has bled! Will I be allowed to stay here with some support?"

"Until her marriage probably, after that it is up to the new earl. There is something else to consider."

Eleanor felt her innards twist. Something in her cousin's tone was ominous.

"The Earl had brothers, did he not?" Robert asked.

"Yes."

"Then Ela is all that stands between one of them and immense wealth. The world can be a dangerous place for a defenseless girl."

"They would kill a girl?" Eleanor found it hard to believe that a brother of William could do such a thing. Their marriage may have been loveless, there was nothing unusual about that, but she was fond of the old man. She respected him as a man of honor and kindness.

"If one child, who you never met, decided your fate between poor obscurity and all the wealth and power you could dream of, what would you do?"

"But you said yourself, she's under the protection of the King." Eleanor clung to the comfort of this realization, avoiding in her own mind the question her cousin had posed.

"This is true, but two things: Richard is not in England, and girls die every day without malice. One would simply have to make it look like an accident." Robert walked to a window and looked out onto the Salisbury Plain as if he could see the danger approaching somehow. "Tell me of William's brothers"

"One is mysterious. Neither William or anyone in his family would speak of him. I've heard whispers that he wanders the woods tortured by the devil himself."

"Is he the oldest?"

"No." Eleanor said. "He was the youngest of the three."

"Who is the elder surviving?"

"Walter—a monk at Bradenstoke—I sent a messenger to inform him." Eleanor replied.

"Stupid woman!" Robert roared, his face flushed with a sudden rage. "You sent for me because you knew you needed counsel, yet you rushed into the most obvious danger right in front of your face!"

Eleanor flinched, but the blow was not physical this time. "It is done. What must we do now?"

Ela could hear the sounds of servants throwing open doors and tossing about draperies. It was a ritual played out so many times before that it was a wonder they ever turned their backs on her. Peeking through the doorway at the base of the staircase, Ela could see that her mother's cousin was in the great hall. She clenched her fists until her fingers and palms hurt. Robert was sitting in Papa's chair, caressing the arm rests. How dare he? One day she would teach Robert that he was not man enough to sit in Papa's chair. But now, she wanted to go where she was not allowed to go. She would not waste this opportunity on a little man. Keeping her back pressed to the stone, she shuffled out of the landing then bolted into the courtyard.

A fat scullery maid waddled into the open space directly into Ela's path. Mopping her sweaty forehead, the woman at first looked suspicious, then turned away as if to say that she desired to see nothing. The young Countess of Salisbury resumed her dash. Likely, the maid cared nothing for the trouble Ela's servants would catch if her disappearance were discovered. If anything, such an event would guarantee that Ela's mother would not cast her critical eye on food preparation that day.

There was no way Ela could sneak past the guards at the gatehouse. Her only course of action was to cease running and looking around. Instead, she stood tall and straight, walking calmly across the moat bridge, into the village, as if no one should think anything of it. Sarum Castle, after all, did belong to her now. For that matter, so did the village and the people who lived in it. If any of the guards gave a thought to the fact that the girl never left the castle unattended, her confident manner held them silent on the matter for a few precious moments.

Once in the village, Ela darted from alley to fence post, from parked wagon to pickle barrel, always keeping the moat in sight on her left side. Eventually the moat led her out of the village and into the cathedral grounds. She again shifted into a dead run, bolting between the bishop's palace and the outer wall of the monks' cloisters. Upright stone slabs and crosses hid her from any prying eyes that might spy on the most guiltily acting innocent in Sarum.

At last Ela made it to her destination. Churches, especially cathedrals, were built so that their altars were to the East, toward Jerusalem. Consequently, the main entrance for the non-clergy was far to the West, at the foot of the nave. In the case of Sarum Cathedral, this meant the entrance represented the westernmost point on the hilltop. A few careless steps in the wrong direction, and parishioners would tumble down the hill, onto the plain below.

Pressing her entire body weight against one of the two oak doors, each four times her height, she managed to make her way into the nave. She was gratified to find the space empty of priests, or anyone else for that matter. Ela gazed upwards in awe, as she always did, at the cathedral ceiling. She had visited larger cathedrals; everyone knew that the limited space available in Sarum meant that their holiest place was a relatively modest building. Nonetheless, it always seemed to Ela that the ceiling reached to heaven. She loved the pattern: yellow diamonds within green ones, those in turn within blue; all the colors of a sunny Wiltshire day.

Richard Poore, Bishop Poore's younger brother, was cleaning in the choir when he heard the heavy door of the nave scrape open. Curious, and desperate for deliverance from his tedious chore, Poore walked to the great screen which separated the common from the holy parts of the cathedral. He watched as young Ela walked slowly toward him. Clearly she was making her way to the slab under which her father was recently placed.

An important earl, William would have an elaborate tomb

effigy carved. His death, however, was a surprise. Noblemen hardly ever planned ahead and commissioned their effigies in advance. Richard wondered if they believed that they would not die so long as there was no tomb to put them in. The convenient vault where the girl now knelt had been used several times over the years.

Richard liked Ela; she was an impressive student. Only days past her eighth birthday, she was not only fluent in French and Latin, she was even beginning to pick up what seemed a passable ability in the tongue of the native Britons. Why she would be interested in the language of a conquered people, a servant class, was a mystery. The fact remained, it was quite an accomplishment for a female.

Just yesterday, Richard again suggested the creation of a school to his brother. Other houses of worship were giving basic education to promising boys around England; why not us? Herbert was less than impressed with the idea. He was even less impressed when Richard admitted that the Earl's daughter was performing far above the abilities of any of the boys he was tutoring, most of whom were several years older than Ela.

Ela set something green on top of the grave. "Papa, I know you taught me how to live, and how to be a countess, but I'm not ready yet."

The girl was crying, but there was strength in her face as well, strength beyond her years. "I know I have to do what mother says now. I just wanted you to know that I'll never forget your lessons, Papa. I'll be the countess you wanted me to be."

Ashamed of himself for lurking in the shadows listening to the grieving child, Poore went back to his duties. After several minutes, he heard footsteps. By the time he once again reached the barrier he saw the girl walk the last few feet of the nave, toward the exit. He nearly stepped out of his hiding place too soon. The girl turned, walked a few steps back, and half shouted: "I love you, Papa. With all my heart, and then some."

This time, Richard waited until the door slammed behind Ela before he entered the nave and walked to the slab. The sound of his footfalls merged with the still echoing door latch. When not full of human bodies, the nave seemed desperate to hold onto any noise it could snatch. Most of the time the silence in this room uplifted or weighed heavy on any soul found alone within it. Which influence it manifested was determined entirely on the condition of the soul itself.

Richard reached down and picked up the small green object that held his curiosity the last few minutes. "Now what, child, does a dead man need with a cabbage?"

When darkness fell on Bradenstoke Priory, Walter was pleased to find the moonlight unobscured under clear skies. With the brothers having to rise three times throughout the night for prayers, they were all accustomed to falling easily into deep sleep. It was a simple matter to slink across the courtyard, keeping to the shadows, to the priory stables, where he saddled the best horse he could find in the darkness.

A shadowy figure could be seen walking the second best horse the abbey owned across the courtyard and through the pointed arch of the gateway. Up above the walls, looking down upon this skulking shadow, another figure slumped its shoulders slightly.

Prior Mark sighed, shook his head, then lifted a lantern in front of him, passing a stiff parchment in front of the light three times.

In the distance, Brother Andre saw the signal and leapt onto the back of the priory's fastest mount. Horse and rider spun one hundred eighty degrees and disappeared into the night, galloping toward the Southeast.

Ela had not slept well all week. Darkness held no distractions to keep her from thinking about her father. She decided to seek comfort in the castle's private chapel.

Something deep within urged her to eschew the family chapel of St Nicholos. Perhaps it held too many strong memories of father, perhaps it was the chance that mother would be in it, perhaps it was too large for her mood. For whatever reason, Ela decided to descend to the lower floor and explore the servants' chapel.

Pushing the door aside, Ela saw that there were candles burning inside the chapel of St. Margaret already. Only twenty feet long, the few candles were sufficient to cast a pleasant flickering glow on the carved arcading of the chapel walls. Painted on the front wall above the altar Ela saw a depiction of Margaret escaping the dragon's belly. A woman who was able to protect her own virtue, as well as her faith, seemed an excellent choice of intercessor for the night.

Ela was not alone in the chapel; the welcome figure of Friar Philip stood before the altar. She had not seen him about the castle since that terrible day. Between the shock of father's sudden death and the busyness of the days that followed, she realized she had seldom wondered what came of him.

"May I join you, Uncle?" Ela asked.

"Ah. I am pleased that he told you." Philip responded, his back still to the girl. He then turned and placed a hand on Ela's left shoulder. "I hope that you find the peace here that you seek. Enough to sleep perhaps?"

Ela was quiet for some time. Finally she spoke. "What does God want from me?"

Philip's mouth spread in a slight smile. It was not a hearty smile showing lots of teeth, but it was warm nonetheless. The little grunt further spoke of appreciation for, and consideration of her question.

He settled into a kneel on one knee to speak to her without looking down. "As for your life's journey, none can know that. The book of Micah tells us, however, what God requires of each of us." Philip stood and walked to the Bible on the altar. Flipping through the pages, he found what he was looking for. "Here. Read this sentence, Ela. Obey that, and you will have a life well lived."

"Will you stay with me, Uncle? At least for a few weeks I mean."

"That could be awkward to arrange without revealing our relationship to your mother's family. They cannot know that I am your uncle."

Ela's shoulders slumped, and she studied the ground in front of her feet.

Philip rested a hand on her shoulder. "Remember though, I am a simple wandering friar; you never know where I might turn up." He winked at her when she looked up.

"Thank you!" Ela wrapped her arms around Phillip's waist and buried her cheek in his stomach.

"Not at all, Ela. It is my debt of honor to watch over my brother's child." He gave her shoulders a squeeze, then separated himself. "I'll leave you to your prayers now."

After Phillip left, Ela lit a candle, then read the words:

What is required of you by God? Do justice, love mercy, and walk humbly with your God.'

Ela committed the verse to memory. *Fewer than twenty*

words, and worth more than a thousand sermons.

Chapter Four

Walter enjoyed a leisurely ride across the Salisbury Plain. He recognized landmarks here and there he had not seen in many years. Most of all, he felt a tingling ecstasy as he savored open space. Seven years was a long time to be confined inside monastery walls.

Picking up the River Avon north of Sarum, his weariness intensified as he came near the village of Avesbury. This was one of the villages of Wiltshire where his family maintained homes. The child rival of his was born here. Walter found a shady bank and led the horse to water.

Taking some stolen bread and cheese from a saddlebag, he sat on the ground with his back against one of the upright stones which encircled the village. There were many such circles on the Salisbury plain. Nobody was quite sure why they were built. The most interesting, and complex, of these was Avesbury's neighbor just a few miles away. Though much smaller, it was finely crafted, with massive lintel stones bridging many of the upright ones. Walter's contemplations grew foggy, and within minutes he was sound asleep.

Walter awoke to the sounds of rustling and harsh whispers.

He slowly opened his eyes to see two outlaws rummaging through his saddlebags.

"Good day, monk!" Another voice uttered to his left.

There was at least one more member of the gang tasked with guarding Walter. He considered himself fortunate that they did not simply cut his throat as he slept. *Wouldn't that have just been my luck?*

"You are welcome to share my food, my sons," Walter said. "You must be starving to risk your immortal souls robbing a man of God."

Walter risked a look in the direction of the third man. He stood alone. It appeared that there were only three thieves.

"A generous offer, Father. We'll be having a look at your purse as well."

"You will be disappointed I fear. I am a simple monk on a mission to deliver sad news of my abbot's passing." A believable reason for his presence, Walter's lie at the same time killed off the sanctimonious Prior. "May I stand? My purse is tucked behind me, in the small of my back."

"Aye, but watch yourself. Those robes don't mean shite to me." The guard showed Walter a short double-edged knife.

As soon as Walter stood up, his own dagger became visible to the outlaw. "I'll be having that, monk! God's blood, I thought you churchmen were men of peace!"

"Of course." Walter tried to sound appropriately frightened.

He slowly drew the dagger from his belt. Before the man could give further instruction, Walter tossed the dagger into the earth, two feet from his opponent's right side. The thief did exactly as expected. He looked away from Walter, bending to retrieve the fine blade.

The scraping sound the sword made, coming out of Walter's sheath, blended into the whistling noise it made arching through the air. Three thuds followed in rapid succession. First was the sound of the blade making contact with the man's neck, then came his head bouncing off the ground, followed shortly by his body crashing on the bank.

The entire incident transpired in less than three heartbeats. Walter turned to face the other outlaws before they realized what happened.

Their mouths fell open when they surveyed the scene. Their partner's body gushed blood in pulsing torrents that formed a small tributary to the Avon. His head was still rolling down the bank. In front of them, a wild-eyed monk swung a shining broadsword back and forth. Without discussion, they both chose a strategy of retreat.

After they had run thirty yards in the opposite direction, Walter released his adrenaline through a primal victory scream, then laughed. Wiping the blade on the headless corpse's tunic, he shouted after the others, "Thanks for that! That's the most entertainment I've enjoyed in years!"

Richard the Lion Hearted was in a foul mood. The King paced back and forth within his tent like the great cat of his epithet. A visible path already showed on the ground where he did his pacing. At well over six feet tall, he was always imposing; when his ruddy face flushed, wise men fled elsewhere.

Richard's seneschal, Walter of Coutances, did not possess that option. He was, however, experienced enough to ride out these moods, knowing that a calmer, happier Richard may emerge tomorrow. Thus, the news the seneschal put before Richard that day would all be positive. Nothing of the other sort was urgent.

"A messenger has arrived from the coast, your majesty. Two hundred English knights have landed, also some infantry from Wiltshire."

"Excellent. And William?"

"He is with them and in good health," the seneschal said. "There is more news from Sarum, Lord. Earl William FitzPatrick is dead."

"How?" Richard asked, stopping his pacing and looking to Walter.

"I am informed that there is no reason to believe it was not a natural death."

"Good." Richard resumed pacing. "Had he issue?"

Normally a king would know whether such a rich vassal produced an heir. This vassal, however, held all of his land in England, a place Richard paid little attention to.

"A daughter only. She is a child of eight years."

"Interesting. Bring my brother to me the moment he arrives in camp," Richard said. "I wish to take his counsel."

"As you wish, my Lord."

Walter stretched his spine as straight as a mast as he rode over the moat bridge into Sarum Castle's square. He cheated an extra inch or two standing in the stirrups without making it obvious he was doing so. In his imagination, he could see and hear the procession of vassal knights that ought to be accompanying him as he came to take his rightful place as Lord of the Manor.

He resisted the impulse to look upwards toward the windows of the Earl's living quarters. Walter was sure that he could smell the fear that certainly must be gripping his departed brother's women as they looked down upon him from the windows above.

The square was unusually quiet. Only a couple of foot soldiers stood sentry at the castle doors. Three servant boys loitered about, waiting to see if the Monk would require service for his horse. One other horse was tied to a rail on the opposite side of the square. Otherwise, the atmosphere was calm and silent.

"You there, soldier! Inform the Lady de Vitre that her brother-in-law, Walter FitzPatrick, would speak with her."

"I am sorry, good fellow, the Earl's family has gone on a journey. They left at first light," the soldier replied.

"What do you mean left? Where did they go?" Walter's voice broke as he spoke, and his thigh muscles relaxed settling himself into the saddle. Even with this setback fresh on his mind he was conscious that, to the soldier's mind, Walter had just shrunk before his eyes.

Whether the soldier noticed the man's change in stature or not, he did not react visibly. "They travel to visit the lady's family in London."

"London?" Walter considered routes such a journey might take. *That would certainly take them north, along the road I just traveled.*

It was highly unlikely that the party took a different route that would have caused him to miss them. Was this soldier lying? Was he misinformed? Now what? Would he be allowed to stay in the castle? Could he take control of the estates without dealing with these troublesome women first? Was there even anyone here who would recognize him after all these years? His knowledge was limited due to his seven years of isolation in Bradenstoke. He needed counsel; was there a potential ally nearby?

Walter realized that he had been sitting in the saddle wrestling questions for several moments. This soldier, who already witnessed his shrinking, must think him slow witted as well. As he prepared to take his leave of the soldier, he was struck dumb and his stomach twisted. Walter witnessed Bradenstoke's sub-Prior, Brother Andre, saunter from the castle, take a large bite from an apple, walk wordlessly past him, cross the square, then untether the horse. Andre mounted the mare, turned her around with a tug on just one reign, continuing to eat the apple with the other hand, before finally acknowledging Walter with a nod of his head. "Brother."

Andre rode out into Sarum at a slow trot as Walter bobbed on a wave of fresh rage.

A thought struck Walter. He turned his horse to leave the grounds as well. As an afterthought, he turned back to the sentry. "Thank you, my son." No good could come from alienating any member of the garrison through rudeness.

The two brothers embraced, pounding each other on the back. Roughly the same height, there was a noticeable resemblance. But where Richard's hair was reddish blond, William had the dark hair and complexion of his mother Ida.

"I am sorry to keep you from rest after your journey, William."

"Not at all, Brother, it is good to see you." Longespee said.

Shouts of "Heave! Heave!" caught the Plantagenets' attention. Hordes of workmen scurried over the hill high above Richard's tent. A stone block as tall as an average man was being levered into place on the growing wall of Richard's latest castle, Chateau Gaillard.

Seeing that all was going well, the King turned his attention back to his brother. "It is good to see you as well, William. Come inside, have some wine to fortify you."

Inside, Richard poured William a glass of a particularly good production from his own estates in Brittany. "William, Philip has renewed hostilities."

"So I gathered from our recall from England."

"It seems that he takes issue with my little daughter. You see the construction continues splendidly?"

"Indeed it does. Gaillard will command an impressive position."

"I will show you the plans. I designed the castle myself; it will be impregnable."

Richard motioned his brother to join him at the map table. "But first, I need to open another front against Philip, make him divide his forces. Have you any ideas?"

William took a seat and thought for a moment. So pleasantries were already over. Richard was in an impatient mood. No matter, he was prepared.

"Actually, I have been mulling over something which has occurred in England," William said. "It may well be of relevance. You are aware of the success of a certain agitator in London? William Fitz Osbern I believe his name is."

Richard cocked his head and grunted. "Yes. So strange you should mention him, he came here to pay homage to me only last week. He swore on oath that this peasant's revolt of his has no quarrel with the crown, but is directed solely at the corrupt merchants of London. I believed him. I have always considered those dogs to be nothing but peasants with aspirations above their station. You believe that I should be concerned?"

"No, not at all. I believe you are right to dismiss this revolt. But I also believe it could bear lessons for us."

Richard leaned forward, dangling his goblet between his knees. "How so?"

William settled back, stretching his legs and taking a sizable gulp of wine. He felt the warmth of it spread through his chest and gut. "It seems to me that the merchants of Flanders, especially Bruges, are far more powerful than those in London. Flemish merchants deal almost exclusively in cloth."

"Of course! Bruges merchants! They get their wool supplies from England!" Richard was no fool, he simply needed wise counsel to direct his thoughts away from direct military conflict for a moment.

"Not only that, but in their avarice they have foolishly become dependent on our wheat." Longespee continued. "Without it, they would starve."

"So if I were to cut off wheat and wool shipments to Flanders, its merchants would revolt."

"Thus forcing the Count of Flanders to change sides against Philip to appease you," William added.

"Opening another front, outflanking Philip to his north, forcing him to split his forces."

"Exactly."

Richard could hardly contain his excitement. He took up his pacing again, continuing to deepen the rut in the middle of the tent. William sat in silence, sipping his wine as Richard worked the plan over in his mind. The King would think several counter steps ahead at every possible turn, looking for a flaw: a lesson learned from the game of chess.

"Will the English nobles who make their profits from selling the wool to Flanders revolt as well?" Richard asked.

William was ready with the answer before it was asked. "You pay them a fair price for their wheat and wool yourself, then store it. The Count will come into line swiftly, you can then turn the supply back on. A temporary expense, easily justified as a cost of war."

Richard nodded. He shook the hand with the goblet in it toward William, index finger outstretched. A few drops of wine fell into the rut in the floor. He resumed pacing.

A few minutes later Richard declared the plan brilliant.

His mood soared like a falcon on the hunt. He called for his seneschal and order him to obtain three women for his bed that night.

When the seneschal had left, Richard smiled and began his finger wag once again.

"William, our father's provision for you was not sufficient."

"He did not have to recognize me as his son at all. I thought the Honour of Appleby to be quite generous."

Richard held up his palm. "Yes. Yes. Perhaps when you were a child. You have proven yourself valuable to the Crown since then."

William's eyebrows lifted, a tell he knew was not lost on Richard. The King was well aware how unexpected such words could be, coming from the Cor' de Leon. Many men would kill, and often did just that, in order to hear those words. Life changing gifts often accompanied them.

"There is an earldom available in England. There is none I trust or value more than you to have it. I wish to install you the third Earl of Salisbury."

William knew that his tournament host had passed. He was working through what he knew of the Earl's family. He knew he should be replying when Richard continued.

"The title belongs to some whelp of a girl by right of suo jur. She will be your bride."

"Ela is to be my wife?"

"You know this child?" Richard asked with amusement.

"We've uh… we've met."

His response could have been construed to be morally suspicious. William could see the thought pass through Richard's mind, reflected clearly in his arched brows; that thought was just as quickly dismissed.

"There you see? Obviously a marriage made in Heaven!" Richard laughed and drained his glass.

Chapter Five

Just as Ela began to smell the faint odor of smoke from the fires of Petersfinger, her party heard the expected whistle followed by the rustle of a branch three horse lengths off the cart path.

Robert and her mother had acted with haste when the kindly monk arrived from Bradenstoke. Ela was kept far enough away that she could not understand the lowest whispers. The tone, the gesticulations, and the odd words which the adults could not manage to control the volume of, all painted a picture. It was not a peaceful picture like the image of Adam and Eve in the garden before their sin. This picture more resembled the fearsome image of the couple being cast out, eyes downcast and arms contorted to hide their shame. Indeed, the trio's dawn journey with only coarse bread and young cheese with which to break their nightly fast felt very much like they were cast out. England's newest countess wondered when, or indeed if, she would see Sarum again.

Once in the brush, Ela recognized one of her servant girls, the one who finished dressing her in the hall on the morning of the tournament. A boy of similar age, whom she did not recognize, took charge of the horses, leading them back in the direction of Sarum. The girl climbed through a gap in the border fence and set off on foot across a common grazing field. Robert indicated that Ela and her mother should follow. Eleanor de Vitre slipped through the fence with surprising grace, considering what a decidedly unladylike action she was undertaking.

Ela smiled for what must have been the first time since Papa's death and dived through the hole with unacceptable pleasure.

Ela could see the servant girl was several steps ahead, leading the unusual procession at a remarkably brisk pace. The dive through the fence was doubtless already marked to her account, so she did not wish to push her luck by running. She did, however, double her step in order to come alongside their guide.

"Where are you taking us?" Ela asked.

The older girl looked at her briefly with a blank expression. "My parents' home."

Ela felt the chill of the terse reply, but she decided to try again. "Thank you for helping us."

"Your mother paid well."

"You've lived in our house for a long time, is money the only reason you would help us?" Ela understood the family's personal servants to be the most fortunate of all peasants.

Again the girl looked at her for several seconds before replying. "Why else?"

"Perhaps gratitude?" Even as the words left her mouth Ela realized they could have come from the mouth of her mother.

The girl looked back to verify their distance from the adults then whispered hoarsely. "Spoiled little bitch. I have dressed you, brushed your hair, prepared your bed, washed your clothes, for near two years now. So tell me, Lady Ela, what is my name?"

Ela stopped suddenly from the shock of the words slapping her face. She didn't know. Two years the older girl took care of her, and she didn't know her name. The nameless girl never paused, she marched on toward a farmhouse on the edge of Petersfinger. Ela was soon overtaken by Eleanor and Robert.

"What did she say to you?" Eleanor asked.

"Nothing."

"You look as if you have been struck. I would have seen her hit you, so she must have said something."

"Forget it. I deserved it."

"You are noble and she is a peasant; we must never allow the lowborn to speak to us harshly, Ela."

"Mother, what is her name?"

"I have no idea, what does it matter?"

"I was just trying to remember. Forget it."

Her mother may have replied, Ela though was transported to her father's private work chamber. Most times, after playing silly games with her for some time, he would sit her down and teach her something about the responsibility of being an earl, or a countess. Sometimes it was a bit of his own wisdom, other times it was a Bible verse the priests never taught. *Whatsoever you do to the least of these, you do it unto me; whatsoever you fail to do for the least of these, you fail to do for me.* A tear ran down Ela's cheek as they arrived at the open doorway to the peasant house.

The building was long, about the distance Ela could throw a small stone, and was made of wattle and daub. Ela once spent a lazy summer afternoon watching a home like this being built in Avebury. Thin strips of wood were woven into panels, which were then set into wooden frames; this waddle was then daubed with a mixture of mud, dung, and straw. Finally, the building was whitewashed with lime to make it waterproof. Otherwise, the mud and dung would dissolve in the first hard rain. The roof consisted of thatched reeds from the river piled two feet thick. The thatched roof extended nearly to the ground.

Watching one being built was one thing, this was the first time Ela ever entered the home of a peasant. It was one large room, perhaps fifteen feet deep and thirty feet long. Ela was amazed at how clean the family was. Their floor was simply earth, though hard-packed and well swept of any loose dust. There was a blazing fire in the center of the room; smoke drifted below the underside of the roof. She could see a small hole for the smoke to escape, but it was not as effective as the fireplace chimneys of the castle which expelled smoke as quickly as it was produced. Then again, she could see cuts of meat hanging from hooks set into the wooden framing arches. The meat was drying in the pooling smoke, so perhaps this arrangement was more advantageous than she first thought. The smell of smoke mixed with a sickly sweet odor that reminded Ela of animal barns. Looking to her right, she located the source of the second odor. A short waddle and daub wall ran widthwise to her immediate right. Beyond it, Ela found herself staring into the bored eyes of a small cow chewing her cud. Inside the cordoned off area of the room she saw two goats and several chickens as well.

"In summer we just bring them in at night, right now they stay in all day." The servant girl's voice was flat and unguarded, as if Ela should find nothing unusual about keeping livestock in your house.

"May I pet the cow?"

The girl shrugged and led her through the gate at the far

wall.

"Tell me your name— please."

"Abigail."

"Abigail," Ela repeated the name as if trying on a new dress to see if it fit. "I am ashamed that I did not know it. My father would be disappointed in me."

Abigail's features softened at the mention of the Earl. "I am sorry for your loss. Earl William was always fair."

Ela desperately wanted to share things her father taught her, lessons she obviously did not learn properly. This softening presented an opportunity to tell Abigail things that would help make up for her own self-centeredness; but every lesson was taught in secret, and Ela swore not to tell.

"What are you two doing?" Robert was already changed into peasant garb. "Never mind. As long as you are behind that wall, change Ela into these." He tossed Abigail a drab woolen dress and very old soft leather shoes.

Abigail's features hardened again as she set about the task.

"I am sorry for the way my mother and her cousin speak to you," Ela said.

Abigail continued to work in silence.

"And I am sorry that I used to do the same; I won't do it anymore— if I ever return."

Abigail looked her in the face for only a moment but remained silent some time. Finally she asked, "Why all this fuss?"

"Robert says my uncle wants to kill me; mother believes him."

Abigail stopped her work. "And you? Do you believe it?"

"I have never met him. But now he is a monk by necessity, not choice. If not for me, he would be an earl and very rich. So yes, I believe them."

Abigail nodded. "I owe you an apology too. Maybe you

are not as lucky as I thought."

Ela studied the simple room/home. Though poor, it was warmer than the stone chambers of the castle ever got. Abigail's parents beamed with pride for being of service to the nobles, who ignored them. An infant sat laughing carelessly in a corner, safely away from the fire. "No. Perhaps I am not."

"And you are certain you would have seen them?"

"Absolutely certain," Walter replied.

Bishop Poore held his hands in a steeple in front of his face whenever he was deep in thought. He rested his chin on his thumbs for another minute before making his pronouncement. "Robert de Vitre has taken control of the lady and the girl. He has removed them in order to avoid direct conflict with you, and to maintain his influence."

"Taken them where?"

"There are only two alternatives as I see it."

"Yes?" Walter's speech betrayed his impatience, and lack of composure. Though noble, even a brother of Earl William, the humble monk appeared easily manipulated.

"The family homeland or Richard's court. Either way they shall cross the channel."

"Then they leave England without explanation. Could I take command of my brother's garrison in their absence? Would the men follow me?"

Again Poore waited an extra beat or two to reply. "Yes, but it would be a temporary victory at best. Richard would intervene. If they deliver Ela to his court, he might even see your actions as treasonous."

"What would you advise?" Just as the Bishop expected, Walter spurned subtlety in his hopes of winning an ally. "I would, of course, be most obliged to you if I was to made

Earl."

Poore did not respond at first. Though he manipulated the man into offering the bribe, Walter FitzPatrick presented a most unsavory character. The threat to Ela's life, though unspoken, was too obvious to ignore. Any alliance he entered into with this man would be unholy indeed. Now that it was offered, the Bishop began to regret his maneuver. At the critical moment of decision, he saw the new cathedral rising from the Salisbury plain. Its glory would surpass those of Wells and Lincoln. With the right earl in place, that dream could become a reality.

Finally Poore decided to keep his options open with the would-be earl without directly advocating murder. "You must appeal to Richard directly. Meanwhile, I will petition the Archbishop to advise the King in your favor. Make for Rouen with haste. I believe," Poore added, "the speediest route to France would be to ride through the New Forest and make for the Cinque Ports. At least, that is if one was disinclined from being recognized."

"Understood. Thank you, Bishop Poore, I hope that we will be longtime friends you and I." Walter strode from the Bishop's chamber.

Bishop Poore remained seated, still resting his chin within his steepled hands. He suddenly felt that he needed a very long bath.

Despite the overwhelming sadness Ela felt at the loss of her father, and then her home, she was still able to appreciate the adventure she found herself on. This journey brought her into contact with new experiences as well as unfamiliar sights, smells, and sounds. It was as if she was transported into one of her books. There was one difference, though. Heroes and heroines in books were always noble like her. A daughter of an earl would never expect the opportunity to see the world though the eyes of a commoner.

"It will be growing dark soon," Robert said. "We will stop at the next inn for the night."

"With a clean bed and privacy?" Eleanor asked, though Ela didn't think her mother sounded very hopeful.

"Neither I'm afraid. At night it is especially important to maintain our disguise; we sleep with the peasants."

"Making camp along the road would be preferable."

"There is greater safety in inns, madam. That is why they exist."

Eleanor had complained several times already of affronts to her dignity as a lady. Whenever the issue of Ela's safety was cited, however, she inevitably complied.

As her guardians deliberated, Ela could see up ahead that they were about to overtake another party of perhaps a dozen souls stopped beside the road. After drawing closer, it was apparent that the group was filling water flasks from a nearby stream. Ela just caught herself before crying out when she noticed a familiar form within the group.

"Hail and well met, friends," Robert offered in his best attempt at a peasant drawl.

General greetings echoed from the group. A tall, heavily built priest appeared to be in charge of the party. "Fellow, God grant you good day."

"Father, it appears your flock is also on holy pilgrimage," Robert said. "May I inquire what shrine you seek?"

"We are bound for Santiago de Compostella. And you my son?"

"Only Paris, Father, a more modest goal."

"A pilgrimage, humbly undertaken, will enrich your spiritual lives no matter the length. We will all cross the channel from the same place, shall we combine our numbers?"

Robert hesitated for only a moment. "We would be thankful for the increase."

Philip met Ela's gaze for only a moment. A nod of the chin imperceptible to all others in the assembly was the only acknowledgment that would pass between uncle and niece for several days.

Walter pushed the stolen horse hard this time. His previous leisurely pace allowed his young adversary to slip his grasp; he would not make that mistake again. Daylight was slipping away fast, however, and it would be extremely easy to miss them in the black of night. Darkness would force him to stop and sleep until dawn. Until then, he would make up as much distance as he possibly could.

Rubbing the horse's head, he leaned over and spoke into its ear. "I hate to be so harsh with you, friend. Just a little further and you can rest."

The Bishop's advice was, of course, intended to send him on an unstated mission. Portsmouth to the south of Sarum was the nearest port city. Obviously, it would be quicker, and certainly safer, to obtain passage to France from there. This land journey through the New Forest was the path Poore believed Ela's family took. The Bishop knew what Walter would do if he caught up to them.

The foolish priest undoubtedly believes he can still stand blameless before his god after I have spilt her blood.

Philip was fortunate that his curse woke him before attacking in earnest. That was so often the case. Likely his perpetual antagonist thirsted for more meaningful battle than an unconscious friar could offer. At any rate, he was able to stumble out of the encampment without raising any alarm. The night watch, and any light sleeper who may have awoken, simply believed he was going into the trees to urinate.

His precautions were, of necessity, rudimentary at best. They were just enough. Sprawled on his back in a small clearing, the pummeling and lurching of his muscles was settling into a slower, less dramatic pattern. There would be new bruises and a cut or two on his face that he would have to explain the next morning, but he had survived the fight once again. He did not yet have the control necessary to respond when he heard a barely familiar voice speak.

"Hello, Brother. I see the struggle continues."

Though still only able to influence the spasms in the direction of the voice, it was enough to get two or three glimpses of his elder brother. How strange he looked in that tonsure, and wearing hard years on his face.

It would still be some time before the curse would release him fully, but Philip was aware of his surroundings, could process the images of those brief glimpses. Walter's sword was drawn. Philip's vulnerability could hardly be greater; he could literally offer no defense.

What was to gain? Philip was younger than Walter, he was no threat to the inheritance of their brother's estate. Then again, a witness to treachery and child murder is a threat, and his elimination would weaken the protective ring around Ela.

"Damn you, Philip," Walter said. "Why must you always be such a pain in my arse?"

"Ah yes, you are unable to speak still." Walter kneeled near Philip's head. "You know it used to scare me to the bones, these fits of yours. Why? Could it be I once loved you?"

A primal guttural outburst was followed by the sound of

steel sliding along leather. "I swear to you, Brother," Walter hissed, "the girl dies. And if you stand against me, you will die too. For your goodness, I relent this last time. But be it known, you have received the last measure of mercy I am capable of."

When his opponent with whom he did not share blood relented, Philip was left exhausted and sore. As expected, he looked around him and found no sign of kin. The curse's nature allowed for doubt as to whether the interaction had ever actually occurred. Just as doubt grew, however, Philip raised himself to sit upright on the damp leaves. In doing so, a small object dropped from his chest onto the ground near his hip.

Even in the minimal moonlight, Philip could make out the wax seal of an Augustinian priory. It would be that of their family's legacy. It was not a sentimental gift. Walter left it behind as he meant to claim the seal of the earldom in its place. Of this, neither man believed the message to be misunderstood.

On the eighth day of their journey, Robert tried to hurry the assemblage along as a dog herds sheep. He knew no whistle or call, however, that quickened the pace of the devout committed to a lengthy pilgrimage. Despite his best efforts, the sun was getting low in the sky by the time they came upon the village of Hauekehurst.

The legitimate pilgrims began to vocalize dreams of sipping ale by a roaring fire.

"We should continue on. We could reach Rye before dark," Robert said.

"What's your hurry?" One of the young men spoke for the thirsty. "Rye will be there in the morning."

"There may be a ship leaving at first light," Robert replied.

"If we arrive tonight, we may be able to secure passage."

The tall priest who led the pilgrims studied the village and the setting in which the inn stood then nodded. "Well spoken. Perhaps it would be best to press on."

"Are you both mad? Even if we could find a ships' schedule at that hour, we would then have to travel on to the port the ship was leaving from. France will be there for later ships, friends," the younger man replied.

Robert realized that there was no reasonable argument he could offer to travelers prepared for a journey of many months. He couldn't very well explain that they were being pursued by a monk bent on murder could he? "Of course, you are right, my friend. I am letting the excitement of the pilgrimage muddle my thinking."

Sometime after midnight, a lone figure stumbled out the front door of an inn and staggered toward Hauekehurst.

"A word, my son."

The blurry-eyed man stopped short, cocked his head like a curious dog, and studied the darkness.

"I'm looking for some of my flock." Walter stepped out of the shadows just enough for his robes to be visible. "Is there a group of pilgrims in that inn?"

"Oh, yes Father, they've gone to bed already."

"That is well; for we have much to accomplish tomorrow. Tell me, my son, they rest in those rooms, the ones above the hearth I assume?"

"Yeah, yeah. There's a lot of 'em. They got the whole upstairs."

"Fine, I will visit them in the morn. You look like you need rest, my son. God be with you."

"Thank ye, Father." The drunk tottered in the general direction of his home.

A pity. So many innocents in the wrong place on the wrong night. "Don't despair, my children," He spoke aloud toward the upstairs windows. "It is for a good cause."

Half an hour later the inn was engulfed in flames. Throughout the village, houses gorged panicking occupants into the streets. At first, the unbearable shrieks from within the structure dominated the cacophony. Three flaming bodies leapt from windows onto the street below, all of them were men. Eventually the screams from above stopped, leaving a stunned and sober silence amongst the villagers on the street, interrupted only by the crackling of flames and pops of exploding timbers.

Nothing could be done to save the structure, or the poor souls trapped inside it. Instead, efforts were directed toward creating a firebreak, pulling down neighboring buildings. The town, at least, would be saved. Several men stayed up and kept watch as the structure collapsed and burned to embers. One wore brown robes and an indecent grin.

Chapter Six

Of the three men who managed to jump from the burning building the previous night, one died within minutes, another would be dead before noon. The other suffered a broken leg, and would be tragically scarred for life, but would survive. The survivor watched numbly as a holy man administered last rites to his brother.

"Why, Father? Where was God?"

"I'm only a monk not a priest, you needn't call me father," Walter replied. "As for your question, it's a very good one. God created a perfect world for his children where things like this couldn't happen. It was man who brought sin into the world. Because of our free will, God must allow sin's consequences to have their days upon the Earth."

"But we were all seeking him. We were on pilgrimage."

Not all were friend. If you were correct, then you would have been saved. "Perhaps your friends will then have a shorter journey to his presence for it. God's ways are mysterious."

"If only I had listened to Michael."

"Who is Michael?" Walter asked, standing up and stretching his sore back. The expiring man's path was now clear to his maker's presence.

"A man of our group who tried to persuade us to continue on to Rye last night."

"I see," Walter replied. *Probably Robert. Poor man. Wish I could tell him it wouldn't have helped; it would have just been the next inn.*

"At least his family survived," the injured man said.

Walter's world shuddered as if in an earthquake. "Survived? I didn't see anyone get out but you three."

"Michael and his group continued without us. I thought he was mad. Imagine such a small group risking the road as night was falling. Angels must have whispered in his ear. Maybe God did intervene, I just wasn't favored. Michael must be holier than me."

Walter had long stopped listening. "This man's family—were there children?"

"One girl."

"How old?"

"I don't know, seven or so. Why?"

There was no time for social pleasantries now. He was behind once more. Damn! It was almost noon; if they made Rye before nightfall, then they've seen a schedule of ships sailing by now. They may be dockside already.

"What happened?" A housewife asked the injured man, handing him some bread and cheese. Her daughter carried two mugs of beer.

"Hell if I know," the man answered, watching the monk disappear down the wooded lane. "Mind if I drink his share?"

"Why are we taking the ship from Dover?" Eleanor asked her cousin. "The ship leaving from Romney makes port closer to Richard."

Robert continued to lead the FitzPatrick women through the village of Rye. "We are not going to Richard. We are going to join our family instead."

"Ela is a ward of King Richard; to steal her away is treason!" Eleanor was now becoming suspicious of her cousin's motives and wanted to throw herself under the King's protection.

"Richard is at war. He is always at war. It would not be wise to bother him with our problems unnecessarily. We will get Ela safely to our family's estate, then send word to Richard. He can send for her in his own time."

That seemed reasonable, yet Eleanor was still suspicious. She was also angry that he did not tell her about his plan from the beginning. She stopped suddenly, halting the group in the middle of crossing the market road.

"Robert, I have been absent for some years. Tell me, is our family loyal to Richard or to Philip?"

"To Richard of course."

The hesitation was short, barely noticeable. Eleanor caught it. She also observed a nod of the chin before he spoke. It was a lie.

"Nonetheless, I insist that we go to Richard."

"You insist?" he whispered.

"You insist?" he shouted.

Eleanor did not flinch. "I do."

"And what makes you think you have any say in the matter?" Robert's shout attracted notice from people on the street. His tone now kept their attention riveted.

"I am Eleanor de Vitre; widow of William FitzPatrick, Earl of Salisbury; cousin-in-law of William Marshal, Earl of Pembroke," she responded in a clear, firm voice. "And loyal subject of his majesty King Richard!"

They were still dressed in disguise, but nobody laughed

at the woman's assertions. Her regal posture and speech convinced all. It was difficult to hide a high-born lady, impossible if she did not wish to be hidden.

"Are you insane?" Robert hissed, his face inches from hers.

Men reacted now. She knew without looking that all the men on the street were coming to her rescue. Robert stepped back, and bowed his head slightly.

"As you wish."

Eleanor relaxed as her cousin stomped away, then looked to her left. Ela was staring in amazement. *So, perhaps my daughter shall learn that she is not the only one to have learned a thing or two from her father.* Ela smiled at her, Eleanor winked in return.

Ela's party was taking advantage of a hearty midday meal in a local public house before setting off for Romney, from where the next ship bound for Caen would leave. None were under any delusion that the argument over their final destination was resolved. Caen could be a convenient port of entry for either Vitre or Rouen.

Nobody took notice when a rather average looking villain in dusty tunic entered the house and asked for a mug of ale. Obviously he traveled some distance recently, but there were countless such travelers in a town like Rye.

"From where have you traveled today, friend?" The fat serving girl set the mug in front of the man, sloshing some of the precious contents on the stained table.

"Tunbridge. By way of Hauekehurst, the town from which I bring sad news."

He spoke loudly, wishing to be overheard. Less than half a day's walk from Rye, events in Hauekehurst would be of interest to many here. The unremarkable peasant would enjoy some glory in being the messenger bearing bad news. Heads turned around the room, particularly those of a man, a woman, and a girl.

"Pray tell then, stranger, of what sad news do you speak?" the girl prodded.

"Do you know of an inn, sitting on the edge of the town, along the Rye road?"

"Yes, I know it."

"It is no more, burned to the ground last night. I have heard there was great loss of life."

"God have mercy on their souls," she said, then turned back to her work. There were a few murmurs of agreement and then the peasant's moment was over.

"Robert!" Eleanor said, swallowing a gasp. "Do you think?"

"Undoubtedly."

Ela's stomach dropped. Uncle Philip stayed with the rest to maintain his anonymity. She barely knew him, yet somehow he felt like a link to her father.

"Those poor people," Ela whispered, saying a silent prayer for her recent travel companions. She liked them. Suddenly the implications occurred to the girl. "They died because of me!"

Robert looked around the room. Ela's last sentence was spoken too loudly, but it did not appear to have attracted attention. "Quiet child!"

She did not bother responding. Her face was pale and she retreated into her own thoughts. It was possible to swallow the stab of loss over her newfound uncle; her part in the deaths of so many innocents was too much.

Robert leaned in close to both of his charges. "We must hurry to Romney. We are safer with the ship's crew than on the road. Walter may not know that he has failed, but we can't assume that."

Late that afternoon, a monk quietly passed through Rye. He obtained information about possible passage to the continental mainland. Of three ships sailing from different ports the next morning, only two seemed of interest to him. Dover or Romney? The monk stood for some time at a fork in the road. Finally he hurried off down the road toward Romney.

By first light Walter reached Romney. He breathed in the sea air. To him it smelled like death, full of decay and rotten fish. Squinting hard, he wondered if it was the other side of the Channel that he saw on the horizon. It was possible to see the other side from here on a clear day. Before long, activity on the quay revealed which ship was about to sail that morning.

"I would join you on your journey, my son," Walter shouted from the dock to a young sailor busy about the ropes on deck.

"Ye all but missed us Padre, still, likely they will take ya on fer a price. Talk to the purser." The boy pointed to a tiny building of rough lumber forty feet up a sharp slope.

Walter hoped talk of a monk trying to secure passage would not make its way through the ship while he was inside. Toward that end, he wished to negotiate as quickly as possible. He would not haggle on price.

Inside, the smell of the sea mixed with those of stale ale and body odor. A tiny shack, perhaps fifteen by fifteen feet, it contained a half dozen rough looking men. They were all hairy, probably of Saxon or Viking decent. Walter instantly sensed that they were hostile to Normans. A thick plank rested on two upturned barrels forming a makeshift table.

"You here for our souls or our money, monk?" the purser sitting at the table growled, garnering appreciative hoots from the others.

"I believe you are departing for Caen shortly." Walter ignored the insult. "I seek passage."

"Trunks?"

"No baggage but saddlebags I can throw over my shoulder."

"Four marks."

The price was exorbitant, he may have to seek out and punish this man one day. "Very well." He hoped that he sounded ignorant, unaware that he was being cheated.

Passage arranged, Walter asked the question he had been holding in at great pain. "I wonder young man, is there by chance a family onboard? A man, woman, and young girl?"

The purser pondered for only a moment. He replied without looking up from his table. "No. No children on this voyage."

Walter held the coins that represented the agreed price in his hand.

"You want to go or not?" The man looked up now.

Damn, it was Dover after all! Well it's impossible to get there before that ship sails, I might just as well get across the channel.

"Of course. I am sorry, my son." He dropped the money in the purser's hand.

Walter made his way out into the sunshine and up the gangplank. It was another setback, but the chase wasn't over yet. After some beer, his spirits were raised, and the crew were astonished at what good company the monk proved to be.

Chapter Seven

"Who, by God's throat, does he think he is?" King Richard bellowed to no particular individual. None of the gathered barons cared to offer an answer.

William Longespee, however, didn't fear his brother's mood. "It is doubtful that he understands what he has done. Lady Constance may not have warned him sufficiently."

Richard calmed. This latest outburst of Plantagenet temper was triggered by the actions of one Ranulf de Blundeville. Still lacking a son of his own, Richard decided to once again name his nephew Arthur as his heir. Arthur's mother lost no time obeying the summons to bring Arthur to Rouen. Along the way, however, her second husband, Ranulf, abducted them both, imprisoning them in Brittany.

"He soon will understand what he has done. When in his arrogance he styled himself a duke, he suffered exile by the hands of his own people. Now he will taste my wrath." The King's declaration was accompanied by a slamming of his fist onto the table with such force that a wine goblet and knife rattled.

"Rightfully so, Richard," William replied.

Looking around at the handful of military advisors circled about him, the King relaxed further. Making the inevitably aggressive decision moved Richard into a familiar and comfortable space.

"Gather an army three times larger than needed. I will lead it personally. We march at daybreak."

"At once, Sire!" Several vassals shouted, scurrying to carry out orders.

The King considered why he had been so upset. He was bored with castle building; smashing an enemy army sounded like fun about now.

It was Eleanor's idea. The third ship to set sail from a Cinque Port that morning left from Hastings bound for La Rochelle. Robert was quick to agree. Ela's mother told her that the route from La Rochelle to Rouen would pass extremely close to Vitre, which was why her cousin agreed to the change in plans. There was, according to mother, another place along the route. Ela was told to pray fervently that a certain individual was in residence there, though no further detail was allowed her.

"This is a much more civilized way to travel is it not?" Robert asked. The little band was properly attired now, having exchanged their pilgrim gear for proper clothing in La Rochelle. They also rode strong French riding horses.

"Yes, my cousin. It is such a relief," Eleanor replied.

Ela continued her silent struggle to come to terms with what happened to her uncle and the true pilgrims back in England. Eventually her father's voice penetrated the anguish speaking one of the many lessons he taught her over the years. It would do no good wallowing in pity, for the dead or for herself. All that mattered now was what could be done in the future. The words of the passage Philip gave her repeated themselves in her brain. 'Do justice, love mercy.'

Throughout the initial days of the journey, as they rode unmolested through the New Forest, the focus was on mercy. The threat from an uncle she never met seemed a vague notion, born of her mother's legendary caution, plus she placed no trust in Robert's counsel. She would show mercy to her uncle, even if he did prove himself overly ambitious. Now the other pairing echoed more loudly: 'Do justice.' Those innocent pilgrims, and kind Uncle Philip, deserved justice. Could a girl give it to them? Ela decided that she would do justice one day. Her father believed women possessed the ability. Why else would he have invested such time in teaching her court politics and estate management? Ela would believe it too and prove Papa right.

On that pivotal day, they were about to leave Cholet behind them with Angers as their day's goal. When they had come upon Cholet the previous day, Ela cried. Eventually, though, tears were replaced with a smile. For the first time since her father died she felt a little less broken.

Her mother kept watching her, yesterday more than ever. Was it possible her mother actually knew that Cholet was named for the Latin word for cabbage, a staple crop of the area?

Ela noticed something else, her mother was glancing about much more often that day. It seemed as if Eleanor was expecting an encounter as much now as back in England. Did the adults obtain some information they were keeping from her? Ela shifted her attention to study Robert, but he appeared as calm as when he first disembarked at La Rochelle. Was he simply subtler in his concern? Unlikely.

"Woe there!"

Two armed men on horseback trotted from behind overgrowth near the road in front of them. Another pair was behind them before they could bring their horses to a halt. Ela was frightened at first, but then she noticed that her mother was smiling. *When will I stop being surprised by her?*

"Identify yourselves please, good people." An older man, about thirty, was in charge.

"I am Robert de Evroux, soldier. I travel with my sister and her child on our way to our family home."

"That is a lie!" Ela heard from beside her. Robert and Ela both gaped at Eleanor.

"Before I answer with truth, I would know whom you represent," Eleanor demanded. "I am hopeful it is a lady I well know and love."

Ela knew now that her mother tricked Robert. She obviously managed to send a message to someone along the route without his knowledge, but who? Ela had no idea; she sat back in the saddle enjoying the little drama playing out for her.

"We come at the command of Eleanor, mother of King Richard of England, ruler of Aquitaine and Poitou in her own right," the leader answered. "It is our mission to locate the Lady Eleanor de Vitre and to bring her party to the Queen's household at Fontevrault."

"I am the lady whom you seek, and we shall gladly visit her majesty, Eleanor of Aquitaine."

As they all moved off in the direction of Chinon, Ela was thrilled. She had heard a great deal about this most remarkable woman. A few weeks ago, Ela would have been convinced that her mother would consider her namesake a vile heretic. Eleanor of Aquitaine was known to be worldly, to put it diplomatically. *Her mother knows the Queen? And loves her?*

"Well shite!" Robert muttered.

86

New friendships Walter nurtured amongst the ship's crew paid off as soon as they made landfall in Caen. Sailors inquired dockside for information of a young girl traveling from England. Within two days the informal spy web assured Walter that the family did not board the Dover ship either.

"What do I do now?" Either they hid and let him pass by, or they took the Hastings ship bound for La Rochelle, far to the South. They likely aren't seeking Richard if that is the case.

He decided to stay in Caen a few days, making use of his eager spies. While he waited, Walter sought out a tailor. Although possible that his monk's robes proved useful thus far, he was tired of the costume. Spending freely, he obtained clothing that better suited his stature as future Earl of Salisbury.

Word began to filter in of later ships that made the crossing. None bore the sought for passengers. News abounded in Caen, as well, of Richard's move to crush the supposed Duke of Brittany. If he could not deal with the brat Ela as he desired, he could at least use this knowledge to be first before the King. The more he contemplated it, the more he believed that it was now his best course of action.

Chapter Eight

Eleanor's household at Fontevrault Abbey was a modest one by her standards. She did not take the veil, but lived as a guest of the Abbess. Fontevrault was unusual in ways that suited Eleanor of Aquitaine. Its founder was a fiery preacher named Robert d'Abrisell. He decreed that, though having both male monks and female nuns within the same house, the abbey would forever be ruled by a female abbess. It was this preacher's opinion that women were superior to men in administrative abilities, an unusual position to say the least.

For her part, Eleanor of Aquitaine was as much an anomaly as this order. Being the richest heiress in Europe, she was married off at a young age to the King of France, Louis VII. Growing unhappy in this marriage to an unusually religious king, she managed to extricate herself, ostensibly on the grounds of consanguinity. It was clear to all, however, that she made arrangements for her next marriage before the first annulment was obtained. To make matters worse, her new husband was related to her just as closely as Louis was. Nevertheless, she married Henry, the Count of Anjou, who would later become King of England. Throughout her long life, there were countless such examples of Eleanor acting very much as she pleased and not at all like a woman, much less a lady.

"Good Morning, Your Majesty," Ela greeted the semi-retired Queen. Though somewhat in awe of the most famous woman in Christendom, Ela was fortunate to be too young to be intimidated by her.

Eleanor smiled. "Good morning, my child."

Even at such an advanced age, well over seventy, the woman's smile was full and white. She was famous for her beauty throughout her life. There were still vestiges that hinted at what splendor she portrayed in her prime.

They were alone in a secluded rose garden on the Abbey grounds. The grand old lady wore thick gloves and carried a small pair of pruning shears. It struck Ela as odd that the former queen to two kings, and mother of a current, enjoyed a pastime of labor, but this fact further improved her estimation of the lady.

"I was told you requested that I join you."

"That is correct, Ela. I would like to get to know you more. There is much in you that reminds me of my younger self, I think we could be great friends."

"Friends, Your Majesty?"

"First off, my friends do not call me their majesty. But I understand your mother's name is Eleanor; that might prove confusing. So child, what shall you call me?"

"Madam?" Ela suggested.

"No no. Something more personal. I have been given many nicknames over the decades; some I would rather not resurrect." Eleanor gave the girl a wink.

"What were some good ones?"

"Well, for instance, on the second crusade I was called

both Penthesilea and Golden Foot."

"On crusade? You accompanied the army?"

"Accompanied hell, I took the cross, child!" Eleanor rested her fists on her hips in mock outrage.

Glancing at the girl, Eleanor chuckled. "Close your mouth, Ela, you're going to swallow flies!"

"Penthesilea was Queen of the Amazons was she not?" Ela asked.

"Very good. You are as well educated as I have been led to believe." The Queen then sighed and looked off into the distance over the river valley. "You should have seen me then, Ela. The day I took the cross, my maidens and I rode around dressed as Amazons, swords and all. We threw sewing thimbles at the men who were reluctant to join the crusade. After that, the priest ran out of crosses; he ended up ripping up his own cloak to make more!"

Eleanor returned to the moment, shook the shears in the direction of her young friend and said, "Never forget the power you have to manipulate men by challenging their courage. That is your first lesson, my Violet."

"Violet?"

"Yes. You see this bush I'm working on now?"

"Yes, Maam."

"It's a rose of Sharon. I brought it back from the Holy Land myself. When this garden blooms, you will be in awe of the shades and scents that will clash for your attention. You will join me here often during your stay at Fountevrault. In this garden you will call me Rose, and I will call you Violet. Take heed my council, store it in your own heart. Tell no one what you hear. Can you do that, Violet?"

"Yes, Maam—yes, Rose. My father shared many secrets with me. I've never betrayed one," Ela said, not masking any pride.

"That is good, Violet. I knew your father well. He was a good man," Eleanor said. "I would like to think that I may have had some influence on his enlightened view of women."

"I was surprised to learn that my mother knew you. You knew both my parents?"

"Of course, Violet, I knew them while I was imprisoned in Sarum Castle all those years. They were kind jailers."

"Prison?"

"You did not know?" Eleanor appeared puzzled for a just a moment. "No, I suppose it would not be popular family history for your parents to instruct you in. I have spoken with your mother, your bedchamber was my cell."

"But why?"

"Under orders of my husband, King Henry."

"Your husband imprisoned you?" Ela asked.

"Another lesson perhaps. Don't judge his memory too harshly though, Violet. I did encourage his sons to revolt against him."

"He must have deserved it then!" Ela offered.

"Thank you for your confidence, my child," Eleanor said. "Perhaps he did. More likely, though, I was wrong. His temper caused much suffering for many, but overall he was a strong king and a good man. I have been wrong many times in my long life. The best lessons you can learn from me come from my failures."

"My father told me the same thing," Ela whispered.

Eleanor of Aquitaine removed the glove from her available hand and cupped Ela's chin in her palm. "Your father was wise as well as good. Failure is always the best teacher."

It was not going well for the petitioners. A handful of

brave, or foolhardy, souls requested audience before King Richard in Brittany. Unfortunately for them, he was in his foulest mood of the year.

As it happened, before Richard's army arrived, young Arthur's tutor persuaded Ranulf to let the boy go. All would have been well, but that the scholarly man considered Paris the place for the boy to learn. Thus, he took Arthur to be educated with Philip's son. He unwittingly delivered Richard's chosen heir directly into the hands of the King's mortal enemy.

Now one last man waited to enter Richard's temporary court; he would not be warned off. The King was briefed of the man's petition and requested that William Longespee bring his two bodyguards from the tournament into the hall for this particular audience.

Though there were several nobles arranged about the hall, Richard was instantly recognizable. Walter genuflected immediately within the door, then twice more as he made his way to the King.

"Who are you and what do you want?" To most, Richard's words would sound gruff. To those trapped for the day in this room, it sounded as though Richard's rage was waning.

"I am Walter FitzPatrick, your majesty. Brother of William FitzPatrick, the Earl of Salisbury."

Richard shared a furtive glance with his brother William. "That is who you are, now what do you want?"

Walter forged ahead undaunted. "I fear that I bring distressing news, Sire; my brother, the Earl of Salisbury, is dead."

"I am aware of this," Richard countered, his face betraying no emotion. "My condolences on your loss."

"Thank you, your grace." Walter realized that he should not have been surprised at the efficiency of the King's sources of information. "Are you also aware that my brother's daughter has been abducted?"

That registered. *So your sources aren't that good it seems.*

William Longespee fought himself for composure as well. A surge of protective emotion turned his insides. It was not the threat to Richard's intended gift; that much he was certain of. No, this was something at the core of his being. He knew this child, he liked this child, this child had been kind to him, but most of all THIS WAS A CHILD! If someone truly meant her harm then they would feel his blade.

"Explain," Richard replied.

"Your majesty, the girl's relative Robert de Vitre has taken control of the family and they have left England. As they have lied about their whereabouts, I assume that they did not have your permission, and that they have infringed your rights as liege lord."

Richard said nothing in response.

"Therefore, the de Vitres have, by their actions, renounced all claims to my brother's inheritance."

Richard sat and considered this in silence for some time. "And you are the eldest surviving brother I assume? You wish to make claim to the earldom?"

"Yes, Your Majesty."

"You yourself used the word abducted," Richard motioned a finger in Walter's direction, as if tapping the man's chest. "Even if she went willingly, she is a child and could have no idea the ramifications of this action. Moreover, at eight years of age, she was hardly in a position to object."

Walter could see that his initial gambit failed. It was a long odds gamble anyway. There was always the fallback plan. And how did Richard know Ela was eight?

"You may not have heard monk," Richard said, with

heavy emphasis on Walter's position. "that I myself was abducted and unjustly imprisoned during my journey from the Holy Land. I too had a relative more eager to take up my responsibilities than to find and rescue me."

Tension congealed in the hall like goose fat. The King was magnanimous in his forgiveness of his brother John, but a month never passed without Richard reminding everyone of his excellent memory. The Cor d' Leon was aware of every nobleman who supported John during his attempted usurpation.

"Of course Ela's restoration is my most eager desire. I would be happy to manage the estates on your behalf until she is found, or the worst is confirmed," Walter replied. Even with the bulk of profits going to the crown, someone must run such vast holdings. Why not him?

The King now stood and walked down to face Walter. Richard looked him directly in the eyes as he spoke. "You are willing to see to it that the domains of Salisbury are run efficiently?"

"Perfectly."

"On behalf of your niece and myself?" Richard said.

"Yes, Your Majesty."

"You will send all profits to me so long as the girl is my ward?"

"Yes, Sire. All of them." Walter replied.

Richard took one step closer, bringing his face close enough for Walter to feel, and smell, the King's breath. "Is there anything more heinous than a lying monk?"

Sharp pain gripped Walter's chest. At first, he thought it was the effect of the King's words. Then he tasted something tangy and his vision blurred. Trickles of warm liquid ran from his bottom lip. Walter's brain never had the chance to interpret the signals it was receiving from throughout his body; the best it could do was a general realization: 'Your life is at an end.'

Richard stepped back and let the lifeless hulk collapse to the ground. He pulled the dagger from Walter's heart and wiped it on the corpse's fine new clothes. "You should have stayed in your cell, monk. It might not have been much of a life, but at least it was life."

"Have this carcass sent back to Sarum. It is to be hung at the gates as a message to any other aspiring earls," Richard said.

Servants appeared and rushed to carry the body from the room.

"William, your bride may have been abducted."

"May I have leave to rescue her, Richard?"

"I'm sorry, William; I cannot spare you, particularly when we do not know precisely where she is. I suggest you send a loyal vassal in your stead."

William knew now why Peter and Talbot were present.

"Is there a volunteer?" Richard glanced at the two men.

"Yes, Your Majesty!" Both men spoke in near unison as each took a step forward.

"This will be a noble quest. You will travel the breadth of as many dukedoms and principalities as necessary to find this girl and return her to court."

Two knights again spoke in unison. "Yes, Your Majesty."

"You may not return without the girl or proof that she is no more. There could be no greater honor in chivalry than to be given such a quest. Are you worthy?" Richard asked.

This time only one answered quickly. "I am, Your Majesty!" Peter declared.

Talbot reflected.

Richard looked at him. "And you?"

"It is too great an honor to declare my own worthiness,

Your Majesty," Talbot answered, his voice faltering. "Please, Sire, ask this question of your brother William Longespee."

Richard drew his sword and walked toward the two knights. William was about to cry out to his brother when the King spoke. "Well said, good knight!" He clasped Talbot's shoulder in a sign of extreme favor. "But I already know your worthiness."

"And your lack thereof," Richard hissed at Peter.

Peter went white. "Your Majesty?"

"William Marshal observed you hiding behind his observation platform at Sarum," Richard thundered. "While my brother fought outnumbered. William?"

"I know, Peter. The Marshal exposed you that day. When presented with testimony from the Earl, your accomplices admitted that you were in alliance," Longespee confirmed.

"And you declare yourself worthy of a knight's greatest honor? Kneel!" Richard said.

Peter hesitated.

"Kneel!" Richard roared. "A good death is the only honor you have left."

Peter knelt.

Richard immediately calmed then turned his back. "William asked me to spare your life. So I am faced with a dilemma. Do I choose to be known for mercy, or as one who should not be betrayed?"

Richard gave his answer. A duke at whose feet Peter's head rolled picked it up by the hair, held it straight out in front of himself, and shouted. "Behold the head of a traitor! Thus be to all traitors! God save the King!"

Richard handed Talbot a bag of gold coins then strode out of the hall, only briefly stopping at his brother's side to whisper. "Sorry, William."

"My dear Violet, what have you been told of your grandfather's death?" the Queen asked one morning in the garden.

"Only that he was murdered while serving the King." Ela never knew her grandfather, he died long before she was born.

"That is true," Eleanor said.

"Did you know him too?"

"My child, 'knew him' are not the words."

Ela was not sure what was going to follow. Rumors of Eleanor's many romantic exploits were legendary.

"He died to save me," Eleanor said.

"To save you?"

"I was on a progress through my territories, not that far from here in fact, to bring certain rebels in line. Several of my vassals were unhappy with my lord Henry."

Ela nodded. She was interested to learn more about her grandfather, the first Earl of Salisbury. Henry's effect on noblemen of the southern feudatories was also a common theme over the last few weeks.

"Your grandfather, another valiant young knight, and I were enjoying a hawking hunt near Lusignan. Suddenly we were set upon by Guy of Lusignan and his brother Geoffrey. Earl Patrick was not wearing any armor. At his own peril, he put me on his fastest horse and bade me make haste for a nearby castle."

Though she knew the end result for both parties, Ela hung on every word.

"Thanks to him I was able to escape. I heard later that he was hurriedly attempting to put on his hauberk when one of the cowardly knaves ran him through, stabbing him in the back."

"The other knight as well?"

Eleanor half giggled despite the sadness of the tale up to this point. "Oh no. The other young knight still lives. He was twenty two years old that day. He must have battled like a wild boar fighting off a pack of dogs. He was a late son, fourth if I recall, of some minor English nobleman. What a fighter though, I watched him fight in tournaments. Eventually the numbers were too much for him, and he was wounded. The fiends refused to treat his cuts. It would have satisfied them to see a valiant man of honor sent to his tomb from rotten wounds." Eleanor spat like an old man into the flower beds at the memory of them. "I ransomed him at obscene cost."

Ela was suspicious that she knew where this story was going. "And you took interest in his career from there no doubt?"

"Indeed! And who do you think that strapping young man was, Violet?"

"William the Marshal!"

"None other," The Queen confirmed. "So wonder not why I have chosen you to be my dearest young confidant. I have extreme confidence in, and affection for, your family. Your father, though my jailer, treated me kindly and respectfully. His cousin fought a small army to protect me. His father laid down his life to save his queen. I would move the Earth to give you a good life."

Ela was embarrassed by such praise, but couldn't help but feel pride in her family's history. "It would be my honor to follow my family's example and serve you loyally as well."

"My time is coming to a close, Violet. If you would serve me, support my sons," Eleanor replied.

Ela considered the request for a moment. "I will do my best Rose, but aren't your sons usually fighting each other?" Not many men in the realm would have dared ask such a question of the Queen.

Eleanor sighed deeply and shook her head. "You speak truthfully. Support the crowned king unless your heart, or the word of God, commands you otherwise."

"I will. With all my strength," Ela vowed.

Chapter Nine

May 12, 1198

"Piss honor!" Talbot spat for the hundredth time, leaning on his pilgrim's staff.

The sun was directly above him, and though barely twenty years old, he felt as if he needed that damned staff as much as a great-grandfather.

He was dressed in humble pilgrim wool having walked to and fro, like this, for the past two years. Still, with Richard's coin purse growing light, there was no trace of Ela's whereabouts. Corresponding regularly through Church communications, he was certain that Ela's family never contacted the King's court either.

All the romance of a chivalric quest wore thin long before. When could he go home, maybe get a bride of his own, maybe even some romance as well? Looking out across the brilliant green fields, he could see in the distance the placid Vienne River as it flowed past the community of Chinon. Recently whitewashed walls of the royal palace glimmered in the sun. Talbot was grateful that Richard was not currently in residence, though the King frequently spent a good portion of each year at Chinon Castle.

Neither the prosperous village, nor the massive battlements hovering above it were Talbot's destination this day. His instructions were to not return to court without completing his quest, yet he needed replenishment of funds. He hoped that the solution to his dilemma lay twelve miles from here. One of the reasons that Chinon was a favorite residence of Richard was its proximity to his mother; the King could visit and take council with her easily while staying here.

Eleanor was fabulously wealthy, steeped in the tradition of chivalry, and fond of handsome young men. Perhaps she would be agreeable to further funding his quest. Clinging to this hope, Talbot gathered up his fortitude and set off westward following the course of the Vienne toward Fontevrault Abbey.

Richard indeed visited his mother at Fontevrault multiple times over the previous two years. Through subtle inquiry, Eleanor learned the King's plan for Ela. It was the Queen's point of view that her own fondness for the girl overrode Richard's strategy for the time being. It was not that she held any ill will toward William Longespee. She readily agreed to educating several of Henry's bastards alongside her own sons, including Richard. After all, she was not innocent of marital infidelity. How could she criticize a man for the same sin?

Ela, however, was only a child. Richard, and therefore William, could wait. As a queen, she was never actively involved in the raising of her own daughters. In her advanced years, she wished to pass something of herself on to future generations of women. This was a misogynous culture they operated in, constantly stifling contributions, and very personalities, of the fairer sex. Like a cultural Amazon, Eleanor successfully battled these limitations all her life. Seeing her own time drawing to a close, she was resolute that spirit, that spark, would not be extinguished with her.

And so Eleanor did not volunteer information of Ela's whereabouts to Richard. When he visited, the family was always conveniently absent. Her deception would eventually have to be revealed, of course. Plantagenet temper would undoubtedly flare. The thought of it bored Eleanor. Over the decades, she witnessed enough of the famous family trait to know how temporary it was, and Richard was always her favorite son. She would soon be forgiven. Eleanor was solely responsible for Richard's ransoming and the restoration of his realm. He was as close to her as a strong man could be to his mother. The girl and the lady de Vitre, therefore, spent two happy years in the Queen's own household.

Talbot saw the tower of the Abbey church come into view above the treetops. Out of habit more than anything else, he moved off the road and approached under cover. Creeping low out of the tree line and taking cover in some tall grass on the opposite shore of the fish ponds, he began to mock himself. *What are you doing fool? You've been at this quest too long man! This is the Queen's residence not some common manor house. What if you are caught skulking around here?*

He was about to turn and backtrack through the woods in order to continue on via the main road, when he noticed a girl approach a pond from the opposite side. She looked to be about ten years old. Suddenly he was transported back to a tournament two years previously in Sarum. The girl meant nothing to him at the time, but he saw her at least twice. Could that be her? *Oh you have lost it now haven't you*

Talbot?

The girl tossed stones into the pond. The more he studied this girl's face the more he thought he recognized her. Talbot then began to review what he knew, and more importantly what was rumored, of Eleanor of Aquitaine. Could anything be beyond her? Furthermore, she doubtless knows that Ela and her rights are meant for a man born of the love of King Henry for another woman. Perhaps that provided motive enough for such a game.

Talbot determined to treat this as his first possible sighting and implement the ploy he dreamed up over those many long months of endless walking. Carefully, he crawled back to the trees, opened the rough shoulder sack he carried, and began to take off his clothes.

"You may enter, good man," Eleanor offered.

The man approached her across the grand hall, or what passed for grand in such a relatively humble dwelling, with perfect courtly manners. He was dressed as a troubadour in bright blue doublet and green tights. The Queen had not kept a good troubadour in her household for many years now. They were a delightful entertainment both as intended and as playthings. She hoped this one was talented; he was certainly young and good-looking enough.

"Who are you, Sir?" Eleanor asked.

"My name is William, your grace. I am a humble traveling troubadour. I know countless songs and lais, many inspired by your legendary beauty, which I beg to perform for your household."

"Many of your profession have sought a place in my household. The greatest of our age included."

"A daunting competition to be sure. I only hope to be of some pleasure and amusement."

"By all means then, young man, favor us with a song."

Talbot stood in the middle of the room encircled by the Queen and her retinue. He lifted the lyre and began to sing.

> *'The sweet young Queen*
> *Draws the thoughts of all upon her*
> *As sirens lure the witless mariners*
> *Upon the reef.*
>
> *If all the world were mine*
> *From the seashore to the Rhine,*
> *That price were not too high*
> *To have England's Queen lie*
> *Close to my arms.'*

All was quiet for several moments. Talbot willed his breath into submission, as beads of sweat formed on his forehead. Finally, the Queen nodded her head once, then the assembly broke out in applause and cheers. The counterfeit troubadour acknowledged all the admirers about him, paying particular notice to one young girl near the Queen's left hand. The girl seemed to have enjoyed the song, but she wore a quizzical expression as well.

"I would hear more of your repertoire, William. Please lodge here with us for a time."

"Of course, my lady. It would be the greatest of honors."

"Very well. The steward will show you to your chambers. Be prepared to entertain us after evening meal."

"Yes, your majesty."

As Talbot was exiting the hall, the Queen spoke loudly enough for him to hear. "And let that be a lesson to all of the ladies here of the sincerity of a man's complements.

Neither of the men who wrote those lines in my honor ever laid eyes on me!"

Talbot chuckled to himself. *Touché, my Queen!* He already liked the old lady. Perhaps at least some of what he'd heard of her could be true.

The next morning was clear and bright. Ela and the Queen, as was their custom, worked and talked in the Abbey gardens. Over the years these encounters developed into part classroom, part strategy session, and good part genuine friendly chat. Ela now knew Eleanor of Aquitaine's heart better than any person alive, other than the Queen herself. She also loved the lady dearly. These garden sessions were the girl's most cherished moments.

"Rose?"

"Yes, Violet?"

"I have seen the new troubadour before, but he was a knight when I met him last," Ela said.

"Really? Where have you seen him?"

"At the tournament in Sarum the week my father died. He was traveling with the tournament champion."

Eleanor remained stooped over a rose bush, not looking up. "I see. So we have met our friend William Talbot. I did not expect him to be so talented a musician. He fooled me brilliantly."

"William Talbot?" Ela was rarely surprised by the Queen's knowledge or intuition anymore. "You know him?"

"I have heard of him yes. I have been expecting him, though we have been sheltered by his good sense until now."

Ela no longer prompted the lady to continue. She knew Eleanor would tell her what she was going to tell her in time.

"He was sent on a great quest by the King." Eleanor said.

"A quest?" Ela grew excited. Quests featured heavily in

the books she read. Courtly love and chivalry led to quests in tales of Arthur, of Tristan, and many others. "What is his quest? Can we help him?"

"We can definitely help him," Eleanor answered.

"Wonderful! What is the quest?"

Finally the Queen stood and faced her young friend. "You are, my dear."

Ela's excitement turned to puzzlement. Eleanor did not explain, merely held the girl's gaze and let the last two year's lessons do their work.

It did not take long for Ela to work the puzzle out. "The King is looking for me."

"Yes"

"Because he wishes to award the Earldom of Salisbury, which is my right, to one in his favor."

"Precisely," Eleanor replied.

"Do you know who?"

"I do."

Ela nodded her head several times, chewing on her bottom lip. "How old is he?"

Eleanor rocked her head back and laughed out loud. "That's my girl! I'm heartened that was your first consideration."

Ela smiled in return.

"He's not an old man, very early twenties I believe." Eleanor said.

"Handsome?"

"I believe so. I have not seen him for many years. I can speak from experience, however, that he comes from solid stock," Eleanor offered a sly smile.

"From experience?"

"Yes. He is a son of my late husband Henry."

"A bastard?" Ela asked.

"Yes, but do not let that bother you too much, child.

Remember, King William was a bastard too."

"What is his name?"

"It is also William. They call him William of the long sword."

"Longespee?"

"Yes," Eleanor said, examining Ela's smile. "I take it you know him?"

"Yes." Ela forced her face into a neutral expression. "He was the champion I spoke of earlier."

"Good. A champion, of king's blood, and obviously of agreeable countenance."

Ela flushed red as the Rose of Sharon not yet in bloom.

"All that remains now is to decide if we are ready to allow these men to believe they have outwitted us," Eleanor said, "Are you ready to reclaim your inheritance, Violet?"

Ela grew sad. They were now discussing her leaving the Abbey, and her dear old friend, perhaps forever. "I would miss you terribly, Rose. Do you think I am ready?"

Eleanor stood silent for several moments, gazing upon her young protégé. "Yes I do, Ela."

"Then so do I, Eleanor."

The pair embraced for several minutes with Ela's head buried in Eleanor's bosom. "We're both weeping so much," Ela said. "If men saw us they'd think us silly weak women."

"Let them," Eleanor whispered.

Chapter Ten

Talbot's jaw hung open. He walked by the fish ponds scheming a way to find himself alone with the girl when he heard a soft high voice behind him.

"You're hairier now than you were at Sarum."

"My lady?"

"I remember you from the tournament," Ela declared, putting an end to any coyness the man might attempt. "You are William Longespee's friend. You fought valiantly."

"I... I have been traveling for some time. It is difficult to shave on such a journey."

"Of course. I am glad I do not have to worry about such chores."

"You remember my lord as well then, even his name."

"I do. He was so valiant, handsome, and sweet."

Undoubtedly her lord Longespee would not appreciate the last adjective, but it was important to encourage Talbot to reveal his mission. If he believed Ela a silly girl in love with a man she only met once, he might believe she would go with him willingly.

Talbot's mind raced. This was the opportunity he was

trying to create. What if she reacted badly? He was in as good a position as he would ever be to abduct her: close to the gates and without her being missed. He committed to the gamble.

"Can I trust you with a weighty secret, my lady?"

"Oh, a secret! Yes, I'm good at secrets," Ela said.

"I am on a quest; one ordered by the King."

"How thrilling! What is it that you seek?"

"I believe I seek you," Talbot said. "You are Ela of Salisbury are you not?"

"I am!" Ela affected the surprise Talbot expected. "You seek me?"

"I do," Talbot said, bowing low. "King Richard wishes you to come to his court without delay. You are to be married."

"Me? Married?" Ela asked in a singsong manner. "To whom?"

"To none other than the valiant, handsome, and--what was it—sweet? William Longespee."

"He fell in love with me at Sarum! He begged the King for my hand!"

"Precisely!" Talbot said. His expression included a wide smile, bordering on laughter.

"I must go to the poor man at once," Ela said, laying her right hand on her chest. "How his heart must break at our long absence."

"Agreed."

"Meet me here tonight, a little past nightfall. We will leave this very night."

"Very good, my lady Ela of Salisbury, future wife of my Lord, William Longespee. Until tonight." Talbot turned and sprinted toward the Abbey.

Ela watched the man's swift retreat and giggled. *Eleanor is right. They are fun!*

Talbot paced in the darkness. Did the girl change her mind? Would she raise the alarm? Certainly it was a lot for a young girl to consider leaving her mother to run off and marry a man she hardly knew. Did he overestimate the power of Ela's imagined love?

Then he saw the girl, and the three horses she led over to him.

"What is this?" Talbot asked.

"Why this, my dear Talbot, is a horse. So are these."

"You stole horses from the King's mother?"

"No silly, they are mine," Ela replied.

"Well that's good. Did none see you?"

"No. The abbey guards only secure valuables, the chapel, and the lady. Besides, I can't go without my things."

Talbot now saw that one of the horses was loaded down with bags. "You women do start early with your baggage trains don't you?"

"I learned from the Queen. Shall we be off?"

Talbot led the way down the lane. Ela waved her hand behind her head in the direction of the Abbess' guest lodgings. Without looking, she knew the wave was being returned by an elegant woman: a woman Ela would never forget.

It was the first week in June when Talbot and Ela arrived at Rouen. They stayed the previous night in a nearby monastery so that they could launder their clothes and arrive at court as clean as possible. Now they rode directly to the castle where Talbot was delighted to learn that the King was presiding over submission of petitions. It would make for a dramatic and glorious culmination of his quest. Only the memory of the last petition session he attended tempered his excitement.

He found the seneschal and inquired of the King's mood. Years of travel emboldened the knight. The seneschal was accustomed enough to calculating Richard's frame of mind that he found nothing offensive in the question.

"His Majesty is in high spirits. I trust your return will only add to the atmosphere in court. Welcome back, William."

"Thank you, sir."

"You will, of course, go straight to the front of the queue. We shall take you in as soon as the current case is complete." The seneschal offered a rare snippet of humor. "I expect the petitioner to survive."

"That is good to hear. And may I officially introduce you to Ela of Salisbury?"

"A pleasure, my lady Ela."

"Good to make your acquaintance, sir," Ela offered.

"Where did you find her?" Walter of Coutances asked, turning back to the male member of the pair.

"Would you believe Fontevrault Abbey?" Talbot asked with a sigh.

The seneschal went white. "How long were you there?"

"A little over two years, sir," Ela replied.

"Oh the Blessed Lady. I've been there during that time!" Ela grinned. "I know."

"Let's hope it doesn't come up," Coutances muttered to Talbot.

Just then a jubilant minor nobleman backed out of the hall, acknowledged the seneschal, and trotted off.

"It is time." The three of them entered the room together. "My lord King, William Talbot returns triumphant with the lady Ela!"

Richard clapped his hands together. "Splendid! Well done, young Talbot."

"A thousand thanks, your majesty." Talbot bowed low.

Ela scanned the semi-circle of nobles and warriors flanking the King and caught sight of her intended husband. His smile reminded her of that first one back in Sarum. She averted her eyes and studied the stone floor on which she stood.

"You shall be well rewarded for your persistence in this endeavor. William, let us waste no more time. Marry this girl today in my private chapel."

"Yes, Brother."

"Tell the rest of the petitioners to come back tomorrow. We will have a wedding and then a marriage feast!" Richard bellowed.

William did not have a proper permanent home in Rouen. Therefore, Ela found herself that night in a hastily prepared bridal chamber in Richard's castle. Though her mother was not allowed to know about her faux flight from Fontevrault, the Queen acted as a surrogate in explaining what to expect on her wedding night. Ela was still quite nervous, especially since Eleanor said it might be painful the first time. The Queen, however, made it very clear that the act of lovemaking was something she very much enjoyed. Indeed, that much Ela knew already; Eleanor's libido was internationally famous.

Ela steeled her courage as the door opened and William walked in. "Good evening, husband."

"Good evening, wife." William shook is head. "When I awoke this morning it was just another day at court. Tonight I have a wife."

"I did not expect quite such a rush myself, though I held the advantage of being the surpriser." She could sense that William felt awkward around her. Eleanor anticipated this;

he was twenty-two she was ten. If he was not apprehensive, he was not the man both women thought him to be.

William then noticed books stacked on a table. "These books belong to you?"

"Yes, my father gave them to me."

"You can read?" As soon as the words left his mouth, his cheeks turned red.

She did not laugh or mock him. "Yes, French and Latin."

"I am married to a scholar! You have managed to keep these with you through all your adventures these past two years?"

"I believe the general consensus was that it was easier to deal with such heavy baggage than to deal with me without it."

William laughed. "I'm beginning to understand who I have joined myself with. Heaven help me!"

Though not as awkward now, silence once again pervaded the room.

Ela decided it was time to take matters into her own hand. Following the directions of her mentor, she stood before William and slowly began to undo the bodice of her dress. She wished for some, any at all, breast development to offer.

William reacted in horror. "Stop, Ela!"

"But we must." She was horribly embarrassed that he was so uninterested. "We must consummate the marriage so that you can become earl by my right."

"No Ela, it is enough that we spend one night together in the same bedchamber. Our union will be legally assumed to be consummated."

"Oh." She felt relieved and rejected at the same time.

"Ela, I have no doubt you will one day be a desirable woman, and I will consider myself fortunate when I become your true husband. But for now you are a child, I cannot know you intimately until you are a woman. I would kill any man who could do such a thing."

Ela nodded. "What do we do now?"

"It has been a long day for both of us. Get into bed and I will read from one of your books."

With the stress of what would happen relieved, Ela at once felt very tired. She was happy to obey her husband's first command by curling up on the bed under a thick woolen cover.

"Ah! The lais of Marie de France!" William said.

"Yes. Father gave that to me shortly before I saved you."

"I had the situation well under control as I recall," he said, chuckling. "Nonetheless, we shall never speak of it with anyone else."

"Yes, husband."

"You will meet Marie," William said.

"You know her?" Ela raised herself up on one elbow.

"She is my aunt," he replied, as if the King being his brother meant little in comparison.

Ela fell onto her back again. "I should like to meet her soon."

William walked over and sat on the bed throwing his legs up on top of the cover beside Ela. He began to read aloud Marie's poem of Tristan. Within minutes he could tell from his bride's rhythmic breathing that she was fast asleep. He closed the book, looked affectionately at the sleeping girl, and touched his lips to her forehead.

"Good night, little one," he whispered.

He rose only to blow out all the candles in the room then got back on the bed. *A wife that has spent two years studying under Eleanor of Aquitaine. I do believe that my life just got a lot more interesting.*

Part the Second:

Wife

Chapter Eleven

Sarum 1208

A tall young woman strode out through the castle gate, a parcel of crushed flowers held to her nose against the stench of the teeming village. She made haste toward the city gate, wanting to leave the hilltop behind.

At over six feet tall, she towered over most men much less women. Self conscious of her height to a fault, the only flaw a spectator ever found in the woman's physical appearance was a pronounced stoop as she hunched to appear smaller. Convinced that people stared at her thinking her a freak and a giant, in truth all who caught sight of her held their gaze longer than was seemly due to her surpassing beauty.

To see her inspired everyone, men and women, to attempt to memorize her face. Long reddish blonde hair was hidden within netting bundled up behind her head attached to a veiled headpiece. Soft unblemished skin of her face showed, as well as her high cheekbones and bright green eyes. A flawless smile often brightened her countenance, gleaming from a wide mouth and full soft lips. Today though, under the gaze of so many who stopped work to bow and to stare, her face was set in a look of pure concentration. She continued without pause through the city gates and down a path which followed a terrace on the ancient hill-fort of Sarum.

Ela was now twenty years old. Though not yet a mother, William and she had enjoyed some years of true married life. The pair came to love each other very deeply, a fortunate if somewhat rare stroke of luck for a couple joined for political reasons. Once again alone in Sarum, with William off serving at the itinerant court of King John, Ela retreated to a tiny clearing in the woods that blanketed the hill. It was her favorite spot to sit and read. Today she carried a large volume which contained the collective letters that she received over the course of the previous decade.

The book was, oddly enough, the suggestion of Ela's mother. The two grew closer over the last few years.

"If you love books so much, why not have your correspondence bound?" Mother asked one day. "That way, you can look back upon it as a chronicle of your life."

It was a brilliant idea, and this volume was now Ela's most prized possession. As was her custom when having a new entry bound, Ela opened the cover and began reading at the beginning.

February 10, 1199
Copenhagen

My Lady Ela,

I am overjoyed to hear the news that you have returned to your home at Sarum. Despite word you may have received, I was not in the Hauekehurst inn when it was lost to fire. My pride holds that you may have suffered some small grief to hear that I had perished. I would have assured you of my survival had I, as many of your acquaintance, known where to send word. May this letter find you well, and may the Lord grant that we should see one another again in this life.

Friar Philip

Ela smiled. Uncle Philip's letter was necessarily formal, as it was likely to be read by others. They were indeed reunited. He was now living at Sarum Castle, no longer a friar but a philosopher. Philip told her of many adventures that he found himself in during those two years he searched for her. Philip and Talbot were brothers in a common mission though neither knew it. They even crossed paths on two occasions. It was chance alone that brought Talbot to Fontevrault first.

March 7, 1199
Fontevrault Abbey

My Dearest Violet,

I have the tremendous pleasure to be in the company of your handsome husband this week. Do not worry, I will not corrupt him through my legendary powers of seduction! I am convinced that he is a good man. You know full well that it would take an impressive man indeed for me to consider him worthy of you. I confess there may not be a better choice in the realm.

I must share with you a sadness which has recently befallen me. Both of the daughters born of my marriage to Louis have passed from this Earth within a short period. In fact, I learned of both deaths from the same messenger. Though I was never close to either girl, born as they were in my selfish youth, I have been struck by this news. It seems that I am forever mourning my shrinking family.

Remember what I taught you, as I remind myself: suffering is inevitable, but joy is a choice! I will pray that God receives them into his presence and take comfort in the memory of a girl I chose to be closer than a daughter.

All of the monks and nuns of the order who knew you send their love and greetings. Particular love comes your way from the Abbess and myself.

Your Friend,
Rose

April 18, 1199
Fontevrault Abbey

My Little One,

I must confess that when you first tasked me with writing letters detailing my adventures and feelings, I considered it a silly chore. Surprisingly, I have come to find this a helpful exercise to put events occurring around me into perspective. I thank you for giving me this assignment. This is, in fact, my fifth attempt at composition. Momentous events have torn me away until now; I pray this time I am able to complete the task.

I am sure that you noted with interest that I am writing this on Easter Sunday from your former home at Fontevrault Abbey. Your most beloved Eleanor is in good health but as you will see as you read, she suffers greatly from emotional pain. Barely one month ago I was here in the company of my brother Richard under much happier circumstances. He was here to enjoy his mother's company and to receive her wise counsel. This provided a most welcome opportunity for me to renew my acquaintance with the great lady, and for us to share our mutual affection for our common friend. You should find within this package separate letters written at the lady's dictation for your benefit.

In parting from the Queen those short weeks ago (though it feels much longer), we set off for a village called Chalus one hundred miles to the South. While plowing, a peasant churned up a treasure of gold buried by some accursed Roman a thousand years before. Minor nobles, vassals of Richard and Eleanor, were beating their breasts over whose right it was to possess this treasure; as if there was a chance any of them would hold it long. Our brother Richard became obsessed with obtaining this hoard for himself, and would not be dissuaded.

Upon seeing our party approaching the village, these fools shut themselves up inside, having locked the gates against their King. It was, at the time, an amusing diversion to lay siege to this little castle. On the 26th of March, however, we made a most tragic error in judgement. Thinking ourselves safely out of range, we reconnoitered a corner of the castle walls without benefit of armor.

There was upon the castle battlements a young man who carried in his heart enmity toward Richard sufficient to charge his weapon with superhuman tension. The bolt missed Richard's heart by inches and lodged instead deep into his shoulder. A captain of the mercenaries by the name of Mercadier attempted to remove the bolt, but we found that the tip had struck so hard that it was imbedded within the bone itself. The shaft broke off leaving the arrowhead still within the wound. Mercadier then set about cutting with a dagger and shaking the tip about, to the King's astonishing agony, in an attempt to dislodge the offending fragment.

That regrettable task accomplished, we sought as best we could to clean and close the ugly wound. Unfortunately, we were unsuccessful and the gash soon festered. Within days it became clear that despite Richard's splendid constitution, he would not recover. You have not witnessed such lamentation from mighty warriors as you would have seen the day we gave him up.

The boy (for he was indeed nothing but a boy) who launched the missile was found and brought before the King. Richard asked the boy what wrong his king did to him to provoke this regicide. When the boy replied that Richard slew his father and two of his brothers, the King was greatly touched. Not only did he command that the boy be allowed to go his way unharmed, Richard presented a generous gift of money in order that he could live out his days in comfort. Such is the grace and kindness my brother often showed which is so often overlooked.

A messenger was dispatched to fetch Queen Eleanor and bring her to her son's side. I do not wish to trouble you more than necessary, so I will not speak of Eleanor's countenance when she arrived and saw her favorite son in such condition. Though she rode with haste normally reserved for one a quarter of her age, she only arrived a few hours before Richard passed. The lady did give passionate counsel to her son that he should change his choice of heirs, as Arthur was too attached to the French King. Richard, whether in agreement or in one last act of filial duty, instructed that all of his territories should pass to his brother John instead of his nephew Arthur.

One week ago, on Palm Sunday, we buried my brother at the foot of our father Henry at Fontevrault as was his final wish. I can assure you that Richard was, in the end, grieved by his actions in warring against his own father and rightful king. A mother and a brother comforted each other in their loss of a mutual relative. Little did we know then, however, how clear it would be seven days later how much the kingdom would mourn the loss of Richard's strong leadership.

John arrived on Wednesday securing the King's treasure at Chinon, though he required the aid and intervention of his elderly mother to accomplish it. Traveling on to Fontevrault the same day, he made great show and pageantry of insisting upon paying his respects to his father and brother at their tombs. Great inconvenience and trouble was inflicted upon the Abbess, one I know whom you hold in great regard and affection, to authorize the opening of the sealed chamber.

Ela, my little one, I am filled with a sense of foreboding for the future of the realm which is our home when I reflect upon the events of today. In my heart I wish to ignore them. I certainly gain no pleasure in documenting them upon parchment. In the end, however, above your desire to know all that keeps me from your presence, I know that what I have witnessed today tells me that peace will not for long reign in England. We must be prepared for what is going to transpire in our beloved land.

Today, Easter Sunday of all days, my brother King John once again refused to partake of communion. Bishop Hugh of Lincoln preached a sermon which the King interrupted no fewer than three times asking him to finish quickly so that he could eat! Later the Bishop was showing us the marvelous relief sculpture that I am sure you remember well depicting the Last Judgement. As Hugh pointed out the saved being received into heaven, John ignored him and pointed instead to the damned falling into eternal torment. His words then sent shivers down my spine and even still leaves a cold stone in my belly. "Show me rather these, whose good example I mean to follow!" he said!

We have upon the throne of the Holy See a strong Pope. John, in his apostasy and arrogance, cannot long avoid a confrontation with the Church itself. England will no doubt find itself under the same unenviable affliction that France now suffers, that is an interdict.

What can I do? My only other choice is to support a child who is fully under control of the King of France. I must be loyal to my brother, though in my heart I believe him wicked and a fool.

And so I bring this troubling message to a close. Pray, my little one, that my next correspondence is a happier one. I send this, as well as Eleanor's sealed letters, in the capable hands of our friend William Talbot. I send him to you as an aid in the work you take on at such a tender age. It is clear that I will not soon be able to spend significant time in Sarum. Therefore Talbot is tasked with crushing under foot any opposition that might arise owing to your sex or your age. Manage our lands well, little one. With Talbot standing behind you our subjects will heed your words as if they fell from the mouth of the King himself!

Your Affectionate Husband,
William Longespee

Ela paused to consider how wise her husband was. The

letter reminded her that William indeed predicted the interdict which England now found itself under. Defying Pope Innocent III, John installed his own choice as the new Archbishop of Canterbury after the death of Hubert Walter. Now because of this foolish pissing contest, no services or rites could be performed in the kingdom. Newborn babies went unbaptized, people died every day without benefit of last rites.

It was a dark time for those who took their only comfort in life from the Church. Even with a greater understanding of scripture and the faults of Mother Church, Ela knew it was an intolerable condition for a Christian nation to be in. Neither peace nor profit could long endure. She turned back to the precious book and continued reading.

April 18, 1199
Fontevrault Abbey

My Dearest Violet,

You will know by now that since writing my last letter I have buried yet another child. For all his faults, and believe me I am well aware the many sins he has to atone for, Richard was always the dearest of all my offspring. I have borne ten children in my lifetime, now only three remain alive. Of those three, one is the least of my sons and another, my namesake daughter, resides in far away Spain. But never mind, I have you closer by and for the moment I borrow your husband's shoulder to weep upon.

I fear that I will also now have to come out of my self imposed (and deeply desired) retirement. John is not as strong as Richard was, and many nobles on both sides of the channel hate him. He will need my help in securing the crown.

May you never bear the grief which has been my constant companion.

Your Rose

April 22, 1200
Fontevrault Abbey

My Dearest Violet,

I am overjoyed to be able to write to you of happier times. Though true I have buried another daughter, as Joanna passed during childbirth here in the Abbey, she gave her life to the service of God beforehand. She took the veil and died a sister of the order and is buried, along with the son who did not survive, here near me. All of this took place soon after my last letter.

Since then, however, I have spent some joyous weeks with my daughter Eleanor. John has concluded a five year peace treaty with Philip (a welcome relief in itself), the terms of which included the marriage of France's heir to one of John's nieces. It was my happy task to cross the Pyrenees in winter! I claim my right as an old woman to complain with biting irony though in truth I have seldom seen happier times.

Reaching Toledo in January, I was able to stay two months at my daughter's court. She has done a marvelous job, I could not have done better, of blending the superior culture of our Aquitaine and Poitou with the best of the Eastern courts. It is a splendid realm blessed with natural beauty, bounty from the Mediterranean ports, and my daughter!

It was my opinion, and you know how accurate my instincts are toward people, that the younger of Eleanor's two still unmarried daughters was a better choice. I saw something in her that I have not seen since you left me two years ago. She has that spark that makes her like us, my Violet. Thus, I ventured out across the mountains with young Blanche of Castille in my care.

The only trouble on the return journey came, as you'd expect, from swaggering men. Mercadier met me and insisted in bolstering my protection with his manly presence. You will remember that he was the mercenary leader present at Richard's last battle. In any regard, not two days later he and another mercenary captain got into a heated argument. No doubt there was some disagreement as to which of them possessed the larger penis! The result was more senseless death as Mercadier is now buried just outside Bordeaux. I beg you child, train your William well! They are all capable of such stupidity, don't be fooled in thinking your man is smarter than the rest.

Back safe, I am thankful for having seen my daughter Eleanor again. That, and meeting many more of my grandchildren, was a joy I did not expect to receive in this lifetime. With peace between our realm and Philip assured, I am confident you and William will be able to enjoy some of your good young years together. These are better days indeed!

Your friend,
Rose

August 24, 1200
Bordeaux

My Precious Little One,

Today I have attended the wedding of my brother King John. Seven weeks ago he was advised by Eleanor to visit the territory of the troublesome Lusignans in a show of force. At a reception, John caught sight of a girl of thirteen years by the name of Isabella. The flames of love burned instantly within the King's heart (or at least loins) as if from one of your chivalric tales. Alas I am afraid that the romance is not so perfect as troubadours would tell it, as I don't believe his love is returned.

The merry side of this tale is that Isabella was intended as the bride of Hugh de Lusignan. John and the girl's parents arranged by trickery to get her out of Lusignan in order to spirit her off to Bordeaux Cathedral to marry the King instead. Imagine Hugh's reaction to such humiliation. Fitting retribution for a perpetually devious family! Eleanor has shared with me that it was these dogs who murdered your grandfather.

I can also report that John intends to bring his bride to tour her new lands in England by the end of the year. In his happiness, some say stupor, he desires to share his joy with me and thus is sending me on ahead. I will be arriving soon and look forward to renewing my friendship with you and Talbot and to see the work you both have achieved in my absence.

Affectionately,
William Longespee

June 10, 1201
Chateau Gaillard

Dear Ela,

It seems I may have underestimated the traitorous Lusignans. They continue to stir up trouble throughout Normandy. John was amused to order his commanders to attack every castle belonging to the family. All is progressing well in those endeavors, but I begin to have a bad feeling as to where this will lead.

For the moment, Philip is rejecting the Lusignan faction's appeals. As you know, however, the French King has a precarious relationship with the Vatican. Innocent has only recently lifted the interdict on France, and Philip dares not offend the Holy Father by breaking his oath to John. Should His Holiness grant Philip legitimacy for his bastard children, however, I believe the way would be clear for Philip to use the current conflict to his advantage. The consequences of France entering openly into this dispute could be grave.

All of this over the enchantment of a thirteen year old girl! The world is a safer place, as you continue your emergence into womanhood, that you are safely married and out of the sight of powerful men. The pretty girl I left behind will one day be a dangerous beauty! What is it they said of Eleanor in her prime? Excessively beautiful? Such reflection reminds me, I charge you to stand up straight. Do not be embarrassed that you are taller than other girls. I would not like to have a wife I could carry around in my pocket anyway! You notice I no longer call you little one? Hah!

With regret I must inform you that I have heard your beloved Eleanor is unwell. I have not been able to see her myself yet, but will endeavor to do so at my earliest opportunity. Let us hope and pray that it is a temporary illness. Though she is of advanced years, we can take comfort in her strength; her perseverance; and let us be honest, her stubbornness.

Take a fast ride on the plains for me when the weather is fair. I miss our riding and hawking days already. Perhaps I am suffering enchantment as well!

With Affection,
William

August 6, 1202
Chinon

My Dear Ela,

It has been too long since I have been back in England. No doubt you have changed yet again. You are now of proper marriage age! By my next homecoming you will no doubt be a woman more desirable than I ever imagined those years ago in Rouen. How tall are you now? Hopefully I will not have to stand on a box to kiss your lips!

I'm afraid my account of recent events will once again be an ominous one, though at least this time I have hope. Your dearest Eleanor of Aquitaine was recently in route to stave off the illegal transfer of her province of Poitou by that dog Philip when her grandson Arthur learned of her travel. Following the rash and devilish advise of the cowardly French, Arthur proceeded to undertake the obscene action to besiege Eleanor at the castle of Mirebeau!

Imagine the octogenarian Queen taking refuge in the crumbling keep without proper provision of food or water. Arthur, as many have done before him, underestimated our good lady! Eleanor was able to sneak out two messengers before the castle was surrounded. One found John and me just leaving Chinon. The fool vacilated once again not knowing what to do and incapable of manly action. Having some measure of the love and affection you hold for the Queen, I took my brother aside and beat him mercilessly in the face!

You may never have known your husband the way God intended. You can guess that it was entirely possible that John would have my head. Luck was with me, however, and my blows produced the desired effect. John then took command of the troops and we rode with haste to his mother's rescue.

Never have I enjoyed a battle more, Ela! We stormed through the city walls and found that whelp and his keeper Hugh de Lusignan enjoying a breakfast of roasted pigeons while Eleanor went hungry. The bloodletting was all too short as we overwhelmed them in an instant. Instead, the knaves were transported through the streets in oxcarts.

Today your beloved Eleanor is back safe at Fontevrault, her lands are secure, and we hold Arthur in our hands. Philip himself must admit his cause is lost! For this reason I am hopeful of soon being allowed to return to my own lands and see you, my now womanly bride.

Your Affectionate and Anticipating Husband,
William

July 13, 1203
Caen

My Beloved Wife,

Disaster is at hand! Normandy falls before Philip as if her castles were made of sand. Meanwhile, despite the urgent beseeching of his few remaining loyal vassals, John does nothing! If he were to act like a man now, Philip could be defeated. Our father Henry or our brother Richard would have beaten him back past Paris all the way to the Rheine by now!

What's worse, I despair of hope that the rumors are unfounded. John most certainly murdered our nephew Arthur. And that during holy week! I believe my family accursed, that each man is tainted by the death of innocents. My father will forever be associated with the death of Thomas Becket, though in truth he did not desire it. Richard's death resulted from the revenge of a boy too familiar with his sword. Now John kills his own nephew, though the boy would surely have forever been a thorn in the side of the King as long as he lived.

Ela, I must explain the nightmare which woke me that night when last I was with you. I was too proud and our love too new at the time. You have become my confidant, however, and I will not keep anything from you. When I was younger, not much younger than you are now, I was a carefree boy. Boisterous and arrogant, I was convinced I was in control of the world about me. One day I was practicing with a bow and arrow in a country churchyard. Carelessly, I made a difficult shot and the missile missed the target high.

What woke me that night is the memory of what my foolishness caused. The nightmares have subsided as I have aged, but occasionally they return. A reminder, no doubt, from our Lord that I might keep my faults in check. The arrow struck a baby! Not more than six weeks old, it was suckling at its mother's breast. The sight of the ruined baby and the sound of the mother's cries haunt me equally. The stains you find on this parchment are my bitter tears that I still shed twelve years later.

And so you know now what ghosts haunt your husband. I pray you do not hate me. That child is the product of my family's curse, it is the innocent I slaughtered. Perhaps it is for the best that my weak brother (they now call him Softsword) squanders his inheritance. We do not deserve to rule such a vast realm.

Pray for your husband and his family. Pray for God's will for their realm.

Your Adoring Husband,
William

April 3, 1204
Fontevrault Abbey

To the Gracious Countess Ela of Salisbury,

Greetings. It is my final act of service to our great and noble lady Queen Eleanor that I write this sad letter. I regret to inform you that Eleanor passed from this world two days ago. Take consolation, my dear lady, that the Queen left all consciousness of the world about her behind and was quite oblivious to her surroundings. She never heard the news of the fall of Chateau Gaillard. I praise our merciful Savior that Eleanor never learned that the Angevin empire she did more than any man to forge is no more.

I leave you with one final secret which I hope will warm your heart and comfort you in your time of mourning. Knowing her death was approaching, our lady commissioned her own effigy which she now rests under.

It is a work of art to be sure. A casual observer will see our lady laying sedately upon her back reading what one would assume to be a devotional book. If ever you visit the Abbey again, take a closer look, Countess. For if you peer over the lady's shoulder, you will read words written by your aunt Marie de France. Yes! Our lady reads for eternity, though she was truly a devout sister in her old age, the lai of Orfeo! Written as it was to tell the tale of your childhood abduction and the quest of Talbot, it was her humor to read the story in which she is assigned the guise of a fairy king!

My Warmest Regards,
Peter de Blois

Hearing rapid hoofbeats coming from the foot of the hill, Ela closed the book in her lap and gazed closely at a pair of riders coming around the curve of the hill in front of her, beginning to climb the path to the main entrance of the town above. She recognized them instantly. It was William Talbot and William her husband! All melancholy disappeared as she jumped up and sprinted to intercept the riders before they could reach the gates.

"William! William!"

Both Williams brought their mounts to a skidding stop and stared at the half wild creature running toward them. Skirts of her dress pulled up just below her knees, Ela's veil fell away allowing her hair to fall about her radiant face.

"Ah. This one's for you, my liege, I think I'll go look for mine," Talbot said, quickly directing his gaze back to the road.

"I believe you'll find her in the chapel, William," Ela offered between gulps of air, as she arrived at the roadside.

"What are you doing here? You did not send word that you were coming home!"

"When one is offered a chance to get away from court one acts!" Longespee replied. "Here Talbot, take my horse with you. I will walk with this amazingly beautiful madwoman."

"Careful my Lord, I am a married lady. And my husband is a jealous man!" Ela said.

"Tough?" the Earl asked.

"A brut!"

"Ok, I miss my wife too and I think I'm about to be sick! I'll see you two later?" Talbot asked.

"If the Countess lets me out of her bed," Longespee answered.

Ela flushed red for a moment but recovered. "Speak like that again and you will sleep with your horse!"

With that Talbot rode on laughing and Ela leaped into William's arms.

As a parched man guzzles an entire jug of ale, thus Ela and William embraced and kissed as if desperate to take in the essence of their long absent lover. Finally, arm in arm, they began to stroll toward the gate and their home beyond.

Not wanting to break the mood, but confident it could be quickly recovered once they arrived in their chambers, Ela broached more weighty matters. "What news from court? Does John still refuse to accept Stephen Langton?"

"He does. There is no end in sight for the interdict. John avoids all clerics fearing that any one of them will deliver his own excommunication."

"Has he not learned anything from your father's struggle with the Archbishop?"

"It would appear not. Our father chose a man for Canterbury that he thought would cooperate in bringing churchmen to secular justice. I believe that Thomas Becket truly would have been happy with this goal if it would not have elevated the King above the Church. Now John wishes to control the Church through his own man de Gray."

"Though not for such a noble cause as justice."

"I fear not." William was not at all offended by the slight to his brother's honor. He and his wife understood each other's views and agreed on most.

"Even if he could win a dispute with the Pope, would John have any better luck controlling his Archbishop than Henry had with Becket?" Ela asked.

The scandalously affectionate couple were passing through the gates into the crowded town, yet neither made any move to release their interlocked arms. Indeed they interlaced the fingers of their opposite hands and rested them at their shoulders. William acknowledged the obsequious bows and greetings of his serfs with the simple nodding of his head.

"I believe so. Thomas Becket's devotion came as a surprise to everyone. I dare say it might have come as a surprise to Becket himself judging by his life before ordination. That is a moot issue though, John is no match for Pope Innocent."

"So if we conceive our first-born this afternoon the child will be born without benefit of baptism?"

"Much can change in nine months. Innocent will not want to keep England under strict interdict for too long. The people could lose faith."

Ela considered her husband's words as they walked and decided further politics could wait. Now was the time for releasing the flood of love and lust for William which she could not long control. Still she couldn't help trying to torment him a little.

"Perhaps it is too great a risk," she stated seriously. "We should not make love until the crisis has passed."

William stopped suddenly. Looking into Ela's eyes he saw

that she was teasing him. Then they dropped each other's hands and arms, and Ela ran giggling from him. William chased after her. He could see that his prey would soon trap herself in the dead end of their private bedchamber.

Chapter Twelve

Ela and William enjoyed several blissful days before the responsibilities of lordship intruded upon their time together. A minor manor lord at Wilton raised a hue and cry against a man named Thomas. Claiming bodily injury, as well as burglary, the case at first seemed straight forward. Then Ela heard the identity of the accused. Thomas was a loyal servant of her father, one she knew throughout childhood up until her exile. She was certain that this man was incapable of committing the crimes he was accused of. As Sheriff of Wiltshire, William called both parties before his court at Sarum.

Accused and accuser stood just in front of the dais, so that though standing, they had to look up into the faces of the seated Earl and Countess.

"George of Wilton, you have made an appeal of felony against this man Thomas. Testify to the nature of your appeal," William said.

"Sir William, this knave broke into my home with a hatchet. In the course of defending my wife and house against attack, I was grievously wounded in the shoulder."

William turned to face the accused. "And you deny this assault, Thomas?"

"My Lord, I admit that I accidentally cut this man's shoulder with an axe. But it was not near his home, and I was only defending myself from blows he was visiting upon me!"

"A likely story! He even admits the wound." George's face was set in an expression of shocked outrage but he was oddly pale.

William studied each man. "This wound, it was examined and measured the night of the hue and cry?"

"It was, Earl William," George said.

The subsequent testimony revealed a wound that, though drawing blood, would be ignored on any battlefield, with the soldier expected to fight on.

"Was there any evidence of the event taking place at George's home? Damage to the doorway for instance?" William asked the jury.

"None, Sir William," was the reply from all witnesses.

"I know this man Thomas," the Countess interjected, "he is not the sort of man to commit such a crime!"

William glanced at Ela. Though alone together it was understood that he greatly valued her counsel, her speaking out here was anything but helpful.

"People can change, my lady. Especially when hunger becomes a motivator," William looked into Ela's eyes before turning back to the jury. "What is this man's source of income?"

"Sir William, I am a merchant." Thomas became much more animated at this line of questioning. "The late Earl left me a generous sum in his will, with which I put myself in business. I suffer no want. I have no motivation to risk my life in burglary, even if I had no fear for my own soul."

Several witnesses came forward to confirm Thomas' account. It appeared he owed no outstanding credit to anyone.

"So this wealthy man broke into your home, without damage, and willfully assaulted your person with a sharp axe, leaving a wound so small a cat could lick it clean?" William grinned while holding George's stare.

Seeing his case unravelling, and his opponent enjoying the sympathy of his liege lords, George remained silent for a minute, thinking.

"My lord, Sir William," George began with feigned courage, "as this crime was a breach upon the King's peace, perhaps we should present it to the royal justices when next they visit Salisbury."

William recognized this ploy for what it was. Furthermore, he was confident that he had mitigated the outburst from Ela by clearly stating the weaknesses of George's case. Still, technically George was correct. According to his own father's laws, a breach of the peace fell under the jurisdiction of the King's Justices.

It was a significant advancement for justice within Henry's empire. Justice was important to Henry. Recognizing that each petty manner lord administered legal proceedings independently, Henry realized that there was no consistency under the law. Now, thanks to Henry's efforts, England had the beginnings of one written set of laws that were applied to all of its subjects equally. Unfortunately in this case, this good thing could be manipulated by men such as George to further torment an innocent man.

"Very well," William answered. "In the meantime, you are to stay well away from each other. I have heard, George, that you have had Thomas arrested three times for the same alleged offense. Each time he spent money keeping himself free. Do it again, and I will personally throw you into this castle's dungeon until the justices arrive. Do you understand me?"

"Fully, my Lord."

"Thomas, tell us what really happened. Hold nothing back." Ela led both her husband and Thomas into private chambers wasting no time on pleasantries.

"My Lady, truly I am at a loss what wrong I have done to George to make him despise me." Thomas stood before the noble couple spreading the palms of his hands before them, looking to each face for hope. "We spent Whit Sunday together in great merriment."

"In an alehouse no doubt," Ela asked.

"Yes, Countess, in an alehouse."

Oh the insufferable weakness of the English for drink. Would they ever learn the trouble it brought them? Ela hoped one day a generation would see the folly of its parents and moderate their intake. "Proceed."

"It was on our walk home that George began to beat me with his fists. At first I thought little of it, that it was the effect of drink," Thomas began.

"And then?" Ela loved the man, believed him innocent, but though several years her senior, she could not help speaking to him as a child.

Thomas accepted the patronizing tone. "Eventually I tired of accepting the blows. I pushed away with the axe I was carrying."

"Why were you carrying an axe?" William asked.

"George borrowed it, he returned it to me that night. His had a split handle."

"Hmm. Continue."

"Well, I pushed away with the axe a couple of times. On

about the third time I nicked his shoulder with the sharp edge. I didn't mean to. I stumbled from being a little drunk."

"Then?" Ela asked.

"That is all there is to tell. He ran off and the next I heard of the event was when friends told me of the hue and cry."

"That's it? That is what has been blown into a felony before the royal justices?" William's brows were furrowed.

"Before God, Earl William, that is all I know," Thomas replied.

"And what did you do after being told of the hue and cry?" Ela asked.

Thomas looked down at his feet and shuffled. "I ran, Countess. I ran for the coast."

Ela blew out her breath. She believed Thomas' story entirely. She believed it first because of what she remembered of his character, secondly because her father liked him. What rung most true was that he was a man admitting cowardice to her. "That was a mistake, Thomas."

"I know, Countess." Thomas still studied his feet.

"The mystery remains," William continued, "why George has made such an issue of a drunken tussle with a friend. What else has transpired between you?"

"Very little, my Lord. We only recently became friendly."

"How did it happen?" William asked.

"George just came up to me at the alehouse one day and we started talking."

"When?" Ela asked.

"Maybe a week before Whit Sunday."

William frowned. "Had you business dealings previously?"

"No, my Lord. I knew of him of course, but we never interacted personally."

"Nothing at all?" Ela demanded. "Think Thomas, anything could be important."

"Well…" Thomas said. He held the syllable out to a ridiculous level, as if he was reluctant to continue.

"Well what, man?" William shouted. "I am attempting to help you for my wife's sake, but I warn you not to try my patience!"

The outburst was enough to fully loosen Thomas' tongue. "His wife, my Lord, I knew his wife."

William and Ela shared a meaningful look. Now they were getting somewhere.

"When you say knew, Thomas," Ela spoke again as if to a child. "Would you by chance mean that you knew her in the same way the Bible speaks of a man knowing a woman?"

This was shameful to the point that it broke down his shy mannerisms. He looked the Countess directly in the eye this time. "It was before they were married! I swear!"

Ela rolled her eyes and came close to smiling. Only the seriousness of the situation suppressed her amusement. She looked at her husband and silently pleaded to him to finish this interview.

"Tell us about that, Thomas," William said.

"She came to me for several small loans during her previous marriage. We… we succumbed to temptation."

"Go ahead."

"Sir William, I made confession of this sin. The priest ordered me to break off relations and assigned me penance."

"Naturally," William said. "Tell me, Thomas, how did the lady in question respond to your repentance?"

"Not well at first," Thomas admitted, but hastened to continue. "But she must not have been too upset. After her first husband died she proposed marriage to me!"

"What?" Ela gasped in spite of herself.

"She proposed marriage to you?" William asked.

"Yes, Sir William."

"And what did you think of this?"

"I was thrilled. She is of noble birth, plus I thought perhaps it would atone for our earlier sin. She is also quite beautiful."

Ela shook her head, but again it was her husband that continued the questioning. "So why is she married to George?"

"Because the priests forbade marriage, Sir William. They said that a couple who have committed adultery may never marry each other."

Ela was still shaking her head. This time not with the foolishness of men but with the outright idiocy of so-called holy men.

"And that was the end of it?" William asked.

"Yes, my Lord. I never spoke to the lady again."

"This helps us, Thomas. Go now. We will talk again later."

"Yes, my Lord."

Thomas rose and walked to the door. Ela stopped him as he was halfway through it. "Thomas?"

"Yes, Countess?"

"Your family. I don't recall much; were they of Oxford?"

"Yes, my lady. There is only my father, mother, and brother," Thomas replied, confused. "My father was also a freeman, but he didn't have enough to give both of us a start. It was determined that I would find my own way. I was eternally grateful to be accepted into your family's household."

"Yes. I recall something else about your brother."

Two couples were riding at a cantor across a seemingly endless field of emerald green. None could hold onto any care on a day like this. The skies were clear, the temperature that perfect point where when standing still it warmed the skin, when riding the breeze was cool.

Ela was the first to see the stones rising up out of the horizon. "There!"

She tightened her grip on the reins and kicked her horse's ribs. With a jolt, Ela sped ahead of her companions as the horse began to gallop. Her husband took the bait and entered the unannounced race with gusto. Talbot held his motion just in time. He looked at his young wife Anne while standing in the stirrups, body hunched over his horse's neck. Anne was a very proper lady and could not bring herself to such exertion.

She smiled at her husband and nodded her head. "I'll be fine, William. You go ahead!"

With that, Talbot put his all into the hopeless cause. The Earl and the Countess each benefited from several seconds head start, and it was hard to say which of the two was the better rider.

Earl William closed the gap, but in the end Ela's start was too much to overcome. All three reared up at the stone circle laughing. By the time the proper lady arrived, the racers had most of the picnic meal set up on a fallen stone.

"All right then, Anne," Ela began when they were all comfortable and eating. "Tell me how these stones came to be as they are."

"I hoped that you would tell me, Countess. I am not from this area."

"Oh, but that's just it, my dear Anne, we don't know. It is a game I play with everyone I bring here. Both my Williams surrendered their own tales. Now it is your turn."

Anne showed no reaction to Ela's familiarity with Talbot, but considered the query for a moment. "Well, the shape is not a cross. Therefore, it is not a ruined church."

"Do not the Templars build their churches as circles?"

The Countess asked.

"Indeed. But they have brought this habit back from the Holy Land only recently. This ruin has to be too old to be built by Templars."

"Quite right!" Ela agreed. "But they build them that way because the Temple Church in Jerusalem is round do they not?"

"I believe that you are correct," Anne replied.

"Then could not some ancient Christian missionary have such knowledge?"

"Perhaps," Anne considered Ela's thesis. "But I still don't think so."

"Why not?"

"There are no small stones that could have been the church's walls. No Christian would have set up an open air circle of stones as a church."

"Could they have been carried off to build some other buildings?" Ela asked.

"Too far, and too clean."

"Meaning?" Ela asked, though she nodded as if she already knew what Anne meant.

"The nearest stone buildings are many miles from here. Besides, if the wall stones were hauled away, no people would be so thorough as to leave nothing behind. There are not even any broken or misshapen building stones."

"Brilliant!" Ela clapped her hands. "But if not a ruined chapel, then what?"

"The Romans."

"Out here?"

"Perhaps there were villas in the area. The land is bountiful and flat. We are also not far from Bath. There would have been a road close by," Anne replied.

"Indeed! But alas I can see no villas, and as you must

concede, visibility is tremendous."

"Not all villa owners may have been rich enough to build in stone. Perhaps there were wooden structures that are no more."

"Well said. Then what is this place?" Ela asked.

"That I do not know, it might have been a meeting place. More likely it is a temple to a false god."

"Then we picnic within a pagan shrine?"

"Perhaps," Anne whispered.

"What would the church say of us?" Ela asked.

"It's only a guess, I'm probably wrong." Anne looked about and fidgeted.

"Well, if it is pagan, we are innocent in our ignorance. But to be safe, let us stroll to the Avon. It is just down this way directly out of the open horseshoe." Ela didn't want her young friend to feel ill at ease.

Anne's spirits seemed to lift with this suggestion. William Longespee felt a sting on his right hip. Looking about him, he caught sight of Talbot, sword drawn, shifting his weight from left to right foot. A silly grin Longespee had not seen in many years, lit his face. He realized that Talbot had struck him with the flat part of the sword.

"Pray tell, William, third Earl of Salisbury, how badly has the idleness of peace slowed your blade?" the younger knight taunted.

"I'll show you slowed," Longespee said, drawing his own long sword. He looked at his wife.

"You two run along and play!" Ela laughed. "We'll bring your horses."

Bellowing war cries, the two grown men set off very much like little boys. Later they would insist it was training. "One must be in constant practice of the martial arts," One or the other would claim. They probably even believed such nonsense themselves. In the meantime, they presented a ridiculous though thoroughly lovable sight.

"Countess?" Anne spoke as if to a strange noise in a dark night.

"Do not call me Countess when we are so safely alone, Anne. Please call me Ela."

Anne looked a bit shocked at the request, but obeyed. "Ela, you truly love Earl William do you not?"

"With all my heart," Ela replied. Then thinking a moment, she added the part she only ever said one time before. "And then some."

Ela glanced at Anne's face and read her expression. It was not sad exactly, but somewhat frustrated. "You don't love Talbot do you?"

"No," Anne replied, sounding ashamed.

"Don't worry, It is nothing to fret over. In fact, it is still early; you may well grow to love him."

"Perhaps."

They walked silently for some time until evidence of the river in the form of dense greenery rose from the horizon. "Do you dislike him?"

"Oh no! I respect him. I'm even fond of him. I just don't love him."

Ela nodded her head. "You love another?"

The girl stopped and looked at Ela, her eyes wide and face paler than normal. The Countess drew the girl close and hooked her arm in her own.

"Do not be afraid, dear Anne. I will never betray your secret. Who is it?"

"He was a servant boy from the village where I was raised," Anne began, suddenly very animated.

"A servant?" Ela failed to suppress her disdain. Her father taught her that she must act for the good of her people,

151

even to care for them. To look after their welfare was one thing, to be joined emotionally was quite another.

Anne pulled away. "I have said too much. I am just being foolish. William Talbot is a good man, an honorable knight. I will be happy with him."

"No please!" Ela said.

It was clear, however, that the door was now closed. Ela pondered the exchange as they walked in silence. Just how different are we, nobles and serfs? What did the Lord's brother James say? The book from which Ela was given that lesson so many years ago came back to her. 'True religion is this: look after the fatherless and the husbandless.' But was it enough to look after them? There were harsh words for how rich men and poor men should relate to each other in there as well. Those words the Church never taught, but Ela knew them. Once you know them, can your soul survive ignoring them?

Ela was seven months pregnant when the justices finally arrived at Sarum. The trial of Thomas did not go well. It was clear to William and Ela that George managed to bribe some witnesses. Though the justices were technically outside the influence of even the King, they listened with interest to the Earl's account of the earlier testimony.

When at last they were prepared to give their verdict, William insisted that Ela stay in their chambers. William held a strong opinion what the outcome was going to be, and he feared for her health as well as their unborn child. She obeyed without argument and prayed fervently in her chamber as the rest gathered in the great hall.

"Thomas of Oxford," the chief justice began, "of the crime of burglary we find you innocent."

Murmurs erupted within the hall.

"Silence!" the justice bellowed. "However, of the crimes of bodily harm, and more importantly disturbance of the King's peace..." His voice trailed off and he paused dramatically. "There is still question. We leave the matter to God."

The murmurs revived, this time of a different tone. Thomas' knees buckled and he nearly fell. William tensed and he attempted to grip the handle of his sword for comfort. He found it missing. As lordship of the hall belonged to the justices while trial was in progress, even he could not wear a sword in his own hall that day. When his grip met air, he felt as naked as the day he was born.

"Trial by ordeal then?" George asked.

"No," The justice glared at him. "By combat."

There were two ancient methods for determining guilt or innocence. Trial by ordeal, and trial by combat. In trial by ordeal, Thomas would be required to pick up an object of iron heated until it glowed red. He would be badly burned, of course, but then God would speak through the damaged hand. If the wound healed, God declared the man's innocence. If it festered, he was guilty. Even if he survived the festered wound, he would be executed.

Trial by combat was more straight forward. George and Thomas would fight to the death. It was assumed that God would insure that the righteous gained victory. George claimed his wounded shoulder did not permit him to duel.

"Your wound was always slight, it has had more than sufficient time to heal," the Justice declared.

"Of course." Although George did not want to fight, William saw no real fear in the man's face. Thomas was a merchant, after all, he was never trained to fight with a sword. George always managed to avoid battle, he paid scutage instead, but he was trained in his youth.

"The only open space in Sarum is the yard of the cathedral," the Justice continued. "We will move the trial there at once."

Bishop Poore was present in the hall. "My Lord Justice! I must protest. You cannot defile the house of God with this bloodshed!"

"It cannot be helped, Father. Besides, it is in the pursuit of God's verdict, the churchyard is a fitting place."

"My protest stands. Do this and you risk excommunication!"

"Do not threaten me, Bishop Poore, we answer to the King. Your Pope has forfeited the Church's rights." The Justice showed no sign of fear or anger. He replied as if discussing some obscure point of law with one of his clerks. "You are fortunate His Majesty still extends his grace. The cathedral's estates can be seized at any time."

Poore blanched. William found it difficult to comprehend that his brother's evil could extend that far, and yet he did believe it. *Truly we must be in the last days.* He considered the arguments spread by friars that the biblical phrase 'time, times, and half a time' pointed directly to the year 1260 being the end of time. *Could his own brother be the antichrist?* Whether or not Poore entertained the same thoughts, the Bishop decided not to press his complaint further.

Thomas was dragged through the narrow lanes of the crowded village. No one jeered as would be normal for an accused criminal. Most of these people knew him from his time in the late Earl's household. *They know, at least believe, that I am innocent.*

There was no chance the villagers would intervene to save Thomas. Even if they entertained the possibility that they could get him away from this party, the castle's garrison was moments away. The King could not tolerate an assault upon his justices. The village would be leveled and its occupants slaughtered.

It was a dismal afternoon. Light rain had fallen for the last several hours and still continued as the two combatants were thrust into the only patch of grass the hilltop afforded. Thomas slipped on the wet grass. He held a borrowed sword in his hand clumsily, never having touched such a blade before, much less fought with one.

Thomas glanced around the circle of gathered witnesses, few faces could be made out in the crowd, obscured as they were by the saturating drizzle. William lifted his hand in front of his body, helping Thomas find him. For a moment the two men's eyes locked. William seemed to communicate that the warrior wished he could fight this battle for him, that at least he should have taught the merchant how to handle a sword. But William did not believe it would come to this. Thomas bowed his head in recognition, offering exoneration to the Earl.

Without warning, the order was given to commence and Thomas was thrust into battle against a man he once thought a friend. George advanced on him, Thomas blocked the blow with his own blade. After several such parries, he realized that George was playing with him. Everyone in the crowd must have known it long before him. This battle resembled the imagined sword fights of young boys playing at warfare with sticks.

George stepped back and circled around Thomas, grinning. When the nobleman waved to the assembled spectators, it was too much for the merchant. Thomas put all of his hope in the sudden belief that perhaps the idea behind this ritual was correct. Surely God directed the arm of the righteous. Hope surged within Thomas, he felt it physically flow through him, tingling his muscles along the way.

The innocent merchant cried out in righteous indignation at the false testimony spoken against him as he hurled himself and borrowed steel at the liar. God did not intervene. He appeared to take no notice of the little human ritual playing out on the rain drenched churchyard of Sarum. Thomas felt the sword in his own arm easily pushed aside then felt his tormentor's blade slicing through his left cheek all the way up into his eyeball.

Reeling, he stumbled and fell flat on his back. He brought his free hand up to his face and realized that his left eye was ruined. Blood flowed from the long gash, he could taste it. The smell of it filled his nostrils. He knew that he was finished.

"Cry Craven!" he heard the crowd shouting.

He was surprised to realize that he still held the sword in his right hand; he threw it away. Throwing up his hands in supplication, he admitted defeat. George looked crazed at being forced to stand down without delivering the final blow. The crowd stepped in to stop him.

Finally Thomas gathered enough sense about himself to sit up in the mud and realized that the justices were huddled together in impromptu deliberation.

Eventually their leader turned to the crowd and gathered himself up to full height before speaking. "Clearly our Lord has indicated this man's guilt."

Shouts now. Thomas couldn't make out any words.

"However! We believe God desires mercy in this case."

Thomas dared hope.

"He has indicated the punishment He requires."

The murmuring was loud. Thomas struggled to interpret God's message from the battle.

"He has caused the sinner to be half blinded already in

the fight. Thomas will be allowed to go free, but his eyes and testicles remain!"

Such mutilation was all too common in England. William recoiled in horror almost as violently as Thomas. It was not just that this butchery was going to be performed on an innocent man. This was also a reminder that his brother John ordered this same punishment be carried out on their nephew Arthur. It was John's vassal, Hubert de Burgh, who stopped it. In charge of the boy, he not only refused to carry it out, he stood with drawn sword before weak minded vassals who were prepared to carry out any order of the King.

Could William follow Hubert's example and block this injustice? No. De Burgh risked death himself, and Arthur was royal. He realized that news of John's order would cause widespread rebellion throughout the kingdom. He was right. By the time John found out what Hubert did, he desperately needed to produce Arthur unharmed to stave off revolt. Yet the King still raged against the man who saved him, before ultimately granting forgiveness.

William's father, Henry, sought fairness and justice through his courts. This foolish trial by combat was becoming rare, but it was still officially recognized. Thomas was a merchant. Born a commoner, he built a good life for himself, but he could never be anything but common. The Law did not allow for exceptions for the lower classes. There was nothing even a powerful earl could do. For only the second time in his life, William felt truly helpless.

He stood in witness, barely seeing, as a group of George's supporters immediately carried out the sentence. People could see William standing in the rain on a bleak April day in Sarum. William, though, was transported to a sunny July day in Normandy. He saw the bloody baby, heard the wails of its mother, and above all, saw her eyes when she looked at him.

When the nightmarish vision passed from sight, William saw that the deed was done. People were filing away. George and his friends were laughing, no doubt on their way to an alehouse where George would be buying rounds. A group of boys were playing in the mud, kicking stones between them. William realized that it was not rocks being kicked about, but Thomas' testicles.

For a moment William wanted to call down all the fear of the heavens upon these vile brats. Before he could do it, he was repulsed by the level of inhumanity he could find in these young children. Suddenly he hated his sword, hated war, hated all the suffering he saw and caused in his lifetime. What was once merely unavoidable consequences, now felt real and personal.

Thomas lay where he fell, covered in mud and blood. The sounds that came from him couldn't be properly categorized. Wails, moans, what difference? William stooped and picked the mutilated man up in his arms. Standing tall and dignified, he marched through the streets. At this time, this moment, his honor meant nothing. The only thing that mattered was caring for Thomas, giving him a reason to live.

Hundreds of villagers witnessed it. Mouths agape, they watched as the godlike William, third Earl of Salisbury, carried the lowest of them past the houses, through the gates, and into the castle. Despite the rain coating all their faces, those closest later swore that Earl William was crying.

Chapter Thirteen

"It's rather distasteful isn't it?" Anne bore an expression of absolute horror.

Ela chuckled. "It's not what I would plan for my day, but it is our duty. Come, everyone else is gathered for the examination. I need another attractive young woman and you fit the requirements."

Anne followed Ela to a chamber within the keep, walking as if being led to the gallows. Inside the chamber stood two royal officials, a very solemn looking priest, and a woman who appeared to be around the same age as Ela and Anne, mid-twenties. Her robes were made of linen trimmed in fur, but the linen displayed visible weave and the furs were of squirrel. She was noble then, but of modest means.

These participants of the disgusting ritual parted to reveal a rough bed on which lay a man of about forty years, who looked only slightly more mortified than Anne. She guessed that this borrowed room belonged to a sergeant of the guard, he would be the only one to have a private chamber. Anne knew all the players' roles if not their identities. The royal officials were justices who traveled the kingdom enforcing the King's law. The priest was on hand to prevent proceedings from devolving into sin. The noblewoman was the accuser of her husband the defendant. Ela and Anne were there to determine the validity of the woman's case.

After they took their places in the semi-circle around the bed, one of the justices began proceedings. "Simon de Fonte, you are accused by your wife of impotence. Wise matrons have been brought here to determine the case. Open your robes."

Simon most unenthusiastically complied, revealing an area of examination much hairier than William Talbot's. Additionally, the volume of flaccid mass was smaller than that of Talbot's on the chilliest of nights. The justices turned their backs on the bed/stage, whereupon the lead justice spoke again. "Ladies, please."

The wife proceeded to remove her own robe and climb into bed next to her husband. After several minutes of stroking, kissing, and various other encouragements, no change was evidenced upon Simon's accused member. Ela then warmed her hands at the torch, exposed her own chest, placed the man's hands upon her breasts and stroked the member herself. No change. Anne was sure she would be expected to go next when Ela stepped back and closed her robes. "The virile member of Simon de Fonte is indeed useless."

Whereupon the justices decreed that Simon was accursed for being unable to better serve and please his wife, and the lady was granted release from the marriage. All hastily made their departure accept the priest and Simon. Ela stopped at the door after the others filed out. "I am very sorry."

Simon straightened himself in an absurd attempt at dignity. "It was not always so useless, Countess. I was kicked in the crotch by a horse some months ago. Things have never been the same."

Ela sucked in her lips and nodded.

Ela found a white faced Anne waiting in the hall. "Thank you, Ela."

"Not at all. Of course the wife would never have said anything, she got the verdict she wanted; I'm only relieved the priest didn't insist you participate actively."

"I feel sorry for that poor humiliated man," Anne said.

The two friends walked down the corridor towards the exit of the keep; Ela knew without asking that Anne wanted to take a walk along the castle ramparts.

"Yes, he claims to have lost his ability in an accident. A most regrettable business, still it is over now. You must understand the wife's position."

"What do you mean?" Anne stopped and looked at Ela, appearing almost frightened.

"Surely you can understand, if Talbot was to suddenly fail to perform, insisting on a real husband?"

Anne studied Ela's face, then resumed walking, looking down. "Yes. Of course."

Ela remained silent as they left the keep and strolled along the western wall. When they turned left and continued on the south side, she was certain they couldn't be overhead. "Anne, do you worry about not having children?"

Anne studied the paving stones passing underfoot. "Of course I want children..."

"Is your William as Simon?"

"It... it is not that it doesn't... no."

"It happens you know. Between perfectly healthy men and women. We will pray with renewed vigor, you and I together."

"That won't help."

"Anne, of course it…"

"Oh I guess He's done it before."

"Anne, stop speaking in riddles," Ela said. "What are you saying?"

"Nothing. Forget it. I must use the latrine, excuse me." Anne strode toward the stairs of the southeast tower leaving a very perplexed Ela staring off toward the swampy lands south of Sarum.

Words are active creatures; they do things. They may build up or tear down, they may soothe or injure, they may excite or bore, they may enlighten or breed ignorance; but they never rest, never just sit there. And once released, they can never be put back in their cages again.

Sir Geoffrey Mortain rode out of Winchester a free man. Before leaving the castle, he paused beside his horse to strap on his sword belt. Looking up toward the royal apartments, he recognized an angry face staring down at him as that of Countess Ela of Salisbury; he presented Ela with a crooked smile. The glare of pure hatred returned amused him further; he suffered no comprehension of the formidable enemy he had gained that day.

When William returned to their temporary quarters, he came prepared for a storm.

"Mortain received a royal pardon from John," William said.

"In exchange for what?"

William began to change out of his regalia of office. "He paid a fine."

Whenever Ela was truly irate she would not know what to do with her hands. She would clench them, then realize she was doing so and relax them; then she would raise her arms and shake her hands in front of her face as if willing a throat to magically appear before her. Finally she would grasp her head in both hands. "What price did John put on those girls' lives?"

"One hundred pounds."

She watched him as he poured a cup of Rhenish wine. "John has daughters, yet he can forgive that monster for a little gold."

"He has royal daughters; Mortain restricted his abuse to daughters of peasants."

"Restricted?" Ela asked. "What makes you think he will stop? He has money to pay more fines."

William sat down at a table and sipped his wine. "He knows he is being watched, I warned him harshly."

"What he did to those girls, those devices he kept in the dungeon, that was pure evil. Do you really think that kind of desire can be denied?"

"If there is a next time, he will not reach the King for protection."

Ela pulled a second chair close to William. "His people fear him; how will you know?"

"I have organized the grieving brothers and fathers into well motivated spies. If another girl goes missing, I will know about it within two days."

Ela nodded but did not smile. She was proud of her husband for his initiative and determination to bring that arsehole down, but her anger lingered. "So then another girl must suffer, perhaps die."

"There's nothing more I can do; I wish there was more."

"Who will protect the English from Norman justice?" Ela asked.

"Ela. We will, you and I, you just need to be patient. It takes time to—"

"Tell that to Thomas."

Ela instantly calmed, too late. The pain in William's face struck her to the core, but the words were out. She apologized, he accepted, but the words took up residency in their marriage.

Ela ordered Anne to take a seat in her private chamber in Sarum Castle. Fond memories of playing at ball with her father, him reading to her, and her to him, intruded on her mind as they always did in this room. But today's discussion was to be serious. She could no longer ignore her friend's sullen countenance at court. Already tears streamed down Anne's face, produced solely by the authoritative tone of Ela's voice.

"Out with it then. What is wrong?" She maintained the harsh tone, there would be no running away this time.

"I'm… I'm…"

"Yes?"

"I'm with child!"

"But Anne," Ela placed her hand on Anne's knee. "is that not wonderful news?"

She could see that there was more to the story, and it was still dammed up. "Anne!"

"It's not his!"

Ela stood in utter shock. She stared, mouth agape, but said nothing. Slowly she walked over to the window, unconsciously placing her writing table between her and Anne. She remembered the conversation at the stone circle years ago, the suspicions raised that day on the ramparts after Simon de Fonte's exam. "This commoner you loved, you have found another. You fornicate with him?"

"Yes!" Tears flowed still faster, but there was a palpable sense of relief accompanying them.

"Still, you can't be sure. It could be William's."

"No. It isn't," Anne replied.

"How long?"

"I have seen the wise woman in Wilton. She says almost three months."

"Well then, William has been here that long and longer!"

"Ela, we haven't…"

"In three months?"

Anne looked away, remaining silent.

Ela pulled the chair from behind the writing desk and plopped into it. "You told me that day on the wall that he wasn't like Simon."

"It's not that."

"Then what is it?" She found herself shouting again. "I grow very weary of dragging information out of you, Anne. I will hear the whole truth today, here, now!"

"He doesn't love me. He never loved me!" Anne yelled back.

"Does he love another?"

Silence.

"Speak!"

"Yes."

"Do you know who?" Ela asked.

"Yes."

"Who? Tell me."

Anne paused, entwined her fingers and squeezed her hands together tightly. When the pain came the confession flowed out of her.

All blood seemed to leave Ela's head, her feet and hands grew cold as well. The name danced about the room, twisting in the air, poking Ela in the chest. It owned the room for what seemed to both women like minutes. "Anne, are you sure?"

Ela woke to William's cry of anguish and felt the dampness of his cold sweat beside her. Some nights she protected his pride by pretending to sleep through it, others she would hold him, stroke his head, and tell him everything was all right. Her soothing powers were never more than temporary measures, however, as the nightmare always returned. Ela recently decided to treat her husband's torments like the barber-surgeon, who must cut away healthy flesh in order to remove an arrowhead.

"Tell me about it, William," Ela said.

"What?"

"The dream, is it always the same? Is it always just as it happened, like a memory?"

It was a cloudless night, but here at their manor house in Avesbury, the windows were narrow slits, the home fortified against the native English. Very little moonlight breached the defenses, leaving the couples' faces hidden in shadows.

"Yes, always just as it happened," William answered.

"Describe them to me."

The silence of shadows. Faced with a man with a blade, intent on doing harm, William would know no fear. Ela knew he feared her now. Tears, even a cracking voice, would seem far worse to him than a cut that exposed a bone.

"What more is there to say than what I have already told you?"

"They were peasants, were they not?" Ela asked.

"Yes."

"Serf or free?"

"Serf."

"Yours?"

"Yes."

"The baby, was it a boy or a girl?"

"A boy," William said.

"Tell me about the mother, what she looked like."

The sickly sweet smell of the many sheep occupying the surrounding fields rode the breeze circulating within the chamber.

"It is when my gaze lifts from the baby to the mother's face that I always wake up."

"What do you remember?" Ela asked.

"She has a typical peasant face: fleshy, dull, but not unattractive, ruddy complexion, reddish light hair. What does it matter?"

"Just that you look at her, that you do not turn away." Still Ela withheld her comforting touch, left him to his shadows. "You made confession, did you give the priest details?"

"Every detail there was to tell."

"And what did he say?"

Silence of shadows.

"I am absolved. The child was born my serf, therefore I suffered the greater loss than its mother, for I lost a lifetime of labor. At that, it was just as likely he would have died anyway. The mother will have more children, all peasant mothers lose some."

"I would like to find and personally beat the damned fool for saying your loss was greater than the mother's, but otherwise what he said was mostly true, though rubbish counsel."

A snort, not quite humorous, but close enough to indicate that her mental surgery could be successful. "Oh? And what spiritual counsel would you offer, my wise wife?"

"What happened was a horror, and it was your fault," Ela said.

Silence of the shadows.

"But the fault was that of stupidity not malice, and all young men are stupid," Ela continued. "Our actions have consequences, in this case those consequences were soul-crushingly severe. It is done. The boy cannot be brought back. What truly matters now is what you do with the experience."

More silence, but the voice that spoke next was not William's, it was the voice of hope. "What can I do?"

"First, see that it never happens again. You already learned the lesson for yourself, and have taken great care in the use of weapons since. Go further. Advise your men of harsh penalties for carelessness with any weapon, particularly drawing a weapon of any sort when drunk; then follow through if your rules are broken. Second, the child would have lived a hard life. If the mother indeed had more children, make them free, and give them land to farm. Finally, churches and monasteries are all good and fine, but build something directly related to your mistake. Build a home for widows, and a place of care for orphans."

Touch was no longer withheld, and the next hours were more passionate, yet more intimate, than any they had ever shared.

Chapter Fourteen

May 30, 1213
English Channel

Five hundred ships, in arrowhead formation, bobbed in the channel waters off the coast of Flanders. The weather was grey but calm, the sun threatening to burn away the thin canopy of cloud hanging over the coast. Each ship in this fleet was a cog. Hulls were open, without decking, carrying a single mast in the center. When the tall man who stood in the lead ship, the one that represented the tip of the arrow, eventually gave the command to hurl the fleet into action, a single square sail would be hurried up each mast. At this moment though, no sails were up and the trailing fleet maintained formation through the muscle power of sailors and soldiers at oars.

England now had a navy. Her king cowered on the Isle of Wight, unsure of the loyalty of any number of dangerous men on the English mainland. Norman nobles of all rank were livid at John for the loss of almost all of their ancestral land in Europe to King Phillip of France. John enjoyed little respect and few friends. To his credit, however, when Count Ferrand of Flanders saw his land invaded by Phillip, in retaliation for his entering into a pact with John, the English king deviated from his standard pattern and acted decisively. He ordered his newly built fleet, England's first, to Ferrand's rescue.

As was his modus operandi these last four years, when King John was desperate for a victory he called upon the man he trusted most in the world: his half brother, William Longespee. Much of William's time during the years 1210 to 1212 involved winning land for John in Ireland. Poor consolation for the loss of Aquitaine or Anjou, but land was land. William understood irony. Just when his youthful zest for warfare had been fully extinguished, he was called upon to become England's greatest warrior. He was categorically successful.

Now the threat facing the kingdom came not from land, but from the sea. Phillip had a fleet at least three times larger than that of England. That French fleet was currently menacing Flanders. Through fortune, or perhaps the grace of God, the previous evening a portion of that fleet became visible to the English while the setting sun at their backs cloaked their own presence.

Mere months previously, William began his new career with no greater understanding of the sea than any other military man in England. Only fishermen and merchant trader crew knew anything about boats, and they were less than worthless when it came to war. John needed a warrior in command. So now William was an "amir al-bahr" (commander of the sea).

Longespee stood at the bow of the lead cog, grasping a rope attached to the forecastle to steady himself. The ship was so new he could smell the resin from the fresh cut oak of the prow. Prior to his commission, ships were of little interest to William. They were a means of crossing the channel, little else. Though still not as familiar or comfortable as a fine warhorse, he could appreciate the qualities cogs shared with those prized steeds.

Great power was present in these constrained cogs, just waiting to be released. The creaking and bobbing underfoot was not at all unlike the feeling of muscle and sinew of a horse beneath you that anticipated a charge. As with any noble, especially one of royal blood, William was raised with an appreciation of his family history. His people were Normans. The word literally meant "North Men", and was given to them by Phillip's French ancestors. Weary of surrendering an annual bribe of gold coins to the troublesome raiders that would go "a viking" through their lands, the people of Paris offered William's forefathers a far greater bribe. For an oath that they would settle into a peaceful life, the men of the north were given a substantial portion of fine arable land.

So the seemingly incongruent feelings of comfort and thrill that were simultaneously waxing in William's soul were probably the same emotions his ancestors felt. The emotions were part of him because those raiders were a part of him. The thrill of the sea lain dormant for generations as war was predominately a land event, and always secondary to agriculture.

Even his cogs were reflections of the viking era. Just like those ancient longboats, they were clinker built. Each plank overlapped the one below, then sealed with pitch. Though stouter, they were still a similar shape, with a flat bottom giving the ships a shallow draft. This allowed them to go where other large ships could not, such as venturing up rivers. Finally on the forecastles that replaced the pagan figureheads heraldry icons were fixed. Shaped like shields themselves, these icons were a nod to the shields that the raiders would fasten to the sides of their ships when they went a viking.

So William was experiencing some kinship with those raiders from the north who terrorized Europe and Asia all those years ago. This day's goals would be different, though. There were two missions at play. One, of course, was to come to Ferrand's aid on land. More important to England, however, was the mission William and John agreed in private council. Phillip's fleet must be destroyed.

For uncounted generations, the Saxons used horses as a means of getting troops to a battle. Once arrived, they would dismount and fight on foot. The Normans now ruled England because of an innovation. They stayed on their mounts and used them as partners in battle. Today William considered that past battle, his own family history, as vessels always used to transport troops to a fight would instead engage in combat themselves. But would the success of such innovation be replicated this day? The commander of the first English fleet could not be described as overconfident.

One thing was certain, however, if the day's experiment met with disaster, nothing would stand between Phillip and England. It was a very personal risk. Without the English navy, nothing stood between the French nobles and William's land. Nothing would stand between French soldiers and Ela nor their children. Regardless of the English fleet's fate, the French fleet must not survive.

Three small fishing shallops approached the English fleet head on. Though rowing faster than any fishermen had pushed these vessels before, William silently urged them to further haste. He was anxious to make contact with these boats, for onboard were no fishermen but English spies. Leading that spy mission was the man William trusted just as John trusted in him: William Talbot.

Even before Talbot's shallop came alongside, a rope was thrown down for him to grasp. He half climbed, was half hauled aboard the flagship.

"Well, Talbot, could you see why the French fleet rests outside the harbor?" William Longespee asked.

Words gushed from Talbot's mouth as if in a race. "Actually, they are in the harbor as well. In fact, the harbor is so full of ships they couldn't fit another in. What's more, there are even more ships beached along the shoreline."

"God's blood! How many are there?" William asked.

"Easily over fifteen hundred. We are outnumbered over three to one in ships."

The significance of Talbot's report could not have been greater. Over fifteen hundred ships meant the entire French navy was in or near the harbor of Damme. Despite the impact of the general report, William did not miss his friend's exact wording.

"You said in ships?"

"That's the great news, only the ships outside the harbor have full crew, the others only skeleton. Almost all of Philip's forces are either holding Bruges, or besieging Ghent. Their navy is virtually defenseless!"

Longespee spared three heartbeats to grasp his friend's shoulder, smile, and nod. He then turned and lifted his head toward the men in the crow's nest atop his flagship's mast. "Raise the attack banner! Set the sail!"

Sailors leapt to action. The sail dropped to full extension and caught a gusting breeze before even being secured. The hull of the ship jolted and creaked in shock at being woken from slumber. Soon it began to pull away and bolted toward the port of Damme. The rest of the fleet sprang to action as well, hastening to join the fight.

In less time than it took to eat a good meal, they were close enough to read the fear upon the faces of the French sailors. Without firing an arrow, William steered his ship amongst the three hundred enemy vessels outside the harbor. Sailors surrendered before he could make the demand.

"You may have the ships, allow us only our lives!" they cried.

Longespee immediately repented the disappointment which churned his guts at such success without conflict. *Have you forgotten that you no longer relish bloodshed?* These men were not so cowardly, only pragmatic and underpaid.

Transferring the French sailors to as few ships as could safely hold them, he sent them on their way. English sailors manned the captured ships, while William maneuvered his own fleet to where his knights could disembark outside the village of Damme.

Meanwhile the French ships trapped at port repositioned as best they could to form a makeshift castle island huddling close to the city, effectively extending its walls into the harbor.

Longespee stormed aboard the first beached ship he reached, sword at the ready. He soon realized, however, that these beached ships were not guarded. What they did have, was vast treasure.

"Knights set a perimeter! The rest of you start transferring all the goods you can move onto our ships!"

With the sun nearing its highest point for the day, the beached ships were gutted of every good thing they carried. William ordered the hulks be prepared for firing. Torches and fires to light them were made ready. The great amount of smoke that would result from the firing of so many ships, however, would alert French forces of the disaster they faced sooner than was necessary. Instead, William turned his attention, and the bulk of his men, toward the flotilla in the harbor.

Men climbed aboard their ships. "Knights on the port side! Longbows to the crow's nests and castles. As many as will fit and still be able to draw a bow. Stand by the quicklime, and for God's sake be careful!" Longespee ordered.

A caustic byproduct of superheating limestone, quicklime was most often used in mortar. Its characteristic of reacting violently with water, however, proved an interesting tool in a naval battle. As a powder, it could also be sent out upon the wind to debilitate the enemy should any get in their eyes. That, of course, was a dangerous tactic. Winds could shift.

Longespee once again took the lead; his ship would be first into harm's way. "Forward!"

Once again William noted with satisfaction that his creaking vessel followed the point of his sword as obediently as any steed.

"Archers fire at will!" he shouted to his right, then to his left. The command was relayed throughout the fleet.

The longbow was a recent adoption of the English army. Developed by the Welsh, the English found it a formidable weapon when faced with it on the wrong side of the battlefield. The bow itself was approximately six feet long, crafted from a single cutting of the yew tree. The Almighty Father favored Britain with this special gift. Yew heartwood provided tremendous compression, whereas the sapwood added remarkable tension. Thus a single cutting of wood, skillfully done, provided the best of both necessary qualities.

It was this brilliant design that William was counting on. The draw strength of the English bows allowed far greater range than the French weapons. Archers in their ships' raised platforms let loose arrow after arrow at the incredulous French.

The first arrows struck down unsuspecting frenchman who did not consider themselves within range. Lessons were soon learned, however, as their commanders shouted orders to take cover. This was exactly what the English hoped for, as they then sailed on unopposed to engage in close combat. Longespee's vessel attacked the center, others fanned out on either side.

"Deploy the hooks!" William shouted.

Long poles with wicked iron hooks stabbed the air up and down the English line. The weight of the hooks tipped in the air then crashed down upon the French ships. Hooking upon side rails, or smashing through the wood of the ships themselves, poles grabbed hold. Soldiers crouched and coiled, clutching swords. Sailors grabbed hold of the grappling poles and pulled with all of their might. Soon each English ship met its opponent, men shuffling to maintain their balance through the shock of the impact, and praying that the sound of cracking timbers represented only superficial damage to their own vessels.

"Board!" Longespee cried, leaping onto the French ship.

Archers in the platforms held their fire as friendly forces flooded the French decks. Each bowman kept an arrow nocked, scanning for a clean target or an Englishman in trouble.

The vast majority of the fighting now was man to man, sword to sword. William realized that the French forces he battled were made of sterner stuff than those who surrendered on sight. Of course, these also benefitted from time to think, to plot, and to encourage themselves.

William cut down two men on the first ship, but was forced

to take cover before leaping onto the next. The French ships were bunched together in circular layers like an onion. Each set of side walls was another barrier from behind which French archers could fire. He shouted orders to hold back until English forces all along the first layer could advance together, lest the speediest become outflanked. English archers moved from their own vessels to the high points of the first line of French ships in order to drive off their opposite numbers.

This strategy worked quickly on the second and third rows. Flood the next deck, kill everyone who dared stay behind to fight, then bring the archers forward to force the French back again. By the time the whole line finished the third exercise, however, Talbot yelled in William's ear that French soldiers were flooding back into Damme. No doubt these were forces that encountered sailors whom William had spared fleeing inland.

William ordered half of his troops from each ship to return to the shore with him, leaving Talbot in command of those still pressing the navel attack. William again split his land forces, each half sailing to opposite shores in order to attack Damme's walls from the north and the south.

Sailors were commanded to pull away each layer of the onion as forces moved in so that each row of ships they took became the new seaward wall. Sailors were of no use in battle, and each row of ships that sailed out of the harbor took with them more and more of the threat to England which had loomed so large when the sun rose that morning.

Now as the sun neared the treetops, William ordered both land and sea attacks broken off. Three hundred additional captured French ships, laden with supplies including fine wine and olive oil, were on their way to England. Surprise no longer an issue, one hundred beached ships were set ablaze and soldiers warmed themselves before these conflagrations rather than campfires.

Satisfied that a proper night watch was set, William Longespee laid out on the beach to sleep. One third of Phillip's navy was destroyed or added to England's number in one day, with remarkably little loss of English, much less Norman blood. William made the sign of the cross for those who did fall that day. Their loss would not feel little to their people, but William's family went to slumber in more safety this night. It was a good day.

Content, William opened the private door in his mind, leaned against the frame, and looked out upon the green fields of Salisbury. He saw young William running with a wooden sword, pretending to take Jerusalem from Saliden. Petronilla and Ida ran in circles chased by puppies, both giggling. On the beach, the prone William reached inside his cloak and touched a lock of Ela's hair. As if called, the Countess came and stood by her Earl at the doorway. She took his hand.

At first light the battle resumed. Captured Frenchmen confirmed that Philip's gold for paying his troops was held in the innermost ships. Spurred on by this information, the English forces fought like berserkers. By noon it looked as though victory would be complete.

Leaving Talbot in charge of the forces continuing the assault on the ship wall, Longespee took personal command of the left pincer attacking the northern wall of Damme. Under his leadership, the French forces were driven back within the city walls. English forces, out of convention, began to take up siege positions.

"We've no time for a siege, men!" Longespee shouted. "Fan out! Find the weakest gate!"

William joined in the search. Vividly remembering the day Richard received his mortal wound, he kept well away from the walls and zig zagged as he ran. Unfortunately, there was little cover, only sandy soil of the reclaimed sea floor. He envisioned himself from the perspective of a soldier aiming a crossbow at him.

Crouching behind his three quarter length shield, he scanned the crest of the wall for movement. Suddenly his eye was caught by the strange sight of a scarlet cloth being waved an arm's length below the top of the wall. As he watched, the cloth disappeared and a rope cascaded to the ground from the same spot.

A mercenary captain ran up to William's right and planted his own shield overlapping the Earl's. "My Lord, did you see the rope thrown?"

"Yes, but we must be cautious. It is possible a Flemish citizen was able to get onto the wall. It is equally possible that it is a French trick."

"Agreed."

"What word from the East?" William asked.

"All gates are sufficiently defended to hold us off for several hours. It is likely Philip will return before we get in."

William nodded and considered the options. A few years before, there would have been no question. He would have boldly taken the chance to scale the city wall and leap into battle with whatever opponent he might meet, should he be fortunate enough to reach the top.

That was then. Fighting for fighting's sake belongs to the bravado of youth. Now he valued a life worth going home to, a beautiful wife, children to watch grow up. John was a coward and a bully, he was not worth dying for. There was, however, a greater issue to consider. The destruction of the fleet was far from complete, and was not yet certain.

Furthermore, the army now ravaging the lowlands was the very one intended for England. Philip gathered these forces to invade William's island home. Only the Pope's intervention impeded Philip's plans.

Given their personal history, it was unlikely that the Pope's threats would hold the King of France back indefinitely. These troops, ships, and payroll still represented a very real threat to the peace and security of England. A vision of French troops landing at the Solent and marching northward galvanized William's resolve.

"Gather the three best warriors you can find and follow me!" He ordered.

With that, he dashed for the wall where the beckoning rope dangled. All the way he anticipated the dull but painful blows of projectiles bouncing off of his chainmail, or the searing white-hot pain of a bolt piercing a metal link and penetrating into his flesh. Still nothing hit him, nor could he see or hear anything striking the ground around him. It only took one well placed bolt he reminded himself. Again the lesson of Richard's end was not squandered.

William thudded into the wall with such force that the air was forced from his lungs and he dropped to his knees. He forced himself by sheer will to keep the shield above his body while gasping for breath. Lungs still burning, William evaluated the situation. Still no thuds in his shield or the ground around him. He was up against the wall now. Out of sight, he should be relatively safe, if not spotted during the sprint.

If seen, surely he and the ground around him should be bristled with arrows and crossbow bolts by now. He decided to risk peering straight up. Nothing. Only the rope disappearing over the top of the wall.

"A good leader leads from the front," William whispered

to himself. *So why the hell have I never seen John near me when my heart is pounding!*

He grabbed the rope and began to half climb, half walk up the wall.

Clare's heart pounded with such force she could feel the blood rushing in spurts throughout her body. She suddenly felt very cold. *That's because you're sweating like a spit turner.* She crouched behind a barrel, shifting position as a patrol walked past. The blessed mother answered Clare's prayers. How else to explain seeing the backs of the two French soldiers moving steadily away?

Incredibly, the pounding multiplied when Clare heard the telltale rustling sound right behind her. She froze. *Oh God, don't let him stick his head up now!* He did.

"Wait! There's a patrol passing!" she whispered as forcefully as she dared.

Turning back to the soldiers, she nearly wet herself when she saw them standing motionless mid-step. She ducked her head behind the barrel just as the men turned their heads in the direction of the noise.

Your fate will be decided in seconds. You could have just stayed in your room, even enjoyed an upturn in business. But no, you had to be a hero!

She was sure they would come back. It seemed they could not help but hear her heart pounding and labored breathing even if they were blind to the rope. Either way, why not go back and investigate the noise you heard? It's only fifteen yards!

Just as she thought she could risk a peek, she heard the tiny snapping sound as one of the soldiers stepped on something dry.

"You there! Behind the barrel! Step out, we know you're

there!"

"Shite!" Clare gasped.

"How many?" a disembodied voice whispered. She had forgotten about the man hanging from her rope.

"Two," she whispered back.

The word barely passed her lips when she fell back behind a blur of blue and steel grey. A massive hulk of a man exploded over the wall, rolled over the barrels, and stood on the battlements. In less time than it took Clare to blink, the stranger appraised the threat.

The guards were not so experienced, and they didn't have surprise on their side. In a moment one man lay gurgling blood and the other's head rolled past the barrel she was pressed against.

Clare screamed. She did it without thinking; death was familiar to her, but not death accompanied by such carnage. Her scream brought commotion from the gates below.

"Stairs!" the man yelled.

Clare came to her senses and pointed behind them several yards. "There!"

The man grabbed her wrist, pulling her from her crouched position beside the wall. He kept hold, dragging her along behind, as the pair raced down the stairs and into an alleyway.

Now they were in her world. "This way!" Clare said, shaking her arm free of his grip and grabbing a handful of his tunic in turn.

Shouted orders echoed at them from the main streets. They could hear rattling steel as men in chainmail ran by a few yards away. Clare led them by back roads and through empty market stalls. At one point they found themselves exposed as soldiers ran across at an alley's mouth. Clare knew they looked ridiculous with their backs pressed against the wall. As if they could simply melt away this man's bulk!

"They'll be searching the side roads soon," the man said. "We have to get hidden."

"Nicht scheisse?"

As soon as she said it she feared the man would strike her, even kill her on the spot. Instead he looked shocked for just a moment then broke out into a massive grin. "No shite!" he replied, then winked.

Great! She'd risked everything to let the English into the city and what'd she get? One huge but clearly mad man. By the looks of his clothes he's even noble. *What the fuck kind of nobleman leaps over the battlements first?*

She thought about explaining to the crazy man that he was a lone warrior in a city occupied by an enemy army. Perhaps this wasn't the time to be enjoying himself! Deciding that would take too long, and perhaps be fruitless effort, she grabbed his wrist and ran.

The hand picked assault force began their run across the killing zone just in time to see the rope fall away from the city wall. They immediately fell back, projectiles thudding into their shields as they retreated.

"Sodding French!" the leader yelled when they reached a safe distance.

"What do we do?" another man asked.

"We are messengers now. We have to get word to Talbot that he's in command."

"I have more news for him." A third soldier said. "A runner just came from the Ghent road. Philip is on his way."

William allowed himself to be drug deeper inside the city of Damme. They were clearly in the stews. This was a port city, there would be an ample supply of prostitutes. In a moment they were disappearing into one of the shabby little rooms off an alleyway.

The young woman pressed herself against the bolted door. She seemed to have a convenient spy hole from which she could study the alley. *Likely a secret of the trade.* William was not shocked by this environment. After all, he was in his late twenties by the time Ela reached an age whereby she could be his wife in more than name only. His needs until then were met either by women like this or by equally sinful encounters with other men's wives and daughters.

"Have anything to drink?" William asked.

The girl turned to him. Her expression reminded him of the way visitors looked at the madmen sitting in the streets of London.

"Don't you realize we could be killed at any moment?"

"I see no point in dying of thirst before then. What is your name?"

"Clare," she pulled down a clay pot and poured beer into two wooden mugs. "And you?"

"William."

"Just William?"

"Is that not enough?"

"I've met a lot of Williams," she replied without shame. "None wore fur lining nor silk."

Then she looked at his shield. Her eyes suddenly appeared twice their original size.

"Ah! You've found me out. Lord William, Earl of Salisbury at your service." Clare still stared at the shield. William blew out his breath. "So you know heraldry I take it?"

"I know that one," she muttered. She appeared decidedly confused, as if pondering what was appropriate to say or do. Eventually she curtseyed.

William laughed out loud. "I think our alliance has progressed beyond that." He held his mug in front of him.

"To Clare!"

Clearly still a bit confused and a lot intimidated, Clare finally followed his lead and raised her mug as well. "To me!"

Talbot's impulse upon hearing of Longespee's fate was to take command of the ground forces and get them into the city, by pure force of will if necessary. Unfortunately, Longespee wasn't the only one encumbered by newfound wisdom born of responsibility. He was now in charge of all the forces. Thousands of men were relying on him. Now that was a thought!

Reluctantly Talbot pulled back from the fighting and climbed to the crow's nest of an English cog. The navel battle was unfolding just as planned. But he knew that his best friend and leader was alone in an enemy occupied town, plus there was the ominous shimmer on the Northwest horizon.

William Talbot made the smart decision, the prudent choice. As a general, and as a tactician, he was acting brilliantly.

It made him miserable.

Clare slipped back into the room and closed the door behind her. Checking the spy hole, she nodded that all was well.

"What is happening?" William asked.

Several hours had passed since he first entered the city. By the sounds, it was clear something significant was occurring. Before long townspeople began venturing outside their homes to receive news. Clare went as well. They discussed finding a disguise for William, but abandoned that plan as pure madness.

"The French have returned from Ghent. They have driven your forces back to their ships."

She expected him to take it badly. Anger or sorrow, she wasn't sure which. Instead he simply acknowledged the facts without visible emotion.

"'And the search?'"

"They mentioned that one soldier got into the town. We are to give him up immediately if we are harboring him. They sounded rather indifferent; I don't think they have any idea who you are."

"My ransom would be extreme. There would be a reward." William looked at her without threat. He would harbor no malice if she were to turn him in; certainly he would not harm her.

"Hmph. And leave this life?" was her answer.

Clare was rather squat, a tad over five feet and carrying some extra pounds. She had a pretty face, though, with blond hair and ice blue eyes. Far from the cliche of the fallen woman with deadened soul, there was a brightness and appeal about her. At least there was now that she was not wallowing in fear.

"I never did ask you, why did you help me into the city?" William asked.

"The French invaded my homeland, you were fighting on our side."

"But why you and nobody else?"

"Oh, that," Clare said, leaning back against a post, arms crossed on her belly. "Because Philip promised us that Damme would be safe. He would be attacking Bruges and Ghent, maybe others, but he wanted the port unharmed. If we cooperated, we would get out of this unscathed."

"I see. And none here have family in harm's way?"

"Many, but I guess letting you into Damme wasn't going

to help other towns was it?"

"True. So that brings us full circle. Why did you help us?"

Clare seemed to find that a very good question. She was taking a few moments to figure out the answer when new commotion erupted outside. Screaming and crying echoed down the alley louder than when the French assault first began.

"What's that?" she asked, as if William should know any more than her.

He did. William opened the shutter on the one window in Clare's home and sniffed the air outside. "Philip's word."

The fires were started at each of the landward gates simultaneously. Whenever a group of villagers ran toward a gate, they were met by an equally panicky mob running away from it.

William gripped Clare's hand tight. "This way! Get us to the harbor!"

Clare was coughing from the suffocating smoke about them. It was slowing them down too much. William drew his sword and hacked into his own outer mantle. He smashed into an impotent water barrel and soaked the cloth strips.

"Here, put this across your face, it will help." It aided breathing but did nothing for the stinging of their eyes.

As they rounded a corner, William tackled the girl to the ground just as a dockside warehouse collapsed in front of them. Every timber was ablaze. He could feel the heat cooking his flesh, though his shield was raised against the heat and floating embers.

"Those people!" Clare screamed.

Several members of the mob were crushed beneath the flaming wall when it collapsed. Others rolled on the ground, their clothes in flames.

"There's nothing we can do for them now! Which way from here?" Longespee said, holding her right shoulder in his hand like an iron bar in a blacksmith's vice.

Clare focussed, looking about, willing herself to think. Finally she shook her head. "That was the last route!"

William refused to accept defeat. Structures that took weeks or months to construct were vanishing to flames in seconds. There was no time for thoughtful planning. "To the wall!"

They were off again. Backtracking and working their way west whenever possible, they emerged into the open space along the city wall. To the left there was nothing until you reached the harbor. Docks blazed there. To the right, twenty yards from them was another staircase.

William took three steps at a time. It was pointless as Clare didn't have such long legs. He wouldn't leave her behind so stopped every few steps to wait for her.

When they reached the top, William surveyed the situation in full circle. Seaward he saw that his fleet had pulled away, closer to the mouth of the harbor. They probably did that when Philip's forces poured into the city and bolstered the ranks of the shipboard defenders. That allowed the French to move their ships away from the quays. They couldn't sail out, but they wouldn't be swept up in the fire either.

Toward the city, little could be made out through thick black smoke. Muted flames glowed beneath the smoke like sunsets on a stormy night. Afternoon was waning. The real sunset would soon compete with Philip's creation.

"Lord William, look!"

Clara was pointing out toward the harbor. Away from the huddled fleets of the English and the French, a lone ship was speeding along the Northern coastline. On the bow castle of each ship were engravings in the form of circular shields.

It was an artistic as well as practical acknowledgement of the cog's ancestry, when Vikings fixed their battle shields to the sides of their longboats. On the front of this particular ship was a representation of a blue shield with six golden lions rampant. It was an exact match of the shield that rested at Williams' feet, the heraldry of the Plantagenets. It was his own flagship making for the harbor.

William peered over the edge of the wall. There were no rocks that he could see, water lapped up onto the wall's foundation stones. "Is this harbor dredged?"

"What?" Clare asked.

"Is there a gradual slope, or has the seafloor been dredged to allow ships to come closer in?"

Clare's expression morphed from quizzical to terrorized. "You are not serious!"

"Oh yes I am!"

He was smiling again.

"I hate when you smile! It means you are crazy!"

William dragged her along the wall as close to the actual quays as possible. Throwing off his outer cloak, he began to pull off his chainmail. She looked away.

"You're shy for your profession."

She shot him a look that made him regret the flippant remark.

"Sorry, that wasn't funny. Ready for a swim?" William asked.

She studied him like he was an animal she had never seen before. He was stripped down to his underclothes but was putting something back on around his neck. Clare examined the object suspended from the necklace. It was a lock of reddish blonde hair. He saw what she was looking at.

Forcing the smile from his face, he put one hand on Clare's shoulder, more gently this time, and held up the lock with the other. "I'm not crazy, and I intend to get home to the woman this belongs to."

Clare swallowed hard then nodded. William lifted up his shield and waved it back and forth. Soon his ship changed tack, heading straight for them.

"Time to go!"

"I can't! You go, I can survive the fire here. The French won't kill me, they'll have use for me." She looked down at her feet but William could see her face looked as if she'd tasted vinegar.

"I can't take that chance. I've grown fond of you."

"I'm not jumping!" Clare yelled.

"Very well." He hooked her around the waist and hurled her over the wall.

She seemed to hang there, four feet away from him, in midair for just a second. Fear and anger battled for control of her face before she disappeared. It made William chuckle to think what Ela would have done had it been her flung into the sea.

He propped his shield up against the wall. It would infuriate Philip to find out who had been within his reach, but escaped. Climbing up onto the outer wall, William looked down into the surf fifty feet below to see where Clare was. She resurfaced and was flailing her arms about wildly. She was a bit to his right, so he shifted left. Wishing for a moment that there was somebody to push him, he leapt into the air.

It is a paradox well known to warriors that only when facing death does one feel most alive. The next few seconds provided William the most vivid sentience of his life. First came the inevitable physical manifestation of the human fear of falling: the feeling that his stomach was trading places with other internal organs. When he plunged into the water all the sounds of fire and panicking people suddenly disappeared, replaced by unearthly silence. Then came the cold.

William surfaced, shook his head, and took in blessed air. He then felt a sharp sting to the right side of his face. Clare was right in front of him. Had a peasant, a prostitute at that, dared strike him?

"Don't you ever do that again!" Clare scolded.

"The situation isn't likely to come up again is it?" He replied.

William's ship began to pass a few yards away from them. Through the bobbing of the ship's wake he could see a man on deck toss a rope. "Get behind me, wrap your arms around my neck and hold on!"

Chapter Fifteen

June 3, 1215
London

"You speak treason." Longespee pulled his shoulders back thrusting his chest out to obtain maximum effect from his already imposing physical presence.

"Come now, William," Archbishop Langton answered, "We both know that at the rate your brother is losing territory there may soon be no kingdom left to commit treason against. Our plan will save the country. You could say it is the most patriotic course of action."

William could offer no answer for that argument; Langton was right. William stood before the Archbishop of Canterbury and a handful of English Barons who were in open revolt against King John. They crowded the great hall of the Tower of London. City leaders, including the mayor, had invited these rebels into the city, throwing open the gates, lending significant credibility to their cause. John was no longer able to treat them lightly and William was sent here to negotiate.

"My family has a long history of brothers fighting each other." He let out a long breath and studied a document on the table, though he couldn't make out any of the upside down writing. "I have no desire to resume the tradition."

"I understand, William. Perhaps there is a way you can serve your country first without offending either side," Langton replied.

William cocked his head and pursed his lips slightly. "Go on."

"Convince John to issue a charter of rights voluntarily. There are at least two factions within the rebel Barons' camp. Some want nothing less than his removal, but there are enough others that could be satisfied with a restatement of the rights they enjoyed under your father. Satisfy that group, and the hard liners will be too weak to continue."

"What kind of rights?" William asked.

"Simple things: relief on inheritance taxes, stop seizure of land for petty debts, London's liberties, that sort of thing."

Nothing in that list was unreasonable. "Nothing more unusual?"

"I'll be honest, William. Many of us distrust John." Langton glanced around at the others listening quietly. William followed his lead, none avoided his gaze. "Some things, particularly the price of scutage, will require the consent of a counsel of barons."

So that's it. John followed up the loss of Angevin lands on the continent by scurrying back to England and imposing mountainous scutage fines on the barons. The traditional payment nobles offered in order to be excused from military obligations was a long established practice. John, however, was characteristically imprudent in exercising his rights. *Now they want him to cede authority to raise funds to a committee of landowners.*

194

"I will recommend he issue such a charter."

"Excellent, we can ask nothing more." The Archbishop smiled and placed his hand on the Earl's back. "Come William, I will walk you out."

The exit of the tower was on the second floor. A wooden staircase led to the ground that sloped down to the Thames. In case of assault, the staircase could be demolished or burned, making access difficult for the attackers. William watched one of the ravens which made this hill its permanent home as he walked beside the Archbishop. Langton obviously wished to discuss something further in private; he wasn't sure if he wanted to hear more.

"Look, William," Langton said. "The ravens remain. There is hope for the kingdom, yes?"

"Hmph." Longespee grunted in return. It was said that if the ravens ever left Tower Hill, the kingdom would fall. He was in no mood for wives' tales.

Langton nodded in recognition of the Earl's mood. "William, will John listen to you?"

"I cannot say. My brother can be--unpredictable."

Langton nodded, not changing his expression in the least. "If he doesn't, it will be war."

"I know."

The Archbishop halted. "Will you back him?"

"Yes."

"You are loyal to a fault. I believe you understand our demands to be just."

Clergy and Lord looked each other eye to eye. Longespee said nothing.

"If you led this rebellion, William, we would win. And I don't have to remind you that we've had a bastard king before," Langton said.

"I meant what I said inside. That lust does not burn

within me."

"Exactly why you would make a fine king. All I ask is that you think about it. I know that besides loyalty and honor, you also desire a strong England and protection of your lands, that you be able to pass them onto your own son."

William nodded, the Archbishop walked back up the hill toward the keep. Though true they wanted him to join them, there was also an implied threat in what Langton said. If William backed John, then should they lose, the new regime could take his title and lands away. Everything he possessed in this world depended on being on the winning side. He mounted his horse and began to trot toward St Bartholomew's hospital in the Northwest corner of the city.

Smithe's field stretched away from London's Northwestern walls. At this point in early June it was trampled down and dusty. Friday, as every week, the field would host a horse market. Ela planned to purchase some new mares to take back with her to Sarum.

She had just finished her tour of St. Bartholomew's hospital, and now the Prior was going to show off the new church under construction next door. It was not a cathedral. London's cathedral, St. Paul's, was just a five minute stroll from here. It too was still under construction, London being a major source of employment for Europe's stonemasons.

Prior Matthew was a funny little fellow. Six inches shorter than Ela, he looked older and frailer than his fifty-five years. His complexion was ashen. Add to that his grey hair and grey robes, and he presented a ghostly persona. The only distinctive physical attribute Matthew possessed was a pair of bulbous blue eyes popping out from the sheet of grey.

"You see Countess, that work continues faithfully, if a bit slowly. Funds have been an issue." Prior Matthew spread his hands, shrugged his shoulders slightly, and pointed those bulbous eyes upwards toward Ela's face.

"I see, Prior Matthew. Still, the hospital's work must take priority. Healing the sick is at least as great a service to God as erecting another big building."

Ela intended to give a gift toward the work being done here before she and William left. That gift would most likely be greater than Matthew even hoped, but in return she was going to have some fun with the little Prior first. Besides, she meant what she said. Ela believed that God was much more pleased with the hospital than he was with the church.

"Yes, well you'll notice that these bays where construction continues are different from those completed earlier. I believe the styles blend well do you not?"

"Yes. Very well," Ela answered.

Ela glanced at what the Prior was pointing out. The church's construction was now in the hands of its fourth generation of workers. Over the last hundred years there was a major advancement in architectural technology and style. The completed bays, which were now in use as a sanctified place of worship, were in the old Romanesque style. The arches were rounded, the pillars thick, and the windows narrow. Recently completed bays displayed the new Gothic style, with pointed arches, narrower pillars, and larger windows. This new style was not just more ornate; it produced a much brighter, more airy atmosphere. It was true that the marriage of the two styles could have created a clash within the interior. The current architect, however, did a brilliant job of merging the two. Only by studying, or having it pointed out, would an observer notice the shift.

All of this was merely a distraction to Ela. She was studying the workmen rather than the product. In particular, Ela gazed above at the ceiling going in. Stones were being raised into place in the highest parts of the walls. Heavy stones were lifted by means of an ingenious crane. The crane was powered by a man inside an open wheel eighty feet above the stone floor. Out of practicality, the man in the wheel was blind. Sighted workers would inevitably look down, which often resulted in such panic that they would plummet to their deaths.

Ela felt pity for the man in the wheel. What would it be like to be blind? Was he born that way or does he know what he is missing? What would she do, how would she feel, if she knew she would never see the fortifications of Sarum shimmering like a jewel on the emerald fields of Salisbury? Her children's faces? William's muscular body? Did the man in the wheel have a family to provide for?

Inevitably, thoughts of blindness thrust Ela's greatest failure into her mind. Had she been alone, she would have yelled out loud at herself, willing herself not to remember the day she failed Thomas.

Thankfully her mental crisis was halted by the sight of a tall but stooped figure appearing from the direction of Newgate.

Ela knew instantly that William was more melancholy than he had been earlier that day when they arrived at the city gates. Periodic bouts with unseen tormentors frightened Ela early in their marriage. Now she understood these spells were always temporary. Over the years she devised clever methods of lightening his spirits. She was almost always victorious over whatever demon fought her for her husband's mind. The thought of improving his temperament made Ela smile.

"Earl William, welcome to our humble priory. I was just finishing showing your wife our modest undertaking. I would be happy to begin again." Matthew seemed to have a sudden burst of energy, no doubt inspired by a belief that a direct appeal to the Earl would be more beneficial than one to the Countess.

"Unnecessary good Prior, but thank you. I would speak with my wife in private."

Matthew's face fell. "Of course, may I suggest the lady's chapel?"

The lady's chapel sat at the North end of the church behind the altar. Ela lit a candle while William paced. "What did they say?"

"They want me to lead the rebellion."

"Is it to be war then?" Ela asked.

"The Archbishop suggests that I convince John to volunteer a charter restoring certain rights."

"And that would be enough for the barons?"

"Enough of them will be satisfied," William said.

"But you don't believe you will succeed?" Ela whispered sideway, still staring intently at the flickering flame.

"Temporarily. John is a fool though. We'll secure his throne then he'll piss it away." William crossed himself, suddenly recalling where they were.

"You're convinced there will be another civil war?"

"Yes." William leaned his forehead into one hand and pressed thumb and middle finger into either temple.

"Husband, your brother does not deserve your loyalty. Why not accept their offer?"

His eyes flashed, but the storm dissipated as quickly. "I cannot."

"Honor in this case may be to the harm of justice and England itself." She kept her gaze upon the altar while her words hung in the air for several moments.

"Is that why I want to lead them? For justice? For the good of England? Or is it for the same reason that drove

John to bribe the Emperor to keep Richard imprisoned, the reason that caused my father to die of a broken heart?"

Ela turned and studied William's face. It was tortured. These were not rhetorical questions, he longed for answers. "Come, let us go to our quarters. I cannot lighten your mood here: God would strike us down."

William glanced at Ela's mischievous grin and smiled slightly.

June 15, 1215

Windsor castle loomed in front of the brothers like a larger version of Sarum. John had just signed the charter relinquishing substantial power to the barons. Most offensive to the sovereign was control over the royal pursestrings. Within the sixty-three clauses, however, was tucked odd little number eight. *No widow shall be compelled to marry* ... Quizzical looks and furrowed brows abounded, but the momentous nature of the event silenced anyone who might have questioned how that clause found its way in.

William and John rode in silence, as they had since leaving the soggy field at Runnymede, alongside the Thames River. Scribes were already busy painstakingly writing out copies of the document to be held at various sites across the country. John suddenly recovered from the humiliation of the day's event.

"William, I need you to fetch me a copy of that wretched charter as soon as possible."

"Of course, but may I ask why? I would think you in no hurry to possess it," William replied.

"I'm not hanging it on a wall you dolt! It goes to Rome by my fastest ship," John said.

"For what purpose?"

"To be condemned of course! You see my brilliant ploy of turning over the kingdom to Innocent as my feudal lord comes to fruition. I am now the devoted defender of the church. Imagine that! Ha! Regardless of how stupid that sounds, his holy ass will declare this charter an affront to the sovereignty invested on me by God himself. What's against the Church cannot legally stand can it? What do you think? Maybe he might excommunicate a few of those cock pustules for me, a favor for Holy Church's most favored son." John raised his eyes to heaven and folded his hands in mock piety.

William interrupted his brother's cackling laughter. "John, if you so quickly void this document, war will be upon us by autumn's chill. I would beg leave to take Ela home to Sarum and spend time with my children."

John's expression indicated disappointment, the far off look in his eyes and the rubbing of his front teeth with his tongue were harder to read. Eventually the King's pride in the way he was manipulating the Barons and the Pope at the same time overcame his hesitation. "Go then my brother the family man. I need you rested. It's going to be a jolly war!"

As John laughed the rest of the way back to Windsor, William felt sicker and sicker to his stomach. At first light next morning he rode off to London. There he obtained John's copy of the charter. As was his right as Earl, and a named participant, he also demanded a copy John did not know about, one that would go back to Sarum with him.

Chapter Sixteen

November 26, 1215
Rochester, Kent

William pinched the dagger's tip between the fingers of his left hand; suddenly his arm extended and his wrist snapped. The blade sunk into his intended target with a dull thud. He walked the twelve paces and pulled the dagger from the trebuchet's frame for the twentieth time.

"What would John say if he saw you attacking his artillery?" Talbot approached and handed William a clay goblet of warm spiced wine.

"Sod John."

"I'll pass thanks. You're drenched, why don't you come inside where it is dry and warm?"

"In the cathedral full of drunken soldiers and horses?" William asked. "No thanks, I think I'd be more comfortable in the rain."

Talbot studied his friend. Though obviously not in the best of moods, he showed none of the signs of impending dark spirits. Indeed, despite the fog and drizzle which half obscured the castle keep they were besieging, Longespee was full of energy, even restless. Draining the last of the wine, William passed the goblet back and resumed his assault on the trebuchet.

Talbot set the goblets down in the grass and pulled out his own dagger. "Anne thinks we're on the wrong side." His blade thudded into the opposite leg of the triangular base.

"So does Ela," William replied. "And what of you Talbot? Why are you here?"

"You are my lord; I follow you." Both retrieved their daggers and reset.

"The King and Justiciar can call me your lord. We both know you are my friend."

Thud. Thud. "Very well. I am your friend; I follow you."

Two more throws passed in silence.

"I have friends in that castle too," William said. "Over the last four years we've fought side by side in Ireland, Wales, Flanders, and France; now we fight our own countrymen a hundred miles from home, while John uses a cathedral as a stable. I'll tell you something, Talbot, I'm tired of it. I'd trade all the gold in that castle to see the golden flakes in Ela's eyes."

"What then? Do we just leave?" Talbot asked.

"Don't think I haven't considered it, but it's impossible. This rebellion will always drag us back until it is settled."

"Your father introduced a common law to the realm. I think that was a great thing. John seeks only to use the throne for personal gain. Meanwhile, his ineptitude has lost us half the kingdom. Our wives are right; we're on the wrong side, William."

William nodded then flung his blade deeper than ever into the beam. "The rebel barons are more wrong. They invite Louis to be their king. Giving England to the French is the greater mistake. I have hope that John's heir will be a better king."

The thick air carried the sound of squealing pigs.

"Sounds like the forty hogs John sent for have arrived," Talbot said.

Ela, wishing to take in the pleasant night air, strolled the ramparts of Sarum Castle. The moon was full and bright; the cloudless night revealed such a vast number of stars that the sky seemed accented not by their light but by that rare black velvet of their absence. Before long Ela noticed the sounds of Philip's muttering and frenetic pacing. Scanning the crest of the fortifications, for the noise seemed to come from above, she found his shadow moving across the flat roof of the keep. It caused her some worry, but she smiled anyway; she would have to check to see what he was up to this time.

"Yes. Yes. Perfect. Could not be better. Hmm." Philip's energetic pacing continued as Ela pulled herself up onto the roof.

"Do be careful, Uncle. What if your illness flared up here?" Ela said.

"Oh Ela, good evening, child. You fret too much. No need to stand near the edge, just high, above the lights."

"What for?"

"This!" Philip held up a cylindrical object which looked like a two foot long section out of the middle of a lance.

"And what is that, Uncle Philip?"

The older man looked confused for a moment. "No name yet. I just made it. It is a… optic magnifier!"

"May I see it?"

Philip bit his lip but eventually agreed. "Of course, Ela. Here. Be very careful. There are glass discs lodged inside see?"

Incapable of standing still, Philip shifted his weight from foot to foot while his beloved niece inspected his handiwork.

"What is it for?" Ela asked.

"Hold this end up to one eye, close the other eye, and point it at the moon."

"Oh my goodness!" Ela looked away from the device and back to it several times in succession. Each time she looked into the tube the moon seemed to step out of the sky to sit upon the ramparts. "How did you do that?"

"You know how you can see your own image on the surface of a still pond?"

"Yes."

"And then how it distorts, parts, like your eyes, get bigger when the surface ripples?" Philip asked.

"In a way I suppose."

"Well I noticed the same thing in glass beads. It seemed to me that with the right shape, and pairing more than one glass, it could be a tool."

Ela handed the wondrous device back to her uncle. "You are very clever."

"Not really, I was inspired by reading the work of the Saracen Alhazen. Thank you again for lending me the book; we are both fortunate for William's choice in gifts."

Ela took the man's arm in hers and hugged it. "Tell me all the new knowledge of the heavens, uncle."

"The night sky is a scroll, on which the glory of God is written in stars. Look at a star child, any star."

"Okay, I've picked one."

"Know now that star, that little prick of light, is many times larger than Earth. It would take you perhaps three years to walk around our world; it would take a lifetime to walk around that star."

She said nothing, just looked at him with a raised eyebrow.

"Yes, most of those little lights are like the sun, just much further away. Some are made of land, like Earth or the moon, but most are made of fire like the sun."

She considered his words, not sure that she believed them, but considered the implications.

"Just think of it, Ela, each star is massive to us, yet in relation to the heavens…" He had calmed under his niece's touch but now grew energetic again as he swept his arms. "In relation to the heavens one such massive entity is of little significance."

"Each star is as a grain of sand on a beach," Ela said.

"Exactly!"

"Or people on the Earth."

"Yet he cares for each of us." Philip's voice was even more full of awe than when he was describing the stars.

"Yes." Ela remembered Anne's love for a peasant. The Bible undeniably said each person was of the same value to God; would she ever accept that thought?

The outer walls of Rochester Castle were breached almost immediately after King John's forces arrived to lay siege. The keep, on the other hand, was testing the royal patience. A hollow square block of stone, with equally square towers, it was susceptible to the repeated pounding of the trebuchets. Three catapults with twenty foot sling arms, each powered by a muscular peasant in a ladder wheel, launched hundred pound stones at the walls once every twenty minutes. Castles were now being built with rounded corners to deflect these blows, but on this target, the process was relentless and the outcome inevitable.

It was not quick. A half-dozen of the most powerful lords in England sitting safely in open rebellion within that tower defied the authority of the crown for weeks. John wanted in fast. To that end, a tunnel was dug under the Southeast corner of the keep. The foundation being pulled away, that tower was now held up by a series of oak timbers.

William Longespee sat on his horse in the middle of a line of knights before the southeast tower of Rochester castle's keep. Morning was waning as men choked on the smoke wafting from the tunnel opening. Interspersed amongst the mounted knights were infantry, some carrying ladders. Here and there a common foot soldier knelt to feel the warmth of the ground around him. Beneath them the fat of 40 pigs was burning away the timber supports that held up the great stone tower. Any minute the undermining would overcome the keep.

Amber glow began to emanate from under the tower. The earth had collapsed into the chamber hollowed out by pick axes over the last seven weeks. Remnants of the animal fat enhanced embers flamed with the introduction of a new source of air. The tower hung defiantly over the maw as long as it could. Just when men began to ask if God himself was holding it up, a deafening crack answered them. The tower leaned out away from the rest of the keep and finally collapsed, like a knight pierced through the visor falls, already dead before he hits the ground.

A line of knights stood, interspersed by men with ladders, ready to charge forward. Behind them archers pulled back their bows ready to fire upwards at any enemy foolish enough to stand so close to the edges of crumbling masonry. All tensed as the dust cloud began to dissipate. When it did, all anyone could see was more stone. The besieged were fortunate. Interior walls withstood the shock, the easy entrance John hoped for refused him.

The Countess of Salisbury was hiding. She would not have denied it; she freely admitted it to herself. In fact, truth be known, she was hiding in more ways than one.

Ela stood in a top floor chamber of Sarum castle, watching her children sleep. William was much like his father in character as well as name. Petronilla and Ida reminded her of herself when she was growing up here, before her eighth birthday. Life was simple then, calm and peaceful. Was it? No, violence and suffering were not invented in the last twenty years. Her life had been idyllic, full of peace and happiness. That was because she was a child, and her joy was looked after by others. To credit the years themselves was a grave disservice to her father, and yes, to mother as well. *I shall visit mother and her new husband as soon as this damned war is over.*

The immediate, more tangible, adversary she hid from was down in the great hall. King John was passing through Wiltshire on his way to Clarendon Palace. Ela found the man repulsive, not physically per se, but loathsome nonetheless. He demanded respect instead of earning it, exploited everyone in his realm rich or poor for whatever he could gain from them. In short, he was a selfish little child in a man's body. What could be more dangerous? A selfish little child in a king's body, his power was ripe for tyranny.

Under the surface, deep down in Ela's heart, she knew she was also hiding from truth. Her father taught her to care for those unable to care for themselves, that great blessing carried with it great responsibility. He considered his serfs almost as his children, not livestock as other lords did. What did she really do for the peasants lately? Had she brought them any justice? And what of Eleanor? The Queen invested heavily in Ela, thinking her fertile ground for raising up a new generation to struggle against misogyny within the culture.

Ela tried to influence her husband. Perhaps in that Eleanor would prefer her failure. The Queen asked her to be loyal to her son, whomever should rule. Now Ela was trying to influence her husband to rebel against Eleanor's last living son. But she must have known. Ela was sure Eleanor knew that John would be a terrible king. It's what she would want if she could see him now. She would want Ela to do something, something extraordinary, something radical. Though the earldom was hers by right, she could not exercise it. The ugly truth was that she was content to let William make the decisions. Being an obedient wife and devoted mother was enough for her. Thank God Eleanor never knew that!

Finally Ela managed to pull herself away from the sight of her children. She would go back to the hall, put in an appearance. She would act the dutiful hostess of the castle. From the children's chamber she walked through her own to the doorway leading to the spiral stairs.

"There you are. I worried you might be ill."

A knot formed in Ela's stomach as she turned around to see John sprawled out upon her bed, a wine goblet still in his right hand. Bile backed up in her throat at the impudence of the position. Not even the throne of England gave any man the right to such presumption.

"Just checking on the children. I'm on my way to the hall if you'd like to rejoin your court." Ela turned back toward the doorway.

"I think not. Stay." It was not a request. "We never get opportunities to talk. You are my sister-in-law after all."

"We have little to talk about. You are a king, I'm just a simple housewife," Ela said.

"Ha! Simple housewife! How droll, how very droll."

Ela stood silent. It was clear John wanted her to say something, to return the volley.

"I think you're very much more than a simple housewife."

"Thank you, your majesty. Your mother was kind enough to say the same." Ela was uncomfortable with the way John was looking at her. She sensed her dignity was in grave peril. Surely bringing the man's mother into the exchange would stifle his lusts. It was a mistake.

John's face went red where Ela expected it to pale. She thought the wine goblet would shatter at any second. "My mother was a bitch who didn't know her place! She poisoned your mind those two years and now you poison William's."

Ela's fists clenched with rage, not for the attack on her but the horrible outburst against Eleanor. She controlled her emotions though, she was in enough danger already without defending her patron. "William has never been anything but loyal to you."

"It's only a matter of time, with your lover's whispers in his ear. Every night I allow him here, those whispers besiege him." John stroked the pillows where they met.

"You've drunk too much wine, John, we'll forget this conversation in the morning."

Ela tried to unbolt the door and flee, but it fought her for only a moment. John was surprisingly quick, falling upon her before she could pull the door open. One hand firmly covered her mouth, the other tore her dress from right shoulder all the way to left waist. Her breasts were completely exposed.

"Go ahead, struggle! I love how it makes your tits jiggle!" His gravelly whisper reeked of rotten food and alcohol. Ela could feel his growing erection pressing against the back of her upper thigh. She fought against panic, tried to think of the best way to hurt him. Could she reach his balls? Could she break his nose by throwing her head back into his face? She decided on the head whip and he released his grip as soon as she made contact. This time she got the door open and was through before looking back to see John pressing both hands against his face.

"Bitch!"

Ela was almost down the staircase, about to burst into the hall, when the enormity of her situation hit her. The hall meant utter humiliation, she was half naked. Could she expect protection? He was the King, and the hall was filled with his court. Her own guards were mostly in the courtyard and on the walls. If she could alert them they would come to her aid. Would they? Would they defend her against the King himself? That would surely be suicide for them. The children! She might escape, accepting the humiliation that went with it, but the children were still upstairs. To go for them she'd have to go back past John.

She slumped down sitting on the stairs and tears began to flow. *No! There will be time for tears later! Think!* Ela searched her brain for a solution. She was smart, if there was a way out of this she would think of it. Nothing came. The children. When would John realize the advantage he held? Absolutely no doubt existed in Ela's mind or heart that he was capable of any evil against her children.

Another fight or rape, her fate awaited her at the top of the stairs. The Longespee symbol was the lion? Well this mother lion was going to her cubs, regardless of what hunter she must get past. Ela stood, pulled the remnants of her dress against her nakedness as best she could, and slowly but deliberately began climbing.

He was not in the bedchamber. She swiftly searched each crevice, including behind the door. No sign. Oh no! She ran to the children's chamber and flung open the door. He stood there calmly. The bottom half of his face was bloody. Then she saw the dagger.

"Pick one."

"John?"

"One child dies for my nose. Then you will give yourself to me in exchange for the other two. Pick one."

"Be reasonable, John."

"That time has passed."

Inspiration struck. "John, what you have done will lose William's service forever. Killing one of his children will make him come after you to the death. Do you want an enraged William Longespee for an enemy?"

This time John did pale.

"Listen. Put the dagger down. I'll give myself to you, you'll have a coupling you'll never forget. Neither of us will ever tell William what happened here tonight."

An offer no sane man could argue with; but John's sanity was severely in question. Seconds passed like hours. Ela released her grip on the dress. A simple movement was all it took for the shreds to fall completely away. He smiled. Three pregnancies had taken some toll on her body, but it was still impressive. She knew that, counted on it. Finally he placed the dagger on a table and walked forward. He grabbed her breasts roughly.

"Please. Not here. I don't want the children to see me should they wake."

"Of course." He smiled again then shoved her hard into the next room.

Ela's stomach convulsed and she felt clammy all over. *Maybe vomiting on the pig will spoil the mood.* He picked up her dress on his way into the room. After closing the chamber door behind him, he began to tear the fabric into strips.

"Get on your knees on the bed."

"What are those for? I told you I won't fight you anymore."

"That's not as fun. Do you know what my dear brother Richard would do with his vassals' wives and daughters?"

Ela knew exactly what he meant. "To rebellious vassals, yes. Richard was never foolish enough to rape the women of his loyal men."

John ignored the sensible argument and its insinuation. "And then what would he do? The Cor de' Leon, the good king. What would he do then?"

"I don't know."

"Don't lie!" John shouted.

Ela swallowed hard but her throat was still dry. "When he was through with them, he gave them to his men." Ela tried to calculate how many likely rapists were eating her food and drinking her wine downstairs.

John grabbed her jaw, pinching his fingers roughly against where her teeth met. Once her mouth was forced open, he stuffed one of the rags inside. Then she was bent over the edge of the bed, her head pulled back by the hair. Another rag was pressed against her open mouth and tied in place behind her head. With a roll that threatened to dislocate Ela's shoulder, she was now bent backwards over the edge, feet still on the ground. John reached down, grabbed her right ankle and pulled it up until her leg was forced up in front of her. He then pulled her right arm forward until it pressed against her leg. He began to tie them together.

Oh God! What is going to happen here? Please God just let it be over. John you damned fool don't leave me permanently damaged or marked, William mustn't know!

There was a banging noise from the direction of the stairs, then John's eyes went wide. When Ela regained some composure, she realized there was a sword pressed against the fleshy part of John's neck. She looked around. The sword was in the hands of Queen Isabella. Behind her was William Talbot's wife Anne; a strung crossbow was pressed up against her shoulder pointed directly at John's temple.

"Step away from the lady, you swine." Isabella's face showed no sign of jealousy, only anger. "I don't care what whore you put that little twig in, but I'll kill you if you rape another innocent noblewoman."

John's mouth opened slightly. It looked like he had in mind to call these women's bluff and cry out for his guards. Isabella's hands moved just slightly and red appeared on the blade, just a little around the edge. He quickly shut his mouth and backed up till he collided with the stone wall.

"Can you move, Ela?" Anne barely looked her way, she kept the crossbow pointed directly at John.

Ela realized that it had been half a minute since she was rescued and her leg still hung stupidly in the air. The knot was not completed, so she was able to easily lower her leg, pulling her arm free at the same time. She untied the gag and pulled the cloth from her mouth.

"Thank you Anne, thank you Isabella. I can never repay you, but you have put yourselves in grave danger."

"Get dressed, get your children, and get to safety," Isabella ordered. "My husband and I will stay here and discuss our marriage."

"Are you sure you shouldn't come with us? We can bind and gag him." Anne risked looking at the Queen. Her face was no longer flushed or pinched, it was now long, her bottom lip covering the top.

"No, it is too dangerous. I can make sure the guards don't come in until you are well away. Besides, my fate is with this--creature."

Ela returned from the garderobe wearing a deep green dress. She wished there was time to bathe, but they must be away. After wakening the children and setting them to dressing themselves, she dug deep into a chest that sat against the far wall. The bag she pulled out contained a healthy supply of gold coins.

Anne led the children down the stairs when Ela paused at the doorway looking back at Isabella. Her heart ached for the lady. She was almost exactly Ela's age, nearing thirty. Would she ever have what Ela enjoyed, a good husband and real love? John was twenty years older and his stupidity did his lifespan no favors. *Favors hell, William is going to know now; the King is a walking dead man. Perhaps Isabella's next marriage will be happy.*

Isabella dared not move her gaze for even a moment, but she didn't need to. "You are very welcome, Ela."

With that, Ela left her home behind her and disappeared into the night. She travelled north, toward London, toward Winchester, toward William.

Chapter Seventeen

October 12, 1216
North Sea, Off the coast of Denmark

For hundreds of years, coastal tides gently gnawed away at the soft sediments left behind by glaciers. Hard basalt now jutted into the deep blue waters of the North Sea unseen by human eyes. Seals and porpoises feasted on cod, haddock, and mackerel which sheltered under the colossal outcropping.

Tiny tremors in the Earth's surface gently nudged the underwater wall. So insignificant were these vibrations that air breathers on the land above barely noticed them. Below the sea's surface, however, fish and mammals suddenly retreated from the continental shelf as small clouds of sand appeared. Within seconds, several feet of the continent's underwater wall broke off and slid to the bottom of the sea.

On the surface, men in a fishing boat felt a lurch and looked about them. Seeing nothing out of the ordinary, they returned to their work. Unnoticed, the surface of the water rippled with a wave just a few inches high, but vastly wide and miles deep. This subtle wave hurtled at four hundred miles per hour south and west. Soon it would collide with the nearest obstacle: the eastern coast of England.

John was miserable. Bathed in sweat, even he was offended by his own stink. He laid on his back in a cart pulled by oxen. On the run from forces of both the French and rebel English, his army was forced to stick close to the Wash to avoid the enemy held towns and castles of East Anglia. He suffered mightily from dysentery, and his bowels were no match for the jostling of the crude cart. Stench from the unhealthiest of excrement blended with the odor of stale sweat, but John was too exhausted to care anymore.

A unique feature of the coastline of Britain, the Wash was a square estuary shared by four different rivers as each one emptied into the North Sea. Along this estuary ran a swath of flat sandy marsh a mile wide. The bulk of his forces, including the slow baggage train, were sent through this thick saturated sand. Not surprisingly, John took an easier route. He would be able to rest tonight in Spalding, several miles inland but still safely off the main road to Lincoln.

With the battle against his sphincter muscle lost, and being beyond worrying about the humiliation of it, John relaxed his body and drifted off into slumber. It was what he most feared. They lived there. Before long they came for him, as they always did. Decaying flesh, swollen and purple, they came to life within John's dreams. They were all there now. Together. Family united by a common goal: to torture him.

He saw them. Most people would struggle to recognize them now, of course, but not John. He knew them instantly. It was dark there. Like gathering dusk. He was in a field. The field was harvested. Only stubble remained. He could see for hundreds of yards despite the darkness. Richard was walking toward him. No, faster than walking. Almost running but not quite. He was definitely getting bigger. John turned around to run the other way. His father Henry was coming from that direction. He turned to his left. Arthur loomed there. Betrayal was the worst of his crimes against father and brother, but he killed his nephew Arthur with his own hands. Arthur was closer. John turned around. Eleanor. His mother, surely she would protect him! But no, she was coming for him too. She never loved him. The others yes. She loved Henry, she loved Goeffrey, and oh how she loved Richard. He was always her favorite. There was no love left for John. The leftover son, John Lackland. John Softsword. He showed them didn't he? The least of them became the King. He never won anything though, only lost. And now they came for him.

"Your majesty?"

They were closer now. Hideous features of death became clearer. They looked the same as they always did. The eye sockets empty, ragged chunks of flesh hung off their faces and arms.

"Your majesty?"

The worms. You could see the worms now!

"Your majesty?"

They're here. They're reaching for me. Will they grab me this time? Pull me away to hell? Tear me apart?

"Your majesty!"

They tore at him. Maggots flowed from their arms, their hands, onto Johns clothes. The maggots spread all over him. There were thousands of them. Despite the horror of those maggots getting inside him through his mouth he couldn't help himself. He screamed.

"Your majesty!"

John awoke suddenly gasping for breath like a swimmer pulled down by a riptide who managed to fight to the surface. He sat up. Screaming, he swatted at his body flinging off tiny creatures only he could see until he finally accepted that the nightmare wasn't real.

Before John's cart were several knights. Beyond them were more men: crossbowmen, pikemen, and longbowmen. They all stared. One scruffy sergeant spat.

"Your majesty. We are sorry to wake you when you are so ill." John recognized the man who was speaking. He was a nephew of the Marshall. Richard Marshall was his name.

Richard signaled to the oxen driver to move forward. He walked alongside the cart until they were out of earshot of the men. The driver secured the beasts' lead straps and quickly disappeared.

"Your majesty, I regret to bring you bad news."

More bad news? More? How much worse can my situation get? John mustered up all the dignity possible to a besieged king sitting in his own watery shit. He nodded to the knight to indicate he was prepared to hear the report.

"The baggage train was making its way along the beach your majesty. Only God himself can explain the reason for what happened next."

"What? What happened?" John

"A wave. An immense wave suddenly leaped out of the sea. It killed dozens of men and dragged several carts with it back into the deep."

John's brain picked the sentences apart, analyzed the words, tried to make sense of them. The simple act of processing language slowed down to the speed of winter sap.

"What was lost?"

Richard looked down, hesitated.

"Your reticence is understandable but unworthy of the household of the Marshall. Despite how you find me now, I am a Plantagenet. Tell me."

"Most of your traveling chapel--and all of the crown jewels, your majesty," Richard replied.

The significance of these items being swept away, especially by what could only be considered the hand of God, was lost on no one. God desired no worship from this man, nor was he to wear the crown. This would be plain to the lowliest foot soldier much less those nobles who, until now, remained loyal.

John simply nodded. "Please take me on to Newark."

"Yes, your majesty."

"Burbondsy is still in rebel hands?" John asked.

"Yes."

"A great pity. Do we still hold Worcester?"

"As far as I know, yes," Richard answered.

"Then that will do."

"Do for what, your majesty?"

"When they come for me, I will no longer run."

"The French? The rebels?"

"No, not them. The others. When I sleep," John said. "I will be dead soon. See to it that I am buried at Worcester. There are saints there; the prophesy will be fulfilled."

Richard didn't understand much of what John said, but he understood enough. The rest was probably the words of the fever. "It will be done, your majesty."

John lingered until the 19th of October. Neither the altar nor the nation's jewels were ever recovered. Thus, when his nine year old son Henry was crowned, he was a pauper king. He did, however, have some advantages. First was that he was placed under the care and support of William the

Marshal. Furthermore, he was not his father. Sentiment ran, partially due to chivalry, that it was bad form to deny a child his rightful throne.

When King Philip heard that John was dead, that the child Henry had been crowned, and that it was William Marshal who acted as regent, he knew Louis' cause was lost. John finally won a battle. He saved England. All he had to do was die.

Chapter Eighteen

April 28, 1220
Sarum Cathedral

Christina couldn't see anything but adults' backsides. Back in the nave she could see some girls about her age hoisted onto their fathers' shoulders. They could see better than her certainly. *If only I were poor.* But such affectionate actions would be unseemly for noblemen such as her father, minor though he may be.

She had been quite excited as this day approached. So far, she had to admit, it was a bit of a disappointment. Christina's family made their way down from London to attend the dedication ceremony for the new cathedral at Salisbury. As soon as they arrived, her parents learned that both the King and the Archbishop of Canterbury were detained in the marches of Wales. This produced a most unchristian stream of profanities from each of her honored elders. Apparently, the purpose of attending this sacred event was to see and be seen by the King. Now she could hear the Latin chants, which meant nothing to her, but could not see any of the pageantry being acted out near the altar.

Standing not far from a side wall, Christina spied a thick Roman window a few feet away, and not too high up. Did she dare? The adults probably wouldn't notice her. There would almost certainly be a coating of dust on the sill, but getting dirty never evoked the horror in her that it was supposed to. She slipped away from her family and slithered between the lower limbs and medium grade silks blocking her path to the ancient stone wall.

It was a warm spring day in England. With the small cathedral filled to capacity, the air was becoming thick and foul. Spinning around the last black silk mantel, Christina felt relief from the reliably cool stones. With a jump, she managed to grab hold of the sill and pull herself up. Craning her neck, she could see to the front of the choir where the priests and the richest people stood.

The Bishop of Sarum was not worth the effort. He was richly dressed of course, and wore extra gold and jewels about his person. The Latin which he continued to speak and half sing was probably special too, but how was she to know? Christina's eye was caught by someone else. At the front, to the left side, was a family. A very tall man stood with his very tall wife. There were a few children about, four or five probably. Christina's gaze went back to the woman. She was so beautiful that it was hard to look on anything else. The lady noticed her too. Their eyes met. Suddenly the lady's face radiated from a dazzling smile. Her mouth was wide, and her full lips stretched flatly but easily, revealing shining white teeth. Her cheeks reminded Christina of puppets from the fairs, so exaggerated but smooth like apples.

In studying the woman's face, however, Christina failed to notice that her grip on the ledge was slipping. Suddenly she was sliding down the wall and landing with a thud on the marker slab of some long dead monk. To ensure, she was certain, that her mishap would not go unnoticed, several wives of the minor nobility gasped and fretted, whispered and tutted after her. Tracing her way back the way she came, Christina rejoined her family and was silently assured that her absence was noticed and that the disruption of the holy service was justly attributed to her score. The faces of neither her father nor her mother bore any resemblance to that of the beautiful smiling lady.

Bishop Richard Poore removed his shoes before leading the procession down the nave, out the door, and along the two mile route to where the new cathedral would be built. The crowd parted, though it didn't seem there was room to make a path for a snake. Not far behind the bishop, the beautiful lady and her family followed.

Coming near Christina's family, the lady stopped and spoke to her father. "The girl must see the next ceremony. It will be much more exciting than this one."

The sight of her father falling to a knee and the sound of him stammering would stay with the girl her entire lifetime. It also put to rest all fear of punishment. Certainly father would never punish her for gaining favorable attention from a woman important enough to make him do that!

The lady was smiling that same warm smile and holding out her hand. "Come child. You will accompany me to the building site."

"If it please you, my lady." Christina curtseyed.

"Come along now. We're holding all these people up." The smile was still wide and warm.

When they had traveled through Sarum and were descending the path which led down the hillside toward the plain to the south, the lady spoke again. "What is your name, child?"

"Christina de Yate, my lady."

"Hello, Christina. My name is Ela."

"Is my father afraid of you?"

Her laugh attracted attention, but no scorn. "Heavens, I should hope not."

"I think he is. Who are you?"

"I am Countess Ela of Salisbury."

"Countess? Do you know the King?"

"I should think so. He is my nephew."

"Oh," Christina's eyes opened wide but she just looked forward for a moment while they walked. "My father is definitely afraid of you."

"Here now. Another one? I must have missed her earlier. What number daughter is she?" The tall man was speaking now. It seemed that he was teasing and joking with his wife. Could such a thing be possible?

"William, meet my new friend: Lady Christina de Yate."

"Charmed, my lady." The big man bowed toward her. "How old are you, my lady?"

"I am eight, my lord."

"I thought as much. You remind me of a girl of the same age I met at this very spot many years ago."

"Not that many years ago." The lady wasn't smiling now, for the first time she appeared stern.

Christina couldn't think of a way to respond for a while. "Who was that, my lord?"

"He is referring to me, Christina." The lady softened already.

Christina looked around. Great numbers of people had made their way to Salisbury from miles and miles around. Most of them were poor. "So many people!"

"Yes. Today is a great event, Christina. The people are excited."

"Why? The King was supposed to be here but he didn't come."

"Oh this day is far more momentous than a chance to see a king. We're starting to build a great cathedral, far bigger than that one up on the hill. Just think, it will still be inspiring people to look to God hundreds of years after we're all dead and gone."

Christina considered Ela's words for a moment.

"Not only that," the Countess continued. "but we will be building a new city around it, with the biggest close in England."

It seemed the cooks were the only souls missing out on the great event. Noble stomachs waited on no man, food must be prepared for the post-service feast. Carrying a bucket of slop half as big as he was, a ten year old spit-turner lurched toward the privy pits between the kitchen and the courtyard house. Noticing something on the ground near the inner wall, he set the pail down and walked over to investigate.

Long hours in the kitchen had fortified the boy's stomach, he was well familiar with butchered animals. This was different. One of the common ratter cats was cut open. No dog did this; it was clean and deliberate. Each internal organ was placed carefully beside the corpse, more or less in the same pattern they were found. The cat's face was pealed off, exposing the skull.

"That's just pure meanness that is." The boy knew he could count on being timed, so he hurried back to his chore and never bothered to tell anyone what he saw.

Another ten year old boy walked out from behind the privy sheds when the kitchen boy left. "Now Tom, haven't you ever heard? Care killed the cat." He laughed at his own joke as he retrieved the evidence and threw it into the cesspit.

Christina watched intently as every segment of the final ceremony played out. Long sermons were preached, songs sung, even a morality play was performed. The Bishop set the first three stones in place for the cathedral's foundation. First was on behalf of the Pope, the second for the absent King, and lastly for the Archbishop of Canterbury. Ela's husband set the fourth. Christina was staggered when the Countess herself set the next. At least a dozen other visiting dignitaries followed her, she was honored above all of them.

After the stone laying, the ceremony concluded with more words and songs. Christina was increasingly struck by the common purpose which caused so many adults to gather from all over the country. The faces of the poor especially reflected joy and awe. Many cried, many fell on their knees weeping.

Suddenly Christina felt something stir inside her, she began to tremble though she felt no chill. Many emotions surged at once but did not conflict; she was in awe, happy, at peace, and afraid. Though of tender age, the girl knew at once what was happening to her. Such a feeling was not the domain of man; she had been touched by the Lord God. There on the plain of Salisbury, with the hands of Countess Ela on her shoulders, eight-year-old Christina de Yate conversed with the creator of the world. She would be a bride of Christ and no other.

It was a marriage contract her father would never have negotiated.

Chapter Nineteen

Roger Talbot knew he should run away. Staying meant almost certainly getting caught, but his legs refused to answer the call. *Just a few more seconds, I'll hear them coming in time.*

Remnants of an abandoned animal pen in a squalid little corner of Old Sarum were ablaze. Flames are fascinating creatures. Creatures being the correct word as far as Roger was concerned. By all appearance they have life, moving this way and that, lashing out with orange fists and daggers. Setting fires is the closest any man comes to creating life.

This particular life was quickly growing more vibrant than Roger planned. Flames were stretching their fingers toward the dry reed roof of the family's previous dwelling. Any second, Roger expected the burning logs to step up on tiptoes to close those last few inches.

A bell chimed behind him; the smoke had been spotted from the castle walls. Men were on their way—time to go. Almost all of the villagers had moved to the new town laid out surrounding the growing cathedral. With no crowds or market stalls to slow them down, the soldiers would arrive quickly. Still Roger held out. *Five more seconds.*

A log fell, and the orange fingers jumped. With naked flame making contact with the dry reeds of the overhang for just a tiny moment, a great crackling sound announced the house's death. A magpie that was nesting in the roof suddenly took flight. Before the bird flapped its wings a dozen times the entire thatched roof was ablaze. Roger laughed.

Hearing shouts, Roger decided his time was up. He could no longer run down the alleyway to his left, and the northern wall, across the yard, was unlikely to be passable either. The only option was to run south until another alley could take him to the main street. The only problem was, that was also the only route for the men coming to fight the fire. Roger ran full into the ample torso of an oncoming soldier. He quickly got his feet under him and attempted to resume retreat, but knight's son or not, the soldier was having none of it.

He grabbed the boy by the throat. "Well, well, another rat runnin from fire. Why do I think you know what been happenin here?"

"Let me go!" Roger kicked at the soldier's groin.

Showing no fear of the consequences for laying hands on the son of a knight, the soldier reared his hand back behind his ear, and letting go of Roger's throat, he cuffed him hard in the face, leaving the boy prone on the ground, Talbot blood oozing from his nose and mouth.

Clare strolled through New Salisbury each morning, reveling in rebirth. Plots of land in regular grid pattern, sounds of chisels on stone from the cathedral grounds, echoing thuds of hammers on wood throughout the town, they all seemed to her to be physical representations of the new life she was creating for herself in England.

230

Upon arriving in Old Sarum after the Battle of Damme, William set her up in a market stall with a room above in which to live. Given the choice of products in which to deal, Clare gravitated to that which was synonymous with her homeland of Flanders: wool. She spent seed money, a gift from the Earl, on Spanish wool, fulled it herself, and sold it on to former clients in Brugges, who used it to make fine cloth. Ten years later, through a combination of good sense and backbreaking labor, she gained respect, and a place in the merchant guild.

As happy as she was with her success thus far, Clare was not happy to sit back and grow fat on the labor of those she now employed to do the hard work. She made plans, big plans, plans that would make the whole of Wiltshire richer, if she could just get people to listen. Better yet, sod the lot. By her calculations the next shipment to arrive from Spain would provide enough savings for her to do it on her own. She would be the richest woman, richest person, in England that didn't carry a drop of noble blood in their veins.

Today, five girls were in tubs stomping the grease out of a batch of Spanish wool within her fulling works on the eastern edge of town. Finding all the girls at work, on time, she walked back toward the warehouse and office under her home on the market square. Along the way she passed her other properties, looking for the boy who should also be working. She found him at the third privy. Clare owned four tiny plots scattered about Salisbury. On each she placed a privy, for the free use of townspeople caught short away from their own facilities. These were a welcome comfort, but for Clare it was not an altruistic endeavor. Piss deposited in her privies was collected, and after being aged for several days, provided the perfect liquid in which her girls trod wool.

The collection boy stopped short upon seeing his mistress

and foul brownish liquid sloshed out of one of the buckets strung from an oak collar about his neck. Clare looked down and found her fears confirmed; her soft cow-leather boots were damp.

"Sorry, Mistress. I am so sorry."

Clare looked at the boy's face, not yet ten years old. She remembered the frightened little girl, an orphan of Flanders, who sold her body to survive. "Be more careful, Thomas. You could get me into more trouble than you can imagine if you spill on the wrong person."

"Yes, Mistress. I promise."

"Well go on then, but for goodness sake walk, don't run."

"Yes'm"

Clare stood in the street calculating the amount of offensive liquid, and the thickness of the leather that rested above her right foot. Was the cold damp feel on her skin inevitable? She was struck by how quickly she had grown soft. Not that many years ago it was her in the tubs, knee deep in the stuff; now the thought of a few drops of fresher waste touching her made her gag. *Fuck it, I'm a damned lady now.* Clare removed her boots, carefully keeping her fingers to the dry spots.

"Good morning to you, Clare."

Clare looked up so fast that she felt a sharp stab of pain in her neck. She stood there in the main street of Salisbury, barefoot, holding a fouled boot in each hand. "Good day to you as well, Lady Ela."

"You are late." Philip did not bother to turn when Roger arrived.

"It is very early."

"A man of few years may surpass his elders if he has wasted none of his hours."

"Is that my first lesson?" Roger mumbled.

"If you possess any ambition—yes."

Philip's experimenting chamber was on the second floor of Sarum castle's keep. The narrow windows provided too little light, their sole purpose was for the firing of arrows at attackers, but his experiments required dangerous substances, as well as silver and gold. Philip could go elsewhere when he desired to pursue knowledge of other physical sciences, but alchemy was restricted to the keep.

Roger scrutinized the contents of a shelf along the wall to Philip's left. The man still stood hunched over a table with his back to the boy. Roger couldn't see what was holding Philip's attention. On the shelf he saw various clay jars with labels. He never showed an affinity for study, but he could read well enough to make out most of the labels: vinegar, urine, arsenic, sulfur, charcoal—

"Do you know why you are here?" Philip asked.

"Punishment."

"Hmpth. Discipline maybe, not punishment. I do not think being my assistant will be so horrible."

"The Countess believes you might help me find—gravitas," Roger said.

"I hope she is right. Undoubtedly, if anything is going to hold your attention it is alchemy."

Roger decided not to respond to the statement.

"So tell me young man, what is alchemy?"

"The attempt to transform cheap metals into gold," Roger said.

"That's not all alchemy is, but it is the ultimate goal; certainly that is what most interests kings and bishops. They want us to invent a way to make them richer than all the other powerful men, but why does the alchemist pursue this quest?"

"To make themselves rich."

"Perhaps for some that is all it is, but for the true scientist there is a far greater reason," Philip said. "Why is gold valuable?"

"Because there is so little of it?"

"Partly, but if farts were rare, would they be valuable?"

Roger laughed despite his desire to appear aloof; then he considered Philip's point. "Also it is shiny, it makes good jewelry."

"Women care about jewelry, what does a man care for that? Besides, copper and tin can be made shiny. Yet men kill to get gold. What is special about gold?"

"I don't know then."

Philip turned to face the boy. "The truth is Roger, most men who dedicate their lives to getting gold have no idea why it is valued; men have simply agreed that it is. But the real reason gold is special is that it is pure."

"Pure?"

"I could take a tiny nugget of gold, smaller than the tip of my little finger and hammer it so thin it could drape this table like a cloth. It does not rust; I can heat it to the highest temperatures known to man yet when it cools, it will return to it's exact form, no change. I can stretch that little bit of gold thinner than a hair on your head. It is perfection, Roger. It is pure."

Roger still didn't understand how a metal could be considered pure.

"When God created the world, he made us pure. Man's sin made the world imperfect. The world has been striving to regain its perfection ever since. If you leave a metal, any metal, in the ground long enough it will turn to gold. The goal of alchemy is simply to speed up the process."

"To help God out?"

"Of course not! Do not speak blasphemy. It is simply man's mission to return to God, to seek him. We do this in our own spiritual lives; philosophers seek to do the same thing in the physical world."

Roger shrugged and nodded, he was not interested in creating godly metal. But if helping Philip meant creating gold, that was at least worth his time.

"Speaking of the physical world— Before you join me in transmutation experiments, you will copy the world itself." Philip directed Roger's attention to a large cloth pinned to the wall opposite the ingredient shelf. It was a square approximately Roger's height on which was an elaborate painting.

"What is that?"

"A cloth of the world; the lady Ela was kind enough to obtain it for me at great cost. See here, this T-shaped blue represents the waters of the Earth; these three land masses are Asia, Europe and Africa. The great walled city in the center is Jerusalem; therefore, the top of the image is the East."

"There is a fourth land mass."

"Yes, we call that Antipodes."

"But where is that?"

"It is the unknown land. You see, the world is a sphere, like a ball. We reach Asia by going East, but it is believed that by going West we could arrive at the same place. The problem is, mathematics tells us the distance is much longer that way. Most scholars assume that, in all that unknown world, there must be at least one other continent, but we do not know for sure."

"No one has ever been there?"

"There are tales. When you study the map you will see creatures reported to live on Antipodes, men very different from us, with their faces in their chests or with heads of dogs for instance. These represent the accounts of men who claim to have visited that distant land and returned. But don't concern yourself with that just yet. I want you to draw a copy, with only the most important elements, in a book I am compiling. I am told sketching is amongst the few talents you have demonstrated."

Roger tensed and he felt his face grow hot. "I like to draw, I am told I am quite good at it."

"Good. You will practice of course. Once you have drawn it to my satisfaction five times consecutively on loose parchment, you will be allowed to set the final piece within the book."

Roger evaluated the simple table, quills, ink, and stack of parchment arranged before the original hanging. *There are worse ways to spend rainy days at least.*

"I had hoped to run into you this morning, Clare." Ela took a sip of weak ale.

"I am pleased you did." Clare sat across the table from her guest. "Perhaps not at that exact moment."

Both women laughed comfortably. Ela treasured her relationship with the scrappy merchant. After her experience in Damme, Clare quickly abandoned pretenses and agreed to friendship with the noble couple. In public, proper formality and distance was maintained. In private, Clare was a commoner Ela could count on for honesty.

"What brings you to my humble shop, Ela?"

"Not so humble, this." Ela breathed deep, enjoying the still fresh smell of cut pine. "I even hear, from jealous mouths, that your latest load of wool sails from Spain on a ship which you own."

Clare looked around the spacious quarters. "It did not

seem logical to constantly give seamen a share of my profits."

"Well done." Ela set the ale down and clasped her hands in front of her on the table. "Clare, I am restless."

"Restless? Hmmm. Now that you say it, I'm not surprised."

"Don't get me wrong, Clare, I'm happy England is at peace. The barons are happy, the French are busy elsewhere, and William is home. I love him, and love having him near me."

"But…"

"But, now he runs the earldom, and manages the estates."

"Which you used to do while he was gallivanting about Europe."

"Yes, so now what do I do with myself?"

Clare pursed her lips and nodded several times. "Well… I have ideas. I was planning to implement them myself, but if you wanted to partner…"

Ela smiled. "I knew you were up to something. Let's hear it."

"It is pretty damned stupid that I have to bring in wool from Spain, across the channel, then ship it back across to Flanders."

"Double risk, yes."

"It's not just that. Look around the countryside some time. We are outnumbered by sheep; but I can't use any of them in my business."

"Do Wiltshire sheep have bad wool?" Ela asked.

"The worst, what there is of it. They're only good for food and shit." Clare covered her mouth with her left hand. "Please excuse my language."

"I've heard worse. The farmers need the sheep to fertilize the fields, though. Without them you couldn't grow bunions in that clay."

"All sheep sh— produce fertilizer, Ela. Wiltshire sheep

don't have particular skill in that area."

"So you want to bring in Spanish sheep to replace ours?" Ela asked.

"Some of them. Keep enough of the old type to provide meat for the shire, I don't want my wool sheep eaten."

"Like you said, you can afford that now. Besides, how long would that keep my mind occupied?"

"That's just step one, staging the battlefield if you will."

"Ah. Go on then, what then?"

"In order to get the grease out, and meld the fibers so that the cloth doesn't fray, you have to pound the wool in special solution. We've always done it using human power, specifically women and girls, and human urine. That's damned inefficient."

"What do you have in mind?" Ela asked.

"There are soils near here that can be used instead of piss, we call it Fuller's Earth, and the River Avon flows right through town. We use the power of that water, through wheels, to grind grain."

"You think you can work wool in a mill?" Ela's tone was hopeful, not incredulous.

"I have watched the builders around town. I think the motion of the water wheel can be made to pound hammers. How different is that from stomping feet? I've even heard rumors it has been done before, in other towns."

"So, grow our own wool, from our own sheep, full more of it, faster, with mill power, and then ship it to Flanders in our own vessel." Ela felt the old fire flowing through her veins again.

"Want in?" Clare asked.

"Does the sun rise in the East?"

Just as the women sealed their partnership, there was a knock on the door. A breathless stick of a boy, his face covered in pox, handed Clare a parchment.

She noted the seal. "It's from my agent in London." With the boy obviously ordered to make unusual haste, she wasted no time in tearing into the document. "God damn it!"

"What's wrong?" Ela asked.

"It's my ship."

"Oh no! Has it sunk?"

"Not sunk, but it was captured by Spanish pirates. Cargo and all."

"What is Ela doing?" Clare asked.

William Longespee watched Ela crouching behind tall reeds with her uncle Philip. The four of them were on the south side of the Thames, across from London, but William and Clare were several yards further up the bank. They were sitting on a spread of wool eating crusty bread with cold pork. The uncle and niece were barefoot in the swampy borders that marked the limit of high tide.

They were just east of London Bridge. Across from them, on the north shore, sat the docks of London's port. Dozens of ships jostled for prime berths from which to unload their cargoes. William watched his wife put Philip's 'optic magnifier' to one eye; he chuckled. "She's shopping."

"Oh Dear, she's serious then?"

"Deadly serious, you can believe that."

"Yes, I suppose I should never have doubted it." Clare allowed a small giggle of her own.

The Salisbury foursome first travelled to Winchester seeking justice. Finding the teenaged King, Henry, as well as his regent, Hugh deBurgh, both agreeable, they then rode on to London. Concealed within Ela's dress was a valuable sheet of parchment.

William chewed a bite of apple, then looked at Clare and

239

grinned. "Philip is quite fond of you."

Clare shook her head, aware that she was being baited. "And I am fond of him, William."

"Well then?"

"I can't."

"He's too old?"

"No, what do I care for age with such a sweet man?" Clare replied.

"Then what?"

"Have you told them? What I was when you found me?"

William stiffened. "It never seemed important. Still doesn't."

"He was a man of the Church."

"The Church didn't want him."

"Would Ela care if she knew?" Clare asked. "Would she still be my friend, much less welcome me as an aunt?"

For a moment, the two sat in silence watching the other pair whom they each loved for a moment.

"Yes, she would care very much," William said. "After time, she would realize the friend she loved is still the same, but that would not translate to family."

"What are you two up to?" Ela yelled from the bank.

"Plotting to put you away in a nunnery so we can marry," William replied.

Ela walked a few paces and picked up the shoes she left on drier ground. "You can have him, Clare. He farts in bed."

Clare made a face as if William just did the offending act. "Eww. Then I don't want him either."

"Looks like I'm stuck with you then, you old hag." He handed each of the new arrivals bread, cheese, and meat. "Still, I suppose being an earl is worth some suffering."

"Still doesn't explain what I get out of the arrangement."

"Have you found a nice fat prize for us?" William asked,

thinking better of a lewd rejoinder, instead letting Ela have the last word in their banter this time.

Ela smiled the smile that, with her wide mouth, took the corners of her mouth nearly out of sight. "No." She winked at them. "I found two."

By the reddish hues of first light, the ship's guards saw the English dock patrol approaching their berth. At first there seemed nothing unusual about this. Indeed, unable to unload their expensive cargo the previous day, extra security was a welcome sight. Even the soldiers were not, at first, threatening; but the guard named Miguel was first to realize that soldiers at an English dock were never a good thing, at least not a good thing if you were a Spaniard.

"God give you good day, men. We need to come aboard on official business," a dock guard called out from the pier.

Miguel recognized this particular dock guard from his many previous calls at London's port. They had even exchanged pleasantries on those occasions. This time he was sure the guard was avoiding eye contact. It also escaped no one's attention that no permission to come aboard was being requested.

"What business?"

"Don't worry. You're not in any trouble. Your employers will have no call to be angry with you," the soldier wearing the most armor assured him, leading his detachment aboard. "Just remain quiet, lay down your weapons, and nobody has to get hurt. You can be on your way to one of London's fine establishments of comfort. We even have a gift that will get you off to a fine start."

"A bribe from a thief?"

The soldier's eyes narrowed and he stepped within a foot of Miguel. "This is a legal seizure. Do you accuse soldiers of King Henry's guard of participating in thievery?"

"No. Of course not."

"That's better." The soldier stepped back. "An English merchant has run afoul of some of your many pirate countrymen. Letters of Marque are issued against any Spanish ships in English ports to compensate that merchant. This ship has been claimed by the bearer."

"We are not pirates."

"I'm sure you are not. Talk to your king about his allowing such a bad reputation for your country. For now, you must leave this ship."

Miguel remained where he stood, not out of defiance, but perplexed as to what he should do.

"Look, you are leaving this ship, one way or the other. My advice to you, is accept the merchant's gift and go have a better day elsewhere. It is up to you whether you run to the ship's captain to report. If it were me, I'd just leave the docks and go have my drinks by Bishopsgate."

Ela watched a band of confused and dejected Spanish sailors shuffling away from the docks, climbing Fish Hill. "Soldier, is the ship secured?"

"Aye, me lady. She's all yours."

Philip's breathing seemed quick and shallow. Meeting his eyes, Ela's fears were confirmed. He nodded his head sharply, and his bottom lip trembled.

"Please leave the ship, but stand guard at the top of the quay for the time being." Ela led her party onboard, looking for a place to prepare in anticipation of the curse, as Ela thought of it. The soldiers were safely out of sight, and hopefully sound, but what to do with Clare?

"William, Philip is going to need a soft place to lay," Ela said.

William grew serious. He witnessed the event in the past, but was not as in tune to the signs as Ela was. After a pause, and a glance at Clare, he set about taking his sword to a bail of Spanish wool.

"What is happening?" Clare asked.

The tough lady merchant sounded as scared as Ela had ever heard her. Could she handle witnessing the next few moments? "Clare, Philip is going to be sick. Perhaps you'd like to wait on the dock. He will be fine soon, no need to worry."

William cut the bail and spread it out on the open deck. Philip lay on his back on the wool, stretching his arms out wide, rolling to first one side then the other. "This should do nicely, William. Thank you," Philip said, his words sounding slightly slurred and shakey. "Clare, please do as Ela suggests. Wait on the dock—please."

"I want to help."

"No! Wait on the dock!"

Ela had never heard Philip shout before. The emotion behind his outburst seemed to cut through his affliction: the command was clear and strong.

Clare stiffened, and her mouth hung open. Her head rocked back on her shoulders, as if it alone, in disagreement with her body, wished to distance itself from her old friend. "Philip, I do not know the nature of this illness, so we will discuss your tone of voice another time. You know me better than this though."

Ela was well aware they were fast running out of time. "Clare, you would be doing him a kindness."

It was too late. Philip began to thrash about wildly. His right hand slammed into the deck hard, despite the cushioning wool. His body tensed, his back bowed into a sharp arch, only his shoulders and ankles in contact with the deck. Clare screamed before Philip's body convulsed again, slamming back to the wooden planks. Ela held his head between her hands, kneeling so that her knees bracketed the man's head, limiting its range of motion.

"A demon has possessed him!" Clare yelled.

"We can discuss theological explanations later, Clare. If that is the help you offer, stay out of the way and shut up!" Ela yelled back.

"Come, Clare, step over here with me. Ela knows what to do for him." William offered a calm harbor as usual.

"Should we not hold down his arms and legs? He will hurt himself."

"No. It is best to let him thrash. He gets hurt more often when restrained. We've given him plenty of room and softened the wood below him. If he should roll to a place where he might get hurt, I will step in."

"This happens often?" Clare asked, more calm now.

William shrugged. "Not so very often. Once or twice a month, so far as I know." William glanced in Clare's direction. "The church believed he was possessed as well. That is why he was defrocked."

Clare remained still, never taking her eyes off of Philip as he thrashed about, except to return Ela's stare briefly. "And why he remained unmarried afterword?"

William hefted his bulk onto a barrel, the spasms were becoming less violent already. "Very likely."

Clare nodded. "And he will be back to normal soon?"

"Exactly the same as he was an hour ago."

She nodded again then looked at William. "Then talk of demon possession is nonsense. It is an affliction, nothing more."

William held out his arm, palm open. Clare returned the gesture and they clasped each other's inner forearms, grabbing the elbow with the other hand. They each looked at Ela. She mopped sweat from Philip's now quietly resting head. She nodded.

Chapter Twenty

December 1225

"Lady Ela, so good to see you again. You are well?" Reimand de Burgh bowed low.

Ela glared down at him from the dais of Sarum Castle's great hall. For several moments she said nothing, her eyes narrowed and her nose involuntarily crinkled. How many times would she be required to welcome this greasy little man? He, his uncle Hubert, and the King visited in September and again in October. In November, it was just Reimand and Hubert. Now here he was back again on his own.

Do they take me for a fool? Should I not perceive their plan? "Quite well, thank you."

Polite return of the inquiry was not forthcoming so de Burgh tried a new tack. "It sorrows me that your Christmas season will not be a festive one, my lady."

"And why is that?"

"My lady?"

"Are you deaf man?" Ela asked. "I asked you why you

believe my Christmas season will not be festive!"

"But… your loss!"

"To what loss do you refer?"

Anne sat beside Ela on the dais. She studied the Countess and smoothed the folds of her dress in her nervous, restless manner. Ela took no notice, at least no care, toward the muttering of the servants and hangers on about the hall.

"Why your husband of course!" Reimand managed to sound almost firm, not as intimidated as before. This newfound confidence would likely pass.

"Ah. I see you are amongst those who would underestimate my William. Others have done so to their detriment," Ela said.

"Countess, there has been no word for months. You must accept reality, the King mourns him, as does the rest of court."

"How touching, but my husband lives."

Anne kept her head lowered, staring at her knees. Ela took her hand.

"My lady, might I have a private audience?" Reimand asked. "I would speak of personal matters."

"No, you may not. It is unseemly for a married woman to be alone with another man!"

"My lady, once again I must point out that, tragic though it may be, your husband is dead. King Henry is prepared to give you his blessing to marry again."

So there it is. "My dearest nephew has always wanted me to be happy. Tell me, sir, has he anyone in mind?"

De Burgh swallowed hard. "My lady, His Majesty has given me that honor."

Anne winced as Ela's grip of her hand tightened. The Countess' face grew crimson.

"That honor is not Henry's to give! Are you not familiar

with the Great Charter?"

Reimand took a step forward and thrust out one hand as if he was about to stare down a mad dog. "Of course, my lady! He gave his blessing only on the condition that you agreed!"

"You clumsy, filthy little man!" Ela released Anne's hand and stood to her full height, further towering over her would be suitor.

All sound in the hall ceased. A far off dog's bark was all that echoed from the stone walls. All eyes soon broke away from the fearsome woman and were directed at the quiet nobleman standing before her. His mouth hung open, unable to produce a coherent sound.

"You de Burghs aim too high this time! My family is of royal blood, how dare you presume any of your kind worthy of me?"

The man grew deathly pale, then red, of shame or anger it was difficult to tell.

"Even if my dear William were dead, which I know not to be true, I would never consider marrying you or any of your family! A match with such a low-born man is unthinkable. Wherefore you must seek a marriage elsewhere, for you find that you have come hither in vain."

Ela stormed up the stairs followed by Anne. Reimand de Burgh was left eviscerated. He fled. Amused servant boys ran to the battlements to watch as he crossed the Avon, not resting his horse until he was out of sight across the Salisbury plain in the direction of Winchester.

William Longespee crouched low within the ship using its port side as a shield against the gale. If a man braved to lift his head above that barrier his words were forever lost to the storm. With the sail stored away, the crew held little influence on the vessel's course. Three men struggled to hold the rudder still on the 'steer board' side. The forecastle was already splintered, both the rudder and mast were in grave danger as well.

"Two weeks!" Talbot shouted in Longespee's ear. "How can a storm last so long if not the hand of God?"

"If God blocks our way, we must carry the worst sinner on Earth." William's eyes held none of their customary glint which usually betrayed his enjoyment of tough obstacles. For the first time Talbot felt genuinely fearful in William's presence.

"Perhaps a sacrifice?" Talbot said.

Suddenly a new noise joined the storm's chorus, it sounded like the crack of a tree being felled. Bodies sprawled in the middle of the cog near the back. They held a plank of wood in common. The plank was what was left of the rudder assembly.

Where one would expect wails, there were none. Men accustomed to the sea instead resigned themselves to their inevitable fate. Prayers subtly changed from physical deliverance to eternal spiritual deliverance instead. Those who had not yet done so tethered themselves to the larger pieces of wood, probable debris that would one day wash up on some shore. It was their best hope for a proper Christian burial.

Longespee stared into his best friend's eyes then stood against the gale. Fighting to stay standing, he made his way to a chest in the center of the ship. Throwing open the lid, he pulled out a woolen bag containing his possessions. In a single motion, he dropped the lid and spun about, flinging the bag in a giant arch. The bag dropped into the sea twenty feet away from the vessel walls. He returned to the side where he began pulling off rings and every other portion of gold he wore, adding them to the channel's treasure.

"Naked you brought me into this world; naked I will return to you, my Lord and my God!"

Talbot stared at his friend ,wondering if, after all they had been through together, it was possible that Longespee could go mad. His actions one could ascribe to impulse. What good were those possessions where they were going? But there was something else. As the Earl looked up to the heavens, rain pelting his face, he was smiling.

"William?"

Longespee looked down at Talbot. He spoke, but the words were immediately seized by the wind and thrown out upon the waters. After reading his friend's face, he bent down low bringing his mouth below the ship's walls. "Be of good cheer, Talbot! We will survive."

Talbot cocked his head. "You think so?"

"There is no doubt about it, my friend, our Lady the Blessed Mother stands in the crow's nest!"

Talbot's last hope splintered within him. "Praise be, my liege." He grasped William's right forearm.

The Earl chuckled and sat back down on the cog flooring, taking no notice to the three inches of water sloshing about. He hugged his knees and rested his forehead on them as if to take a nap.

Talbot was convinced his friend had lost his senses, but as he turned his attention back outside the ship, he couldn't help but think the wind sounded just a bit quieter.

Ela sat at the table in her working chamber reading correspondence from a steward at her Lincolnshire estate. Anne sat near the window working on a piece of needlepoint. The Countess looked up when she heard a firm knocking on the door.

"Enter."

"Mother?"

"William! Is everything well?"

William Longespee the younger didn't answer directly. Instead he closed the door behind him and faced the women, standing very tall. "Mother, is my father dead? Am I the man of the family now?"

"No, William. Don't listen to the futile chattering of servants. Your father will be home very soon."

"It's not just the servants mother, did not King Henry declare he cannot possibly live?"

"Henry is the King, and a good young man. He does not see with God's eyes though. In this instance he is wrong."

"But mother, how can you be so sure?"

Ela looked at Anne, clearly the same question had hung just behind her lips for some time.

"I have told no persons on this Earth, other than your father and Queen Eleanor, what I am about to tell you now. My father entrusted secrets to me many years ago, we were always within this very room when he swore me to silence. Will you both swear an oath that this confession never leaves this chamber?"

Both solemnly swore to take whatever Ela told them to the grave. Ela rose from her desk, walked to the corner by the window, and stroked her favorite falcon that perched there. She reached into a box next to Anne and elicited a small shriek from her friend when she pulled a live mouse out by the tail. She fed the rodent to her bird of prey while she spoke.

"Periodically throughout my life I have been sent visions. Many have to do with death. Recently I have been given a vision of life. Your father lives, you must simply trust me."

Anne and William looked to each other for judgment

upon this information. Both saw that the other wished for something more substantial to hang their hopes on.

"You are welcome here of course, Earl William." The Abbot's face betrayed the trouble William and his men brought with them, though his speech remained diplomatic.

The storm continued to abate overnight and with the morning, the island of Rhe came in sight. Two hours of hard rowing brought the vessel ashore where the crew lost no time beginning repairs.

"I am aware that this island is under French rule. We will endeavor to cause you as little difficulty as possible, but we are grateful for your aid. Who commands the garrison on the island?"

"Savaric de Maloleone, my lord. He commands a sizable force."

"We would not put you at such risk as to launch an assault. We only ask comfort and food until there be a more favorable wind to continue our crossing."

The Abbot nodded in relief. "That is well. What we have is at your disposal."

Christina found the entire matter beyond peculiar. Her parents were delighted to be asked to the Bishop of Winchester's home for dinner. They positively beamed when they realized how few guests were invited. Two servants ushered her here to the Bishop's bedchamber.

"The tapestries are most magnificent are they not, my lady?" The male servant was in his early twenties and wore a perpetual smirk all evening.

"Yes, they are very beautiful. I would, however, have thought tapestries in a bishop's home might portray Biblical stories, not Greek gods." Christina glanced at the girl. She too appeared to be about 14, though the sadness in her face made her look older. The girl also jumped at every little sound.

"You don't know the Bishop well do you?" Still the insufferable smirk. "If he ever commissions his own, I venture geese will feature prominently."

Christina looked at the strange man, not understanding the reference.

"You know… the Bishop's Geese?" The man chuckled.

"Shut your mouth, Gilbert, she has no idea what you are talking about," the young female servant said. "The lady is pure, how would she know of the things you pick up in Southwark gutters?"

The young man grew red and clenched his fists. Apparently he thought better of violence. "Of course. I shall educate you, my lady."

"Gilbert!" The girl cried.

"Silence, girl!" Gilbert raised the back of his hand. "You see, my lady, the Bishop controls the supply of London's prostitutes. They all rent space from him here in Southwark. Under the shadow of the Cathedral, his holiness does an outstanding management work. All the men of the city call the whores the Bishop's Geese!"

"Well, I have seen the tapestries, I would like to rejoin the others now," Christina said.

"Are you sure, my lady? Your father is quite drunk."

Christina turned on the man. "How much wine my father has drunk is of no concern to you! You forget your place, I assure you that when I have told the Bishop of your insolent words you will be severely beaten."

Gilbert just smirked wider, and the young girl wouldn't raise her gaze from her own feet.

"Have you been insolent, Gilbert?"

Christina turned to see the Bishop standing inside the doorway. "He certainly has! And not just toward me; you should hear what he says of you!"

Winchester said nothing. He simply snapped his head to the side whereupon both servants exited the room closing the door behind them.

"Your parents tell me that you are quite devout. You desire to serve Mother Church?" The Bishop said.

"I desire to serve God, your grace."

"Of course. It is the same thing, for to serve the Church is to serve God."

"Perhaps. In any case, we should continue our conversation somewhere else." Christina walked with long strides toward the heavy door. "We find ourselves alone in a bedchamber, both our reputations are—"

"Stay." Winchester grabbed hold of the left sleeve of her tunic as she passed by.

"Sir?"

"There are many ways to serve God, Christina."

It was becoming all too clear. For years the Bishop made no secret of his relationship with Christina's aunt; there were even children involved. Apparently the aunt had grown too old, and Christina had grown old enough.

"Your grace, I have made a vow of virginity. I have promised myself to Christ and none other."

"When? Where?" His tone changed, the sharpness of the questions betrayed concern.

"At Salisbury, the day the Cathedral was blessed," Christina replied.

"And who solemnized this vow?"

"It was silent."

Winchester smiled. "My child, you are not held responsible for such impetuous oaths. The vow is not binding until confirmed by a priest."

"God himself bears witness."

"Christina, as I said, there are many ways to serve God. Are you so sure that He would not have you serve him by bringing comfort to his Earthly representative?"

"Your grace?"

Winchester smiled again, a huge toothy grin. For just a moment Christina saw a wolf standing before her, teeth bared.

"The life of a Bishop is a lonely, arduous one, my child. What you could do for me tonight would renew my strength to serve my flock better in the future."

He thinks me a naive little fool? Christina stopped struggling against the Bishop's grasp. "If we have no fear of God, let us at least take care that we are not caught. Allow me to bolt the door."

His eyes narrowed and he turned his head slightly.

"I swear before God I will only lock the door."

"Alright then." Winchester stepped aside and began to pull off his outer mantel.

Christina walked slowly to the door. Looking over her shoulder, she could see the Bishop bent at the waist, pulling off his tunic. His head was temporarily covered. She threw open the door, hopped into the hallway, and slammed the door behind her. Before the man realized what happened and crossed the space to the door, it was locked behind her.

"Christina!" Bishop Winchester shouted.

"Before God, sir, I told you no lie. I didn't promise from which side I would lock it!"

After the monks of Rhe dispersed from Matins, the 2 a.m. prayer service, the Abbot stored away his vestments as quickly as his weary bones would allow. As he often did at this time, alone in the chilly round chapter house, he pondered what scandal would really come if he was to sleep past 5 a.m. Lauds service. When he turned to exit, heavy eyelids suddenly lost their weight and his heart beat feverishly. Two French soldiers emerged from the shadows.

Chapter Twenty-one

"Damn him!" Ela was pacing again. She circled the table so rapidly that her loosely fitting robes whipped the air, sending correspondence fluttering to the floor in every direction.

It was January now. Christmas was past, the epiphany just concluded, and she was not rid of the de Burghs. This time the uncle was back, Hubert de Burgh, the Chief Justiciar, second only to the King in power over England, was waiting for them in the hall.

"Will the King allow him to torment you?" Anne was fretful as ever.

Ela stopped and rested a hand on Anne's shoulder. "Do not worry. Henry is young, not so strong, and Hubert is crafty, but it will do him no good. William lives. I only have to hold out until he returns."

"When you insulted Reimand you insulted them all, Hubert included." Young William sat beside Anne.

Ela smiled, rage temporarily banished by the sight of her eldest son. At seventeen, he was as tall as his father, but not yet filled out, still thin and slightly awkward. Their resemblance was often remarked upon.

"Do not concern yourself, the insult will be ever so chivalrously forgiven, the words of a distraught widow after all."

"Forgiven yes, not forgotten," young Longespee said.

"Well, if there is to be any peace at all between the families I cannot avoid him any longer. Let us join our guest."

As the trio descended the spiral staircase, Ela could have sworn she heard the sounds of jubilant soldiers echoing amongst the stones. What were they up to now? *Some new method of gambling no doubt.*

"My lord Justiciar de Burgh, so good of you to visit me—again," Ela said, walking to the middle of the dais.

Hubert de Burgh smiled sweetly and bowed. "A great pleasure I assure you. The King sends you his love and warm wishes."

"Please give him mine as well," Ela replied.

"I will. You are well then, Countess? I heard you might have been troubled the day my nephew was last here. Nothing he said I hope, young people can be so clumsy with words."

"Not the words, sir, the message."

More noise, it sounded as though the whole city was shouting. Ela remembered her eighth birthday, thousands cheering for their team at tournament. Hubert too looked about.

"Yes, well, I was hoping we could discuss that matter further," Hubert said. "I'm sure Reimand was insensitive in his approach. Let us leave it for a later time. I am giving a banquet at Winchester in March, I would very much like you to attend. Henry expressed his great hope to see you there as well."

"We accept, my friend!"

Everyone in the room recognized the booming voice

that accepted the invitation on Ela's behalf. From the hall's vestibule stepped William Longespee, third Earl of Salisbury, looking very much alive.

"Should we send for a man?" Christina's mother was losing patience.

"My lady, what would you have me do?" Christina's betrothed, Michael, had just emerged from the bedchamber after an hour. He could only report fervent prayers and the many scripture references the girl shared with him.

"I would have you do what all young people do on their wedding nights," his new mother-in-law replied.

"But she does not wish it. She still insists her body belongs to Christ."

"My daughter shall be deflowered one way or another. If you will not do it, I'll find someone who will, I don't care who does it anymore."

"My lady!" Michael gasped.

"My wife is correct young man. We gave the girl life and paid well for her upbringing, it is time for her to repay us by advantageous marriage," Christina's father added.

Michael stared at the couple before him. His wife's parents were actually demanding that he rape their daughter. The threat of having another man do the job was enough. He hoped that she would not put up too much of a struggle, he had no desire to hurt her. Without a word he went back inside the bedchamber and slammed the door in the faces of his parents-in-law. Undoubtedly they were still there listening, he tried to put that thought out of his mind.

Thoughts did escape him when he realized that he was completely alone.

King Henry was nineteen years old when his uncle,

William Longespee, made his dramatic return to England. At this tender age, Henry was becoming increasingly aware that being a king was not all good food and frequent sex.

"Please be reasonable, Uncle," Henry said.

"Reasonable? I do not wish to be reasonable," Longespee replied.

"Hugh expected you to be angry. It is unfortunate that your anger was so—public."

"The worm wriggled its way to your bosom the moment it fled my home, of course."

Henry smiled and stood. "Come Uncle, it is time my cats had their meal. I prefer to feed them myself when possible." He led William out of Winchester's keep to another tower. "Hugh looked frightened when he reported that you were alive and well in Sarum. I have never seen him afraid before."

"He has cause to be afraid," William said.

"And I, Uncle? Do I have cause to fear you? I gave them permission to woo Ela."

Longespee stiffened; his expression did not soften. "An unfortunate decision, one I do not understand. Justiciar de Burgh obviously swayed you with evil words."

They entered a circular central chamber, surrounded by four doors of thick iron bars. A stack of freshly butchered ox meat sat in the center of the antechamber. At three of the iron-barred doors paced an adult female lion, each eying the stack of meat and licking its lips.

"Look Uncle, don't they seem as though they stepped off our family crest?" Henry drove a dagger into the stack of meat, and held out the three chops it snagged to one of the lions. It pulled all the chops off before tearing into the meat. "Like us, they lack subtlety."

"Hubert de Burgh is a peasant and a churl," William said.

"I understand that the de Burghes sniffed around your

wife, but Hugh has been loyal and extremely effective. I believe before you left for France last year you would have called him a friend."

William's hold on his outrage finally slipped. "He has gone too far; he has grown arrogant."

"Uncle, I have had my share of conflicts with the good justiciar. They grow more frequent and more intense by the month. He has, for all purposes, been king for several years; he would prefer that I remain in the background, forever a child. I grow furious and battle to exert my will."

"Well.." Longespee began.

"The point, my dear uncle, is that when my passion subsides, I am reminded that he has done an excellent job as regent. He also refused to kill my cousin Arthur, and his military endeavors for my father were nothing short of legendary."

Longespee remained quiet until the King finished his self-appointed chore. "You would have me forgive him?"

"No," The King met his uncle's stare. "I would have you apologize."

"For what?"

"You humiliated him publicly at court," Henry said.

"It was his own doing."

Henry took a deep breath, let it out, and nodded. "I suppose he rolled the dice, and lost."

"Do you command that I apologize?" William asked.

"No. You are no average subject. You are the most treasured relative I have. It is your decision. I remind you though, that Hubert apologized for disturbing you."

"Henry, I have no quarrel with you, and you know how loyal I have always been to England's sovereign."

"But?" Henry asked.

"I will have my revenge, or I will disturb all England,"

Longespee replied.

Christina's arms ached already. Slowly, deliberately, she drew deep lung drenching breaths through her mouth. She heard the muffled sound of Michael reporting her as missing to her parents. They checked under the bed, in the trunk, out the window.

"She can't disappear, you helped her!" Her mother said.

"I swear before God I did not. Besides, where could she go even with my help?"

"Could she have snuck past us while we were in the hall?" Father asked.

"Not without being shielded by angels, we were right outside the door," Mother replied.

"Perhaps that is the explanation," Michael said.

Christina thought that, under different circumstances, she would have been happy to have Michael for a husband.

"Have you started believing she is the next Virgin Mary now?" Mother asked.

"My lady, I have had quite enough of your vile mouth. Unless you can tell me some other way my beloved bride could disappear into thin air, I will consider Christ my rival until we can bring this before the Bishop once again. Good day!"

With that the lucrative groom was gone and imperfect parents stomped shouting, spitting, and cursing to their own chamber.

Christina waited a few more minutes before believing they had conceded defeat. Finally she let go of the nail she grasped, dropping to the floor. Peering from behind the tapestry, her solitude was confirmed. Half an hour later she disappeared into the dark countryside, laden with what necessities of life she could carry.

Ela bathed her husband's forehead with water infused with rose petals. Thankfully he was now in a peaceful cycle. Since returning to Salisbury Castle five days previously complaining of headaches, William's health had declined. Headaches increased in intensity, then came frightening fits of delusion in which he struck out wildly at nonexistent enemies. In order to safely stay by his side, Ela on two occasions resorted to having his arms tied down at great distress to herself. Evil humors were then purged by his own body through vomit and diarrhea.

Before long he was too weak to make it to the cesspits behind the kitchen. A dozen chamber pots lay scattered about the room. William lost more blood each time they were used. Diarrhea, vomit, even his piss was stained with blood. Ela refused to allow Brother Thomas to do any bloodletting. If men bled to death on the battlefield, how could the Earl afford to lose more blood?

William's eyes opened, they gazed up at Ela though clearly struggling to focus. "My dearest wife, I have ruined our reunion."

"Hush now, don't talk more nonsense or I'll have you bound again."

"Ela, send for the Bishop please."

"No!" Ela's face radiated fear and she whined the word as she never did before, not even as a child.

"Do it, Ela— for me."

Ela went to the door and ordered a waiting servant to fetch Bishop Poore. It would not take long, everyone knew Poore was awaiting the messenger.

Even with confirmation that they had little time left together, she remained with her back turned for a moment. "He's killed you."

"Perhaps."

"Perhaps? There's no perhaps!" She turned to face him. "Eight weeks ago you walked into this castle in glory, as strong as the day I met you. You survived wars, storms, and shipwreck. The Blessed Mother protected you from all of that, but you couldn't survive a banquet! What am I to believe?"

"You must promise me two things," William said, instead of answering.

Ela stuffed her anger back into its compartment temporarily. "What?"

"First, when the Bishop arrives, leave us alone while I make confession. Second, after I'm gone, say nothing to endanger yourself or the children. You can never prove what you suspect to be true."

"What I KNOW to be true."

"Very well, what you know to be true, you still can't prove it. I would be far more distressed to know you were harmed or the children lost their inheritance. Promise me," William ordered.

Ela did not take the vow lightly. *Do justice, love mercy. Do justice, love mercy. Do justice! I can do justice without making reckless accusations.* "I promise."

When Bishop Poore finished the rites, he found Ela in front of a fireplace in the great hall with all of her eight children gathered around her, the youngest three clinging to her arms and legs.

Poore held as little respect for women as anyone, even less than most as a churchman, but he realized then that he had never seen more strength in the face of any man. "He has confessed. I have gotten him back into bed and he sleeps again."

"Back into bed?" Countess Ela asked.

"Yes, after you left he jumped out and fell on his knees in contrition."

"I did not think he had that much strength left," Ela said.

"His penitence was most sincere, no doubt it alone gave him the strength."

Ela nodded. "Thank you, Bishop."

"The very least I could do." Poore started to leave, stopped at the door, and spoke over his shoulder. "I sincerely wish there was more."

On March 8, 1226, eight weeks to the day after his triumphal entry, William Longespee, third Earl of Salisbury, was laid to rest within the newly completed chapel of Mary within Salisbury Cathedral. He was the first person to find his eternal rest within the cathedral.

Gracing the solemn line of mourners were three bishops, two earls, three barons, and many knights. More remarkable than any of these, however, were the commoners who lined the two miles from castle to cathedral. For William Longespee was a nobleman mourned by all, noble and common alike. Their silent respects drowned out all speech.

Part the Third:

Widow

Chapter Twenty-two

Spring, 1228
Old Sarum

Ela scrutinized the riders approaching Sarum from the North. Numbering less than two dozen men-at-arms, not a knight amongst them, they represented a real threat nonetheless.

Each family, the Longespees and the de Burghs, spent the two years since William Longespee's death sizing each other up, dancing around each other, gaging support from both the amused and the bloodthirsty spectators. The de Burghs threw the first punch. As Chief Justiciar of England, Hubert de Burgh ordered Sarum to supply soldiers, under the command of William Talbot, to put down raids by the Scots in Lincolnshire. No clever ploy, everyone knew that his real purpose was to leave Sarum, and therefore Ela, undefended.

Advisors begged Ela to leave; she refused. Instead, she ordered young William to take his brothers and sisters to Pembroke to entrust their care to her late husband's best friend, William Marshal the younger. She trusted that the new Marshal would send a replacement guard under her son's command. This was not them on the horizon, however, instead Hubert's men were arriving first.

"My Lady, a priest has arrived. He begs that the drawbridge be lowered so that he may enter." The poor little servant girl was so terrified she could barely speak. There were only two men-at-arms to guard the castle ramparts, neither would leave their post for such a message.

"Don't sound so anxious, Abigail. I am the only person in danger today."

"If I may say, my Lady, I fear for you as I would one of my own relations… we all feel that way."

Ela lowered her head, she didn't know whether to smile or cry. "This priest, did he say what he wants?"

Abigail turned her head in the direction of the riders, away from the Countess' face. "He has come to offer confession."

"I have not made such a request."

"He says the Bishop sent him, knowing the danger you are in." Abigail was bewildered by Ela's hearty laughter. "My Lady?"

"Hubert has no intention of killing me, he plans to force me into marriage through rape. My death is the last thing he would want, why would I be in such dire need of confession? Furthermore, if Bishop Poore did decide I needed confession, for greater favor from the Almighty say, he would come himself. He wouldn't send a priest. Come child, let's meet this clergyman of yours."

Both men-at-arms stood on the eastern wall nearest the drawbridge. Their faces were books. Ela read absence of fear, stoicism, but great concern for her. She harbored no doubt in her selection of bodyguards.

A priest stood on the far side of the moat, alone amongst the specters of deserted buildings. The entire village of Sarum was now relocated to the newly laid out town of Salisbury, two miles to the South, surrounding the great cathedral. The quiet which descended upon the ancient hill-fort at first felt eerie and troubling. Ela overcame that feeling and now enjoyed the reduction in stench as well as the sense of space that came from the troops moving their quarters outside the castle.

"Hurry, Lady! You must allow me entry quickly, the riders are nearly upon us. There is just time." The hooded priest spoke oddly, not quite right, as if disguising his voice.

"Lower your hood, *father*." Ela virtually spat the last, clearly ludicrous, word.

The man shook visibly, too witless to respond.

"Stop this ridiculous attempt to become an earl, Reimand. Perhaps the King needs a new fool? I would give you a glowing recommendation, you have certainly earned that." Ela turned and walked away.

One of the Countess' guards lifted the front of his tunic. "Here now priest. You forgot your holy water, lucky for you I have some." With that he made a valiant attempt to reach the counterfeit priest with his urine stream, but the arch fell harmlessly into the moat.

Reimand threw off the outer cloaks of disguise and stood before the castle walls in his most magnificent warrior's pose. The man-at-arms who did not have his hands full reached down and pulled up a crossbow. By the time he ensured the bolt was snugly in place in front of the pre-strung cable, Reimand reassessed his situation and retreated toward the nearest abandoned storefront.

The bolt lodged firmly in his right arse-cheek. "Bastards! You'll pay for this I promise you!"

Hubert de Burgh was no fool, but he knew one when he saw one. In his nephew he found the model by which an army of fools could be built. Reimand was, however, male, unmarried, and close enough in relation to be useful. Amongst the assault team was a competent sergeant with clear assurance that he could ignore the commands of the would-be earl with impunity. The assault upon Sarum, therefore, was carried out carefully, methodically, and in a tactically sound manner.

The barrel chested sergeant assessed the situation and decided to take the time to build several very long ladders. The southern wall of Sarum castle abutted the hill-fort slope, for practical purposes it was impenetrable. Northern and Eastern walls faced the abandoned town. Better yet, to the West was the old cathedral. Ela's men had burned the bridge that afforded easy access between the castle and cathedral the day before. Only a relatively narrow gap remained. With ladders, it would be easy enough to divide and conquer. Though few in number themselves, Hubert's men could easily overcome two soldiers and a handful of scrawny servants. The attack would begin at dawn the next day.

Where to hide the Countess? Ela listened as her guards argued their ideas. The crypt of the cathedral? Being outside the castle, that might be clever. Many bodies were already translocated to the new cathedral at Salisbury; would an empty tomb fool the men? Risk of suffocation made them vacillate.

"De Burgh's men have probably already occupied the cathedral, men," Ela said. "Do not worry, I know what to do. There is a means of escape."

"Please tell us your intentions, Lady Ela, that we may better divert their forces."

"Better still you not know my whereabouts. I know and trust your loyalties, but any man may be forced to talk, if he knows what his tormentors want to hear."

Sarum Castle, indeed the ancient hill-fort itself, veiled a secret passed down through generations of its rulers. This confidential information was even concealed from the Kings of England who nominally owned this land but did not live there. For the hill which Sarum crowned was made of chalk, and hewn into that chalk was a tunnel.

Ela slept in the old great hall that night, the one inside the courtyard house along the northern wall. As light of day capitulated and firelight alone cast dancing shadows upon the stones, Ela remembered happy days past in that room. Occasionally the light played tricks and a shadow would stretch. It was easy to imagine that one was cast by her father, the next by her husband. Before drifting off to sleep, the reality of abandoning her home struck Ela. She wondered when she would see Sarum again.

Just before dawn, cries of alarm bounced along the stone walls and tore past Ela. It was time. She gathered the parcel and the torch that she had placed beside her makeshift bed the night before. A ten year old servant raced to find from which direction the assault was coming while Ela walked to the nearest fireplace and lit the torch. She willed the boy to report quickly, no doubt if the soldiers were serious they would be here soon.

"From the North, East and West, Countess!" The words echoed in from outside and above, the servant being under strict orders not to return to the hall.

Fine. The West was the greatest threat, they would succeed first. But they would come in beside the keep, it was still necessary to cross the courtyard in order to enter the hall. She walked into the antechamber off the dais. There, beside the staircase, a paving slab was already ajar. Ela pushed at the waiting iron bar and the slab shifted further, opening a hole large enough for her to climb through. Once inside, a borehole in the underneath of the paving slab accepted one end of the iron bar. Leaning with all her might, she felt and heard the stone fall into its place.

Ela threw aside the iron bar, and using ropes already tied to the parcel, slipped it onto her back. She needed one hand to hold the torch, the other held firm to a thick rope that disappeared into the distance where torchlight was overcome. The tunnel consisted of a steep slope that descended to the plain far below. After carefully backpedalling a few dozen feet, Ela guessed she was under the moat. Were the men directly above, scrambling over their ladders, or had their paths already crossed unbeknownst to either party?

Every footfall stirred up a new cloud of chalk powder. Dust enveloped her, coated her skin and clothing, and threatened to besiege her lungs. She slowed her pace, so as not to give herself away by choking. There was plenty of time, no need to take the chance of being heard. How many possible hiding places would the enemy check before tearing up stone floors?

After half an hour's steady descent, Ela stumbled and dropped the torch. Dust enveloped the flame like angry ants. The light flickered, regrouped, then died.

Darkness was jubilant.

Nowhere but the grave was its victory so complete. The night's victory was never absolute, there was always a sliver of moon or a few stars to continue the fight. Nothing of that sort existed here, only blackness. For just a moment, Ela was a frightened little girl who wanted her papa. Then she took a breath, considered what to do, and realized she didn't need the light. Perhaps the torch only slowed her down. Now she was free to use both hands to rappel the sheer grade.

When she reached the bottom she found herself in a cramped alcove. Without the torch, all she could do was push hard against the wall where the tunnel maw should be. Soon she found hard stone instead of chalk and threw all her weight behind it. The stone slid a few inches. Light streamed in and more importantly fresh air. Ela put her face to the crack and heaved in great gulps of freshness. Her lungs seemed to be full of chalk, but soon her strength was renewed and she focussed all her weight and effort against the stone's edge. It fell away and she scrambled out onto the green grass field.

Ela dashed along the northern face of the hill, hugging the tree line to avoid being visible from the ramparts above. Finally there was no choice but to sprint the two hundred yards from the western slope to the shaded overgrowth that embraced the River Avon. There were no shouts coming from behind her that she could attribute to discovery. Just a few steps later she crashed into the clearing where the small boat was hidden. All she needed to do was push the boat into the water, climb aboard, and float peacefully into Salisbury.

Instead, all she found was smashed and splintered lumber.

"I'm afraid my men had an unfortunate accident with your craft, Ela. It was never befitting a countess anyway."

Reimand!

His arrogance survived her glare—just.

She glanced at the Avon. If she could just reach it, just a few strides, she could float in the drifting current part of the way then climb out and run along the far bank. It was only two miles to town. Reimand stood directly in her path, with thick saplings to slow her down on either side. There was only one way to go: back the way she came. Ela turned and ran.

She ignored the burning deep within her lungs. The chase wore on minute after minute, though each second Ela expected to feel the man's hands grab her. She didn't know about the wound Reimand suffered the previous day, but looking over her shoulder, she realized the gap was widening. Back across open space, she decided to run along the western slope and around to the South this time. They did not assault the southern wall, and their western assault came from the interior, the cathedral district.

Now what? The Countess stopped to regroup, taking advantage of the space she had gained to think. She could think of only two options. First was a two mile chase across open fields to Salisbury. She was winning the race against Reimand, but what if the men were alerted? Surely at least one of them could outrun her, even with her head start. The only other option was to go back into the town and find a hiding place. Decision made, she placed her bet on the town.

Hubert's men were still focussed on the castle, so Ela was able to slip into Old Sarum undetected. Reimand couldn't possibly be far behind. Everyone would then be searching the abandoned buildings. Where could she hide for longest possible concealment? A sudden inspiration struck Ela. It would be uncomfortable, dangerous, and revolting; and that is exactly why they wouldn't look there.

She ran directly toward the inner bailey, veered left as she approached the bridge, and scrambled down into the moat. Once neck deep in the rank liquid, she scuttled along the outer bank until she was directly under the bridge. The first five minutes would tell the tale. If her dash was detected, then the men would have her soon. If not, then chances were good she could remain hidden for several hours, perhaps she could even make it to nightfall when she would try again to make for new Salisbury.

Reimand's voice suddenly cackled very close and dirt rained down on Ela as he stomped onto the bridge. At first she was sure that she was caught, but then she listened to his words.

"You men come quickly, she came to the boat!"

Another voice came from high above. "And got away from you I see."

"I couldn't run with this damn wound in my leg."

A third voice was familiar. "I didn't shoot you in the leg; I hit you in the arse!"

"Sergeant, I order you to kill that man!"

"I got no quarrel with him. He fought like a knight, I only wish we could have taken them both alive."

"My uncle is the chief..."

"I know who your uncle is. It's his orders I follow, not yours."

A fresh shower of silt fell as Reimand stamped his foot. "Well, she isn't in the castle and I can see for miles in all directions, so she had to come back into Sarum.

"Reasonable. I'll organize the men. We'll start on the outskirts and work our way into the middle, herd her like sheep."

"Fine. Let's just get on with it. I have a marriage to consummate!"

Ela pushed away a turd that floated inches from her face. *If he found me now would he do the deed? For the earldom, probably.*

Time passing proved impossible to measure. Ela dared not peer out to look for the sun or its shadows, she clung to the bank, constantly slipping in the muck and regaining hold. It was best not to think about the source of this slime. Over the decades the moat served as a latrine for the town. Human and animal waste, even carcasses of dead animals, were dumped here. Faced with the option of looking up at Reimand's face contorting with pleasure, the Countess decided this was paradise in comparison. She even smiled at the thought.

Ela had surely been in the moat for hours when she heard them. She could not identify the sound for a few minutes as the rumble grew louder. Then the noise crescendoed, meaning the source breached the eastern gate of the old city. It was singing, loud singing, hundreds of people singing. It was a hymn of the crusades, of protecting Jerusalem from the heathen. Then the singing stopped.

"We have come to see the Countess Ela of Salisbury."

Bishop Poore!

"Maybe you'll have better luck than us, Bishop, we haven't seen her." This was likely the sergeant speaking again.

"Do you surrender peacefully to the people of Salisbury?"

"Why the hell not? I got no taste for this job no more. Throw down your weapons men—all of them."

Ela climbed up the embankment and stood wobbly before the bridge. Her hair was disheveled, her face hidden under layers of chalk and muck, and her clothes were painted the color of sewage. The tears eroding the sediment of her cheeks came from happiness and appreciation, not suffering. Almost every adult in Salisbury must have been in Poore's army, all carrying pitchforks, sickles, any makeshift weapon they could find. On either side of the Bishop stood Uncle Philip and Clare, their infant daughter watching the excitement from a sling on Clare's back.

At the sight of the Countess, the mob fell upon the soldier unfortunate enough to be standing closest to them. Before Ela and the Bishop could regain control, the man was hacked to death.

The next day, after so many baths Ela lost track, a new garrison arrived at Sarum led personally by the Earl of Pembroke. After considering what the Earl's father would have done, the fate of Hubert's men was decided. The town was delighted. With the exception of the capable sergeant, whom both Ela and the new Marshal believed to be truly repentant, the men were shaved bald, stripped of all their clothing, and thrown into the dyer's vats. One week later the survivors marched naked across London Bridge, a bright yellow and green display for the populace.

From hovel to palace the decision was unanimous, round one to the Longespees.

Chapter Twenty-three

Ela sat at her desk in the private chamber of the courtyard house as morning grew in strength. The door was open to encourage the fresh spring air to enter the building. She was not surprised when a large form appeared in the frame and rapped on a post.

"Countess, may I beg a moment?" William Marshal asked.

"Dear William, you are this house's greatest friend. Here you beg for nothing, least of all my time."

The Marshal nodded once and stepped into the room, leaving the door open for appearances sake. "I will of course take my leave at mid-morning meal. I wished to say farewell privately, more informally."

The siege of Sarum was over. Hubert de Burgh was embarrassed but not permanently incapacitated. Sarum's troops, however, were relieved of service in the Marches; they were reinstalled in defense of the castle. As such, the Earl of Pembroke's presence was no longer critical.

"That is most thoughtful of you as always." Ela looked out on the plain north of the hill. "Do you remember that day, at the tournament?"

"I do. I remember being in awe of my older cousin, the free spirited girl with the flashing smile."

"Your father talked of our betrothal that day. If my father had not died so suddenly, we might have been married you and I."

Marshal looked down at the flagstone floor. "I remember, and have considered from time to time what might have been."

Ela kept her gaze on the fields. "I loved William Longespee, was always happy with him, but I believe that if I never knew that love, the alternative would also have been—pleasant."

"If I did not marry Elizabeth so shortly before your husband's death we may have had a second chance."

This time she turned to face him. "How were you to know? It proves that we were never meant to be I suppose."

Marshal nodded once again.

"Well, it may not be God's will for us to be lovers, but what I said earlier is true. You are the greatest friend my family could hope for. I do not know what would become of us, of me, if it weren't for your constant support."

"Do not mention it. You are, after all, family. And your William was my best friend and brother in arms."

"I remember. Go in peace and with my love, William."

"May the Lord bless and keep you, Ela."

The ancient hermit Edwin strived for the hundredth time to speak. Peering up from his bed in the monastic hospital at St. Albans, he gazed at a lovely young face, one that had been a constant presence at his side since the apoplexy first struck. This face attempted to display courage and hope, but the eyes were overly moist and red. With only the left side of his mouth functional, Edwin's words came out as little more than a warbling W sound.

Christina knew what he was saying. "Go. Get away. Flee."

She was fortunate two years ago to stumble into the care and protection of the kindly old holy man. Not once over the years did he glance at her in an unseemly manner as he nourished her physically and spiritually. According to the ecclesiastical courts, however, her vow was not recognized. Michael still held claim upon her as his betrothed.

A taller, healthier version of Edwin approached the foot of the bed. Roger was considered the greater of the brother hermits, no doubt due to his strict submission to the decisions of bishops.

"You must leave him now, I have matters to discuss with you," Roger said.

Christina guessed what this would be about. Giving Edwin's good hand a last squeeze, she followed Roger down the aisle that ran down the center of the long hall. Crude rope-strung beds lined either wall.

"How may I serve you, Brother Roger?"

"Stow the pleasantries, wench. You have never been a bride of Christ, you belong to a mortal man. Only loyalty and love of my brother kept me from exposing you two before now. Your insistence on staying by his bedside did the task for me."

Christina inhaled sharply. "What do you mean?"

"Someone here recognized you. They expect a reward for informing your parents of your whereabouts. I am— informed of much that goes on here."

"Why are you telling me this?"

"You must flee." Roger's previous bluster dissipated. He finally looked into the girl's eyes, which he avoided doing to this point. "It is a final courtesy—to thank you for brightening my brothers life."

Christina withdrew a step. "You must know that there was never anything unholy about our relationship."

"Yes yes, I know. You waste time."

"Where am I to go? I will be little better than an outlaw," Christina said.

"You already are little better than an outlaw. You made that decision two years ago."

A novice strode up beside Roger carrying the satchel in which Christina carried her worldly possessions. She accepted it, thanked the man, for his warning was a kindness however artlessly delivered, and left the hospital immediately. She didn't dare look back.

Leaving the monastery grounds behind her, she wandered in the drizzle through the market of St. Albans' village. Around the square, the buildings' drop shutters were down, resting on barrels. Tents of oiled leather gave some protection of the wares against the rain. It was impossible to read expressions on the faces gazing out from heavy hoods, but Christina suspected each one of watching her, and accusing. Once inside the churchyard, she slumped against the trunk of a yew tree and considered her situation. Certainly she could not go on like this, she feared either her mother or Michael around every corner. The churchyard faced onto the London Road, the most likely direction from which her hunters would come.

Something Roger said troubled her. "You made that decision two years ago." *No I didn't decide that. Betrothal was forced on me. My fate was sealed when I made my vow all those years ago, in Salisbury. Salisbury!* Suddenly Christina recalled the tall beautiful woman who laid a foundation stone, and intimidated her father. The journey to Salisbury was a long one. Christina was homeless and destitute, and no woman was safe traveling alone along the English roads. At least now she had a plan, though, and a goal. She would take her appeal to Countess Ela.

Ela rode her best horse at full gallop all the way from Sarum to the new village of Salisbury. She was too late.

"I came as soon as the messenger arrived, how could it happen so fast?" Ela panted. "Was there no warning?"

"It was the fastest fever I have ever witnessed, Countess," a monk whispered, packing his potions and medical devices into a leather bag.

Philip sat on the edge of the bed, brushing stray hairs from Clare's stark white face. A bowl of pinkish water and red stained rags sat on a nearby table. There had been blood on the body.

"Uncle Philip, I am sorry. Will you stay at the castle for a while?"

Philip stood and turned to Ela. "That will not be necessary. We will be fine, little Ela and I."

"As you wish. The offer stands, should you change your mind."

"Thank you, Ela. There is one thing you can do for me."

"Name it," the Countess said.

Philip rested a hand on Ela's shoulder. "Run the trade will you? I was never any good to her in business."

"Of course, Uncle."

As she approached Oxford, there were two things on Christina's mind. First was her overriding thankfulness to God for his protection thus far. She walked fifty miles due west over the last week, constantly watching for bands of outlaws. Even so, it was impossible to be totally alert to every rustle of leaves or grass and still make any progress. The second thing occupying Christina's thoughts was how she was going to get across the River Thames. There were still provisions of hard bread and legumes in her bag, but no money. There would be a toll to use the Oxford bridge, or any village's bridge for that matter.

Christina's luck ran out a mile southeast of Oxford. Walking along a lane toward the city gates, she could sense that she was close to the river. The perceived closeness to a city like Oxford caused her to quicken her step and be just a little less alert. The man who pulled her into the brush was not much taller than her, and thin, but his grip was surprisingly strong. Pushing her back up against a tree, the man pinned her crossed wrists with one hand and used the other to cover her mouth. The move was so quick and smooth that she was sure the man was well practiced.

"Ok girl, here's what's gonna happen. I'm gonna take my hand away from your mouth, and you're gonna be nice and quiet. Got it?"

Christina regained her composure and nodded her head.

"That's good honey, now we can have a nice chat."

The man did as promised, reaching down and drawing a dagger with his now free hand. He suddenly released her wrists and swiftly moved that hand to Christina's throat. He held the dagger point inches from her nose conveying a silent but clear message that trying to escape could be very unhealthy. Her focus adjusted from the narrow blade to take in the face behind it. It was impossible to tell his age, though he couldn't be too old as the matted hair and beard were bright orange, with no sign of grey. Her initial impression of his body was confirmed; he was short and very thin, whether naturally or due to poor nutrition was difficult to say. One thing was clear, he had not done hard work for years.

"Good girl, stay nice and quiet and you'll be alright."

She wanted to ask what the man wanted but there was no answer to that question that didn't frighten her, so she just stared.

"You see, you're walking along a toll road, precious. My friends and I are toll collectors." The tangled bush of his facial hair parted in a broad smile that revealed more gaps and stubs than actual teeth.

"What is the toll?"

The smile widened even further. "What ya got?"

"I don't have any money."

The man appraised her again head to foot. It made Christina's stomach lurch. "Well your tunic is poor enough, but you talk noble."

He was right of course, her speech always gave her away at the very least. Edwin once told her that she "carried" herself nobly too, whatever that meant. But the nobility was often poor, and her poverty was real albeit self-inflicted. After pondering the best tack for a moment, she decided that the truth seemed as good as any. "I walked away from a wealthy match to give myself to Christ. I have no money at all."

The face bush moved again, he probably pursed his lips, considering her claim, but it was impossible to say for sure. Finally he nodded slowly. "That's too bad me lady, lucky for you we accept other forms of payment."

He was looking at her body again, this time clearly not appraising the cut and quality of her clothing. The weight of his words hit her hard and she vomited a mouthful of sick. It was time to fight. With aim and distance any ruffian would be proud of, she spat the vomit in the man's face and bolted toward the roadway. She heard a ripping sound as the knife caught in the sleeve of her tunic but she didn't care.

She only managed two steps. A wiry arm scooped her

up around the waist and the knife was back searching out her neck. She tensed and pulled her head back, but stopped struggling.

"Now that wasn't very nice noble girl. Time to meet the rest of your new friends."

Her entrance into the outlaws' camp elicited whoops and whistles. Christina was frantic but her faith was strong and her mind clear, she knew God might expect her to be part of her own salvation and to answer the call, she must be clear headed and thoughtful. She could see five more men not including her captor. They ranged in ages from a boy still in his teens to about forty, all ragged, unkempt, and spectacularly filthy. Her gaze was drawn to a hulk of coarse wool and flesh. He was a giant, and out of some comic irony of nature, he was the least hairy of all. His face was very flat, his mouth hung open, and there was dullness in his eyes.

"What d'yah find Cutter?" The oldest outlaw strutted forward, apparently he was in charge here.

"A little noble girl. No money though."

"No money? What good's a noble girl with no money?" He chuckled, Christina saw that this man considered himself quite clever. "Skunk, get some sticks. We'll draw straws for order, boys."

"Draw for who goes after me you mean. I found her and got her here." Cutter possessed a clear sense of fair play.

"That's just cause it was your turn on the road." This counter argument was offered by one of the as yet nameless rogues.

"I coulda just had her in the woods!"

"But ya didn't did ya? Guess maybe you'll learn something." It was the king of the outlaws again.

Christina used the time bought by this debate to study the

terrain. They were all standing in a glade surrounded by thick scrub, poplars, and box trees. As well as the path by which she was drug, there was a second, opposite pathway leading out of the other side of the clearing. Though the land here was all very flat, there was slight but noticeable downward grade to that trail. She guessed that it led to the river. No doubt the men were equal part pirates as well as unofficial toll takers. If they did intercept river travelers, there would be a boat of some kind. The river was the better option if she did find herself on the run. She would be run down on the road, but if she got the only boat into the water, the chase would be over.

"Git yer clothes off, noble girl." Christina looked back into the camp, apparently Cutter's line of reasoning carried the day.

"Listen, like I told Cutter at the road, I've dedicated myself to Christ. I vowed to remain a virgin for Him!"

"Well we didn't take any vows of virginity noble girl, and you aren't dressed as a nun so I say that's just a story."

"And if God wanted you to be a virgin, he wouldn't have sent ya here. Seems you be a gift to us not Christ," the leader added.

"We'll be sure to thank him in our prayers tonight." The teen laughed.

"Now take yer clothes off or I cut them off." Cutter waved the knife back and forth. "In fact, maybe that'd be just fine. Ya probably won't be needin clothes long as ya's with us."

Christina looked around. She was surrounded and time was running out. The only outlaw not part of her human prison was the giant. He stood several yards off, shifting his weight from foot to foot, shaking his head and grunting nonsense words.

The leader followed her gaze. "Don't mind Tiny, he's just tetched in the head a bit. He'll be along to entertain ya later though, those parts work better than his brain."

"I'm a bride of Christ!" Finally the tears flowed.

"No you isn't." Cutter was oddly calm. "We've already hashed that out. Now seriously, you should save your clothes, you'll want them later. Believe me."

Christina looked at Cutter's face, the knife, the ring of outlaws. She untied the hemp belt of her tunic and, as slowly as she believed she could get away with, pulled it over her head. "Have you no fear for your immortal souls?" She sobbed as she folded the tunic and laid it at her feet.

She stood there before these lowliest of men in just her shift. Her nipples were clearly visible through the thin linen. Coolness of the air in the glen added to her humiliation.

"Keep goin."

"Is that really necessary?" She whispered.

Cutter reached out and clutched her right breast. "Yes. It is." He grabbed hold of the linen and tore the thin garment away from her body. "Git down, on yer back."

Christina couldn't believe it. She fought all this time to withhold her virginity from a fine husband, and now she was to lose it to half a dozen filthy outlaws? It didn't make sense. Her faith made its escape where hers was unattainable.

"Now don't be cuttin her, keep her pretty for the rest of us," the leader instructed.

She lowered herself to the ground and fell back, but she couldn't bring herself to open her legs. Cutter would just have to fight that much. She placed the palms of her hands over her already closed eyes. After a pause in which Cutter undoubtedly freed his member from his own undergarment, she felt his hands under her calfs. In one last burst of defiance, Christina remembered the theatrics she had seen boys display when they got hit in the nether regions while playing games when she was a child. She jerked her right leg out of his grasp, opened her eyes to target, and kicked Cutter hard under his erect penis. He reacted with shock, the men laughed hysterically, but she must have missed because Cutter soon recovered. Her legs were wrenched apart and the swollen purple thing stabbed at her. She shifted and it punched her in the mons.

"No. No. Not right. Not right at all. No." The words barely registered in Christina's reality, but they continued growing louder, more insistent. "No. No. Soul. Not nice. Don't hurt girls. Not right."

Suddenly Cutter was no longer before her. He was disappearing before her eyes, hurtling backwards. The outlaws reacted.

"Take it easy, Tiny."

"It's okay, Tiny."

It was definitely not okay, and obviously it wasn't okay with Tiny. Christina could see now that there was a battle in the camp. The violence reminded her of bear baiting. She witnessed a baiting once, and never wanted to see it again. Half a dozen dogs would be set upon a chained black bear and bets made whether the bear would be killed before it tore all the dogs apart. Tiny was a massive bear and the rest of the outlaws were dogs, but these dogs could use weapons. Christina understood that this was the one moment of opportunity that God presented to her, and she was wasting precious moments. She rolled, stood, and ran, like she'd never run before, toward the river, for her earlier reconnaissance served her well.

Crashing through the brush that encroached on the primitive path, she could hear the river ahead of her. Praise God! Her soul began to sing until she heard the shouts and footfalls of outlaws gaining on her. At least some of the men left the battle to recapture their prize. She stumbled into a clearing at the river's edge. Even more unexpectedly, she found herself standing naked before a cluster of men again.

Christina screamed. She instinctively turned to flee, saw the outlaws emerging from the greenery, turned back, saw the new men, turned to either side to see nothing but more poplar trees.

"Get out of the way!"

The command came from one of the new men. Christina stood frozen like a deer that senses a threat, determining which way it should bolt. In a flash, her senses once again came to her and she realized the new men wore livery. They were soldiers. Two men were archers and knelt with bows drawn, their muscles trembling as they held the shafts to their ears. The arrows pointed directly at Christina. She threw herself against a tree and slid down, sitting on the roots.

Before her rump hit wood a whistling sound cut the air, then again and again. She looked to the archers. As an arrow left their weapon, their right hands travelled a graceful but rapid arch, pulling another shaft from the quivers slung on their backs, nocking the arrows on bowstring, pulling, and repeating. Seconds later four outlaws lay in the clearing bristling with shafts and fletching.

"Avert your eyes men. That's an order!" The sergeant turned his head away as well, while Christina retreated behind the tree. "Ahem. Do you have clothing, me lady?"

"It's back at the outlaws' camp."

"Are there more?"

Christina counted the bodies one more time to be sure.

"Two, but one of those helped me escape."

Wordlessly two soldiers were assigned the task to retrieve the naked girl's garment: a man-at-arms and an archer.

"Don't hurt the giant! He is simple but kind!" Christina shouted after the pair.

"What's all the excitement?" From the opposite tree line emerged a young man about twenty years old. He was dressed very simply in coarse wool. He was of medium height, a little on the thickset side, and with a narrow forehead. His otherwise pleasant countenance was somewhat marred by a drooping left eyelid.

"Outlaws, my Lord. We… um… have a visitor."

Christina waved from behind the tree then felt exceedingly stupid for having done it.

"Well hello, maid; well met!" The very humble looking man greeted her with a winning smile. Strange that the sergeant called him Lord. He must be a poor noble. Perhaps he was a clerk of some important man, why else would he have a military escort?

"So what brings you here, maid?" The man continued.

"It's maiden, sir." She saw the sergeant raise an eyebrow. "Still a maiden thanks be to God—and yourselves."

The man nodded.

"Indeed! Praise God! But go on." The strange man sat on a fallen log as if there was nothing at all unusual about this interview.

Again Christina decided the truth was as good a story as any. "I was traveling along the road yonder when I was set upon by a band of outlaws."

"A pretty young lady traveling alone?"

"I am on a quest for aid, sir, I am in distress."

"A damsel in distress? How very chivalric! To where were you traveling on this quest?"

Christina stood up straighter, though she was well hidden behind the tree. "To Countess Ela of Salisbury."

"Ela? Why Ela?"

"She was present the day I made my vow of perpetual virginity before God. She… she was very kind to me."

"She is a kind lady, you could not have chosen better."

Christina nearly ran out from behind the tree. "You know her?"

Just then the soldiers returned and one handed Christina her tunic. "I'm sorry, my lady, the undergarment is destroyed."

"No matter, thank you very much. What of the other men?"

"Both dead. Looks like the giant smashed the skull of an Irishman before the others stabbed him to death. I'm sorry, my lady, I heard you say the giant saved you."

"Yes, he did." Christina said a silent prayer for the big man's soul.

The civilian stood and walked toward the river. "Well if you are properly covered, let us be off!"

It sounded to her like she was invited to join the men, but she wasn't sure. She followed behind the soldiers to shore and stopped so as not to appear presumptuous. Tied there was a sizable barge. More men were aboard it, the sailors apparently.

The friendly plain man stopped and turned to Christina. "Well, are you coming, my lady?"

"Thank you, sir, but where are you going?"

"Oh that's right, we were interrupted. I happen to know for a fact that Ela is not in Salisbury."

"Sir?"

"She is in London, young maiden. And it just so happens that is our destination. Would you care for a ride?"

"Oh thank you, kind sir!" Christina was now completely

convinced this band was sent by God, and ran to the craft.

"If we are to be traveling companions we should be properly introduced. I am Henry of Winchester."

"Pleased to make your acquaintance does not really seem enough to express my sentiment, sir. I am Christina of Markyate."

"Charmed." The man nodded and sat back in a chair in the center of the barge offering a similar seat to his new friend.

"How do you know my lady Ela, sir?"

"Why I am proud to be her nephew."

"Oh!" Christina exclaimed, then frowned slightly. Ela was rich, how was her nephew so simply dressed?

All at once a snippet of conversation from that long ago day at Salisbury dawned on her. She remembered being amused that her father was intimidated by Ela. "Do you know the King?" Christina had asked her. "I should think so. He is my nephew," Ela replied. Henry! Ela's nephew! A bodyguard of soldiers. She looked again at the barge and saw the royal emblem with the three leopards.

"You are the King!"

Henry smiled. "I wish you would tell that to the magnates. They tend to forget. Oh don't kneel. There's no point in formalities between friends."

As they floated down the Thames, Christina came to understand why Henry dressed so plainly. He captivated her with his devotion to St. Edward the Confessor. Considering him the greatest example of what a king should be, short of Arthur himself, Henry sought to model himself after this predecessor. Edward was said to have dressed simply and humbly, thus Henry did the same. Christina was amazed and intrigued by the concept of a humble king.

Drifting past Westminster, Henry told her of his plans to make the Confessor's sanctuary the capitol of his realm. The Abbey would be rebuilt, in Norman style, grander, more impressive inside and out. It would be a fitting monument to house the saint's bones. When he had a son, the next King of England, he would be named Edward. It seemed a bit odd to Christina that the abbey the Confessor built would be torn down in order to honor him, but she nodded politely and said nothing.

Approaching London by river, the city is hidden from the traveler's view until it is upon him. As the barge rounded a sharp turn of the Thames, Christina saw her former home come into dramatic view. There was Temple Church, the round sanctuary of the Templar knights, final resting place of William the Marshal. Towering above it was the newly completed Cathedral of London, St. Paul's. Minutes later the White Tower loomed.

"And soon I will build a great curtain wall encompassing many of the out buildings, including the chapel of St. Peter Ad Vincula. Beyond that will be a moat."

Christina smiled. "It is nice to know there are kings with visions of building, not just warring."

"Oh there will be war as well. I intend to regain our rightful lands stolen by the French during my father's reign."

Christina nodded once again. All this talk of spending. Massive building projects and wars, where was the money to come from?

A sudden splash caught her eye. There in the river, just below the Tower, a great beast was fishing. Christina had never seen anything quite like it. Its form was that of a bear. It was at least three times larger than any bear she had ever seen, however, and was pure white, whiter than any cloth imaginable. It dived down, then came lumbering up onto the rocky beach with a large salmon in it's mighty jaws. Three powerfully built and armed men kept respectful distance while holding onto leather tethers attached to a collar around the beast's neck.

"A gift from the King of Norway. Thankfully it contributes to its own keep, otherwise the cost of food would rival a table full of courtiers," Henry said with a chuckle.

The barge came alongside a dock a few dozen feet further on. The King escorted Christina up the hill, passing the ravens as they hopped and cawed in protest, to the wooden steps which provided access to the second floor of the keep.

A colorfully dressed guard snapped to attention and announced the King, as Henry led her into the council chamber. A few men gathered around great oak tables looked up, some nodded, but otherwise Christina was struck by how under-awed they appeared. All were meticulously shaven, wearing very fine cloth trimmed in various animal furs. None wore visible arms, she saw tall baskets full of swords immediately inside the main doorway. Apparently it was forbidden to bear arms within the royal residence. She soon realized that there were no women in this great room; she wondered both if her quest was incomplete and if she was somewhere she aught not to be.

Henry remembered his guest, looked about himself, and held up a finger to Christina. "Ah! Christina, you no doubt wish to find your benefactor. Gentlemen! Where might this maiden find the Lady Ela?"

"I believe the lady is just there, in the chapel of St. John." The speaker seemed bored but courteous enough.

"Thank you, Sir Peter. Christina, the chapel is around the corner, through the other doorway at the stairs."

"Thank you, your majesty. Will I see you later?"

"I very much hope so, my lady."

There was only one person in the chapel. It was a woman kneeling at the altar with her back to the doorway as Christina entered. Though she could not see the lady's face, the form and obvious height instantly felt familiar. The sight of the lady warmed Christina like hot soup on a cold day. She felt a great weight come off of her, one she carried, unnoticed, since that dreadful day at St. Albans.

The chapel was dim despite the many flickering candles. She could see, though, that it was painted in vivid hues. Each alternating column was either bright white or orange, with each meeting at the roof in sharp triangles of color. In her relief, she must have sighed, for the lady turned toward her. Finishing her prayer and crossing herself, the lady stood and faced Christina.

"Good day to you. I am finished here, I leave you to be alone with God."

"No please! I mean, thank you, I have much to give thanks for, but I have been seeking you."

"Seeking me?" The face was a little older, her countenance slightly sadder, but this was definitely the same impressive woman Christina remembered from her childhood.

"You will not remember me, but I was present with you when the foundation stones were laid for Salisbury Cathedral several years ago."

Ela's eyes raised to the vaulted ceiling for just a moment. "The little monkey climbing for a view? My how you have grown!"

Ela's face betrayed an uncomfortable pity, and Christina was suddenly very aware of her appearance. "Forgive what I must look like to you today, Countess, I was attacked by a gang of outlaws this morning."

Pity changed to horror. "Outlaws? My child, did they…"

"No! I mean, they tried, but I escaped and God delivered me safely to the King's men."

"Well then, you and I will give prayers of thankfulness to the Father and the Virgin, then you will tell me tales of your great adventure."

Christina desperately wanted to escape. The dilemma she found herself in was difficult to fathom. In many ways, she felt as if she was back in the forest glen three days ago. Instead, the clearing was replaced by the council chamber of the Tower of London. Filthy lecherous outlaws were replaced by her greedy parents, poor patient Michael, three different shire reeves, the lady Ela, a mixture of interested and bored courtiers, and one king. The King of England himself was hearing the debate that would determine the course of her life. Furthermore, it just took an unexpected and dangerous turn.

Her parents' local reeve barely finished explaining Christina's legal obligation to Michael when Ela boldly contradicted him.

"The crux of this case rests on the parents' greed to profit from their daughter's body."

Muttering echoed from the stone walls. Some of the until now bored courtiers maneuvered for a better view.

"Should my Lord's court listen to the wails of a woman?" The Reeve sounded indignant, but the blood was drained from his face not flushing it. Behind him, Christina's father looked as if he was barely able to remain standing.

Anger flashed across Henry's face like lightning. The King would have spoken in defense of his beloved aunt's council, but Ela did not require it and kept speaking. "Our Lord the King's great charter states that a woman cannot be compelled to marry."

Hubert de Burgh moved to insert himself into the proceeding. "Correction my lady, the words are specific: widows, not women. Christina is not a widow."

"Quite right my Lord Justiciar, but she has vowed her virginity for the sake of Christ."

"That vow was not confirmed before a priest, and she willingly entered into betrothal." It was the reeve again.

"Hardly willingly, she was coerced, and her vow was confirmed before Edwin of St. Albans," Ela said.

"Who is struck dumb by apoplexy and cannot confirm her story," the reeve replied with a sigh.

"Enough!" All eyes turned to Michael, the wronged would-be husband. "My Lord King, I accept that Christina devoted herself to Christ, and wish only to have the betrothal set aside so that I might take another wife."

"Splendid!" Henry's countenance brightened.

"No!" Christina was the only person in the chamber not shocked to hear the new female voice cry out.

"You are too kind, Sir Michael, you need not surrender your right so easily." Christina's mother looked sheepish, but clearly knew her husband would not speak up to protect their interests.

"Thank you for proving my point. We are all here due to your greed." Ela crossed her arms in contempt.

Spurred on by the boldness of his female constituent, and most assumed by a hefty bribe, the reeve dared challenge the Countess once again. "My Lord King, the Countess Ela is passionate, but she is a woman, and I must again protest her intrusion on matters of law. I have witnessed myself how the lady has been quite wrong in legal proceedings before."

Christina looked at Ela, saw her slightly confused expression come and go, changing to almost imperceptible anger. "Perhaps the good reeve could elaborate?"

"I refer, my good lady, to a trial held in Sarum several years ago. You were adamant in your defense of a former servant. God declared him guilty."

"Of course, I had forgotten, good sir, that you were amongst the King's justices." She turned to the Sheriff of Wiltshire, just a few feet from her. "As were you John of Monmouth, were you not?"

John nodded, looking exceedingly confused and unwilling to be drawn into this discussion.

"His name, should you not remember, was Thomas."

"Yes. Yes. Thomas."

"You tried him by combat, putting the Lord our God to the test." She spoke matter-of-factly, not sounding accusatory in the least, but the words rushed to both men's faces and slapped them hard nonetheless.

"You dare…"

"Tell me, my Lord King, if a man were to grow new testicles and eyes, having been mutilated by order of men, would you consider that a miracle?"

"Most certainly, it could be nothing else!" Henry sounded delighted. Genuinely devout, the very mention of such a miracle of biblical magnitude excited him.

"And would such a miracle indicate that the punishment must have been unjust?"

"Without doubt!" The King said.

"Then if I were to prove that Thomas was restored, would you find in favor of my young friend?"

Hubert, amongst others, began to protest, but the King cut them all off. "Silence! I am the King, we are no longer under your wise regency rule. I will decide personally on this matter." Those who would control the King wisely stood down.

"Well then, Ela, you speak wisely. If it is as you say, I

will affirm Christina's vow personally." Henry scanned the haughty and the obsequies courtiers. "Furthermore, I will dismiss these two shire reeves."

"My Lord King, you plan to hunt at Clarendon this spring?" Ela asked.

"Yes, in three weeks time."

"Then I invite you, and all who require proof before their own eyes, to Sarum. You shall meet Thomas."

"Splendid." Henry looked around the room, intentionally holding the gaze of each who argued against his aunt this day. "We shall visit Sarum on our way from Clarendon in four weeks time."

"You will all be most welcome." Ela took Christina's hand. "In the meantime I should like to take the girl into my protection. May we both be excused to return to Sarum?"

Henry frowned, but acquiesced. "Go in peace, good lady."

"Thank you, my Lord King."

When they were out of the keep, Christina asked Ela about the extraordinary claims the Countess had just made.

"Pray Christina. We are about to try something my husband would not have approved of."

"My lady?"

"Would you agree deception in the name of justice can be righteous?" Countess Ela asked the girl.

Christina thought hard. This was not a simple question. "I should think it can be."

"Good. You are going to visit Oxford after all."

Two unlikely fraudsters sat prepared in the new great hall of Sarum when King Henry and his court arrived. A great banquet was served, including fresh roe sent ahead by his majesty from the hunt. Suspicious officials ate impatiently while Ela and the King spoke of family matters. When everyone was satiated, Ela gave the order to have the trestle tables removed and within minutes the hall was converted into a room worthy of a trial.

Into the room were escorted Thomas' old accusers and other men of the jury.

"You recognize the lady and gentlemen, Stephen Bukerel?"

"Yes, yes. I remember them. Good day to you all," The Sheriff of London acknowledged the group coldly.

"Three of the jury, as my beloved husband, are sadly no longer with us, the rest are all here. Only one other man is yet to join us."

"Thomas aye?" George of Wilton sneered.

"Yes, Thomas. You gentlemen would recognize him, your identification would be trustworthy?"

"I dare say anyone could identify him, my lady." Stephen's joke elicited the desired laughter.

"But if he had not been punished? Would you then recognize him?"

"I hardly find the question relevant, Countess." Stephen grew impatient again.

"Indulge me. Of course you would not be a reliable witness having seem him only for a short time. But these men of the village, they could testify to his identity."

"Yes of course, my lady." The sheriff bowed his head in an exaggerated way.

"Then we are agreed. Thomas!"

From the side door walked Thomas. His eyelids were firmly shut and he walked with a long narrow stick which he swept in front of him. Sheriffs Stephen and John stood on the dais near the King, they exchanged a look and a single nod, but something seemed strange about this man. After years of blindness, he was still rather... robust. Thomas stumbled and leaned heavily on the walking stick to keep from falling. Many of the witnesses, George chief amongst them, laughed out loud once again.

Ela took Thomas' arm and guided him until he directly faced his old accuser George, and the witnesses could all see him well. Thomas stood less than two feet from George and his wife, Thomas's former lover. After laughter died away and the hall was filled with an uncomfortable and expecting silence, Thomas threw away his cane and opened his eyelids wide, revealing perfectly formed blue eyes.

George's wife screamed and fell to the ground. George did nothing to help his wife but stepped away from the frightful gaze of his victim, stammering pathetically. The witnesses stared in wonder. They too were frightened, but although they may have shared guilt, they had shown no malice. They simply crossed themselves.

"I ask you witnesses, is this Thomas?" Ela said.

"It... it is!" All agreed.

"Could it be any other?" Ela asked this in a confident tone, though inwardly she prayed that none would ponder too much on the question.

"No, my lady, this is Thomas, healed."

"You see his eyes. Sheriff Bukerel, will you witness to the completeness of the restoration?"

Stephen Bukerel nodded stone-faced, no other option seeming to be available to him. Thomas walked to him, turned his back modestly and lifted the front of his tunic. Stephen reached under and took hold of the man's privates. He glanced in the direction of the King and the Sheriff of Wiltshire, and nodded.

Ela allowed the chatter to go on and on, rising louder and louder before finally trailing off. "Your majesty, my nephew, these wicked men have declared me unfit to speak of justice for my sex and my judgement of Thomas. See now that the punishment of this man was the real crime, for God has healed him. Heed then me, not this council, for I say to you as I said of Thomas that which is right and good."

Silence pervaded the dais. Chatter erupted again from the hall, but was swiftly silenced by the wave of Henry's hand. "I shall personally confirm the vow of virginity this maiden Christina of London has made. Archbishop Langton will do the same, if he lives still."

None dared object this time. "Furthermore, my servants the Sheriffs of London and Wiltshire have been found to have carried out gross injustice in the King's name. They shall be dismissed."

Henry looked about the hall for signs of rebellion. Finding none, he was emboldened. "Ela, I shall wish to give you the honor of shire reeve of Wiltshire."

The room erupted louder than ever. Henry had asserted himself, then been carried away with his newfound authority. A woman sheriff? Everyone spoke at once, words rambled about seeking an ear to accept them. The only people silent were the King, Christina, and Ela.

Ela did not anticipate this, was not sure she wanted it, but after thinking through the din, decided she'd be happy to act as shire reeve. It would increase even further her ability to bring justice to the shire. "Agreed!"

Hubert pleaded, "My lord, a woman is not capable—"

"Correction, Justiciar," Henry said. "My own father affirmed Nicolaa de la Haye twice! By all accounts she was a fine sheriff."

"She was the only one," Hubert muttered.

"Yes, and now there will be another."

Chapter Twenty-four

William Longespee crashed to the ground. If any evidence of the effect of a hot day on a man in armor was needed, sweat splashing out of the slit in his visor gave it.

A barrel-chested commoner stood over him, holding the pike that delivered the most recent blow. "Again!"

Richard, Stephen, and Nicholas all laughed at the abuse their brother was receiving. His sisters' reactions were mixed. Ela and Petronilla cringed with each blow given or received by William. Isabella, however, completely ignored her needlework, so caught up was she in the excitement of the practice. Young Ida showed signs of following her eldest sister Isabella, fascinated by the flashing lights of reflected steel and the sounds of weapons and armor clanging.

Ela herself struggled to maintain her calm whenever her son took a particularly nasty hit; she didn't often choose to watch him practice. She understood, however, the significant benefit of every blow he received in the parade ground of Sarum Castle, administered by a friend. On the battlefield, past bruises could save lives and limbs.

It was with some relief that she first saw William Talbot

ride through the gatehouse. Talbot, though, barely slowed and gave the sentry only a cursory nod. The soldier wisely decided not to insist on following protocol with the knight, and Longespee family friend. Talbot silently communicated with Ela by a simple tilting of the head and darting of the eyes. She moved to speak with him beside the well, where a groomsman took charge of his horse.

"What is it, William?"

"I have received word of a tragic event within the boundaries of the shire."

Ela's brow wrinkled and she took a deep breath. "Go on."

"A girl of fourteen years was tending sheep on a hillside; it is claimed she was taken by wolves."

"Strange, but not unheard of. It does not sound like a matter for the Sheriff. Tell me the part that has you on edge, William."

"Only a bloody outer mantle cloth and one shoe were found. There is no sign of the body."

"Drug away?"

"So it is claimed."

Ela nodded and paced several feet away, turned, and paced back. "It happened near the manor of Geoffrey Mortain?"

"Precisely."

"Then I will ride out within the hour. William, will you ride with me?"

"Nothing will please me more."

The posse comitatus consisted of William Talbot, his son Roger, William Longespee the younger, Baldric the barrel-chested sergeant, and three men-at-arms. They arrived on the outskirts of Geoffrey Mortain's manor just before noon the next day.

Ela pulled up alongside Talbot. "Well, William, once again

for old times?"

Talbot chuckled. "It has been a long time."

"You men and your long times, I prefer to think it seems like only yesterday."

"Ha! That too."

Forced to spend the previous night in a roadside inn, the group took advantage of the time to have a general council of war. It was decided that the direct approach could lead to disaster; Mortain could bar the gates and hold out for an opportunity to bribe the King. Henry was not as corrupt as his father, but Ela was taking no chances with justice on her watch. Therefore, Ela and Talbot decided to approach and investigate the situation under cover of disguise.

After each took their turns in the brush, Wiltshire's newest peasants walked up to the hillside where the sheep flocks grazed. Their timing was excellent, for the midday meal was the only time these peasants could gather in numbers without drawing unwanted attention.

"Have children been taken by wolves here before?" Talbot asked, accepting a portion of heavy bread and cheese. He had revealed his rank and mission, but Ela was still concealed.

"Not that anyone here can remember. There are wolves, but not in great numbers."

"Aye, and there's plenty of deer and other game to feed them. They've no call to risk hunting humans."

Thus far the elder males spoke, those in their mid-thirties.

"Why talk of this wolf nonsense? We all know what come of my Betsy!" One of the women serving lunch said.

Ela wondered at the woman's control, she spoke harshly, but did not yell.

"He's got her!" The woman whispered hoarsely, jerking a thumb in the direction of the manor house. "We've heard the rumors, what he likes doin! When I think of it, I wish Betsy really was torn apart for beasts' dinner."

Ela paced into the middle of the circle, turned and faced the anguished mother. "If she lives, we will get her back, I promise you."

"And who are you, 'is wife?"

Ela felt a smile surfacing, but forced it down by thinking of the what the young girl was no doubt experiencing. Instead she looked the woman in the eyes, fished around in a pocket and held up an elaborately carved wax seal. "No, good woman. I am the Sheriff of Wiltshire."

The gate of the manor compound remained open during daylight; peasants often brought supplies for Mortain's household. Thus, little notice was taken when a timber cart, loaded with hay, rumbled into the open square.

The compound was built on a mot and bailey plan. Within a timber palisade stood several waddle and daub buildings, a hall, a barn, kitchen, servant housing; no buildings in this household were built of stone. Directly across the square from the gates stood the mot, in this case a tall wooden structure. The tower would only be for use in an attack, the family would live in, or above, the hall.

Ela and Talbot took in the layout, confirming it matched the peasants' description. The dungeon, or whatever Mortain's playroom consisted of, would likely be in or beneath the mot. From the buckboard of the cart, neither Ela nor Talbot could account for more than six guards.

A bald man, with a bulbous nose, as wide as he was tall, waddled over to the cart looking irritated and bored at the same time. "We've plenty of hay, why are you bringing this load?"

"Orders," Talbot grunted.

"Orders from whom?"

Unnoticed by the fat household steward, Ela climbed down and walked around the ox. She leaned in front of the man and held a dagger to his corpulent folds. "From the Sheriff."

The rest of Ela's posse rolled from beneath the hay and out the back of the cart. In less than a minute they overcame the unorganized guards and disarmed them. Ela indulged herself a smile. *Men spend so much time fretting over their complicated battle plans. This was easy; I rather like a little action.* Still, one thing marred the maneuver: Mortain was nowhere to be seen.

Ela briefly considered attempting to take the great hall but thought better of it. "William and Roger, you each take a man-at-arms and search the keep for the girl."

The young men each chose a swordsman and ran off in the direction of the mot, leaving Ela, Talbot, the sergeant, and an archer behind to keep control of the courtyard.

"Geoffrey Mortain, show yourself if you have the bowels!" Talbot shouted toward the great hall.

Soon the front door opened and Mortain casually walked out into the courtyard. He was of above-average height, with long black hair falling about his shoulders. All in all not bad looking, Ela thought, but in appearance nothing out of the ordinary for a Norman knight. He wore a breastplate; it was the only piece of armor he wore, but still, he was hardly wearing it ten minutes ago while lounging about his hall.

Mortain took in the sight of his unarmed guards huddled against the gatehouse, and Ela, before settling his gaze on Talbot. "So you are Lady Ela's faithful dog now are you, Talbot?"

"Faithful servant and retainer of the Sheriff of Wiltshire, and proud of it, Mortain."

"Geoffrey Mortain, I have come to search your property. I do this under authority of the King." Ela would not be ignored.

"For what purpose, Lady Ela?" Mortain managed to sound civil, but he was unable to look Ela in the eye, looking at the ground a moment, then shifting his gaze back to Talbot.

"You will address me as Sheriff today," Ela said.

"For what purpose— Sheriff?"

"A girl has gone missing from your village."

"Ah yes, a most unfortunate business. It is said wolves took her, there are no wolves here," Mortain said.

"It is my belief that a very different kind of wolf took her, one whose mind and genitals are both damaged."

Her gambit worked, he looked her in the eye for a brief moment, his own eyes flashing rage.

"Well then, you had better be right. King Henry will not be pleased to hear you have disturbed a loyal knight's household with false accusations." Mortain turned and walked back toward the hall door. "You will no doubt want to begin with my home?"

"We have begun with the mot tower," Ela said.

Mortain spun, fear showing on his face.

"We will wait here for my other men to return," Ela continued.

Mortain looked in the direction of the tower, though the view was blocked from where he stood.

I've got you, you bastard!

Geoffrey Mortain waived his arm in an arch above his head. Two seconds later Talbot cried out, an arrow protruding from just below his sternum. Ela instinctively noticed the fletching rising inches higher than the entry wound, realized the arrow came from above, and looked up on the roofline of the hall.

"There!" She shouted to her own archer, pointing to the assailant, before pulling Talbot down behind the cover of their oxcart.

Ela's archer let loose a poorly aimed shot, meant to drive his opponent under cover before he could let loose a second shot of his own. Baldric turned to protect the Countess from a charge from Mortain, but as soon as he did, one of the prisoners made a quick move in the direction of their confiscated weapons. The sergeant ran him through.

"Right! That fucker did you all in then!" Not yet bound, each guard represented a reinforcement for an enemy already holding the advantage. Baldric began hacking away. It was precious time, with Ela left unprotected.

Mortain did not charge. Instead, after watching the battle taking shape in his courtyard, he tore off in the direction of the keep.

"William?" Ela managed to get Talbot laid out on his back between the wheels of the cart, the place of maximum cover from the roofline. Flat on his back also proved the position from which he could draw the most breath.

"Go. But please be careful, Ela." Talbot's plea sounded pitiful. Ela knew it grieved him bitterly that he was helpless to protect his best friend's widow.

The enemy archer on the roof was able to make his way along and rise up from an unexpected angle. Each archer took aim at the other as quickly as possible and fired. Ela saw her man go down, struck in the neck. A few seconds later, however, she heard a thud from the other side of the cart. Baldric, having killed or disabled the last of the guards, collected his dead comrade's bow and quiver and joined the Countess at Talbot's side.

"Right. I'm going after Mortain," Baldric said.

"No, you need to stay here and guard Talbot. I'm going after Mortain."

"Me lady! Beggin the ladyship's pardon and all, but 'av you lost your female mind?"

"Sergeant." Ela placed a hand on the soldier's shoulder. "I appreciate your concern." Ela then struck the man as hard as she could across his face with the back of her other hand. "But if you ever speak to me that way again I'll run you through with your own damned sword!"

When Baldric stared at her in shock, she smiled at him and winked.

She slung the quiver over her left shoulder and grabbed the bow. The courtyard was now still, all non-combatants of the household were taking shelter in the buildings. One last look back at Talbot's color, then she sprinted through the gap between the hall and the barn, toward the mot tower.

As she broke into the inner courtyard, Ela could see another battle waging near the keep stairs. William and the two men-at-arms were engaged with more guards they must have found in the keep. She looked about, including on the ground, for Roger, but could not see him. She did spot Mortain standing at the south side of the mot watching the skirmish with interest.

When Mortain saw Ela he laughed, apparently finding the sight of a woman bearing a longbow amusing. *Perhaps you will be less amused with an arrow sticking out of your eye socket.* She nocked an arrow and pulled at the string with all her might. The bow barely flexed.

"Even the strongest men have to put their whole back into drawing a longbow, Countess."

Mortain laughed again then turned and walked briskly, following the base of the mot away from the battle. Ela did not hesitate; she ran after him.

Ela rounded the mot just in time to see Mortain's head and neck disappear into the ground. Confusing sounds swirled all about her. From behind her came the sounds of the battle at the stairs. In between those clangs, grunts, and shouts, were faint but disturbing notes she feared came from wherever Mortain went. She heard a girl crying, then shouts; one voice sounded like that of Roger Talbot.

Ela reached the spot where she last saw Mortain in one minute. She found thick oak doors resting either side of a four foot square maw, a rough cut oak staircase disappeared into a murky cellar. This time Ela hesitated. She realized how foolish it was for her, a woman, to chase a warrior like Mortain into a dim room only he was familiar with. Shouting from the wicked knight and from Roger Talbot did not motivate her to take such risk, though she worried about Roger's chances against the stronger, more experienced Mortain. Then she heard a cry of agony, a woman's cry, and she acted.

Halfway down the stairs, in the dimness, she made out the form of Mortain just two feet from the edge of the stairs. He was standing legs apart, sword above his head. She then saw that he was about to bring the sword down on Roger, who had already fallen. Roger was in terrible danger. With no time to think of a better idea, she used the bow she still held in her right hand as a club, striking at Mortain's elbow. He flinched, in surprise more than pain, and looked over his shoulder, seeking out the new threat. When he saw Ela, he cursed at the irritating woman but dismissed her just as quickly and turned back to Roger. Those few seconds allowed Roger to raise his sword to block, and to climb to one knee.

Ela also used the seconds to think. She raised the bow and hooked one end, where the string met bow, over the raised tip of Mortain's sword.

Mortain's sword cut the bowstring. "Damned bitch!" Ela's efforts slowed down his blow just enough to allow Roger's block to be effective, despite the older man's advantage in strength.

Ela was still crouched on the stairs. Mortain took a moment to turn and push her, making her lose balance and fall back against the cold dirt wall. Those seconds granted Roger his feet. But he was still badly outmatched. Ela felt something dig into her back as she fell against the wall. The quiver! She struggled to regain balance and pulled an arrow from the quiver. Grasping the shaft firmly in both hands, up high near the fletching, she gaged the angle and distance. "I told you, that's Sheriff to you!"

Mortain turned toward her once again, as if to swat at a pest. Ela leapt into the air, pushed the arrow down underneath her, and fell with all her weight onto Mortain's shoulders. The arrow plunged into the knight's neck just above the top of his ribcage. It was the perfect angle, avoiding any bone, the arrow slid easily through his heart and into guts.

The pair collapsed to the floor, Ela quickly rolled off and regained her feet. Roger ran to take control of the fight, but Mortain was likely dead before he hit the ground.

"Are you hurt, Countess?"

"Bruised, and I will likely be very sore tomorrow, but nothing a little rest will not cure. And you?"

"Fine. You should not have interfered. I would have dealt with him myself."

"Of course, Roger, but this was personal." Ela then looked past the young man and saw the girl.

She was tied spread-eagle to an X-shaped cross, completely

naked. At first Ela was relieved to see the girl's head raised, but when she walked to her, she looked into the eyes. "No. No."

There was no spark of life in those eyes. A strap held the girl's head upright. There was a pike sticking out of her left side. Ela noticed blood still seeping down the shaft, droplets falling to a puddle in the dirt. The Countess reached out and stroked the peasant's cheek, still warm.

Ela began to shake violently. "Nooooooo!"

Ela arrived back in the courtyard to find William Talbot still laid out on the ground beside the cart, his face ashen. She marched to the front door of the hall.

"Open this door! I am Countess Ela of Salisbury, Sheriff of Wiltshire. Under authority of the King, I demand you surrender."

She heard a latch scrape and the door opened a foot revealing a blue-eyed young woman of approximately twenty years of age.

Ela examined the pretty face and fine robes. "Who are you?"

"I am Lady Mortain, wife of Sir Geoffrey Mortain."

"Then you are a widow." Ela immediately wished she could reach out and recover the words; she was still livid at her failure to save the girl, and the likely loss of Talbot as well.

The girl nodded. "Who killed him?"

"I did."

"You did?"

Ela straightened her posture, standing a foot taller than the new widow. Pity be damned if the wench was going to doubt her. "Yes, I did, with my own hands."

The girl smiled suddenly, a bright pleasant sight. "Then

you have my unending gratitude, Countess." The smiling widow then opened the door fully. "You there, prepare refreshments for the Countess and her men. You, bring wine, the best we have."

"I have a wounded knight; he needs care."

"There is an abbey a few miles from here. One of the monks is a passable man of medicine. I will send a messenger by fast horse."

"Thank you, Lady Mortain."

A panel of wattle was fetched, Talbot was placed on it and carried into the hall, before the fire.

Talbot could barely move a limb, but he was conscious. Ela sat at his side, Roger stood at his feet, others loitered about the scene, in varying degrees of concern and curiosity.

"I would speak with you in privacy," Talbot whispered.

"Of course. I will leave you two alone," Ela said.

"No. I would speak with you, Ela. Alone."

Roger had not until now betrayed any emotion. At being dismissed from his father's deathbed, he shrugged and walked away. The others in the hall honored the man's request as well.

"William, you should speak with your son."

"He is not my son."

Ela said nothing. She never spoke with Talbot about what she knew. The subject did not come up with anyone these twenty years, not even with Anne. It was not information that could really be forgotten; but it did not seem very important.

Her silence at the revelation was unnatural though. "Ah. You knew."

"Yes," Ela said.

"How long have you known?"

"Since before he was born."

A slight chuckle, that produced a trickle of blood. "Figures. Probably longer than I." Ela wiped the blood from the corner of his mouth. "Do you know the whole story?"

Again Ela was silent. She knew what he meant, had kept the secret he apparently wanted to confess for two decades. "The father? No. I did not care to know."

William looked at her, studied her face. "Not the father— the reason." He turned his face away from Ela, toward the fire. "I am a sodomite, and I desired your husband as I should have desired my wife."

"I know," she whispered.

He turned back to her, more swiftly than his condition allowed. "You knew?"

"Do not be cross with Anne, William. I browbeat her into telling me."

He stared up at the thatched ceiling and hammered beams for several moments. "You have been very kind."

"It was a very sinful thing, William. You didn't just desire him, though, you loved him too. Your sinful desires just never seemed quite as important as your loyal service."

Talbot nodded. "It is growing dark early, I feel a chill."

Ela choked back tears. "William, it is still a bright day, and the fire burns high."

"Ah. Then the good monk has been put to trouble for nothing. Apologize for me will you?"

Tears flowed freely now. "I will."

"Ela?"

"Yes, William?"

"I see him. He looks magnificent. Is there a message you would send?"

"Tell him—that I miss him."

"I will."

Chapter Twenty-five

February, 1232
Sarum Castle

Ela glanced from time to time at the conspicuously empty chair. She and her guests were enjoying an intimate feast in the old great hall of the courtyard house, while the castle staff and the entourages of her guests supped in the larger great hall along the south side of the castle. Trestle tables were arranged in a square in the main area. No one sat on the dais today; all were equal--equal members of the conspiracy.

"Are we certain Henry is amenable?" Ranulf, Earl of Chester, was a brash straight forward warrior of a man. He was also often at odds with the King. As such, he relied on his more diplomatic fellow conspirators for the mood at court.

"For the moment." Stephen of Seagrave was the senior justice at the King's bench. "The unfortunate outcome of Henry's efforts in Wales, and the lack of funds to continue them, have left Hubert weakened in the King's mind and heart."

"Which leaves the Marshal, who can hold back the Welsh, as the keystone of our plan to topple de Burgh. So where is the Marshal?" Ranulf gestured to the empty seat on his left.

Ela allowed men to answer questions so long as their answers were correct. As hostess, this question was directed toward her. "The Earl of Pembroke sent word that he would attend our--gathering. I can only think he has been delayed along his way. I'm sure he will arrive soon."

"Perhaps we should wait until he arrives then."

"My dear Ranulf," Peter des Roches, Bishop of Winchester, seemed to sigh as he spoke. "We must eat, naturally our dinner conversation will involve the topic we have travelled all this way to discuss. William Marshal is a clever fellow, I'm sure he will catch up to us swiftly."

Ela listened as her collection of bishops and earls plotted the demise of their common enemy: Hubert de Burgh. It was a contemptible thing that Henry was so fooled by the man who killed his own uncle. Though he never accepted Ela's testimony in the matter, for the circumstances of William's death could be explained by natural causes, Henry adored his aunt and lavished gifts upon her. He also still listened with patience whenever she wished to bend his ear. Ela was cautious not to become tiresome to the mercurial King. Over the years she nurtured the discontent Hubert sowed amongst the nobility—a whisper here, an introduction there.

Now, five years after her husband's murder, her closest friend, he who might have been her lover, he whom she relied on to bring about the justice she so desperately longed for, was not present. Her assurances to Chester were reasonable. Travel within the kingdom was never completely safe, certainly never predictable. Still, Marshal was never late. Even at the siege, when she was on her own, Marshal's late arrival was earlier than predicted. The forced march from

Pembroke was astonishingly quick.

"We are agreed. It seems there is little else to discuss my friends." It was the Bishop of Winchester again. "It only remains to pledge to each other our personal vows. If the Marshal arrives today we might be about our business within the week."

Hope swelled within Ela's chest again. Now was the time of revenge. Just as the band was finishing their last course a familiar form appeared in the doorway. Relief washed over Ela and as quickly evaporated. The man who walked into the hall was a Marshal, but it was not William. It was his brother Richard. Everyone remained silent, staring with questioning faces.

"My lords, it is with pain I must inform you that my brother and lord, William, Earl of Pembroke, is dead."

April 16th 1232

Half a dozen very confused soldiers tensed when they saw the figures of men and horses in the distance.

"Countess, there are soldiers ahead. They appear a larger group, with horses and armor; we should detour."

"Steady Baldric. Continue on until we can see their standard, I am expecting a friend."

"Aye, Countess." Baldric nodded his head toward his men, and they resumed progress, bringing their horses to only a trot, not the slow canter they maintained before.

Traveling forty miles to accommodate two dedication ceremonies in one day seemed madness. Now it appeared that after all these years of service, the Countess still did not trust him.

"Do not sulk, Baldric, it has nothing to do with trusting you."

How does she always do that? Ela had come alongside the sergeant out of earshot of the other men.

"It is just that you are a terrible actor," Ela said with a chuckle.

"Ah, I see now. It is the young Marshal."

The two groups met beside a tranquil pool formed at a bend in the river. Ela's horses paced into the shallow water and began to drink.

"Hail Countess, God give you good day."

"And you, Earl Marshal."

"What brings you to this lonely stretch of plain?"

"I have dedicated a site for building an abbey for nuns at Lacock. I travel to dedicate another for men at Henton."

"Our meeting is the work of God then my lady, for Henton lies along the way to our destination."

"What fortune, would you attend the ceremony this evening and tarry overnight at Henton?"

"I would be delighted."

"Then it is settled, you shall be my guest. The brothers will not mind; it is a rather fine abbey I am building for them after all."

"It will be good to exchange news as well."

"Yes, Earl Richard, we have much to discuss."

July 9, 1232

Hubert de Burgh loved to walk along the Thames. He especially appreciated these strolls under two circumstances: when the tide was out, and when he needed to think. The Thames is a tidal river; water levels rise and fall in concert with the tides of the Atlantic Ocean in the Channel. When the tide was out, Hubert would often remove his shoes and walk barefoot in the dark wet sand between the cities of

Westminster and London.

On this particular day, the Chief Justiciar of England had much on his mind. As he left the bustle of merchants and laborers serving the expanding government of Westminster behind, Hubert watched new palaces going up along the road that connected it to its sister city, the trading center of London. Every day, less of this stretch of river retained its former tranquility. He could even imagine that, at this rate of construction, the two cities could one day be indistinguishable. Two palaces neared completion. Further along, ground was being broken for still another.

Building. Everywhere I look, more building. Stone floated into the valley at an incredible rate. Along this stretch of Thames River Valley, which offered almost no natural stone, a massive city of stone arose from its clay.

Building on the government offices, a new Westminster Abbey, and a curtain wall around the Tower of London; these were just the government funded works. Palaces and churches grew fatter and soared higher every day. Most men would be inspired but such sights, but Hubert only saw mocking irony as the buildings rose in direct antithesis to his own diminishing position.

He and his family were more like the dwindling countryside between the cities. Though the air was an order of magnitude more pleasant than the malodorous vapors of Westminster, even here Hubert could make out the odor of burning tar on the wind. *Countryside will not much longer welcome me here.*

These were precarious times for the de Burgh family. Young son of a minor noble family who found favor during the wars in Ireland, Hubert rose farther than any man of his time ever did by merit alone. Brilliant and ambitious, he became the trusted friend of one king, and regent of the current. Henry, however, was no longer a child. Like a butterfly strengthens its wings fighting its way out of the cocoon, thus Henry found his own comfort upon the throne by struggling against his justiciar. Still, all would have been well if Hubert had not attempted to add the earldom of Salisbury to his family's fortune.

It was too far to reach. When William appeared alive and well in England, he reacted swiftly and savagely to the de Burghs' move. Hubert understood his old friend's anger, in retrospect, it was probably well deserved. But William's confrontation was humiliating, and so very public. When William soon turned up dead, it took every bit of the justiciar's strength and wits to keep from falling. Most suspected him of murder, the King probably did too, but it could not be proven, and Hubert was very good at his job.

Now he was under threat again. William Longespee's widow Ela was at work, to be sure, but her strong ally this time was the same one that ruined so many powerful men in England before: money. Henry would doubtless be known to future generations as "the builder," but just because he was spending all of the royal revenues on building projects didn't mean he was content to give up the pastime of all Kings of England: warring against France. Hubert nearly fell three years prior over his slowness to build a new navy for Henry. After that he reluctantly allowed the King to lead them all into disastrous campaigns in Poitou and Wales.

Something caught Hubert's eye, so he lifted the hem of his robes to his knees and walked closer to the waterline. Kicking up the sand with one foot, he found that the mysterious object was nothing but a broken hatchet. He could hear some workmen at a nearby palace building site laughing at the absurd display. He ignored them. A year before, he pulled a Roman sword from the sand; it was now one of his most prized possessions. He showed it to the King the previous week while they stayed at his home at Burgh in Norfolk.

Last week. The wheel of fortune saw me rise—last week. At Burgh, Henry made fresh vows of the permanency of Hubert's positions in government as well as his lands and titles. Henry was warm and appreciative of all the Justiciar had done for the throne. Hubert worked tirelessly to restore royal prerogatives lost by John, Henry displayed exuberance in his thankfulness. But that was last week. Henry was a Plantagenet and, as his forefathers before him, was prone to rapid mood swings from utter joy and energy to extreme depression and paranoia.

Engrossed as he was in thought, Hubert was surprised to find that he had walked as far as London Bridge. The surface of the bridge was by now packed solid with buildings. Built with the chapel of the martyred Saint Thomas Becket in the middle, enterprising Londoners soon discovered acres of prime real estate on the stone bridge. Shops and houses now stretched from the northern to southern shores. Unforeseen by the builders, their engineering efforts created two new sports for city dwellers. The many thick stone pillars standing in the river bed supported arches over which the buildings and the road sat. This altered the flow of the river as it slowed, causing a tranquil pooling effect upriver, while the water closest to the bridge battled to force its way through the narrow gaps. The unintended consequence was an artificial rapids.

In winter, the Thames now froze more often and more solidly than ever before where the water pooled. Londoners enjoyed strapping long sharpened bones to their shoes and sliding across the river. Now, in the heat of summer, Hubert watched as two wealthy young men stood in narrow boats borrowed, probably at a small rent, from peasants. They were using long poles to push themselves toward the current. Passing through those narrow arches while attempting to stay standing in your boat was called "shooting the bridge," and this pair appeared to have turned the already dangerous sport into a race. Hubert picked a winner, silently made a small wager with himself and watched. Neither man made it through standing, but both managed to haul themselves onto the far shore alive.

Perhaps this was what the last few weeks were. Hubert "shot the bridge" and came out the other side to tell the tale. But was he standing? Was Henry's tone really that different this morning? Was a conversation really cut short when he entered the hall yesterday?

God's bones, I'm getting too old for this.

July 29, 1232

"It seems you will finally get your way, Ela." King Henry walked with his aunt down the main road through Oxford. Though far enough away to afford the pair at least the appearance of private conversation, the King's guard was sufficiently menacing to keep the people at bay.

Ela allowed a small smile to surface; she never felt a need to play coy around her nephew. "Certainly it would have been simpler if you had bowed to the inevitable sooner."

Henry laughed out loud. Cheekiness of a woman be damned, he adored the Countess. "True enough. Still, I have much to be thankful to Hubert for."

Ela's smile retreated; she bristled at the thought of being grateful to her husband's murderer.

Henry glanced at her, and read her expression. "Your friends Thomases live somewhere around here do they

330

not?"

Ela shot a glance at Henry. Her smile regrouped. "Whatever do you mean?"

"Come now, Ela, others underestimate me; I would not have counted you amongst them."

"How long have you known?"

"I suspected it the day you produced the miracle. Inquiries only took a matter of weeks."

"Hmph. Did anyone else guess?" Ela asked.

"Not that I have heard of. If so, it would appear they were of the same mindset as I."

"That the outcome is of more importance than the method?" Ela asked.

They advanced several steps before Henry responded. "That at least that point of view has some merit."

"I am not certain either. Though I wonder who still walks amongst us, seeing and--loving, who would have been lost to gross injustice."

"And Hubert?"

"What of him?" Villagers and guards alike were shocked at the tone used by the noblewoman in speaking to the King. Henry ignored it.

"William's death cannot be proven to have been murder. Has Hubert received justice?"

Ela did not reply. After a few moments Henry changed the subject to happy trivialities. Though Henry would never know for sure, his parry found its mark; a tiny crack appeared in Ela's anger, and doubt seeped in.

Hubert's survival instinct woke him an hour before dawn every day. If they came for him, they would do it at sunrise; his enemies were so predictable, so trite. A week had passed since his dismissal from court. Still officially the Chief

Justiciar, he was not yet stripped of his titles, but if the King would not see him soon all would be lost.

He was sitting on the roof of the bathhouse, across an alleyway from his own room in the King's House, when they came. Richard Marshal was in the lead, with three men-at-arms, just as Hubert expected. The bishops would never have directly involved themselves in the dirty details of their plot. The monastery was not a viable haven, it was as much a political institution as religious; Hubert planned to get himself to the local chapel on the edge of town. Any accused man could claim sanctuary within the walls of a church in England. Some houses of God had special rules whereby their sanctuary extended for up to a mile and a half around the building itself. He had not gone so far as to seek out one of these, he was content to stay inside for up to the forty days he would be safe. After that, worst case, he would be forced to leave the kingdom; but at least he would still be free. Peter de Roche fled certain arrest and spent five years on crusade. It worked well enough for him.

As quietly as possible, Hubert crawled backwards toward the opposite wall where he had placed a stolen ladder days prior. Before he could lower the ladder into place, commotion arose in the alley. It did not take long to search the guest chamber. Hubert did not have to witness it to picture the look on Richard's face, nor that of the novice monk who was assigned to take him to the Justiciar. *I am no longer young; today I will find out how much quickness is left in these weary bones.*

Abbey grounds, where the baths and the King's House sat, occupied the southeastern quadrant of the city of Bath. Hubert's destination was near the southern gate. His plan was to hurry to the main street that ran north to south through the city. Light was gaining hold; merchants would be preparing for the day's business; he hoped that he could remain far enough ahead of his pursuers to avoid creating a scene. When he stepped off the ladder onto solid ground, however, one glance indicated that route was blocked. Richard and one of his men turned the corner at the street; no doubt the other two were sent to the opposite side of the Abbey.

Prepared for this eventuality, Hubert was on his way toward an alternate route before Richard could realize what was happening. Soon both men broke into a run. With his head start evaporating by the second, the Justiciar burst through the gothic arch and into the close, barely avoiding a pair of elderly monks out for morning contemplation. Far from their typical peaceful devotions, the pair were instead treated to the bizarre spectacle of an English earl chasing the highest official in the kingdom through their cloister.

The Chief Justiciar of England leapt up, placing the palms of his hands onto the crest of a stone wall that separated the cloister from the abbey's orchard. He managed to heave himself up, swing his legs over, and drop amongst the cherry and apple trees. The ledge of the wall was well coated with bird shit, but no matter, Hubert was quite proud of the physical accomplishment; he decided he didn't mind getting a little dirty in the process. For a moment he was reminded of his younger days holding out the siege of Chinon. He defended his city long after all others in the region fell; the honor won there launched his most remarkable career. *Once again I am the hunted one. If I can hold out again, perhaps my position can yet be saved.*

Seconds later he weaved through the fruit trees and found himself at the southern wall. Repeating his act of prowess, with only a little more effort, he dropped down into a courtyard under the curious gaze of a baker and a brewmistress. Taking no heed of curious peasants, he darted between two service buildings as the Earl followed him over the wall. He wondered if the man-at-arms was sent to cut him off, but assuming he exited the cloister to the south, Hubert knew an extra wall stood in that man's way.

Now in the stable yard, a most unwelcome soft footfall reminded Hubert that there was no time for such luxuries as looking where he was going. He was close now. Sanctuary lay through the stables, across another alley, and over one more wall. Perhaps he might even be afforded the opportunity to use a gate this time. As soon as he entered the stable, Hubert heard shouting from the other end. A long shadow, then a man-at-arms came into view in the far doorway. The man was scanning the street, he did not see Hubert yet. Hubert fell to the ground and scrambled under the gate of the nearest stall. Having gone in feet first, he was certain that none of his pursuers saw him go in, but it would not take long for them to guess that he was trapped, and where.

The horse he now shared the stall with reacted to the appearance of its new roommate, but thankfully Richard's wild course through the stable aisle set all the other occupants into similar agitation. Hubert moved to the back and burrowed into a stack of hay, doing the best he could in just a few seconds to cover himself completely.

"You there, did you see him?"

"No sign, me lord!"

"Which direction did you come from?"

"That way."

"How long?"

"Only a moment."

"Then he couldn't have made cover or gotten into the churchyard. I last glimpsed him coming into the stable seconds ago myself."

"The stalls!" The man at arms suggested.

Loud bangs and shouts swelled like a wave down the aisle. Hubert's own stall was entered and exited as the wave passed. Soon the wave washed up on the yard end of the stable.

"Perhaps he hid in a stall and then doubled back?"

"Perhaps. You two look that way, you stand here and watch the aisle, I'm going to check the stalls more closely."

Damn they're all four back on the trail now.

Time was up; Hubert needed a plan. He remembered his Latin studies. *Audaces fortuna iuvat - Fortune favors the bold. Nothing but pure boldness will win this day.* When Richard opened the door of the stall, sword out to stab into the haystack, Hubert was standing next to the horse. He leapt into the air, threw one arm around the horse's neck, and with the other hand grabbed hold of its mane with all his might. Startled, the horse instinctively reared and then charged out of the stall. In the aisle, Hubert slammed his feet into the ground and pushed all of his body weight into the horse's neck. The encouragement was enough to lead the beast to choose the chapel side exit.

Galloping through the door, the horse once again reared as it sought its next move. To its left was only the city wall, it thus turned to its right and bolted. Hubert clung to the horse's left side and found himself suspended horizontally above the alley surface. After a handful of strides, Hubert released his grip and tumbled, finding bones and muscles with the cobble stones. The de Burgh luck seemed to hold, though, as he looked up to see the churchyard gate. Everything hurt, but nothing was broken, he stood and lurched into the yard. He made it to the door and fell through into the church itself.

"I claim sanctuary!"

335

The church's priest was in the nave into which Hubert burst. "This church has a frith-stool, my son."

Damn, not quite there yet. "Where is it, Father? I have little time."

He got to his feet quickly, keeping his gaze on the priest. The holy man pointed to his right and barely whispered. "There."

Hubert took a stride in the direction the priest indicated before searching out the stone bench. In some churches door knockers must be grasped. In others bells must be rung. This one had a special place the accused must sit before sanctuary became official. He found the frith-stool quickly enough, but it was already occupied. Sitting upon the stone was a very comfortable looking Earl of Chester munching an apple.

Hubert de Burgh sat on the bare earthen floor of Devizes Castle's dungeon. He had been in chains since being drug from the chapel and thrown into this pit, but the blindfold was new; he wondered what its purpose was. There were no other prisoners with him, but he was far from alone. Chafing from the heavy chains on his wrists brought about bleeding. Blood, in turn, attracted more than the typical number of rats. God only knew the last time he slept; as tired as he was, the feel of the rats walking on him or licking his wounds never failed to cause him to kick himself awake. A pail sat in the corner, but the guards rarely loosened the bindings to allow him to use it. Thus far he managed to keep from soiling himself, but he long ago gave up holding water.

The reason for the blindfold became apparent when a metallic rattle echoed, causing a scurrying of rats. The wooden staircase creaked as someone descended into Hubert's darkness.

"Good morning, Countess. Or is it later? I fear I have lost track of time down here."

A short pause. "How did you know it was me?" Ela asked.

"My jailers rarely bathe in rose water, my lady. I can't think of another woman who would come here."

"Not Margaret?"

"Bah! Margaret is the daughter of a king. Her wifely duties don't extend below ground." Hubert listened to Ela walk closer. "Please excuse the smell, Countess, my facilities leave something to be desired."

"It was thus in my William's death chamber." Her tone was strong and accusing.

"Ah. Most unfortunate, he was a very good man. I considered him a friend."

"Was the young William Marshal your friend as well?"

"At one time," Hubert replied.

"Your friends have an unfortunate habit of dying young. I should be grateful to be your enemy."

"Ha! Well played, Lady. So what have you come here for?"

"To kill you," Ela said.

"Ah. So it comes to that. Is it important that I die at your own hands, or are you afraid men may botch the job?"

"You and I both know the Plantagenets, Hubert; one never knows when Henry might change his mind."

"Of course, but aren't you putting yourself at risk if that's the case?" Hubert asked.

"I am not here; the guard will be forced to kill you during an escape attempt."

"I see. You managed to get one of your own men guarding the King's dungeon?" Hubert said. "I am impressed."

"He is not my man, he simply can't betray me without admitting he accepted a bribe to leave his post."

"Simple plans are often the best. I'm guessing that the

reason you're taking so long is you're hoping I will beg for my life?"

Silence.

"You once told Reimand that my family was beneath you. I was born beneath you, Ela, but the King of Scotland gave me his daughter to wed. I made myself noble, my daughter is royal; I will not beg."

"Fair enough. I do have one question though," Ela said.

"By all means, ask it."

"Why did you spare Arthur?"

Hubert smiled and nodded in an exaggerated manner. Despite his humiliating environment, he comported himself as if he were still at court. "Ha! That must confuse you."

"I assume you were a better man then, before you became corrupted."

"I spared Arthur because it was the right thing to do. I may have changed over the years, Countess, who of us has not?" Hubert faced the direction he had last heard Ela's voice, and raised his head, intentionally exposing his throat. "I swear this, Countess. I did not kill William."

The rats were growing accustomed to the newcomer; they rustled in the dirty hay near the walls of the pit.

"Why should I believe you?" Ela asked.

"I can think of no reason to offer. I agree that I must appear as guilty as Satan himself."

Hubert listened intently. He expected his exposed throat to be slit at any moment. He was not blind, however, therefore his other senses were not attuned. Ela's breath, the rats, and his own heartbeat were all that was audible for what felt like minutes. Eventually the staircase creaked again, the door opened and closed. Ela left him alive, for now. He was not entirely sure that he was relieved.

Perhaps I should have stoked her anger.

Chapter Twenty-six

"I wish you would reconsider, Henry; I will not remarry."
Ela sat beside her eldest son, facing the King who rested on
the chaise lounge in her private office at Sarum.

"Nevertheless, as long as you are marriageable, I cannot
grant the passage of your land or title to young William. You
must understand, vain though their hopes may be, potential
suitors would cry foul."

"I understand." Disappointment slightly dulled the
bravery in William's voice.

"Well he can at least act as Earl then." Ela respected the
King's position, it was reasonable, and she fully expected it.
"I will turn over command of Sarum Castle soon; would
you please make him Sheriff of Wiltshire?"

"No I will not, nor will you give him command of Sarum,"
Henry replied.

"What?" This was certainly not expected. "You doubt his
ability?"

"No, of course not. But he cannot act as Earl because
you already do."

"I will retire."

"Bullshit!" The King threw up his hands against Ela's reaction, significantly ignoring the quiet subject beside her. "And even if you believed it yourself, if it were even true, nobody else would believe you were not actively controlling the b— young man."

Ela stood and paced to the window, looked out upon the plain. William and the King fell into idle talk, Henry attempting to appease the would-be earl. William was considering options for a position at court when Ela returned to the men. "I will miss this place."

"What do you mean, Mother?" William asked.

Ela's answer made Henry laugh, then he caught himself. "You are serious?"

"I could do with a change."

"The women need more food."

The Abbess of Lacock Abbey sat behind her desk and gathered her thoughts before responding to the initiate before her. Normally the Abbess would not stoop to hear the complaint of a novice, but this challenge was expected, and she could not escape this time. Expected or not, the Abbess knew she was in for a hell of a fight.

Abbess Beatrix set a velum document aside and rested entwined fingers on the desk between her and the novice nun. "There is good reason for the ration size, Daughter."

"Monks do not go hungry."

"That is of no relevance; this is a nunnery, not a monastery," Beatrix replied, without malice.

"Why is it of no relevance? Why should women of the church starve while men grow fat?"

Beatrix took a deep breath before making another attempt. "Daughter, holy scripture provides two models for us to follow. Either we are daughters of Eve, or daughters of Mary. We obviously must choose Mary; would you not agree?"

The novice shifted on her feet but her facial expression did not change, it remained obstinate. "Of course, Mother, but what has that to do with perpetual hunger?"

"Nuns must eat as little as possible, this makes them thin; that way they do not develop the curves that lead to lust, to becoming daughters of Eve. You, of course, will not be held to this standard, you may eat as much as you please."

Until her last breath, Abbess Beatrix never forgot the effect her words produced in the novice nun, Ela of Salisbury. The former countess shuddered, then her face twisted like a gargoyle, then her color changed. First she paled, then she turned red as blood. And the eyes, the eyes were what made the abbey's mother cross herself.

The nuns of Lacock Abbey did not cheer when it was announced at Chapter the next morning that their rations would be doubled; they did not dare, but there were more than the usual quiet giggles echoing from whispering huddles.

William arrived in Egypt in late autumn 1249. Having gone on pilgrimage to the holy land twice, the landscape and architecture felt familiar to him. The seaport of Damietta sat within the mouth of the Nile, on the western arch of the vast delta. Muslim ships were visible, just on the horizon, keeping close eye on the Christian invaders, but avoiding direct confrontation for now. William was fascinated by these ships. He traveled by sea extensively himself, and his father was admiral of the kingdom's first naval fleet. Unlike European ships, these vessels supported two masts with triangular sails. Whereas Christian nations all built their ships with high wooden castles at the fore and aft, the Muslim hulls sat low in the water; only a very few feet of either the port or steer board sides raised above the waterline. William could see the aft section sat higher, but not to an extent that could give advantage to archers in battle. It seemed, rather, to aid in the securing of the triangular sails, the narrowest point of which faced that direction.

The calm azure of the Mediterranean never failed to remind William of the stormy coast of England by its very contrast. This coupled with thoughts of his father, wishing he could discuss the merits of ship design with him, cast a profound shadow upon his mood. Drawing a deep breath of salty air, he forced his mind to other things before the sadness came. It was far too early for such thoughts. He would be away from England, his wife and children, for at least another year. Would it only be a year? Would he return at all? Death on crusade was a very real possibility, from disease if not a Saracen blade. It was considered the most honorable death, one which would atone for a lifetime's sins. But what would it mean to his children? The third William Longespee was almost sixteen, a year older than he was when his father was poisoned.

His mind drifted again. Memories of his father's murder, never properly avenged, brought him back. Now to suppress his rage, he turned to the city and the crops surrounding it to the south and west. Stone walls and monuments here were ancient compared with anything William encountered in England. Men dressed only in loincloths continued to toil in the fields and in the intricate network of canals that took the life-giving, green-coloring water of the Nile out to the fields. Whether by official truce or by assumption, the Egyptians acted as though the change in rulers was of no consequence. This was ever true of the poor. Surely the villains of England took little notice when William's own people, the Normans, overthrew the Saxon pretender king, Harold Godwinson.

All two hundred knights having disembarked, William led his army to the gates of the city. Louis, the King of France, met him there.

"Hail, William Longespee! It is good to see you again. I trust your journey was an easy one?"

"Greetings, good King. I bring blessings from my sovereign, Henry." William bowed low to give proper respect to Louis' status as king and leader of the crusade, but he did not take a knee. It was a calculated distinction, one he considered during the long voyage. Louis was not William's liege lord, he held no lands or honors at the French King's discretion.

"How is your good cousin? Well I hope." Louis continued to smile, showing no offense. Others amongst the French knights gathered about the plaza, however, muttered.

"Quite well thank you. This city is a glorious prize. Did you win it at great cost?" William noted the presence of a particularly hostile looking French knight near the King. He guessed that this was Louis' brother, Count Robert of Artois. Robert was a notorious enemy of England, holding land which formerly belonged to William's own family.

"In truth not a man was lost. The heathen ran before the cross and left the city open."

"Open?"

"Completely. The gates stood open to us in welcome."

"There was no trap, no resistance at all?" William asked.

"None whatsoever."

"Astonishing."

"Now that you are here we shall soon enough venture forth toward Cairo; then we will see greater glory than this! But now eat and drink; renew your strength."

"Halt!"

It was early afternoon when William and his men approached the gates of Damietta. Waiting for them outside the walls was a large contingent of French knights led predictably by Robert d'Artois.

"What now, Sir Robert?" William spoke with unmasked weariness.

"You cursed Englishmen left the city by night without permission. What treachery have you been about?"

"No treachery, Count. We have simply relieved some Saracen merchants of their burdensome goods." Many English knights found this explanation amusing, but no Frenchmen laughed.

"And how did you come to know of this merchant caravan? Your spies?"

William noted that Robert already knew more than he was just told, but seeing no reason why this should be presented as an accusation, he simply pursed his lips and shrugged his shoulders. "Yes."

"You are not here for your own enrichment but as part of the French army. Therefore, you will surrender these goods to us."

Now William was no longer amused. Despite talk of action when the English knights arrived, two months had passed, and still the crusader army remained in Damietta. William grew tired of waiting, and found and attacked a strong tower in which he found a number of wives of Saracen nobles. The ransom doubled William's wealth, even after sharing it with his army. Now his spies had advised them of a rich caravan on its way to Alexandria under light guard. His army was weighed down by the plunder, but now greatly outnumbered by the French, this wealth was under threat by his own alleged allies, though they shared none of the effort or risk.

"These goods belong to those who have fought for them. I was unaware, good Count, that you were of a mind for action. I would be most happy to invite you next time, now that I know you wish to fight."

"Oh I have a wish to fight, William. And I repeat, these goods belong to the French army now."

"I do hope this does not mean that anything foul has befallen your brother and liege lord King Louis? When I left these walls this morning he was in command of the French army, not you."

Robert grew red in the face but, with visible effort, remained still. "My brother lives."

"Then I shall discuss this misunderstanding with him."

"Very well, but the goods stay."

Not wanting his own knights to start a disastrous conflict while he wasn't present, he ordered that each man turn over the goods in his own care, but only after careful inventory.

Louis paced back and forth across his private chamber, stopping at the window each time to gaze out across those calm Mediterranean waters.

"William, please understand my position. My people grow jealous of your success. Your name grows in honor and in fear amongst the heathen by the day."

"If this is true, it is because I have taken action that they know and fear me. You and Robert could also be feared, if you would but leave the comforts of Damietta."

Louis sighed. William had met many kings, all of whom would have flown into a rage at such an insult, but Louis seemed to truly understand the truth of these words, and even more surprisingly, accept them. "Am I to risk the cause of Christ and his Church to give you justice? I beg you to let this pass, and I promise you riches far beyond these when we take Cairo."

"Are the tailed English to obtain a greater share in the plunder then?" William followed the sound of the familiar voice. Robert entered the chamber, unasked and unacknowledged; it should be an inexcusable offense. Again Louis did not bridle.

"Better to have our own hard-fought gains stolen by our Christian brothers? I wonder Robert, who is the greater enemy of the English in this land?"

"You see brother? This Englishman considers allying with the heathen!"

"Silence!" Louis showed the first backbone William had seen in these two months.

Robert's face, in turn, betrayed the first fear. The Count must have realized that he pushed his brother too far. So Louis was not Robert's pet after all.

"You will show respect to our English brothers in arms. We have equally taken the cross, have equally been sent here by his holiness the Pope to injure the Saracens, not each other!"

Robert nodded and dropped to one knee before his brother. "Of course, my lord."

He did not enquire about the goods, both he and William waited silently for Louis to make pronouncement on the case.

"William, I hold you dear and would give you justice if it was within my means. But this brother of mine has stirred up the passions of my army. These goods you have taken today will be divided amongst the entire army, but I give you my word that I will not forget that I am in debt to you."

"You have spoken today of my fame throughout the

land. My name is honored amongst the heathen even as it is dishonored by your men. I cannot accept this humiliation. My own honor, and the honor of my family, cannot allow it. A king must be able to bring justice, or he is no king at all. I will not follow such a leader. We shall leave at first light tomorrow."

Louis again accepted the blows of William's harsh words. "Where will you go, back to England?"

"I have taken the cross, I came to fight Saracens; if you wish to reunite our armies by acting justly, you will find us at Acre."

"My heart aches at this division, William."

"My heart soars." Robert, still kneeling, did not bother to suppress a smile.

Louis drew his sword and savagely struck the hilt into the side of his brother's head. "I said silence! This is your doing, cock sucking fool!"

William felt at home in Acre. The site of one of his uncle's greatest victories, this was his third visit to the area. Although it was the only city still firmly under crusader control, the port and natural harbor ensured the Europeans a comfortable foothold just eighty miles from Jerusalem.

After a hearty meal and a long night's sleep, William took in the early sun on the rooftop terrace of the citadel. With his back to the land, the Mediterranean surrounded him on three sides. He imagined the thumb shaped promontory as an island vessel sailing through the sea. Shaking off the daydream, he turned to the harbor on his left and evaluated the condition of his ships. All was well, luck with storms was with them thus far, and there certainly hadn't been any naval battles. That was a pity, but perhaps he'd get his chance; he rather fancied the idea of fighting on water. One needs variety in life.

"Good to see you again, William." Adelaide stood before her former customer, smiling.

"Word travels fast in Acre I see." William walked over and embraced his old friend. It would be a shocking act in England, but here there was--certain freedom.

Acre was well fortified with brothels. The men that travelled here on God's business were absent from their wives for years at a time; brothels were considered as essential as walls. Adelaide was the result of the trade; her mother was a Saracen prostitute and only God knew who her father was, but he was European. The blend was a success, and so Adelaide had been when she entered the family business. William spent time with her then. Though still a beauty at twenty-nine, she showed a mind for business and was now the proprietress of one of the finest establishments in Acre.

"I have a special girl for you if your lance isn't shattered," Adelaide said with a wink.

"My lance is as strong as you remember."

"Ah, well I'm sure Fatima won't mind."

"You're a wicked woman, Adelaide," William said.

"That's what they tell me, but they never shun me!"

William took hold of Adelaide's right hand. "Come out of retirement while I'm here?"

"You can't afford me, William."

"Wicked," He dropped her hand. "Tell me about this Fatima then."

"Beautiful naturally, young, a little silly, and strong-willed. She came to me when she was thrown out of her community. She was too--independent for them; her father was away, else she would not have lived."

"Sounds like my kind of woman."

"When shall I send her to your quarters?"

"Tonight," Willaim said.

"I suggest mid-afternoon. You will want to see Fatima in full light."

"Intriguing, but I must have evening meal with William de Sounac."

"She will stay in your quarters while you sup. She will stay until tomorrow morning. No extra cost."

"Most kind of you."

"Not at all William; for old times sake."

"William! You were telling us of Louis?" William de Sounac jabbed his guest in the shoulder.

William Longespee felt the jolt as his mind returned to the present. He inhaled deeply while surreptitiously nodding his head, bring his nose close to his chest. The scent of Fatima was still there.

"Yes. They stay fat and happy within Damietta while his brother steals from anyone with bowels enough for action."

The older man nodded several times before speaking. William de Sounac was Grand Master of the Templar order. "Disgraceful. The idea behind this crusade is sound. We have been foolishly fighting here at Jerusalem for generations as reinforcements and supplies flow in from Egypt. Seize the Saracen's richest base and the whole region will be ours. Unfortunately, the only king with enough appetite at the moment is French."

Longespee grunted. "Ah the French, if only they weren't so--French."

The grand master guffawed and began a familiar story from his experiences with visiting Frenchmen over the years. Fatima. She was likely the most beautiful creature William had ever seen. Artists found beauty in bold vibrant colors. William discovered this day that the most luxurious color of all was one artists rarely touched: brown. Light brown skin, dark brown eyes, hair a shade in between, with Fatima in the room, how could a man bear look anywhere else?

She entered his chamber that afternoon full of confidence, yet still appearing innocent. Burnt umber eyes never averted his gaze; her brilliant white smile flashed when natural, but was never contrived. William felt he could read this girl's mind. She did not languish in self-pity over the circumstances that led her here, nor did she blame this man for the needs that created a market. Such attitude imbued her with a quality many would find impossible for one of her trade: dignity.

Certainly she was lovely, but so tiny. Just barely five feet tall, William worried that he could not perform, her appearance being of a mere girl. Soon she disrobed—they always did that too soon—too quickly, but in Fatima's case it was for the best. Though short, she was perfectly proportioned, proving that she was most certainly a woman.

Sounac roared and howled. William guessed that he had come to the climax of his foolish Frenchman story and reacted as he had every other time he'd heard it.

"Robert must apologize to you, William. If he does, the Templars will join you in Egypt."

"A more welcome brother in arms has never been, Sir. But I will not hold my breath for an apology from Robert, better to have it from Louis. His would be unforced."

William's thoughts once again drifted away, to the masterpiece in brown waiting for him on his bed. Talk of the Templars joining in the crusade reminded him of the elder William Marshal, of how he became a Templar in his old age. As a Templar, William could stay here in this warm land with Fatima. Would he miss his wife? Not really. His children yes, but the boys would become knights and would likely join him here. The girls, well they would go off to their husbands' homes soon enough anyway.

Yes. He could do it. Leave everything and live free with Fatima. That face, those breasts, that body seeming to be fully assimilated under him, she was worth everything. He would speak to Adelaide first thing in the morning.

William awoke to find Fatima finishing dressing. "I had hoped for a morning tumble."

The girl smiled at him. "Your time is up."

Longespee winced at the reminder of their current relationship. "I'll pay extra."

"I really must be going."

"I meant what I told you last night. I'll be speaking to Adelaide as soon as possible."

She smiled again. "And when, my mighty warrior, will you be asking me what I think?"

Suddenly the meaning of the smile was not as easy to interpret.

"Well… I just…"

"Have a good day, William."

As quickly and quietly as she entered his life she was gone. Was any of it real?

William rose and stretched, still determined to buy out Fatima's obligation to Adelaide. She was teasing certainly. Of course being his mistress was a dream come true in comparison to a life as a prostitute. A voice of reason, which sounded remarkably like his mother, already whispered in his brain. *What nonsense, you just met the girl yesterday.* He walked over and picked up the scrolls that still lay on the table. A messenger brought the letters while William was at dinner the day before; he ignored them yesterday evening, choosing to focus all his energy and attention on the girl.

Briefly he felt embarrassment for the messenger finding a prostitute in his room, but that quickly evaporated. *Who doesn't use prostitutes here?*

William decided to take the scrolls back to the roof of the citadel to read them in the warm sunshine. He also hoped Adelaide would come looking for him once again.

It was not Adelaide who found him sitting on the edge of the building staring out to sea an hour later.

"I hear you received letters William, from England and from Egypt. Any news you'd care to share with me?" William de Sounac sipped pomegranate juice; he held a second cup he brought for his friend.

"The letter from Egypt brings word from King Louis. He restores all my men's goods, apologizes, and begs me return to the crusade."

De Sounac paused a moment. The news from Egypt was the perfect response, yet William's voice was flat and hollow, it contained no victory. "And home?"

"My wife is dead."

Chapter Twenty-seven

Two days before the English army left Acre, William received an invitation to dine with a man of science by the name of Roger Bacon. The man arrived in Acre late the previous day, and for some reason was eager to make William's acquaintance.

William entered the inn where Bacon arranged a dinner and found it a typical dark room smelling of stale ale and recently butchered pig. None of the clientele at that moment looked like an educated Englishman from a college in Oxford, so William chose to ask for an ale at the front counter.

"Hello, William. My God it is you."

William turned to see that two Englishmen entered behind him, one looked to be around thirty, the other closer to three times that age. The voice that spoke to him creaked in such a way that it could only have come from the older man.

"I am sorry, do I know you?"

The old man's eyes grew wide, but then he nodded. "It has been a very long time."

"Philip?" William asked.

The old man smiled. "Yes, William. How is your mother? Well, I hope?"

"When I left her, yes."

"I have been remiss in writing, but correspondence can be difficult from such a distance."

The threesome were shown to a table set for a fine dinner. "Where have you been?" William asked.

"Roger and I have been studying amongst the Saracen scholars—in Persia. Events in Egypt have made things difficult, we thought it best to leave for a time."

"I regret my part in cutting your enjoyment short," William said.

"So you are part of the invading force?" Until now this young Roger had not said a word.

"I was. The French were my greater enemy."

"Ha! So there is nothing new to tell from England then!" Philip said, placing a hand on William's shoulder, turning his attention away from Bacon in the process.

"My wife died," William said.

"I am sorry, William."

"I am sorry too, Philip. I don't know why I blurted that out. It was not that our story was ever going to enthrall the Courts of Love."

"Still," Philip searched for words. "When did it happen?"

"I received the letter three days ago."

Philip nodded. "Roger, I wonder if you might enquire as to whether the innkeeper could provide fresh figs."

Roger shrugged his shoulders and walked over to the bar, leaving Philip and William alone.

"William, I have known your family a long time."

"Known? You are part of it."

Philip nodded. "She told you?"

"That you are her uncle? Of course."

"Good. Then let us set aside pretense. Something troubles you. And if I recognize a look from your teenage eyes, it is a someone."

William started to bluster, out of habit more than anything else. Finally he realized that there was an opportunity here. He could not have dreamed of a father figure falling from the sky, one from whom he could seek advice. "There is a girl. But she is forbidden."

"Forbidden eh? How forbidden?"

"Every kind of forbidden."

"Saracen?"

William nodded. "And a prostitute." He said it fast, stabbing it into the air like a thrust from his sword. It was the easiest way to be sure he didn't demur. To his surprise Philip's face remained stoic, not a hint of shock.

"I see."

William studied his elder.

"William, it is time I told you a story about your great aunt Clare."

Senior knights formed an auditorium of flesh as they gathered in a circle on the parched field. A triumvirate of allied leaders entered the circle. Robert d'Artois represented the French, William Longespee the English, and William de Sounac spoke for the Templars. Robert, as was his custom, spoke first.

"Let us follow up the enemy who are near at hand and are said to be fleeing while things are going well for us, while we see that our people are full of ardor and thirsting for the enemy's blood, and while the enemies of the faith are despairing for their safety. If anything unlucky should befall us — which God forbid — the unconquerable army of my brother and lord the King will come to our aid at a nod."

Some cheers followed his speech, but only from the French and even of them it was not universal. William de Sounac stepped forward next. Of only medium height, de Sounac was a thickset and muscular man in his late forties. His bushy beard was almost completely grey, with only a hint of brown here and there to remind others of his younger appearance.

"My lord and noble count, we can commend well enough your efforts, your innate generosity and your bravery freely devoted to the honor of the Lord and his universal Church, which we know about and have often experienced. However, we would like and we advise and entreat you advantageously to restrain this fervor with the bridle of modesty and discretion so that we can recover breath a little after this triumph and honor which the Lord has given us. For after the heat and labour of battle we are tired, wounded, hungry and thirsty; and if we are consoled by the honor and glory of our victory, no honor or joy can revive our wounded and exhausted horses. We shall be better advised to return so that, united with the army of our lord the King, we may be strengthened both in advice and aid, and recuperate ourselves and our horses with a little rest. For now the clamor of the fugitives, carried on the swiftest horses, will arouse the Sultan and our other enemies, confident in their strength and numbers, and forewarn and encourage them because of our small numbers and because of the division of our army which they have long hoped for."

Robert, red in the face, stepped forward to reply before William could speak for the English. "See the time-honored treachery of the Temple! The ancient sedition of the Hospitallers! What deceit hidden for a long time, now appears openly in our midst! The whole country of the East would have been conquered long ago had it not been for the Templars and Hospitallers and others who call themselves religious, who have hindered us, the laymen, with their deceit. Look how the permanent exaltation of the law of our Christian church lays open to us. This Templar here is doing his best to prevent it with his fictitious and fallacious arguments. For the Templars and Hospitallers and their associates, who are fattened by ample revenues, are afraid that, if the country is subjected to Christian laws, their supremacy will come to an end. It is because of this that they mix various poisons for the faithful coming here fitted out for the cause of the cross, and kill them in different treacherous ways with the help of the Saracens."

Rage of every man charged the air around. Some shook from rage believing the truth of the Count's words. More still trembled at the insults of a such a reckless fool.

"Why noble count, should we have taken the habit of a monk? Surely not to overthrow the Church of Christ and thus lose our souls through intending treachery?" William de Sounac turned to his standard-bearer. "Unfurl and raise our banner and we shall advance to battle to experience today the uncertain fortunes of war and the chance of death. We would have been insuperable had we remained inseparable, but unfortunately we are divided, like sand without lime, so that we are unfit for the spiritual edifice and, lacking the cement of mutual affection, we shall forthwith become like ruined walls."

William stepped between the sparring warriors. Those amongst the gathered knights who still held onto their senses, looked to the leader of the English to bring reason to the discourse. He waited until shouts and jeers subsided. He paced several steps and turned. Still equal distance between the adversaries, he formed the point of a triangle and faced the Count. "According to the Lord's word, desolation follows from such a schism and division. Let us therefore, most noble count, listen to this sincere and saintly man. He has for a long time been an inhabitant of this country and, taught by manifold experience, he knows the strength and the craftiness of the Saracens. No wonder that we, newcomers, young men and foreigners, are ignorant of the dangers of the East. As far distant as the East is from the West, so far different are the Westerners from Orientals."

Longespee then walked forward and clasped his hand onto de Sounac's shoulder, speaking into the Templar's ear words no one else could hear.

Robert d'Artois, however, was not yet prepared to yield to logic nor reason. "How cowardly these timid people with tails are! How blessed, how clean, this army would be if purged of tails and tailed people!"

The Frenchman insulted the Templars, and now he enraged the English knights, denigrating the entire race. William stiffened visibly and turned to face d'Artois. "Count Robert, I shall assuredly advance unafraid of any danger of impending death. We shall be today, I fancy, where you will not dare to touch my horse's tail."

As Eleanor taught Ela long ago, all men are made fools by pride. All good sense left the small advance guard on the Egyptian plain. Unfurling their banners and putting on their helmets, they tore away from the bulk of their own army seeking further Muslim blood in the nearby city of al Mansurah.

William pushed his horse to its limits as the gates of al Mansurah remained open and inviting like the legs of a prostitute. Even in the insanity of battle and with his wounded honor crying out to beat Robert d'Artois to the fight, William realized he had never seen such a surrender. It did, however, echo the surrender of Damietta as it was described to him; thus he never wavered, but thundered over the bridge and through the yawning gate.

William and his standard bearer, de Vere, were the head of the Christian vanguard. City streets did not allow room for anyone to come alongside, but funneled the riders into a parade of pairs. Fleeing Mamluks safely disappeared down still narrower alleyways. Finally William charged into the market square and reigned in his mount allowing the Count of Artois to catch up.

"You see how easily we have taken the city, Longespee?" d'Artois spun his excited steed a full three hundred and sixty degrees trying to bring it under control. "You cowardly English would still be outside making camp!"

William could think of no reply; leading the charge ahead of Robert was of no consolation when there was no resistance. The market square was painted in vivid hues of exotic spices. So strikingly different from the dull camel colored walls and buildings of the city, it seemed they burst forth into another world. White and red banners of the Templars, deep blues and golden fleurs-de-lys of the French added to the masterpiece as the square quickly filled to capacity with knights. As more and more cavalry pressed in, some market stalls were overturned filling the air with clouds of precious spices.

William was entranced by the smell around him. Cinnamon, nutmeg, saffron, and many other scents he could not identify, seemed to paint a masterpiece every bit as real and artistic as the visual scene. He resolved to write a poem about this place that very night. Suddenly the air was pierced by praise of Allah. From the city walls arose hundreds of Muslim warriors interspersed by villagers.

For a moment bright light of day turned to dusk as the square was shaded by hundreds of arrows. Villagers on the walls, as well as those appearing in upper windows, hurled crushing stones upon the European invaders. There was little to be done. All of William's allies were mounted knights; their own archers were back with Louis on the far side of the Nile. The beautiful canvas became a killing field.

"William, God is fighting against us; we cannot resist any longer. Flee to safety while you still can!" Through the narrow slit of visibility afforded by his helm, William saw Robert d'Artois dismount and scamper toward a mean house facing onto the market square. He was beckoning William to follow him with his sword arm.

After all the blustering and insults, William could not understand why the Count should now have a care for an Englishman. Then he realized Robert wished to guard his own honor; he was fleeing, it would be humiliating if others of his rank did not.

"God forbid that a son of my father should flee from any Saracen. I would rather die happily than live unhappily!" William turned back into the market and to the men who were led as lambs to the slaughter.

Few horses survived, but the knights wore mail and armor. Though many suffered multiple puncture wounds, few were deep enough to kill. William himself counted eight arrows lodged about an inch into his flesh. The wood of his shield was badly cracked in several places, but the rawhide reinforcement held.

"Gather in a circle men! Backs to each other, to the center of the square. Build a shield wall!"

His orders flew from man to man as all gratefully welcomed clear-headed instruction. If the Saracens wanted to finish them off, they would have to come down and do it man to man. Quiet fell upon the scene, broken only by the cries of the surviving horses and metallic rustle of mail. William faced the age old dilemma of helm wearers; without it, he would not survive five seconds; with it, his field of vision was a quarter of normal. He glanced to each side, glad to see de Vere still on his right side, and another Englishman to his left.

Just as the first torsos filled the metal window, William heard one of the senior Templars shout. "For the Church!"

Echoing shouts of the men were soon drowned by the reverberating clang of swords. William cut down three of the enemy, sure that they would never rise, before he noticed that his movement was badly restricted. Unable to turn his head, he thought he must have suffered a crippling blow to the neck. But soon he fell onto his back and through the slit he saw the face of a Saracen that had gotten alongside him; at least one of his comrades must have been killed to allow it. Then he could see the honed tip of a small blade hunting for the narrow outer slit above his eyes. It found the gap, and slowly came closer as it became increasingly hard to keep focus. It was true what they say of time slowing in deadly situations, but this had to be more. This man was taking his time, enjoying it.

William felt the tip puncture his right eyeball before holding there for a moment. "Allahu Ackbar!" William knew the words: God is great.

"Ave Maria!" William spat back. The last sensation William ever experienced was the sound of the blade thudding and scraping against the back of his skull.

Midday service was in progress in the modest church of Lacock Abbey. Sister Agnes was reading from the Psalms of David, a song of an exalted soul, in gallant effort to crack the prevailing feeling of coldness. Coldness of the stones, coldness of the February English weather, coldness rather than light seemed to stream through the narrow windows, licking every corner and every person inside. Candlelight, the only light available, was mocked by the bitter chill. Two novices cried out, eliciting wicked scorn from the more senior sisters gathered at the front of the congregation. Until, that is, the girls pointed to the Abbess who had fallen to her knees. The service was forgotten, as all rushed to her side, but the elderly woman held them back with a thrust out palm.

Just one month shy of her sixty-fourth birthday, Ela was experiencing one of her visions that first began not far from here on her eighth birthday. She saw a host of angels framing a gate of shimmering gold. Before the gate stood the earthly form of a knight, fully clad in mail and armor.

She turned to an angel standing nearby and the messenger turned its gaze to her. "Who is this fine knight who has gained the praise of all heaven?" Ela asked him.

"See now." The heavenly dweller gestured to return Ela's vision toward the gate. The knight turned to face her and though no part of him was visible, Ela saw the image upon the man's shield. It showed six golden lions rampant. "It is your son William, who has gained great glory as a martyr of Christ."

Suddenly returning to the gloomy church of Lacock, Ela allowed two of her senior aides to help her to her private chamber. The sisters listened intently to the description of the vision. Neither doubted the authenticity for a moment; they knew of the Abbess' gift.

"I am so sorry, Abbess." Anne grasped Ela's hands in her own.

"As am I." Agnes stood apart but spoke with deep feeling.

Ela nodded, looking past them. "I have been greatly blessed. My own mother had only me, my second mother Queen Eleanor had, by my age, lost almost all of her 10 children. I have borne eight healthy children and at sixty-four I have lost only one, and that one an offering sacrifice to the Lord. I shall mourn of course, but I consider myself fortunate."

"I thank the Lord that we have your example, Abbess," Agnes said.

"It is fitting the Psalm you were reading today Agnes," Ela replied. "Praise the Lord oh my soul: and all that is within me bless his holy name."

Earl Richard stood before the counting table of the Exchequer at Westminster Palace. The sounds of chisel against stone making its way through the open windows from the building site of Westminster Abbey mingled with the clacking of wooden tally sticks. The kingdom's chief bookkeeper was nearing the end of the pile of sticks on which he would strike Xs acknowledging the Earl of Cornwall's tax payment, when one of the clerks walked over and handed him a scroll.

"A message arrived for you from your chancellor, my lord."

"Thank you." Richard trusted the Chancellor of the Exchequer and so strolled to the nearest window for more light by which to read.

"All is in order of course, Earl Richard." The exchequer looked to the nobleman by the window and noticed the firmly set jaw and pinched expression. Earl Richard was normally a jovial fellow, not withstanding he was paying taxes this day. "Something wrong?"

"Very wrong it seems." Richard continued to read,

silently promising further details to the finance minister in due course.

Every clerk in the hall looked to the Earl as he finished his reading and began to roll the scroll back up, gazing absently out upon the expanding abbey. In the end he didn't bother taking the high official aside. The news would be public knowledge soon enough. "This seventh crusade is a disaster. The weakness of King Louis and the arrogance of his French brothers has brought the Church's mission to ruin. God has seen fit to use the heathen to punish our sins."

"How many of our knights are lost?" The Exchequer stood and faced the Earl.

"All of them."

"All?"

"Every one, plus all of the 250 Templars with them. The Saracens cut off all of their heads, hands, and feet."

"Dear God!" Similar cries rumbled through the hall, but neither official took any notice of them.

"And Louis?"

"Taken prisoner. He attempted to trade Damietta for Jerusalem but it was too late. The Saracens knew they held every advantage. They ported ships across the barren land and dropped them into the Nile south of Damietta. They surrounded our ships with superior numbers and Greek Fire. In the end the port fell, Louis will have to be ransomed, and we have nothing to show for our losses."

"I was going to invite you to stay for dinner. My company would be subdued now."

"Thank you anyway, I feel the only action I can take is to be the one to tell the Countess Ela about William. I will set out for Cornwall by way of Wiltshire immediately."

"God go with you."

Chapter Twenty-eight

The people of Lacock were enjoying a warm midday on the second Tuesday of August 1251. Most able bodied men were out in the fields. Everyone else, women, children, the old, and city tradesmen played and worked in the streets to avoid the stagnant air of their homes.

Donald Smythe's hammer fell off the mark. "Fuckin 'ell!" He shouted, shaking his left hand like a rag.

A few of the mothers in range of the soliloquy gasped. "Mind your tongue, Smythe, there are ladies and children about," Mary of the mill pond yelled.

All the rest of the tradesmen, and a good number of the younger wives, laughed.

"I see the children, Mary. Where are the ladies?" Smythe replied, still nursing his injury.

"Figures you wouldn't know a lady if she walked right up to you, though I can't imagine why she would."

Laughter halted like a ripple, starting at the far end of the road. Silence rolled over the main street.

A stranger was walking through town. The men and most of the children stared. Women were quicker to action, they hustled their children inside the houses and closed the doors fast.

The stranger was dressed in flowing robes of fine linen painted the color of highway dust. A cowel covered the stranger's hair, but the face was visible to all as the stranger passed steadily through town. The stranger stopped and sniffed the air near Thomas the Baker's shop, appeared to consider attempting a purchase, but walked on through the village and up the path that lead to the Abbey.

In the stranger's wake tongues were found and shocked voices echoed behind. "Saints protect us!" "Here now, what is the likes of you doing here?"

The stranger seemed deaf; there was no reaction at all. It was Fatima.

Ela stared at the woman across the table from her. The two sat in silence together for some minutes. The girl seemed to understand that Ela needed time to process the ramifications of the documents presented to her. The Abbess experienced a range of emotions over the last five minutes: anger, disbelief, sadness, confusion, and finally surrender to reality.

Everything about the girl was dark, and very strange. Ela had seen dark people before, men brought from the continent of Africa to London, but very few. Never did one sit across from her defiantly, albeit silently, demanding to be treated as an equal. The hair, eyes, skin, Ela could not deny the girl was lovely; she could understand how her son could be charmed by her, but to this extent?

"The marriage was—Christian?" After so much silence, Ela's voice couldn't help but sound loud.

"Yes. I agreed to convert first." Fatima held the woman's gaze.

Ela nodded. When she was younger, she would have found no trouble in disdaining the girl. As a Norman noble, everyone was beneath her; certainly this dark skinned Saracen would have seemed less than human. But Ela was older now, had learned lessons about humanity. She could not blame this girl for wanting a better life; but there were limits to Ela's compassion.

"I'm sorry you have taken such a great journey in vain. You will not, of course, obtain any of William's wealth."

The girl cocked her head slightly then smiled. "You assume that I have come for money?"

"I admire your spirit child, let's not play silly games with each other. Of course you are here for money."

The girl's teeth were white and even, as if sculpted out of fine marble by a gifted artist. "It was my understanding that he owned next to nothing in England. The Pope had to help him raise the funds to join the crusade."

This candid statement shocked Ela. It was certainly true, but why then did she come? Ela began to suspect that she was underestimating the girl. Picking up the documents again, she searched for the girl's name. "Fatima is it?"

"That is correct."

"It is true—Fatima—that my son had no wealth. I retain the earldom and all our lands as my right. This wealth will pass on to my children, as you can guess, I will have no more husbands. I assumed you were here to claim William's share of the lands."

"Hah! Well that would be an occasion wouldn't it?" Fatima replied. William, as oldest son, was entitled to most if not all the lands. "Can you imagine? A... what? Tenth? A tenth of all England belonging to a Saracen woman?"

The girl's laughter was refined yet robust, Ela liked it, could see it capturing men. But she couldn't join in; though she would never be allowed to exercise them, Fatima's understanding of her rights was disconcerting.

"Fatima, why have you come?"

Those brown eyes softened as if the girl sympathized with Ela's anxiety. "William obtained a fortune in ransoms and plunder before he died. I have brought two-thirds of it for you to give to his children; a third of their portion is on a ship in Portsmouth, a third in Rye, the rest in London. I felt it wise to divide it, should disaster befall any one ship; of course none but a few trusted knights knows what is in the chests."

And so she did, in fact, underestimate this Saracen girl. "That is most noble in deed and wise in execution. Is there nothing that you want?" The question was direct, the tone unmistakeable. William's mother was certain Fatima wanted something in return.

"I wished to see William's homeland, to meet his children, without telling them who I am of course." She was quick to offer assurance but then softened once again. "I thought perhaps there was a way I could make a home here, I have none in the land of my birth, save Acre. That is no place to raise a child."

Ela's eyes widened. "Child?"

Chapter Twenty-nine

June 4, 1256

William Longespee, grandson of the venerable Ela of Salisbury, feared the strength of the sun more than any knight on the tourneying field this day. Suffering mightily from a night of good cheer, he rode out of the little village of Tickhill an hour after daybreak, surrounded by villagers making their way to the tournament grounds. There were few of the customary cheers of adulation coming from this crowd, save a few merchants whose purses grew fatter the previous week. Today William was amongst those without. Knights of this tournament were divided by northern and southern regions of England; and William was of the South. Blyth and Tickhill were situated in the far north of Nottinghamshire, well beyond the reach of any non-noble supporters.

William studied the sky above him and along the horizon. God was not giving anything away yet as to his plans for their afternoon. It was pleasant enough so far, with patches of blue showing here and there amongst mostly white blankets of cloud. It could go any way then, from breaking up into all blue skies to a severe rain. Given the choice, William would choose rain, it fit his mood, and would have less severe effect on his headache.

Officially this tournament was illegal. Under Henry III, tournaments were often banned. In fact, Henry was more creative in suppressing tournaments than his predecessors; he threatened both royal and spiritual punishment on villagers who fed or housed the recalcitrant knights. It was testimony both to the Englishmen's thrill of the sport, as well as its economic benefits, that these royal threats were almost universally ignored. William knew that nobody, villager or nobleman alike, felt any trepidation today; rumors had been confirmed. One of the wayward knights riding out of Blyth to meet him this morning was seventeen-year-old Edward, the King's eldest son.

The tournament changed over the years since William's grandfather met Ela. Jousting became more popular. Often events were staged over multiple days now, allowing for many jousts to take place before the incapacitating violence of the melee.

Midpoint between the villages, two miles southeast of Tickhill, an uncultivated stretch of flat ground was set up with a semi-permanent jousting arena. A wooden wall, three feet high, stretched for eighty yards between two stands of seating and viewing platforms. Those within were already at the lists, claiming the choicest grounds for their colorful tents. Tournaments provided the dyers' guilds their greatest opportunity for showing off, and they never failed to take advantage. Dyers seemed to compete with God himself, attempting to outdo nature, to paint the landscape with hues that embarrassed wildflowers. Peppered about the fields beyond the arena were these circular tents. Sewn together from triangles of vivid cloth, each tent consisted of at least two colors, usually corresponding with the colors of a particular knight's heraldry. Outside each tent's door a flag displaying this heraldry was planted; these same symbols hung as plaques along one side of the barriers that separated observers from participants. William quickly found young Edward's symbol prominently displayed amongst them.

Gilbert began to swing the bell in his right hand as soon as freshly plowed fields announced his approach to another small village. The road to Winchester was rocky and uneven. What soil and clay was present in the road's surface was deeply rutted, telling the stories of untold thousands of carts that passed this way over the centuries.

Such a surface was no great obstacle to a normal, healthy man who walked from place to place. Gilbert was not healthy; he was most decidedly not normal, that is, not in the eyes of strangers. Gilbert's toes were now being impacted by his condition. They were thinner than normal, more brittle. Add to that the fact that he had no feeling in his feet, and he could lose all mobility with one poorly considered footfall.

At the top of a rise, Gilbert decided to rest and study the manor through which his path was about to take him. Certain that there was nobody about, he lifted the grey silk that usually concealed what was left of his face, and looked down the road.

The Winchester Road passed through the village like a dry riverbed, full of stumbling stones left behind by currents that never flowed. The manor house, where the lord lived, was large and made of stone. A small church was also stone. The rest of the village consisted of a few waddle and daub hovels lining the single road. A bush hanging outside one hovel announced that the mistress had extra beer or ale she was willing to sell. Another English village, like so many dozens Gilbert had already passed through, nothing stood out about it. Nothing gave away the temperament of the residents. Some villages let him pass in peace, offering looks of pity; others chased him away, threatening violence. Some merchants accepted his coins, if tossed, along with the goods, from a distance. Others contributed only their scorn at Gilbert's obviously many past sins.

Kindness or rebuke, the answer lay ahead. Everything Gilbert had, or hoped to have, in this world laid ahead. He lowered the death-shroud fabric in front of his face and trudged on.

Success of the southern knights did little to temper the crowd's enthusiasm, as each side accounted well for themselves. After the opening ceremonies, minor young knights clashed. As morning gave way to midday, anticipation rode high as everyone knew the King's son would soon ride. William leaned against the arena barrier wall, feeling much better and in good spirits when he spotted young Edward riding into the arena ground.

The banner he carried was quite similar to William's, and he was about six foot two inches like William, they were second cousins after all. It came as no surprise when the boy nodded in William's direction then rode directly to Longespee's plaque giving it a whack with his lance. Edward was challenging his older cousin to a joust.

There may not have been another knight on the field that day who would try to unseat Edward. It was dangerous business to deliver a lance blow upon the King's heir. After all, what good could come of victory? If the boy was seriously hurt, or God forbid killed, his opponent's name would reach the King's ear swifter than thunder. Should the boy be unharmed, he would one day be king with the memory of his dishonor still fresh on his mind. Therefore, Edward was assured easy victory against any other knight of the South. By challenging the only man his equal physically, and the only one he knew would dare give his full measure, Edward was announcing to his future subjects that he would never take the easy way out.

Unlike the melee, which held little distinction from all out battle, the joust had very specific goals. Each man would attempt to unhorse the other. Failing that, points were awarded for solid strikes to the breastplate or shield. Up to three passes would be run; in this particular tournament unhorsing would end the joust. Sometimes the still mounted knight would dismount and continue the battle with swords, but not here.

Fifteen minutes after the challenge, William settled his mount, Cobalt, at one end of the low wall, facing Edward. Because of the focussed nature of the blows, both men opted for limited armor. Each wore a thick padded coat under a chain mail shirt and finally a solid breastplate covering his torso. Leg protection consisted of thigh and calf plates attached to their saddles. Helmets and mail gloves completed their armor ensemble.

Cobalt kicked at the sand, knowing his part in the coming performance. William felt the power of the steed's tensing muscles under him, and patted its head. "Easy boy."

A young boy stood at the midpoint of the wall with a green flag touching the ground as William took a lance from his squire and set it in the crook of his right arm. An instant later the flag was up and the boy ran for the barrier. Cobalt launched himself toward the opposite end of the wall, requiring no instruction from William, a well trained mount was a partner in the joust, not a tool.

William settled into the rhythm of Cobalt's stride like a sailor adjusting to the effects of a sudden squall upon his vessel. In seconds he drew close enough to Edward to let his lance drop and pick his target spot. Seconds after that, he felt the jolt as both men found their marks. William heard a loud crack from his lance but it did not shatter; Edward's lance also sheared away intact after its initial impact.

As he turned the corner and trotted back to his end, where his team would replace the broken lance, William analyzed Edward's strike. Chalk from the blunting ball confirmed that the Prince struck low, below the ribcage on William's left side. The boy was strong for his age, but he was also inexperienced. William guessed that Edward would overcompensate, and thus the next strike would be high and to the right.

Polite cheers greeted the awarding of points, one point each for an honorable strike, a draw. The cousins settled into their starting points once again, new lances couched, the flag raised, horses galloped toward each other. Anticipating Edward's overcompensating, William leaned out of the saddle to his left and swung the lance into place, stabbing it into the Prince's breastplate. Edward's lance was exactly where William expected it to be; instead of striking solidly into armor, the clay ball affixed to the blunt point shattered on William's right shoulder and the lance itself simply ricocheted off. This time Longespee's lance did shatter into a cloud of splinters. A few instinctive cheers rose from the appreciative crowd before being tempered by realization that they were celebrating not only a point for the opposing team, but a blow to the next King of England.

Strategy for the next pass would be more difficult; William did not expect Edward to overcompensate again. Whether or not he would find the perfect zone, or pick a new spot entirely, William was unsure. He did have the advantage over his royal cousin though. It was now two points to one. If William avoided being unhorsed, and struck his lance anywhere on Edward's torso, he was assured of victory. Helmets were still in place, but a glimpse of the Prince's eyes told William that Edward was struggling to accept what he asked for. Edward wanted to test himself in a fair fight, but now the reality that this meant he could actually lose was sinking in. William considered, for just a moment, that he ought choose the safer strategy and miss in the third round. That was not, however, in his nature; nor did he think Edward would be fooled. If Edward was the man he thought he was, that would provoke a greater anger than losing.

Cobalt bolted before the flag was above the boy's knees on the third pass. The sun came out from behind a cloud, bathing Edward in light as he raced toward William. Sand and dust reflected the light, William aimed for the dead center of Edward's torso, for the sternum itself. Not sure where his opponent's strike was aimed this time, William chose to assume it was anywhere but high and right, as it was last time. He lifted himself slightly up and right. He guessed wrong. Edward aimed exactly where he did in the last round, his lance struck hard directly above William's heart and shattered. William felt no shock from his arm, only the impact of Edward's blow; he scrambled with both hands to grab hold of saddle leather in order to avoid falling off. Just managing to climb back into place, he looked back as he turned the corner to see that his own lance bob had connected.

It could not have been much of a blow, but technically his strike counted the same as the crushing impact of Edward's hit. The tally was confirmed, William won the match three strikes to two. When the pair greeted each other over the wall, it was obvious that, though his first joust was a defeat, Edward was well pleased with his own performance and was therefore not embarrassed. He thanked his cousin for the honest match.

Before William left his cousin to leave the jousting field, another knight whose heraldry William didn't recognize rode in and struck a sword against the plaque of the house of Longespee. It meant another challenge.

"You may defer this challenge, William." Edward turned his back on the overeager new challenger. "Everyone would believe you if you told them I had exhausted you."

William chuckled. "You didn't bring Frenchmen with you did you?"

It was more common in France for jousting tournaments to be personal challenges whereby one knight agreed to fight all comers.

"No, he's an irritable little twat from Lincoln. My father doesn't care for him much."

"Then I shall do my royal relative a favor and spank his arse!"

Edward tilted his head back to laugh out loud. "You do that cousin. God be with you."

"And you."

The future king trotted off the field as the chief official of the tournament approached William's mount. "Would you rest first, my lord?"

"No, I find this convenient, it saves me time changing."

"As you wish."

As William lined up for his fourth consecutive pass, his mind wandered to other things, food and women. It was a critical mistake to underestimate an opponent, to allow yourself a minute of not being focussed. He was surprised when he felt Cobalt spring underneath him. The sun was still out, he felt his hair matted and wet inside his helmet. He thought how glad he was to not be wearing full armor. At the moment the lances dropped to horizontal, William's mind was on the mixed smells of dust and leather.

William's blow on the anonymous knight was a routine strike to the chest, the lance broke. The blow received was not routine. He sensed rather than felt his body reverberating and realized he was pushed too far over Cobalt's right flank. He attempted to call upon his stomach and back muscles as never before, but it was not enough; he was past the point of no return. He was going to miss Cobalt. A knight who managed to unmount his opponent won the man's horse. As he hung midair flinging his arms out to prepare for the ignominious landing, William was already planning to fight for or ransom back his favorite steed.

Something went horribly wrong. William felt the expected impact of his torso, but his legs didn't follow. Suddenly he felt himself sliding and bouncing backward across the field. He realized that his right foot was tangled in the straps of the stirrups. The pain of the blows, head, chest, shoulders, compounded with each stride as Cobalt continued to make for the wall's far end. Then the worst possible thing happened. His body bounced under the horse itself and Cobalt's right rear leg came down on William's neck at the juncture of helmet and breastplate. Everything changed. There was no more pain.

William knew that his motion stopped only by sight, the limited view of sky through his helmet slit. He commanded each limb to move in turn, none seemed to be complying, they didn't rise into view above his face. At the moment of shouting out the "Fuck!" that repeated itself over and over in his mind, the horror compounded. Nothing came out.

Calm down, calm down. Relax. It might be temporary. What if it's not? At least there is no pain. Fuck that, I want pain. Pain would tell me my body is still whole. The sky is gone! Ok, somebody just pulled my helmet off. Everyone's shouting, pulling and pushing at my body. That can't be good. Answer them damn it! Not even my fucking mouth works. Is this just shock? Shit! God give me a do over. Just five damn minutes over please! Two minutes! Just two minutes. Mary, blessed mother of God intercede on my behalf. If this is temporary I'll never lose focus in a joust again!

A monk, he must be a surgeon. Stop slapping me already! Where'd he go? Laying his head on my chest? He must be listening for a heartbeat. Oh God, do I have one? Is this death? No, he said I'm alive! Any pain? Think, focus, Mary mother of God let me feel some pain. Mother! I want my mother! She's dead William. I must have more injuries, maybe they're fatal. Please God, if my body is not restored, let the wounds be fatal. Is it possible? Can a man have no control over his body, not even be capable of speech and yet live? Why were you thinking of women during a charge you fucking idiot? Someone should kill me. They won't though, the Church would say it's a sin. Surely making me live like this is the greater sin? Two fucking minutes back. Is that so much to ask? Take it seriously; you deserve this for not taking the joust seriously. It's not a game! Not really. Women, you think of women when a man is about to ride at you with a lance? Well you'll never have another woman now! Never feel their soft skin, never feel them touch you. God, God, God, one more chance, just one more.

CLANG CLANG

The high tone of the brass bell preceded Gilbert whenever other humans might be around. It served as a warning, to send the fearful away from danger. Most often, however, it served the opposite purpose. It drew the curious to watch him pass. In this village, only a few briefly stared from their doorways, before returning to their previous tasks. Gilbert was encouraged. These people were familiar with lepers, saw them pass by regularly. Surely, then, the hospital of Saint Mary Magdalene must be close.

A small stone dropped in front of Gilbert on the road. He heard a thud before seeing the stone drop, the only indication that the stone struck him.

"I saw it was you, young Thomas, son of Tom the plowman! Your father will hear of it, and be fined!"

Gilbert searched for the source of the rebuke and found a red-faced priest shaking his fist at the back of a fleeing boy.

"I beg pardon for my parish, fellow. The boy will be whipped, his father made poorer, do not doubt."

Gilbert's protector was certainly prepared to deal with him kindly then, if from a distance of about 20 feet, no closer.

"Thank you, Father." Something deep in Gilbert's memory told him that he should request leniency for the boy. Do not all boys take pleasure in the misfortunes of others? Did not Gilbert himself, at that age? Would he have thrown stones if a leper walked through his village?

Gilbert did not feel like being forgiving. After suffering from the disease for so long, suffering too from the meanness of others for almost as long, he was tired of the abuse. That was why he walked this road. He hoped to seek refuge with people like him. If taken in, he would never see another healthy person again; he would live out his days--normal.

"Stop and rest in the churchyard, friend," the priest offered. "There is a recess built into the wall behind the church. Give us the time it takes a man to walk a mile, and there will be bread, beer, and cheese for you there."

"Most kind, Father." Gilbert rarely spoke anymore, he found language laborious. The disease ate away at his skull, collapsing his nose, and causing him to lose all of his upper front teeth. "Saint Mary—"

"Yes, my son. Saint Mary Magdalene Leper Hospital is but a day's journey onward."

Gilbert raised his hands toward the heavens.

"In the wall there will be a package. I would ask that you take it with you," The priest continued. "There is a woman in the hospital whose good works are famous throughout the Shire. We would send her this gift."

"Gladly, Father. What is her name?"

"We know not. Fear not, you will know her. She is called The Yellow Angel."

Ela looked up from her desk as Anne shuffled into the Abbess' chamber. *Can we really be that old, she and I?*

"A letter arrived for you, Abbess," Anne said.

Ela long ago gave up asking Anne to stop calling her by titles. "Thank you, Anne. Please have a seat. How are you, old friend?"

Anne looked grateful for the rest. "Well enough, well enough."

"I have heard you cough more than is to my liking of late. Have you asked Sister Margaret for a potion as I requested?"

"Yes, Abbess. They give some relief," Anne replied.

Ela nodded and broke the wax seal. It was the seal of the King's son Edward. She read the contents in less than a minute, sucked in her lips, and rerolled the parchment.

"Ela?" Anne said.

"My grandson William is dead. Killed in a jousting accident."

"Oh, Ela. I am so sorry to hear it."

Ela nodded again, much the same way as when Anne spoke of a coughing potion. "Such is the way of young men whom I love. So few grow old."

Anne looked as though she was searching for the right response. It would not come; words were not Anne's gift. When the silence grew too old, Anne spoke to kill it. "Such is it with too many of England's men."

"True," Ela replied. "But death is my constant companion. When my father died, I thought I was alone and unprotected. But then mother's cousin protected me in his own way, regardless his motives. I felt so safe with William, when he was taken, I again felt alone and unprotected. But your Talbot was there for me."

Ela paused and studied Anne's face. Was there any pain there? No. It had been over thirty years, and what love she might have felt for Talbot was very different from that Ela and William shared. Still, Ela realized there was business left unfinished all this time.

"I never apologized to you, Anne," Ela continued. "It was my fault Talbot died."

"Why would you say such a thing?"

"Because it is true. I led us into Mortain's stronghold like a sixteen year old boy wanting to impress his warrior father," Ela said.

"You wanted justice, to rescue an innocent girl."

"I allowed that zeal to silence my judgment," Ela said. "If I was more prudent, perhaps Talbot and the girl would both have lived."

"You bear burdens that are not yours to carry," Anne said.

"Perhaps," Ela whispered.

For the first time in their long association Ela saw Anne's face set in defiance. "There is no perhaps! You take too much blame, and claim too little praise."

Ela sat stunned by Anne's boldness.

Her friend continued. "You have protected many people,

and delivered justice."

Ela sat back in her chair and considered Anne's rebuke. "Thank you, dear Anne. I did have more successes than failures. Perhaps that's the best any man or woman can hope for."

The two sat in silence for several minutes.

"So now I have lost a father, husband, son, grandson, and some dear friends," Ela said. "But I am thankful. Eleanor lost eight of her ten children before her own death. I have buried but one son, I am fortunate."

"Who will protect you now?" Anne asked.

"Hmmph. Perhaps the one I hoped for all along: myself."

Anne smiled. "And you do not feel alone?"

"How could I," Ela replied, gripping Anne's wrinkled hand.

Anne coughed several times. When the fit subsided, Ela noticed a drop of blood escape from Anne's mouth.

Gilbert was welcomed into the community of Saint Mary Magdellene after minimal questioning. There was little doubt the fact there was an almshouse available owed to a recent death, but no details were offered and Gilbert felt no desire to investigate the source of his good fortune.

The first order of business when a leper entered a hospital such as this was to perform the newcomer's funeral. It was a stark reminder that the man or woman was all but dead. As far as the rest of the world was concerned, Gilbert was dead the moment he walked through the gate.

He watched his own funeral with fascination. A priest led the Latin incantations, strangers repeated them without passion. The smoke of incense was folly. Few in this room retained the gift of smell.

There were no friends or family present, of course.

Gilbert realized that if this ceremony had been left to its traditional timing, it would have made little difference. *So that's done then, and I am dead. Now nothing remains but purgatory's purgatory.*

As his borrowed mourners filed out, Gilbert remembered the package in his satchel. "Pardon me, Friend."

An old man with a missing foot, and little forehead, stopped his stumbling exit. "Yes?"

"I have a package, a gift from a nearby village. They said that I would know the recipient as The Yellow Angel."

Even a face barely recognizable as such could express sorrow, for Gilbert saw it in the old man's eyes, but there was mischief as well. "Ah. To this community's great loss, The Yellow Angel passed from this world but Wednesday last."

His tragic timing intensified Gilbert's curiosity about the woman. "Who was she?"

Grief was replaced with animated excitement in the old man's visage at the question. "That, young man, is a very good question!" He looked about, to make sure they were now alone. "Some say she was a saint, that Mother Church should waste no time confirming her holiness. Her good works, and kindness, none can dispute."

"But?" It was clear there was more information ready to burst forth, like water from a failed dam.

"Come." The old man grabbed Gilbert by the elbow and pulled him out of the church with remarkable vigor for one so advanced in his leprosy. "I know a secret. Those that prepared her body for burial told me."

"Told you what?" Gilbert was torn between his curiosity and repulsion from the man's gossip. How could one laid so low, the least of all God's creatures still revel in telling salacious tales of the dead? And why did he just encourage the man?

"She dressed in a long yellow robe whenever she tended to those suffering harder than her. In truth she ministered to those who should have been tending to her near the end..." This tangent sounded like a confession. The old man shook it off. "Anyway, that is how she got her name. But not a soul saw her skin until last week when she breathed her last, not an inch of it. Not even her hands."

Gilbert looked at the man, and refused him the extra encouragement he sought. The man wanted to further implicate Gilbert in the gossip, to alleviate his own guilt.

After a long moment, the old man knew Gilbert would not press for the final secret. "She was a Saracen!"

Chapter Thirty

Felicia arrived in the rose garden as ordered, wondering why the elderly lady wanted her there. Though over seventy years old, her summoner stood tall and straight, no hint of the stoop most very old people displayed. Felicia walked down a grass pathway between blooming roses, to where the lady stood with her back to the garden. Felicia wondered whether she should announce herself, clear her throat, or simply wait to be noticed.

While she considered the options, she spotted the attraction which held the old woman's attention. A doe walked out of a thicket down by the river, a young fawn suckled as its mother kept careful watch.

"Beautiful aren't they?"

So the old woman sensed her arrival after all. "Yes, my lady," Felicia answered.

The woman turned to the girl, and for a moment her expression changed. Felicia thought that it spoke of a surprising amount of sentimentality. "My name is Ela, please call me by name, at least for now."

Felicia was shocked by the request, never had an adult

asked her to call them by name. She considered pointing that out, but decided the lady must know how unusual the request was. "I know who you are."

"Do you now? Well, we'll see if I can muster any surprises on that front."

"My lady?"

"Ela." The strange old woman paced to a corner of the garden where there was a cluster of rose bushes of unique colors.

Felicia could see yellow, white, even some with two colors on the same bloom. She couldn't quite understand why she felt like resisting this woman, knew she must obey, feared the consequences of rebelling, and yet still she did not want to call this woman Ela.

After a few moments the lady let the issue pass without Felicia having to say anything. "Don't just stand there, child. Take those shears there on the stool, those are yours now. Come over here and I will teach you to prune roses."

Silently she obeyed the command. Felicia always loved the rose garden. The air in this particular corner was saturated with sweetness, its odor made her forget that the stink of unwashed people and shit even existed. "I think this is what the Garden of Eden must have smelled like."

Ela smiled. "Me too. And the roses didn't have thorns." She turned to a bush with yellow blooms. "Right then. Lesson one: roses are like human lives. Without proper pruning, roses will grow in every direction, with dozens of blooms at once. Problem is: their energy is expended on branch and stem growth, and all of those many blooms are tiny, they don't meet their potential. It is the same for people, Felicia. Some people want to dabble in every possible endeavor, in wanting to do everything, they don't do anything very well. We find the new growth on this bush that looks the strongest, has room to thrive, and then we cut away others. This little red nub will soon be a strong branch with breathtaking blooms bigger than my fist. As you grow into a woman, find what you are best at, a few things, and pursue those."

Felicia was still very confused, but nodded politely.

"Another thing. You see these branches growing out from the base of the bush, near the roots?"

"Yes…"

"These are called suckers. They are worthless. Worse, they rob the bush of its limited energy but will not produce any blooms, even tiny ones. Their only purpose is to grow and grow, doing nothing else. This is activity without accomplishment. Fill your life with useful purpose, Felicia. There are many purposes your activity can accomplish, but the noblest of all is to leave the world a little better place than it was when you entered it."

"Lady Ela, why am I here?"

Ela rubbed her chin for a moment. "What exactly are you asking, child?"

"Why did you ask me to come to the garden? Why did you choose to teach me about roses?"

Ela appeared slightly relieved, then nodded. "What do you remember about your mother?"

Felicia looked to the grass under her feet. "Almost nothing. I can't…" She almost burst into tears, this question coming at her unexpectedly. "I can't even remember what she looked like."

Ela reached out and lifted the child's chin. "Don't be ashamed of that Felicia, you were very young. I myself soon struggled to conjure my father's face, and I was much older when I lost him than you were when you lost your mother. It is part of being human, not a sign of coldness, I loved my father desperately."

"Thank you, Lady Ela"

"She was very beautiful, your mother."

Felicia stared up at Ela and her eyes opened wide. "You knew her? What did she look like? Like me?"

"Yes, but there is much of your father in you as well."

"My father! You know who my father is?" Felicia impulsively reached out and grabbed Ela by the forearm. "Is he alive?"

"No, child. He died before you were born."

Felicia's hopes collapsed, like logs in a fire when the base has turned to ash. "So I really am alone."

Ela cupped Felicia's chin in her left hand. "You have felt alone here? Amongst all the sisters?"

"I do not fit here. I am different."

"How so?"

"The sisters, I see how they look at me," Felicia answered. "No, don't be angry with them, they have never mistreated me. It's just that I can see that I am different, and that they think so too."

"Different in the way you look?"

"Yes, I am darker than everyone else."

"Not so very dark," Ela said

"No, but still darker. Even that skin that never shows, never sees the sun, it is darker than the other girls' faces."

"I will tell you why, if you are sure you want to know."

"Please!" Felicia nearly shouted.

"Are you absolutely certain?"

"Yes, Lady Ela, I am certain."

Ela took the girl by the hand and walked her over to a bench where they enjoyed a broad view of the river. "Your mother was a Saracen, Felicia."

Felicia swallowed hard, and stared at the river for several

moments. "She was a heathen, I won't meet her in heaven?"

Ela finally took the girl in her arms and hugged her tightly. "Yes you will, Felicia, she became a Christian in order to marry your father."

Felicia accepted the embrace and sobbed into Ela's chest for several minutes before setting her resolve and asking: "Who was my father?"

Felicia having extricated herself from the hug, Ela stood, looked off in the distance a moment, then turned to face the girl. "I regret keeping you at a distance these past years, Felicia, it was a flaw in my own character for which I hope you will forgive me. I did not know you felt so alone."

Felicia stared up at Ela as hope once again began to build. These words seemed to say that there was someone she belonged to, even sounded like that person was the Lady Ela herself, but Felicia fought the hope, not wanting to be crushed again.

"Felicia, I liked your mother very much. I understood why my son loved her. I am your grandmother."

August 16, 1261

Roger Talbot felt famished as he sat down to sup with the nuns of Lacock Abbey. Devout but not austere, these holy sisters laid a fine table for their main meal. Roger had arrived two hours previously and gone directly to the grave of his mother Anne. Ceremony performed, with witnesses, he was glad to share a meal with the women and girls, especially the girls. Some he imagined would be quite lovely out of those bulky and severe robes.

"My lord Talbot, I'm quite certain you'll want to visit the Countess while you are with us." Sister something-or-other looked down her long hooked nose at him.

"Does she not dine with you?"

"Alas, she cannot leave her bed. She never will; that is certain."

"That is a pity." Roger shoved a chunk of the Abbey's own cheese into his mouth and washed it down with ale.

"I should think it is; she who has ever been such a friend to your family." Scrunching and pinching her face ever further toward the male interloper, this particular old bag reminded Roger of the wife of the Punch and Judy dolls.

Glancing about the table, Roger could see that the crone's words were impacting the younger, more appealing brides of Christ. They looked at him out of the corners of their eyes, brows raised. "It grieves me. I will go to her now."

Roger stood and made his way toward the exit, not abandoning his meal, but carrying the stale bread trencher with him, he picked at the morsels heaped upon it as he walked. He knew where Ela's chamber was; if he wanted to see her he would have done so already. Still, as he walked, the thought that he happened upon her death bed pleased him. Just inside the cloister, he turned left walking just a few steps before ambling up the staircase.

The stairs were so narrow that he was forced to turn sideways, just as they were designed. This staircase was identical to those in castles, built so that a retreating man climbing step by step would have his right arm, likely his sword arm, free for fighting the pursuing attacker. That pursuer, in turn, was placed at the disadvantage, wielding his sword either in the left hand or awkwardly across his body. Roger parried the air with the bone of a chicken leg.

The chamber was warm with the August sun streaming in through open shutters. The breeze was insufficient to eliminate the smell of old woman. There lay Ela, spent of her famous vigor and energy. Roger walked to a far window and took in the view of Lacock village. Morsels finished, he began to tear off bits of the trencher sodden with gravy.

"You awake Ela—or alive?"

"I live, Roger."

"Oh so you are awake. And you recognize my voice; perhaps you are not so far gone as believed."

"Oh, I am near death, Roger. Is that why you are here? You have not visited me since your mother passed; perhaps you believe there is something for you in my will."

"Now now Ela, no need for sarcasm. I happened to be passing by and stopped at mother's grave. Some old woman felt I should know of your condition."

"I see."

"On my way up it occurred to me; this little circumstance affords me the opportunity to settle a troubling matter for you."

Ela's eyes now opened and settled on Roger. "What matter?"

"I watched you, as you danced the politics of court with de Burgh. Skirmishes between families. You expertly orchestrating his fall. I was surprised he recovered for a time. You brought him down, why did you let him stand up?"

Ela searched Roger's eyes, not comprehending what this was about, not knowing why his tone was so hostile. It was true Anne's son never showed appreciation for all that was done for him, but outright hostility made no sense to her. "In the end, I had doubt."

"Of his guilt?"

"Yes."

Roger smiled. "You were always so superior Ela, but I'll give you credit. Perhaps you were as wise as the sycophants you always surrounded yourself with said you were."

His smile disappeared and was replaced with a sneer. "He was innocent."

"How… how do you know?"

"Because I killed your precious William."

"You?" Her accelerated breathing taxed her failing lungs beyond endurance. She forced herself to calm, to breathe deliberately.

"Yes. I stole arsenic from Philip's lab and poisoned Willam's beer. The stomach ache he arrived in Sarum with was likely nothing but too much fine food after months of deprivation."

Ela lived half her life a widow, even having so little childhood. All the years disappeared in an instant and the wounds were new. Bloody and painful wounds of the soul. "But why?"

"William Talbot lusted after him. He who would be my father wanted to hump your husband. Everyone knew it!"

"Nobody knew it."

"Everyone did! I heard them laughing when they didn't know I was there."

"You imagined it."

"Besides, I was tired of being the charity case. The Talbots lived to serve the almighty Longespees, so smug, so superior to everyone around them. You thought yourselves gods, but can gods be killed?"

Tears followed one another down Ela's face one last time.

"No need to go telling anyone about our little chat Ela. You're dying, madness comes over the dying. A fever you know." He came very close. "Nobody will ever know, or believe."

He popped up straight and walked to the stairs. Before descending, he turned back for just a moment. "Oh, I killed Clare and the girl in Mortain's dungeon as well."

He stepped lightly down the spiraled stairs, gayly reliving the triumphal past few moments.

Though I only knew Countess Ela for a few short hours, I wept bitterly at her funeral. I offered what comfort I could to Felicia. The final visit of Roger Talbot marked the end of Ela's tale, and she called for her granddaughter before her last ragged breath.

When the concluding Latin chants finished echoing from the chapel walls, the sisters filed out. For most, this was a routine funeral mass, they being too young to have known the former Abbess in her active years.

Mother Agnes approached Felicia and me as we lingered near the open grave in front of the altar. She nodded with closed eyes and pressed lips toward Felicia, acknowledging a truth that would forever be left unspoken. "Yolanda, a servant has arrived to return you to your father's house."

"Yes, Mother Agnes," I said.

"I wish you well, child. Go with God." The Abbess turned to leave.

"Mother!" I said.

She turned back to me with a questioning look. "Yes, child?"

"I still do not know. Why did Countess Ela send for me?"

"Did she not say anything to you?"

"She told me all about her life, but not why I was the one to hear it."

Mother Agnes nodded, and for the first time I could recall I would swear she almost smiled. "I believe our good Lady Ela has not yet exhausted her surprises."

The Abbess left Felicia and me alone in the chapel, both more perplexed than ever.

When I arrived at my father's home, he ordered everyone else out of the great hall. I recoiled in fear as he rushed toward me, but rather than strike me, he embraced me with affection I never felt from him before. "You have done well, Yolanda."

The hall was gaily decorated, and I could tell from the sweetness of the rushes covering the dirt floors that they were freshly laid not hours before. "What have I done, father?"

He stepped out of the embrace and looked down at me, holding my shoulders. He smiled then laughed. "I had hoped you could tell me, but it must have been a fine thing!"

"Father, I do not understand."

He released his grip and sobered somewhat. "No matter, we will talk another time. You marry today."

"Today!" I asked.

"Yes. I'm sorry, Yolanda. I would have expected to give you more time, but perhaps it is for the best."

"But who?"

"Did she not tell you?" Father asked. "The former Abbess of Lacock, Countess Ela, you gained favor with her. She arranged a husband for you: a very rich and noble Wiltshire knight."

Father then grew very serious, a countenance I was much more familiar with. "Her correspondence was quite clear on two conditions to this gift. First we are never to mention to the bridegroom that you were at Lacock or that we knew the Countess."

I felt a niggling headache grow behind my left eye as I struggled to understand what scheme the Countess had set in motion for me. "What is the other condition?"

Father shuddered then stood very tall. "That I do not yet know. Before the ceremony, you are to receive a letter written by Lady Ela, hand delivered by the priest." He snorted. "It is my opinion that she did not trust me with this information."

Just then a man entered the hall. He was graying, older than father, but not without appealing countenance and manner. "Well then, is this my bride?"

"Ah, sir. Indeed, this is my daughter, Yolanda." Father bowed to the man. "Yolanda, greet your husband to be, Sir Roger Talbot."

Yolanda sat on the rough wooden stool in her cell. She rested her arms on the simple table that represented the only other piece of furniture in the room. Candlelight flickered nearby as she rubbed and flexed her aching fingers and wrists. The piles of straw which were her bed for the last two weeks called to her. She was weary and night was some hours old.

Still, Yolanda believed she was fortunate. Though her father disowned her, and no one would be giving the guards money to provide proper meals, she was not in the Tower dungeon. Her cell was on an upper floor of the Salt Tower. She remembered the description of Hubert de Burgh's prison which Ela told her, and she had written down. She was thankful that, though the straw had not been changed, it contained only her own smell.

She was guilty of the greatest crime a noblewoman could commit. Yolanda murdered her husband in the bridal bed, she did not deny it. Each time a soldier's footfall climbed the stairs she tensed, wondering if they were coming to take her for execution. She prayed fervently that they would grant her the beheading her station afforded her, but it was entirely possible they would decide she deserved to hang.

Just as she was about to blow out the candle, she heard heavy footsteps coming up the stairs. *Surely they haven't come for me at night. Executions usually take place at dawn.*

An iron key scratched its way into the lock and turned. When the door swung open there stood a soldier. He was not a guard she had seen before. His hair was long, but not as sweaty as most. His clothing was of reasonably clean green wool with a velvet collar. "Come with me, Miss."

Yolanda opened her mouth to scream, but stopped herself. She would remain noble until the end. She owed it to Ela.

The soldier followed her down the spiral staircase, and directed her to walk along the curtain wall that faced the Thames. She sucked up deep breaths, soaking in the salty smell of high tide. Fires flickered here and there along the south bank. If these were the last moments of her life, Yolanda was going to take in every available sensation.

She expected to be sent to her left, down onto the green by White Tower. Through the darkness she saw the ravens, descendants of those that complained of the intrusions of Earl William and of Christina all those years ago. Instead, she was led to the right, into another tower.

She was marched down a flight of stairs and placed in another room. This one was warm, several large logs burned in the fireplace. There was a basin, clean rags, and clean clothes laid out on a bench.

"You'll wash yourself and put on clean things, Miss," The soldier said. "You need not have a care, you will not be disturbed until you are properly covered again. But do not dally, be quick." With that he left, closing the door behind him.

Yolanda wondered at what all this meant. Perhaps father forgave her after all and paid for a nicer prison. In any case cleanness was not a gift she was going to turn down, or let slip away. She quickly stripped and set about scrubbing every inch of skin she could reach.

When she was done putting on the new robes she rapped her knuckles on the door. "I am dressed."

The door opened, and the same soldier stood ready. "Come with me, Miss."

Up the staircase again, she was told to keep climbing past the entrance level, up another flight of stairs. For the first time the soldier did not appear bored. He straightened his own clothes and inspected himself. "My Lord! The girl."

The door opened. A hatchet faced man about her father's age looked at Yolanda. His eyes drifted down from her head to her feet. After a moment he opened the door wider. "Come."

Yolanda stood in a fine bedchamber with tapestries on the walls, a massive oak bed with burgundy covers dominating the room. The floors were of the finest green tiles. To her left, she could see a small private chapel with gold alter pieces. There was another man kneeling in front of the altar. He crossed himself, genuflected one last time and stood. Walking into the main chamber the man waved his hand at hatchet face. "You may go."

"Yes, Sire," hatchet face said and quickly made his exit.

He called this man Sire, and Yolanda noticed the drooping eyelid. She remembered hearing, and writing, of this man's description. "Your Majesty," she said, curtseying low.

"Take a seat, Yolanda," the King said, offering his own fine chair to her, while he himself sat on a large oak chest with steel bands.

Yolanda noticed that on the bed sat a fat scroll tied with scarlet ribbon. She recognized the scroll. It was the one she spent days writing on, the reason her fingers and wrist ached.

"It appears my dear aunt put you to great trouble," Henry said.

"She made it my choice, Your Majesty. Her final letter absolved me completely if I refused."

"I see," Henry said. "I am not surprised, I could not believe for a moment Ela would risk your life without your free will. I know something else without a sword's edge of doubt."

"My Lord?" Yolanda asked.

The King looked her straight in the eyes, like few men ever did. "That she knew you had the steel to do it."

Yolanda smiled. "Thank you, Your Majesty."

Henry nodded. "One time, and one time only, tell me what happened on your wedding night."

"When my vile husband approached the matrimonial bed, I pulled out a long dagger hidden under the covers, and plunged it through his neck, behind the breast bone, into his black heart, just as Ela did when she killed Mortain with the arrow," Yolanda said. "As I looked into his shocked face I whispered to him. 'Roger Talbot, I send your soul to the depths of hell for the murder of William Longespee.'"

Henry stared at the girl, showing no emotion at all. "Tell me, Yolanda, have you any remorse for killing your duly wedded husband?"

Yolanda thought for only a moment. It appeared the King was offering her a way to save herself. If she showed remorse, would that save her? Would she be allowed to live if she apologized for offending all the noble men of the realm in this manner?

"No, Your Majesty," Yolanda said. "I suffer no remorse and do not beg mercy. I am proud to have served the cause of true justice. Let the King do with me as he sees fit, and may God have no mercy on Roger Talbot's soul; I have every confidence he will have mercy on mine."

The third King Henry of England stood, opened the

oak chest he had been sitting on, and placed the scroll of testimony in it. He closed the lid, and secured it with a heavy iron lock.

"The soldier will take you to a proper chamber for the night, Yolanda" Henry said. "In the morning you will be declared not guilty; you will be granted possession of Talbot's goods and land. You will also find that the good Countess Ela mentioned you in her will."

Yolanda came close to feinting. She could not stand right away, even though she knew she had been dismissed from the King's presence. He waited patiently while she gathered her wits.

Finally she walked to the door. As she grasped the handle Henry spoke again. "Tell no one what you have told me about that night, Yolanda. We take that to our graves you and I."

"Yes, Your Majesty," Yolanda said. "And thank you."

Henry joined her and opened the door for her. "Justice has been done; let us now love mercy."

Author's Notes

Ela of Salisbury: Do Justice, Love Mercy is a work of fiction. Most of the characters in this novel, however, were real people. It was my desire, as closely as possible, to follow the historical record. As one with an abiding fascination with history, I will attempt to parse "what was" from "what could have been." Those who only read historical novels for the story may stop now, those who want to know more about the facts please read on.

First and foremost, my desire to write this book came from my desire for people to know about Ela, Countess of Salisbury. Ela was very much a real woman who led a most remarkable life considering the era in which she lived. But to meet the real Ela, let us review the events of this story.

The Tournament:
When Richard the Lionheart took the throne, tournaments had been outlawed in England for many years. His father, Henry II, lost at least one son to a tournament accident. Richard re-instituted the tournament, but with limitations. Ela's father, William, the second Earl of Salisbury, was placed in charge of issuing licenses to those who wanted to

sponsor an event. There were also only five fields in England that were named as official grounds that could receive a license to tourney. The land between Sarum and Wilton was one of those five. It seems only natural that the nobleman in charge could hold tourney at his own base.

Strangely though, there is no record of a tournament ever taking place there. I have adopted the archeological maxim "the absence of evidence is not evidence of absence." Though we have many records of various tournaments, we cannot delude ourselves to think that all accounts have survived intact over eight centuries. It is reasonable to assume there were events at Sarum, but any connection with Ela's birthday celebrations (themselves not standard medieval observances) is fiction. The order and description of events at tournament, however, are told with strict adherence to the records we do have from the era.

It is a testament to the medieval technology of armor production that deaths were relatively rare at tournaments. Indeed most accounts of deaths describe accidents such as trampling, or being drug with a foot caught in stirrups rather than from jousting blows. Though the lances used in tournaments were blunted and designed to shatter, consider that modern research indicates that a couched lance blow from a mounted charge (such as the one experienced by William) carries approximately 6000 foot pounds of force. This is comparable to being hit by a car traveling 70 mph.

Ela's exile:

With only one exception, all accounts of Ela's life include the story of her being "abducted" by relatives on her maternal side to protect her from potential harm at the hands of an uncle. Many believe that because the one account which gives a date for Ela's birth, as well as timeline for her betrothal and subsequent marriage to William Longespee, does not mention this exile, that it never happened. I argue that this one account is almost certainly wrong about the date of her birth and therefore cannot be taken as the definitive record at all.

To be sure, it is such a great story one wants it to be true. There are disturbing aspects to consider, however, if you want to make this assertion. For instance, the story of William Talbot searching high and low throughout Europe dressed as a common pilgrim bears a more than passing resemblance to the story of Blondel looking for Richard while he was held captive in Germany after the third crusade. My response to this argument is that the story as it relates to Richard makes less sense of the two. The Holy Roman Emperor was very angry with Richard after the humiliation the Lionheart put him through at Acre. He could have killed Richard in vengeance, instead he ransomed him for a massive amount, perhaps more satisfying a revenge in the end. Faced with those two options, why would he instead just hide Richard away safe and well for years? No, I submit that there is at least the possibility that Ela's story was adopted into Richard's legend rather than the other way around. Indeed, it has been postulated that Marie de France's tale of Orpheo was based heavily on Ela's tale. In fact, one of the strongest cases for identifying Marie holds that she was a sister of Henry II and therefore an aunt of Longespee and in-law to Ela.

A difficult mystery presents itself when accepting the historical reality of Ela's childhood disappearance. No account tells us where she was for those two years. The story of Ela's relationship with Eleanor is sadly pure conjecture, one I will take up shortly. It was quite reasonable for Ela's relations to fear for her safety. Though she was immediately a ward of the crown, and therefore under King Richard's protection the moment her father died, Richard was not in England. Famously, Richard probably spent less than eight months total in England in his whole adulthood, at least his reign. He hated the place. If one decides that a man faced with immense riches could rationalize the relative impotence of an absent king, the question remains why not just take her to Richard? All accounts state that they did take her to the mainland, to what is now France. Richard was there, fighting in Brittany. Could they not have simply taken her to court, placed her under the King's physical protection? Instead they hid her from even him, an act of treason punishable by death. Why?

During my research I was delighted to find that the annals of Eleanor's life provided an astonishing coincidence. Eleanor lived to the remarkable age of 83. During that time she was almost constantly on the move. For the period of Ela's alleged absence, however, there is no record of Eleanor ever leaving Fountevrault Abbey. It is the only time in her entire life that she stayed in one place that long, even considering her imprisonment by Henry. It was too much to ask for, and I joyously solved my mystery. It is made up, but I would love to think that it was true. In an age when women were not only considered property, but to be mentally retarded and immoral as well, there was during each of the 12th, 13th, and 14th centuries one incredible woman who defied all odds to be powerful, independent, and respected. To me, those women are: Eleanor of Acquitaine, Ela of Salisbury, and Isabella the "she-wolf" of France. To link two of these women I admire was delightful serendipity.

The odd case of Thomas:
The story of Thomas is real. His association with Ela

and William, however, is fictitious. The story, in effect, is borrowed. Thomas did live, suffer the fate described, and amaze all with his healing, but he was from Eldersfield and his fateful accident with the axe took place nine years later than I have placed it. What does one do with accounts, purported to be serious historical records, that describe a man growing new eyes and testicles? My explanation is easy and has a somewhat modern TV cleanness to it. Academics, on the other hand, try to explain it from a medieval perspective. If one assumes that Thomas never left the village of his birth, then people would know if there was a twin brother. People did have the opportunity to move about more than we tend to think they did. Regardless, academics have postulated that rather than grow new eyes, Thomas' optic nerve repaired itself enough that he could distinguish various shades of light. The optic nerve's ability to do this in the absence of an eyeball is factual. Once you explain away "vision," then it is easy to assume some simple objects, even animal testicles, were sewn within his scrotum to fool the magistrates.

Whichever explanation is true, the people of the age believed a miracle occurred. And since this miracle corrected an injustice carried out due to trial by combat, it had a positive effect in pushing this barbaric practice further into obscurity.

The Battle of Damme:

The account of the battle is true with the exception of William's adventure within the city walls. It was a remarkable victory for England and in my view deserving of more attention and instruction. England was, at the time, under just as much threat of invasion by France as she was by Spain three hundred years later. Victory at Damme secured the island kingdom from invasion in the same way as did the defeat of the Spanish Armada. Furthermore, the fleet under the command of Longespee is deserving of recognition as the first English Royal Navy. All that it lacks is the romantic association with naval guns, having occurred a few decades before the introduction of cannon.

John attacks Ela:

It has been a mystery why William suddenly rebelled during the First Baron's War. The easiest and most widespread explanation is simply that he saw how the war was unfolding and wanted to be on the winning side. I reject this simplistic drivel out of hand. Nothing else in William's life or character remotely resembles such action.

Another, more considered, explanation is that William was acting as a double agent to learn more of Philip and Louis' plans. This makes sense, and though William would have considered the task dishonorable, it certainly fits John's character to have ordered it.

I have chosen a third option, the one I do believe to be correct. This story actually comes from King Philip. It was he who explained William's defection as having been caused by John "attempting to seduce" his wife. I put the phrase in quotes as it was a common euphemism of the period to describe what we would label rape or attempted rape. Given William's unwavering loyalty to both Richard and John in turn, regardless of how foolish their decisions, or the extent of the opposition, an attack on Ela better explains such a complete reversal.

William's tragic accident:

The accidental killing of a baby at its mother's breast during archery practice as a young man is fictitious as it pertains to William. This event is, however, adapted from an actual tragedy. Once again this story comes from St. Albans. If you visit St. Peter's church in St. Albans today, you will see just north of the churchyard a row of almshouses. The rooflines of these houses are decorated with triangles clearly representing arrowheads. These homes were built by a very wealthy nobleman as homes for widows. The arrowhead designs were a reminder for him of the greatest mistake of his life. As a young man, he was practicing with a longbow in the churchyard when he carelessly shot high, missing the target. Rather than a baby, he instead struck and killed an elderly widow. This obviously haunted him his entire life, hence the building of homes to aid and comfort other widows later in his life.

The Virginity of Christina:

Christina's story is a wonderful one borrowed from another time. She actually lived in the previous century (early 12th.) Her childhood religious experience occurred at St. Alban's Abbey. We have a detailed account of her life because one of the great historians of the age was a monk by the name of Matthew who lived at St. Albans. Christina, therefore, was a bit of a local legend. The accounts described of two of her fights for virginity, against the Bishop as well as her betrothed, are accurate to the historical account. In this case I cannot be accused of 21st century storytelling, that is exactly how medieval chroniclers told us they transpired.

The Murder of William Longespee:

There certainly was suspicion at the time that William was murdered. Without technical ability to prove it, however, nothing was ever done. The chronicler Matthew of St. Albans named Hubert de Burgh as the murderer many years after all parties were passed. We now know, with some level of reasonableness, that William was in fact murdered. In 1790, William's tomb was moved to its present location in the nave of Salisbury Cathedral. In the course of that event, workmen opened the coffin and were presented with the macabre view of a perfectly preserved rat resting within the man's skull. This rat can be viewed today at a museum within the cathedral close. Knowledge that arsenic was a preservative did exist at that time and further added to suspicion. Subsequent centuries brought modern testing that was carried out on the rat's corpse. What is scientifically proven is that the rat ingested an enormous dose of arsenic. It is circumstantial evidence by which we deduce the rat died of arsenic poisoning by eating William's brain, and that he must also have died of arsenic poisoning. Strong, if circumstantial, evidence indeed.

The murder mystery I have unfolded is fiction. I decided early on that it would be too difficult to write anything readable based on guilt of the prime suspect. It is very strange when you consider that William and Hubert were friends, or at the very least cooperative peers, and that Hubert was the protector of Arthur. Did something else happen, unrecorded by history, to cause a falling out between the pair? In the end, the most likely explanation is that the humiliation William rained down upon Hubert was enough. Hubert rose far above his birth, William's confrontation was a very real threat to that position.

Good Kings and Bad Kings:
It is a well recognized anomaly that the British hold such affection for King Richard the first, given that he so despised England. One must understand that during his rule the kingdom consisted of as much land in what is now France as it did the island of Britain. Richard considered

the mainland territories not only more pleasant but more valuable as well. Hence, he spent only eight months in England during his time on the throne.

Despite national hero-hood, strong arguments are continually made against "Good King Richard." He is painted as of very bad character. Certainly one cannot argue against the fact that by our modern standards Richard would be considered a war criminal. His slaughter of prisoners at Acre cannot be defended by 21st Century man. Richard did not live in the 21st Century, however, he lived in the 12th Century. The fact is that Richard could not feed a large group of prisoners and still withstand siege. Furthermore, Richard tried to exchange prisoners with Saliden, offering the Saracen leader favorable terms. It was Saliden who refused this offer from tactical motives.

It is also remarkable to me that Richard was willing to forgive John after his brother's clear attempt to usurp the throne. Whether all for respect of his mother Eleanor, or because Richard remembered his own attempt to seize the thrown from their father, I argue an evil king would never have welcomed his scheming brother back to court. In the end, I am sympathetic to Richard as a historical man in the context of the world he knew. It does not mean I do not abhor some of the things he did, particularly his treatment of women.

Going into this project I must confess I expected to be kinder to John. I believed that I would find through research that he was a better king than history portrayed him to be. My conclusion, however, is that history, even the Robin Hood myth, got him about right. I do argue that he deserves credit as the creator of the Royal Navy, no small honor for the island nation. He is also recognized as a very good administrator. Curiously, it is also true that John appointed, then confirmed, the first female 'Shire Reeve' (from which the word sheriff is derived) in English history. Other than that, he truly was an awful king. Inaction, self-absorption, pettiness, if it is a negative trait in a leader you can find it in John. I leave it to some other writer to "give John a break." I planned to, but just couldn't do it.

The assault on Sarum:

This story is fictitious as it pertains to Sarum and Ela particularly. It borrows heavily, however, from a wonderful petition to the King which still exists in the National Archives at Kew. This petition could be described as a medieval equivalent of a request for a restraining order. Another noblewoman complained to the King about a certain knight who was fervently trying to convince her to marry him, even by the method of rape. The knight came to her castle disguised as a priest. When this ruse failed, he left but returned soon after with a number of friends and proceeded to attack the castle; whereupon the lady was only able to escape her fate by hiding in the moat. Her petition to the King simply asked him to make the knight leave her alone, a reasonable request it would seem. Sadly, there is no decision recorded on this particular document, so we do not know if she was granted relief. I sincerely hope this scoundrel received a stern royal "cease and desist."

The attempt to woo Ela was real enough during William's prolonged absence and assumed death. It is not known, however, if these attempts carried on after his actual demise. Furthermore, the tunnel dug into the chalk hill of Sarum is also very real.

William Longespee II on Crusade:

There is a great deal of frustrating contradiction in the

records concerning the events of the seventh crusade as it pertains to the English contingent. Sadly, the main annals, written by the English source Matthew Paris, have enough known inaccuracies to render them unreliable propaganda. Nevertheless, the death of William, blamed largely on the arrogance of the French (particularly Robert d'Artois), had a massive impact on the national psyche. Its influence would be felt in the animosity toward France for centuries.

Both the capture of the "tower of ladies" and the merchant caravan are events told in the annal of Matthew Paris and as such are suspect from a historical perspective. The battle(s) of al Mansurah I believe to be largely accurate, taken from reliable sources, with only a seasoning of the much more interesting account of Paris. I have included this seasoning not just to flavor the novel, but to put the event into the perspective of the English as they would have seen it.

There is a general agreement that Robert d'Artois was largely to blame for the disaster. All appearances indicate that he overstretched the crusader forces in an attempt to grab greater glory for himself at the expense of his brother King Louis IX. Interestingly, the chief opponent of that theory was Louis himself. He accepted the blame for the collapse of the seventh crusade. Though an admirable trait for a king of the period, I believe such accountability, in this instance, is unfair. Certainly Louis IX never ordered his advance force to tear off on their own before the bulk of the French army could cross the Nile. Robert's pride and arrogance did severely weaken the crusader army, wiping out over six hundred elite knights, a blow they were never able to recover from.

Philip the Philosopher/Roger Bacon:

The presence of Roger Bacon in the holy land in 1249-1250 is a contrivance of mine. This does, however, coincide with a mysterious absence of the man in the historical record. It is an established fact that we do not know where he was during the years 1247-1256, a mystery speculated on by various authors over the centuries. My theory is based on the fact that at this time ancient learning was being reintroduced to Europe through Arab scholars and scientists. Roger Bacon seems to me the type of man who would seek knowledge wherever possible, even amongst the muslims.

Philip's studies in the philosopher's arts are also based heavily on Roger Bacon. Bacon described both building what could only be called a telescope and manufacturing gunpowder. Both of these seemingly anachronistic accomplishments occurred in the same region of England during the 13th Century. Roger studied, and became an instructor, at Oxford; he could have been influenced by such an eccentric philosopher as Philip. There was no shortage of philosophers; and though their chief preoccupation was alchemy, they tended to spend great amounts of time and effort on theology, the physical sciences, astronomy, and astrology. Renaissance began in Europe far earlier than generally accepted.

Holy Anorexia:

Ela's conversation with the original Abbess of Lacock is fictional, but the debate was very real. Medieval nuns believed that there were but two models in the Bible of whom a woman could follow: Eve or Mary. Eve represented everything wrong with womankind. She, and therefore her entire sex, was responsible for original sin. Women were not just a temptation, but active assailants of man's virtue. Women then, were the ones who thought of nothing but sex, who could not control their desires. A reversal of roles from our beliefs to be sure. Mary, on the other hand, was considered eternally virginal. To follow Mary's example, many nuns maintained themselves just barely on the right side of starvation. This practice has come to be known as holy anorexia, a practice known to have not been followed at Ela's Lacock.

Death of William III:

The account of the death of Ela's grandson is largely accurate from the perspective of the bystanders. My account of William's inner thoughts as he lay paralyzed and unable to speak are, of course, by their nature speculative. He did, though, die from injuries incurred in a joust outside Tickhill; and he did linger for many hours paralyzed, unable to communicate. It is also true that this tournament represented the public introduction of Prince Edward, who would become the famous King Edward Longshanks, the "Hammer of the Scots" of Braveheart fame. The personal joust between William and Edward is my own fancy; I found no record to indicate the individual matchups that occurred on the day.